A

WINTER CHASE

The Mercer's House Book 1

A Regency Romance

by Mary Kingswood

D1096903

Published by Sutors Publishing

Copyright © 2022 Mary Kingswood

ISBN: 978-1-912167-42-5

V3

Cover design by: Shayne Rutherford of Darkmoon Graphics

Author's note:

this book is written using historic British terminology, so *saloon* instead of *salon*, *chaperon* instead of *chaperone* and so on. I follow Jane Austen's example and refer to a group of sisters as the Miss Wintertons.

About this book: A family in trade moving up in the world. A family of landed gentry stepping aside for them. And the sons and daughters caught in the middle.

Julia Fletcher is the unimportant daughter of the Fletcher family, with neither beauty nor wit nor accomplishments, but always in a scrape. Somehow she never manages to get through the day without breaking or spilling or tearing something. She's quite the despair of her stepmother. She's looking forward to their grand new home because it will give her a vast estate to roam over without getting into too much trouble. Or so she hopes.

James Plummer is the younger son of an impoverished baronet, forced to sell the imposing family home to the upstart newcomers. James doesn't mind that; he's the local clergyman so he's snug in his rectory, with a curate to do the dreary business of the parish and leave him free to wander about with a gun or a fishing rod. It's all pretty boring, though; his family, his neighbours, his dull daily round... nothing very exciting happens. Maybe the Fletcher family will liven things up a bit? And outspoken hoyden Julia Fletcher seems just the one to shake things up... maybe a little too much for everyone's peace of mind.

This is a complete story with a happy ever after. A traditional Regency romance, drawing room rather than bedroom. Book 1 of a 6 book series.

Isn't that what's-his-name? Regular readers will know that characters from previous books occasionally pop up. There are mentions in this book of several Sagborough residents. The Harbottle family (including Nell, her son Louis and Nathan) of Percharden House were seen in *The Widow*. The

Marfords, Lord Carrbridge's extensive family, were seen throughout the *Sons of the Marquess* series, and in *The Seamstress.* Mr Malpas, the mayor of Sagborough, his wife and daughter Emmy were in *The Seamstress.* Lord and Lady Craston (Ferdy and Fanny) were in *The Seamstress.*

About the series*:* A family grown rich in the wool trade. The landed gentry they've displaced. And the gentle daughter whose beauty will open the door to an even greater prize - the nobility.

The Fletcher family is moving from Yorkshire to a mansion in the south of England. After generations in trade, can they escape their roots and be admitted to the leisured world of the gentry?

Their new home is Chadwell Park, in Hertfordshire. **The Mercer's House.**

Book 0: The Mercer: the rich merchant and the poor widow. *(a novella, free to mailing list subscribers).*

Book 1: A Winter Chase: the wild daughter and the reluctant clergyman.

Book 2: A Spring Dance: the flirtatious son and the prim paid companion.

Book 3: A Summer Game: the mischievous daughter and the strait-laced gentleman.

Book 4: A Michaelmas Truce: the cross spinster and the even crosser bachelor.

Book 5: An Autumn Courtship: the intellectual son and the flighty socialite.

Book 6: A Christmas Betrothal: the beautiful daughter, the unhappy son and the lost lover.

Want to be the first to hear about new releases? Sign up for my mailing list at marykingswood.co.uk.

Note: hi-res versions of the family trees are available at my website under Extras.

Table of Contents

The Fletcher Family

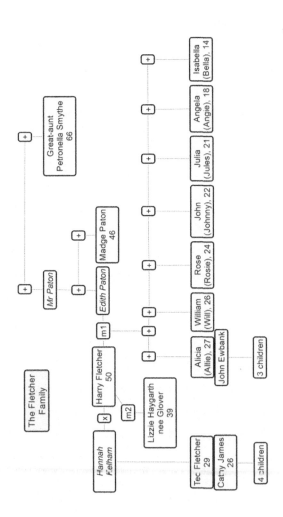

The Plummer Family

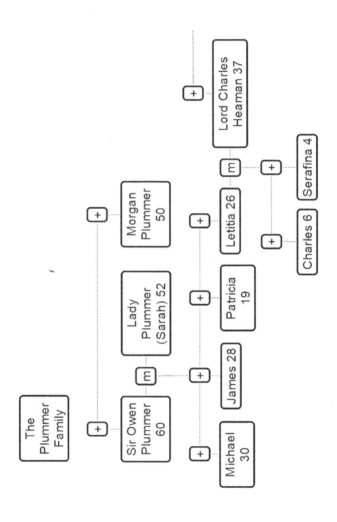

Prologue

CHADWELL PARK, HERTFORDSHIRE

THE FIRST DECADE OF THE 19TH CENTURY; OCTOBER

Sir Owen Plummer had commanded his entire family to assemble in the library at Chadwell Park. Not that he would ever be so ill-mannered as to express himself so. He would be greatly obliged if they would attend him, or some such, but to James, the clipped, brisk tones of the former military man always sounded like commands. No more than ten years in the army and thirty out of it, but Sir Owen was still a soldier at heart.

They were all there, at any rate. Mother was weeping, of course. She wept constantly these days, trickles of tears flowing gently down her face to fall unheeded onto her bosom, perpetually replaced with more of the same. Where did all that water come from? It was a mystery to him. Michael looked ill, but then he always looked ill nowadays, a thin, pale shoot of a man. Letitia looked angry and her husband worried, but since those were their habitual expressions, James took no notice. To complete the array of his predictable relations, Patricia's face was as blank as a slate, and Uncle Morgan was topping up his brandy glass already and it was only eleven o'clock. Lord, what a boring lot they were!

James wondered briefly what they thought of him. Nothing, probably. He doubted any of them thought about him at all, and certainly not now. He, after all, was the only one unaffected by their impending doom, with his snug rectory and his ample tithes and no one but himself to support or to please.

Precisely as the clock struck eleven, Sir Owen entered the room, his eye raking over the assembled Plummers, lingering only momentarily on his wife. He took his position in front of the fireplace, the fire still unlit despite the season. It was the rule now.

"All here, I see," Sir Owen said. "Good. I have news from Simons. He has found a buyer for the Park." Mother gave a convulsive gulp, but Father continued without so much as blinking. He was used to it by now. "It is a Mr Fletcher, from a place called Sagborough. Near York, seemingly. Simons went up there to talk to the fellow, but I chose not to mention it to you in case nothing came of it. Simons has now talked to Fletcher and they have agreed terms. Firstly, he is prepared to pay the full price for the Park, no quibbling or caveats. He has the money, too. Simons has talked to the bank. The other consideration is that he will take the Park exactly as it is, with the furniture and art work, and will retain all the servants, apart from the few we will take with us. That is a huge relief to all of us, I am sure. He will take over the village cottages, leaving us with all our tenant farmers, and he will very generously allow us to shoot and hunt and fish on Hall land for our own table. That will please you, James. All things considered, it is an excellent agreement for us."

"What sort of a man is this Fletcher person?" Letitia said. "Please tell us that he is a gentleman."

Sir Owen hesitated long enough for Mother to utter a low moan.

"He is — or was — a mercer, a highly respected man in his home town, who has now relinquished all his business ventures. He has recently remarried and his wife is a gentlewoman, so he wishes to keep her in a suitable manner. Simons tells me that Fletcher himself is only moderately educated, commensurate with his position in society, but his children have all been properly educated. His sons attended Harrow and Cambridge, and his daughters had governesses and masters of art, music, dancing and so forth. The usual things."

"Hmpf! Not a Whig, is he?" Lord Charles said. "Never do to have a Whig in the house, sir. M'brother would be mortified."

"Your brother has nothing whatsoever to do with this, Charles," Sir Owen said tersely. "Mr Fletcher has no political allegiance, seemingly, and it would hardly matter to me if he were a screaming zealot. He has the money to buy the Park and get this family afloat again, so buy it he shall."

"But a *mercer*, Papa," Letitia said. "The shame of it! You will not expect us to receive them, I trust."

Mother uttered another moan of distress.

"I not only expect it, I shall insist upon it," Sir Owen said. "We cannot take the man's money and then snub him socially, and if you and your husband dislike it, Letitia, you are quite at liberty to find someone else to support you. Go and ask Charles's brother to provide you with a house and put food on your table and educate your children. It is hardly unreasonable to expect a marquess to take care of his own brother's family."

Letitia bristled. "You know perfectly well why we cannot, Papa."

Hoping to forestall a repetition of a very tired family argument, James said quickly, "When does Mr Fletcher want to take possession, Father?"

"Not before January, and the weather may delay him further, but we must be out of here by Christmas, I feel."

"I do not know how we are all to squeeze into the Manor," Letitia said fretfully. "It will be far too crowded. It was by no means over-large just for Charles and me, but with so many extra, and the disruption..."

Sir Owen's tone became even more clipped. "Patricia has already contrived the disposition of the rooms to minimize the inconvenience to you, and to repeat, if you dislike the new circumstances, then you are perfectly free to make alternative arrangements at any time."

"Are there young children, Papa?" Patricia's soft voice was a striking contrast to Letitia's shrillness and Sir Owen's brusque tones.

"Hmm, let me see." He leafed through the several pages of the attorney's letter. "The eldest daughter is married... there are two sons, grown... ah, here we are. Four younger daughters... the youngest is fourteen."

"Almost grown up," Patricia said disappointedly.

"But the older girls are not without interest. Listen to this. *'All the daughters will have very good dowries of twenty thousand pounds apiece from their father, and the eldest, who is a rare beauty with the most charming manners, has an additional thirty from an aunt. I cannot understand why she has not been snatched up already, but dare I suggest that this presents a wonderful opportunity for Mr Michael Plummer? I do not scruple to say that the young lady will be a sensation in town, and since it is Fletcher's intention to participate in the season next spring, it is highly recommended that your son move swiftly to secure the lady's affections to himself.'"*

Michael snorted in disgust. "A mercer's daughter! I should hope I am not so desperate as all that!"

"I tell you now, Michael, and this applies to all of you who may be thinking upon similar lines," Sir Owen said, his voice growing harsh, "I will not have this supercilious attitude from any of you. We are not so high in the instep as to refuse Fletcher's coin, so we will treat him with every courtesy. Such men are the very backbone of England, sterling men of worth, honest and loyal and hard-working, helping to keep the country prosperous and thriving. They provide both goods and employment, and they frequently go on to become mayors and aldermen and justices of the peace and members of Parliament and even knights of the realm in time. So we will deal kindly with the Fletcher family, even if we do not choose to make intimate friends of them, and Michael, if you disdain a pretty and well-behaved young woman with fifty thousand pounds merely because her father was once in trade, then you are more foolish than I gave you credit for."

"Father, I beg your pardon," Michael said, his pale cheeks flaming up at this reproof. "I spoke intemperately. I will get to know Miss Fletcher, and if she should be all that she is described, then I will consider the prospect of matrimony seriously, you have my word on that. Beyond that, I cannot undertake to venture as yet."

"I ask no more than that," his father responded in genial tones. "You may find that she will do very well, and since James shows no inclination to secure the succession in your stead, and Morgan must be regarded as a confirmed bachelor at this point, I should be glad to see you settled. It would be a weight off my mind, to be sure." He chuckled. "One of you had better make a push for the baronetcy that your great-grandfather worked so assiduously to obtain. No one wants Cousin Sydney to have it, after all this. Well now, that is all settled, and I shall write today to instruct Simons to draw up the papers. Michael, James, I should like you to stay, but the rest of you may go. Letitia, Charles, you will dine with us tonight?"

"Thank you, Papa," Letitia said colourlessly.

One by one they ambled out of the room, too well-bred to whisper to each other until the door was closed behind them, but James knew that Mother and Letitia would have their heads together before they reached the morning room. Uncle Morgan refilled his brandy glass before he left.

Sir Owen poured three small glasses of port, of identical amounts, and handed them around.

"I suppose it is useless to ask whether you might reconsider before taking such an irrevocable step," Michael said.

"Quite useless," Sir Owen said.

"If the Park could be let instead of sold, if only for Mother's sake..."

"My mind is quite made up, Michael. We still have the Manor, after all, which is the Plummers' ancestral seat. The Park means nothing to us — an extravagant monstrosity built on vanity, which I shall be glad to be rid of."

"It is our family home," Michael said. "We grew up here, and Patricia was born here. Mother adores the place."

Sir Owen said nothing, for the arguments had been gone over a hundred times already.

"This is my fault," Michael said glumly, and that, too, had been said a hundred... a thousand times.

"It is *not* your fault, brother," James said, before their father could speak. "No one blames you, not in the slightest. It was not to be, that was all."

"But if I had done what was expected of me—"

"You would have been desperately unhappy," James said. "Let the past go, Michael. What is done is done. You will all move back to the Manor, the Fletcher family will fill this house, by the sound of it, and we will all grow accustomed to the change."

James and Michael walked to the rectory together, as was their wont after any family gathering, so that Michael could relieve his mind of its accumulated grievances and James could soothe his brother's restless spirit. So it had been since they were barely out of leading strings, and so it would no doubt be as they descended into old age. There being only two years between them, and having suffered the indignities of tutors, school and university more or less in tandem, they were as close as any two brothers could be.

"Will they be dreadfully vulgar?" Michael said. "They are bound to be, I suppose. It cannot be otherwise."

"The father, possibly," James said, "but the rest of them will be perfectly genteel."

"How can you say so? You cannot possibly know that."

"Unless matters are very much amiss at Harrow and Cambridge, the sons will be gentlemanlike, and the daughters have no doubt had the best governesses the north of England can provide. The stepmother is a gentlewoman, according to Simons. So that leaves only Mr Fletcher himself."

"The mercer," Michael said in sepulchral tones. "Chadwell Park occupied by a man in trade. It is beyond belief."

"*Formerly* in trade," James said patiently. "He is retired now, and wants to see his family rise in society. Such men are everywhere, Michael. Naval men return to shore with fortunes in their pockets, the East India Company is turning out nabobs by the score and men of industry turn their mills and manufactories into cold, hard gold. Meanwhile, the sons of the aristocracy lavish their inherited fortunes on mistresses, horses and games of chance, or in our case on a grandiose country house in the Palladian style. Are we to spurn those who have risen to fortune by the sweat of their own brow? Our own ancestors were no better, they just got their foot in the door a few centuries earlier, that is all. The Fletchers may not talk quite as we do, or know how to bow to a duke, but they are not to be despised on that account."

"Ah, there speaks the man of the cloth," Michael said.

"I hope I would say as much if I were not ordained," James said. "I shall not despise the Fletchers, at all events. I shall judge them by their actions, and at least they will bring fresh faces to our stale society. They will liven us up, I am sure, and if the eldest daughter is all Simons describes her to be, with fifty thousand pounds to her name, well, I have a very pretty little rectory that she may be mistress of, if she wishes."

"You would not marry one of the mercer's daughters," Michael said, although he said it half as a question.

"Why should I not?"

Michael spun round to face him, grabbing his arm in a painful grip. "Because if you had been minded to marry an heiress, you could have done so any time this past two years and spared us the grief... the *humiliation* of giving up our home. But then you have never cared about the Park, have you? *You* do not lie awake at night wondering how we will survive the shame. *You* do not dread seeing strangers in our home. *You* do not have to struggle every minute to appear not to mind. Damnation, James, you have not the least sensibility."

"Well, no, not much, I admit it. But if I do not care greatly about the Park, I do care about my family, brother, and I know that Father will be relieved of that dreadful desperation now. He hides it well, but financial worries have ground him down remorselessly since Grandfather's death, and now he will be free of all that. For the first time, his income will exceed his expenditure, and there will be a little money to set aside for Patricia, perhaps. And we still have the Manor, which is our *real* home."

"I shall hate it," Michael said morosely, shoulders hunched, as they began to walk again. "We shall be cooped up together, all six of us, and Letitia's horrid infants. What a life!"

"There is plenty of room at the Rectory," James said.

Michael's eyebrows lifted. "Truly? Are you in all earnest offering me a home?"

"Of course. Why not? I did wonder about Patricia, for Letitia will treat her just like a servant, you may be sure, but the horrid infants are a great attraction to her, for some peculiar reason. But you are always welcome, you know that."

"You have never mentioned such a scheme before," Michael said, eyes narrowing in suspicion.

"I never thought you would be interested."

"Of course I would be interested! Although... it would be cruel, do you not think, to leave Father to the tender mercies of Morgan and Charles? I should never be able to enjoy an evening at the Rectory, knowing they would have to call upon one of the women to make up a four for whist."

"You could walk over there every evening after dinner," James said. "In fact, there would be little walking to be done, since I dine there more often than not."

"No, I could not abandon Father. It is important in the hour of his great loss to support him in every way that I can, do you not agree?"

James sighed. "Of course."

"And I am the eldest son — the heir. It is my duty to be there."

"I am sure you are right," James said.

"Well, there is the Rectory now, so I will leave you, little brother. *Au revoir.*"

And with a quick wave, he was gone, leaving James to shake his head in affection. His brother would never change.

Whistling, he continued on to the Rectory.

1: Leaving Sagborough

SAGBOROUGH, WEST RIDING

JANUARY

Julia had endured fourteen farewell dinners, each more tedious than the last. As if it were not enough that every day must be spent kneeling before a trunk or box or portmanteau, folding and tucking and wrapping, but every evening they were all to don their finery, or what remained unpacked, and venture out to be congratulated or condoled, according to the opinion of the person offering the sentiment. There were those who thought they were entirely mad to leave the blessed country of Yorkshire to venture into the decadent south. There were those who envied them their opportunity to climb the ladder of society a little. And there were those who were no doubt glad of their going, or foretold catastrophe, or wished them gone long since. They all *offered* good wishes, but Julia took leave to doubt the sincerity of many of them.

Their final evening at Sagborough was spent in their own home, but if they had expected a quiet time, a respite before the rigours of the journey, they were mistaken. Everyone who regarded himself as a particular friend came to wish them a final farewell, and it seemed they had a great many particular friends, for the drawing room was full, and the parlour next door almost so.

Allie was cross, of course. The house should have been solely hers, as she whispered to anyone who would listen. As the eldest daughter of the family, the abandoned family home should rightfully have come to her, and not to Ted, who wasn't even a legitimate son, for all he'd taken the Fletcher name. Now they were all to live together, Allie and Jack, and their three bairns, and Ted and Cathy with their four, all crammed in together, and Cathy ruling the domestic sphere. But Pa had been unmoved.

"You're a Ewbank now, Allie," he'd said, smiling ruefully at her. "You made your choice, and you must live with the consequences. Ted's my son and my blood, just as much as you are, and he bears the family name, too. I want a Fletcher to have this house that's been ours for so long. Four generations of Fletchers have lived here, and it's right and proper that it should pass to a fifth. Will won't need it, for he'll inherit this grand estate of ours down south, and Johnny's well set at Cambridge and needs nothing from me, so Ted's the best person to have it. He's got the warehouses to manage and the business to tend, and he can do that better from here. He's the only Mr Fletcher of Fletcher's Import and Export Company now, and he needs to live according to his position in this town."

"But it will be so crowded, with two families living in a house intended for one."

"It's generous of Ted and Cathy to offer to share," he said. "It'll save you all a bit of money, and you must approve that, the good little housewife that you are. In time, Jack will have enough saved to buy you a house of your own, but it's a good arrangement for now, and I shall be glad to think of you all living in this house, where we've all been so happy. Be content, Allie."

Ted and Cathy seemed rather stunned by their good fortune, but the papers had been drawn up that day, with the whole family watching.

"Bridges are burned now and no mistake," Will had whispered in Julia's ear as Pa signed his name with a flourish.

"You ought to be cross about it," Julia whispered back. "You're the eldest legitimate son, the family house should be yours."

Will had shrugged. "I'll get a better one. Chadwell Park... I shall be master of Chadwell Park, in the far distant future, and I shall like that very well, I assure you."

That evening, the two stood a little aside from the crowds thronging the drawing room.

"Aren't you the least bit sorry to be leaving?" Julia said to him. "You have friends here, and favourite rides, and... and female friends."

Will laughed. "I have other friends, friends I made at Harrow and Cambridge, and I shall make more. And there are females in Hertfordshire, I am certain. What about you? What will you miss?"

"My walks, I suppose, but there will be hundreds of acres of walks in Hertfordshire. I can't wait!"

"No friends?"

"My *real* friends are going with me — Rosie, Angie, Bella, you, Johnny. Pa and the new Mama, too. I shan't be leaving anyone behind that I regard as an intimate friend. Unlike Rosie. How will she manage without Belinda Jupp? Look at them, weeping together over there."

"They will write each other huge letters, every page double crossed," Will said with a shrug.

"It's not quite the same," Julia said thoughtfully. "And poor Ricky!"

"Ricky Jupp? Ricky the apothecary?"

"He's been in love with Rosie for years," Julia said. "You must have noticed it."

That brought another shrug of Will's elegantly clad shoulders. "Half the young men of Sagborough have been in love with Rosie for years. The Star of the North, they called her in York, remember? She is by far too beautiful to be constrained by Yorkshire, and especially she should not throw herself away on an apothecary. She will be a huge success in London, and have the eligible men of the *Beau Monde* at her feet, you may be sure. Rosie will marry very well indeed, or I am a Chinaman."

"What about you, Will?" Julia said slyly. "Are you going to marry very well indeed, too?"

"Certainly I am… but not yet. I am only six and twenty, Jules, and I want to enjoy myself before getting leg-shackled. I shall not even consider matrimony until I am thirty. At least!"

"Well, I don't plan to marry at all," she said robustly. "After all, who would have me? I have no accomplishments, I trip over things and always have a tear in my gown. Oh, and I speak my mind. What man of sense would want a wife like that?"

"Plenty of men want a wife with some spirit in her, little sister," Will said, affectionately flicking one cheek. "You may be surprised."

"Perhaps, but not these high-born southern men. They won't want a mouthy Yorkshire lass."

She laughed, and Will laughed too, although he shook his head at her. "We shall see. Marriage comes to all of us in the end, it seems to me."

~~~~~

The road south was not as dire as Julia had imagined. Will and the new Mama had managed it all between them, planning the route, sending most of their luggage on ahead, so that they travelled in easy stages, with horses and meals and overnight stays all arranged in advance. There were three carriages, all of them excessively comfortable, and there were hot bricks for their feet, fur-lined wraps to snuggle into and baskets of dainty comestibles to cater for the slightest pangs of hunger.

Only the weather was a concern, but they were fortunate that the week they had chosen turned out to be the mildest January anyone could remember. Every time they changed horses, the head ostler or the innkeeper or the cook would wander over to them to express astonishment at their travelling at all so early in the year, but wasn't it remarkable how benign the weather was? Apart from an occasional shower of icy rain, they completed the journey to Hertfordshire with nothing at all to trouble them.

The only element of travelling that drove Julia to distraction was sitting still for hours on end. She shared the smaller carriage with the new Mama, Pa and Rosie, and although it was beautifully appointed and could not be more comfortable, it was still the greatest trial to a taller-than-average girl who was not accustomed to sitting in one attitude for more than five minutes at a time. If Julia sat at all, she liked to stretch her long legs out and be easy, but there was no stretching anything in the carriage without bumping into a leg or a brick or the hamper.

As if that were not enough of a trial, there was the talking. Rosie was no bother at all, for she said nothing, merely gazing wide-eyed out of the window as the miles rolled past, and Mama said very little. But Pa had Carey's Itinerary with him, and he insisted on reading pieces from it for every place they passed through. No hamlet was beneath notice, for often there was a Norman bell tower or unusual spire to the church, and if that failed, there was bound to be a manor house or a court or an abbey nearby to be described and wondered at. And all the while, Julia was trying not to fidget and wishing she could leave the carriage behind, no matter how comfortable, and stride out across the winter-bare fields and under the leafless trees and stretch her legs.

The only relief she obtained was the short period after they halted for the night, when there would be an hour, perhaps, before dinner and she could rush away into the dusk, with Will and Johnny to bear her company, and make sure she never got lost.

On the fifth and final day of their journey, they were permitted to sleep late and enjoy a leisurely breakfast. They were now only an hour or so away from Chadwell Park, and had notified the servants that they would be there at noon, so there was no great need for a swift departure. As if to bless their arrival in Hertfordshire, the sun shone from a cloudless sky as they turned out of the inn yard. Julia gazed about her with satisfaction. The countryside was not, to her eyes, particularly interesting at this season, and the flat terrain was not enticing, but surely there would be good walking to be had, even within the grounds of their own estate?

They passed through the modest village of Danes Green, which boasted a handful of nondescript cottages and a rather fine church, and then there was a great stone arch and ironwork gates thrown wide, and a little line of people bobbing up and down outside the lodge as they turned in, and a long curving drive.

Mama was all a-flutter, for this was *her* lodge and *her* drive and *her* avenue of stately beeches, and when glimpses could be seen through the trees, *her* house, too, and a lake and a wide vista of empty grounds just begging to be explored. Pa was his usual smiling self, pleased that Mama was excited, but not himself overwhelmed. Rosie's eyes were huge. Poor Rosie! Julia sincerely pitied her, for everyone expected her to marry well, and hoist the whole family a notch or two up the ladder of success in society. What a burden to lay on so gentle a person. Julia was grateful that there could be no possibility of such expectations as far as she was concerned. If she were to marry at all, it would be to the vast astonishment of all who knew her.

The carriage rumbled through more formal gardens and then to the house itself. It was huge, that was Julia's first thought. Even though she had seen the plans and the sketches of the front elevation, yet the edifice rose majestically above them, strong and solid and overpoweringly massive, with two wings to either side making it enormously wide.

As they drew up at the foot of the twin sets of steps that led up to the front door, a number of servants streamed out of the house to take up station there. On the steps to the left were the indoor servants, bewigged manservants in livery and maids in neat, plain gowns and aprons, and on the right, the grooms and gardeners, she presumed. Two servants came down to the carriage door, a superior looking manservant who was presumably the butler and a woman wearing the chatelaine of a housekeeper.

Julia was about to descend as soon as the carriage door opened, but Mama's hand on her arm held her back.

"In the proper order, dear," she said, smiling.

Oh, yes, everything must be done in the proper order now. Julia had almost forgotten that the change in their circumstances changed everything else. They were landed gentry now, and all must be done in the appropriate manner. Whatever that was.

Pa descended first, and then gave his hand to Mama. Then Rosie, and then Julia. Last, as befitted her lowly status. Of course, the second carriage had disgorged its occupants at once, all higgledy-piggledy, Angie exclaiming at the size of the house, the boys pretending they were not in the least overawed by it, Bella huddled against Miss Crabtree, Aunt Madge sour-faced, as usual. One would imagine that a mansion would at least be something she could not complain about, for it could hardly be too small or too ill-appointed or too inconvenient, being so modern. But no, she could always find something about it to despise, no doubt.

Pa and Mama went past the line of indoor servants slowly, so that each could be named and respond with an appropriately servile curtsy or bow. Then nothing would do for Mama but she must be introduced to all the outdoor servants, too. As if she would remember the names of the third under-gardener, or the boy who swept out the stables! It was ridiculous. But she seemed to think it necessary, and Pa watched her in affectionate complacency.

Bored, Julia turned away from the house to look at the grounds. The remains of a fine frost lay on shaded parts still, and icy cobwebs on the shrubbery shimmered like diamonds in the still air. Beyond the formal grounds, all dismal dark greenery, trimmed to rigid shapes, there was the open park she had been promised, the grass sloping gently up to a line of trees, interrupted by a short stretch of wall and what looked like a gate set into it.

That gate called powerfully to Julia. A gate was a promise of something beyond, something unknown but enticing.

"May I go for a walk?" she cried out. Everyone turned to look at her. "Please? Just to stretch my legs."

"But you will want to see the house and choose your own room," Mama said with a small frown creasing her smooth brow. "Surely tomorrow—"

"I don't care about the room! Rosie may choose for me… or you, if you wish. I've been confined to the carriage for days now, and I shall run mad if I don't walk somewhere."

"Perhaps if Will or Johnny—"

"We have to see to the stables," Will said.

"Let her go." That was Pa, ever the peacemaker. "She'll be the better for some exercise. I only wish I could go with her."

"But the ways here are unfamiliar," Mama said. "What if she were to lose her way?"

"I shall only walk up to that gate there," Julia said. "You will be able to see me from the house at every moment. I shall not go further than that, I promise. Oh *please* may I go?"

Pa looked at Mama, one eyebrow raised. She laughed, and said, "Oh, very well then, Julia. There will be nothing but bustle for an hour or two yet, but do not stay out long in this cold weather."

"I won't," Julia cried, turning away with a wave almost before the words were out of her mouth.

She was free at last! With eager steps she sped along a gravel path between beds brown and bare at this season, balls of drab green standing forlornly at the corners, and then a rose garden, already pruned almost to the ground, and finally the lawn. Another path wound down to a narrow part of the lake, spanned by an arched stone bridge, and then up, up, up to the woods and the intriguing gate. What would be beyond it? A dark, mysterious forest? A river... a vast uncrossable lake... wild moorland, filled with curlews and pipits... mountains, even? No, probably no mountains. They were a very long way from anything that might properly be called by that name. But hills... there might be hills.

It was farmland. At first, her spirits plummeted, for what could be duller than cows and bare grain fields? But when she looked again, she saw more, a great deal more. There *was* a river, now that she looked more closely. She could catch glints between the leafless branches of a line of trees some distance below her which could only be water. Another line of trees probably marked a road, for it led to a small hamlet, the smoke rising vertically from several cottages.

Nearer at hand, a tiny cottage peeped through an untidy hedge. From it, a man in rough clothing emerged and walked steadily up the slope towards her, a gun in one hand and a tidy haul of game dangling from his belt. The gamekeeper! One of the estate workers, one of their own people. Someone who would not disdain the newcomers from the north, the mercer and his family, because his livelihood depended on them.

She waved cheerily to him. He looked up, saw her and smiled. He had a kind face, she thought. A friendly face. She clambered onto the gate and waited for her first new friend to reach her.

~~~~~

There was a girl sitting on the gate. As soon as James emerged from the hut, he saw her leaning on the top bar, watching him. Then she waved, and climbed up to sit on the gate, one leg swinging, a merry smile on her face.

He had never seen her before, that much was certain. As he drew nearer, she called out merrily to him, "Good day to you, sir! That looks like a good haul. What have you there?"

"Nothing too exciting, only pheasant and a couple of ducks. There were some woodcock, but they got away from me."

She was an odd sort of young lady, he decided. Her clothes looked expensive if not exactly fashionable, but her pelisse and the gown beneath it were both mud-bespattered, and loose tendrils of hair escaped from a rather battered bonnet.

"Are they for the house... I mean the Park?"

"That's right."

"Oh good, because I like pheasant. It's a pity about the woodcock, because that's one of Pa's favourites, but maybe you'll have more luck tomorrow."

"Maybe I will," James said. Her lively face and enthusiasm made him want to smile, and at least he now knew who she was. "You must be a part of the Fletcher family."

"I am! We just arrived an hour or so ago, but I couldn't bear to be indoors, so I came out for a walk."

"And only got as far as the gate to the High Field."

"Is that what it's called? I don't know the names of anything yet. I would have walked further, but the new Mama didn't want me to go out of sight. She thinks I'll get lost, but I never do. If I walk from one place to another, I can always turn round and go back the way I've come, can't I?"

James laughed. There was something so open and artless about her that he could scarcely resist. "Do you like your new home?"

She shrugged. "I haven't seen much of it yet. I've left that to Mama."

He knew she was one of the sisters... one of the four. But which one? The eldest was a beauty, allegedly, but this girl, although pleasantly featured, would never be described as such. But she was so open that he had no hesitation in asking her directly. "So which Miss Fletcher are you?"

She laughed merrily. "The second one. Well... strictly speaking, the third, but Allie, the eldest of us, is married and left behind in the West Riding. Rosie is the eldest unmarried, then me — I'm Julia, then Angie. And Bella, but she's still in the schoolroom. There are two boys, Will and Johnny. Oh, and Aunt Madge. Mama's sister. Our real mama, that is, not the new one. The new Mama is the one who wanted to move here and be gentry. The rest of us would have been quite happy to stay in Sagborough, but Pa wanted her to be happy and so here we are, and lucky for us this place was for sale, I suppose. Although unlucky for the Plummer family, who got into debt and had to sell it to us. Our neighbours, now. Oh, but you must know them, of course. What are they like? Are they quite horrid?"

James knew perfectly well that he should tell her at once that he was a Plummer himself, but the mischievous streak in him intervened. He had not enjoyed himself so much in an age. Life was so boring, as a rule, and here was someone who was not in the least boring. It was deliciously amusing that she had no idea who he was, and was not on her best behaviour. She would find out his name soon enough, so where was the harm? "I would not say they are horrid," he said cautiously. "In fact, they are very pleasant people."

"Pleasant, are they? I hope that's true, and they don't despise us too much. They're very grand, though, aren't they? The father is a baronet, and that's like nobility, isn't it? Mama says not, but I'm not sure if she's right about that."

"She is quite correct," James said. "A baronet is gentry — just like your family, although a little more distinguished, perhaps."

Miss Fletcher brightened. "Is that so? Well, I hope we get on with them. We have to learn to get on with all these high-ranking people because Rosie is to marry a title. She is a great beauty, you see, so her destiny is to marry a lord and drag us all up into good society in her train, although for myself I'm not sure I want to be dragged up. Or could be, come to that. I dare say *my* destiny is to marry the local parson and deliver beef jelly to all the poor families of the parish."

"There are worse fates than to marry the parson," James murmured, trying very hard not to laugh.

"Are there? I can't think of many." She shivered.

James was instantly alarmed for her. It was January,

after all, and a bitterly cold day for a gently-brought-up young lady to be sitting about on gates.

"You will become chilled if you linger much longer here. Let me escort you back to the Park. I have to go that way anyway to hand over my efforts for the day."

"Oh, that's kind, although I won't get lost, you know. If I look back the way I came, I can see the house very clearly. But if we are both going the same way, perhaps you can tell me about the neighbours and the village as we walk."

And so they ambled slowly back down the hill, and James managed to tell her a great deal about the parish without once mentioning the church or the rectory or the fact that he was himself the rector.

2: Chadwell Park

The gamekeeper took Julia to a low building to one side of the house, which she immediately identified as the kitchens, from the distant banging of pots and the glimpses of still room and scullery on either side of the door. A harried kitchen maid took charge of the birds, with a bobbed curtsy and a surprised glance at Julia.

"Thank 'ee, Master James," she said. With another puzzled look at Julia, she disappeared into a side room.

The gamekeeper laughed, his face alight with amusement. He was young for a gamekeeper, Julia thought, who had imagined such people to be weather-beaten men of mature years, grizzled and grey, chewing twigs between gloomy prognostications on the prospects for rain. This man was not above thirty, with pleasant features and hair of an indeterminate brown that fell in soft curls around his face like a halo.

"If you follow this corridor a little way and turn right just past the cheese store, you will find the passage to the main part of the house. When you come to the stairs, go up and you will come out beside the breakfast room. The entrance hall is just a short distance further."

"Thank you, sir, and for your company. I dare say we shall meet again."

"I imagine we will," he said, grinning as he bowed low. Then, with a cheery wave of his hat, he was gone, closing the outer door behind him.

She had no difficulty finding her way as he had directed, emerging into the main house in a broad passageway lit from far above by some kind of window set in the roof. Several doors led off to either side, all of them closed. At the far end, wide stairs looped upwards past high windows. There was no one in sight.

Walking slowly down the passageway, she found the massive entrance hall, rimmed with marble pillars, its floor tiled in an intricate pattern. So grandiose, their new home! Not like the comfortable familiarity of their Sagborough house. A wave of nostalgia washed over her momentarily, but she resolutely banished it. It was strange just now, but they would grow accustomed and if the local people were as friendly as the gamekeeper, they would be very happy here.

There was no one about, but voices emanated from behind one of the closed doors, deeper male rumbles, and one higher voice that might be Mama's.

Julia turned the knob and pushed open the door.

Many pairs of eyes turned to stare at her. Pa and Mama

were there, as well as Angie and Johnny, who grinned when he saw her. Will was leaning negligently against an elaborately carved marble fireplace, looking very much at home. There were three complete strangers sitting stiffly on chairs with gold-painted arms.

"Oh! Julia!" Mama cried. "Goodness, child, must you come in here in all your dirt?"

Julia gazed down at her travelling pelisse. It *was* rather stained, now that she looked at it.

"I beg your pardon, Mama," she said. "I shall go and change."

"Well, now that you are here, you had better meet our neighbours, and the former owners of our new home. Lady Plummer, may I present to you our second eldest daughter, Miss Julia Fletcher? Julia, this is Lady Plummer, Sir Owen Plummer and Mr Michael Plummer."

Lady Plummer, her back ramrod straight, inclined her head slightly in icy acknowledgement, but the two gentlemen had risen at her entrance and now made her formal bows.

Julia made her curtsy. "How do you do, Lady Plummer? Sir Owen. Mr Plummer. Pray forgive my dishevelled appearance, but I could not wait to enjoy the freedom of your lovely gardens after five days of confinement in the carriage."

"That is entirely understandable, Miss Fletcher," Sir Owen said, "although of course they are *your* family's gardens now, not ours. I sincerely wish you many pleasant walks there, and in better weather than January affords."

"You are too kind, Sir Owen," Mama trilled, a smile fixed

on her face. "Too tolerant, when it must be the greatest grief to you to see your family home occupied by strangers."

"It is no grief to me, I assure you, Mrs Fletcher, and I very much hope you will not be strangers for long. Did you walk far, Miss Fletcher?"

"Only to the gate to the High Field. I met the gamekeeper there, who told me the name of it."

"The gamekeeper?" Lady Plummer straightened even more, sounding startled. "Is he better? The poor man has been practically bedridden for months now, but then he is over eighty, so it is only to be expected."

"Over eighty? Then this man must have been his son... or grandson, perhaps?"

"Billings has no children."

"An under-gamekeeper? Apprentice?"

Sir Owen chuckled. "Miss Fletcher, I believe it is possible that you may have encountered our younger son, James. He is often out with a gun."

"Oh yes, the kitchen maid called him Master James!" Julia laughed heartily. "Well, how foolish of me! Now that I think about it, he was remarkably well-spoken for a gamekeeper. So he is your son? He never mentioned it. What a good joke, but he was bringing pheasant and duck to our kitchen, you see, so what else was I to think?"

"Really, Julia!" Mama said, flushing a little. "How could you possibly think Sir Owen's son was a gamekeeper? I must apologise for my stepdaughter, Lady Plummer, Sir Owen. Her manners as yet lack a little polish, I regret to say."

"No need at all for any apology, Mrs Fletcher," Sir Owen said, smiling. "It is an understandable mistake, for James wears the most disreputable garments when he is out shooting, and no one would take him for a gentleman in the least. Mr Fletcher has been so very obliging as to allow us to shoot on his land, both for our own table and for his, and James has taken this licence to heart. But perhaps you gentlemen shoot, or mean to take up the sport? We would be delighted to show you the best coveys, if so."

"I shoot a little," Will said eagerly. "I should be very glad of some advice on the sport to be had here."

"It would be our pleasure to introduce you to the best this part of Hertfordshire can offer. I cannot speak for James, but Michael and I will be out tomorrow. Perhaps you would care to join us, sir?"

While Will responded with enthusiasm and Mama fluttered under these pretty courtesies, Julia looked from one to another of the Plummers, these people who had lived in Chadwell Park until a few short weeks ago and were now their nearest neighbours. Sir Owen was a man of the most gentlemanly appearance, tall, upright, his manner of speech clipped but not in an unfriendly way, she thought. Whereas Lady Plummer dripped with disdain, her mouth set in a rigid line that would almost certainly melt into a sneer if she allowed her dignity to drop for a fraction of a second. The third member of their party, Mr Michael Plummer, must be the eldest son and heir. He was perhaps thirty, tall, like his father, but pale and spindly, his expression nervous.

Sir Owen said something to Angie, but before she could respond, Julia said, "Where is Rosie? Shouldn't she be here too?"

An expression that might have been exasperation crossed Mama's features. "She could not be found. The footmen have looked everywhere. When you have changed out of your muddy clothes, perhaps you might see if you can find her."

It was a clear dismissal, which Julia was not loath to obey. With a quick curtsy, she scurried out of the room, although she had no idea where to go. The bedrooms would be upstairs, no doubt. Quick steps took her to the stairs, which she took two at a time. Up above, more doors lined the long landing, all closed. Shrugging, she began to open one after another. The first two were empty, the furniture shrouded in holland covers, although she saw the schoolroom boxes piled in one of them. In the third, she surprised two maids busy making up the bed. Johnny's boxes sat opened on the floor, half emptied, but there was no sign of his valet. A fire burning fitfully did nothing to drive away the chill. The two maids stared at her, seeming not unfriendly but not welcoming, either.

"I wonder—?" she began, but an exclamation behind her caused her to spin round. The housekeeper stood there, a pile of towels in her arms, her expression downright hostile.

"What are you doing here?" she said frostily, making no attempt to curtsy.

"Looking for my room," Julia said. "Perhaps you can—?"

"I have no idea," she said curtly. "The young persons chose their own rooms."

"Yes, but—"

Johnny's valet came in at that moment, carrying a ewer of steaming water, and Julia smiled in relief. "Ah, Matlock, which is my room, do you know?"

"Aye, t'one directly across t'way, Miss Julia," he said, his Yorkshire accent a little burst of home. "I'll show you."

"Thank you." He held the door for her, but Julia paused, turning to the housekeeper. "What is your name?"

"Mrs Graham, miss."

"Do you know who I am?"

She flushed. "You're Miss Julia Fletcher, miss."

"Correct. That makes me the daughter of your master and mistress. If you should encounter me in future, you will kindly remember that, and curtsy to me. You will also teach the maids to do so. Is that understood?"

The housekeeper turned beetroot red. "Yes, Miss Julia." She dropped into a curtsy, and the two maids did likewise, as Julia swept out of the room.

Her own room turned out to be very much the same, except that the bed remained unmade, her boxes unopened and the fire was as yet unlit. She shivered, not used to such neglected rooms. At home, her bedroom had a fire burning all day at this time of year.

"Glory be, these rooms are freezing," Matlock muttered, kneeling to light the fire. "What they're about not making up t'beds or lighting t'fires, I can't think. It's as if they weren't expecting us."

"What are things like below stairs, Matlock? Are they helpful?"

The valet looked up, wrinkling his nose. "I wouldn't say that, exactly. If you ask where summat is, they point you t'right way, but they none of them go out o' their way to show you anything. Too busy rushing about themselves. There, that'll warm things up a bit." The fire blazed up cheerily. "Shall I send Sarah to help you change, Miss?"

"No need. She'll be busy unpacking Rosie's things, I expect. I can manage for myself."

When he had gone, Julia threw off her pelisse and bonnet, opened her boxes and dragged out the first day gown that came to hand. Changing quickly, she ran fingers through her tousled hair and scooped it into a simple knot. Then she sat on the bare bed and looked around the room. Devoid of any personal touches, it was a sad, soulless place, and it was all hers. She had never in her life had a bedroom to herself, but she would share with Rosie and Angie no longer. That had been agreed before they left Sagborough. They would have to double up if there were visitors, but otherwise they would sleep alone. How strange that would be!

Restless, she crept out of the room again, and looked about her. The housekeeper and maids were busy now at the room furthest from the stairs, so perhaps she could creep downstairs unnoticed and have a look round while Mama and Pa were busy with the Plummers. She had reached the head of the stairs and was just about to descend when she heard a sound, muffled but unmistakable. Someone was sobbing quietly nearby.

All the doors were closed, but there was a curtain draped to one side of the staircase. Lifting it, Julia discovered herself in a strange room with big windows that curved above the stairs, the walls lined with busts on plinths and little groupings of miniatures, medals and a pair of swords. Following the curve, she came to a straight section, the walls hung with numerous paintings. And there, tucked behind a nearly naked statue of a Grecian woman, she found Rosie, hunched up on the floor in floods of tears.

"Oh, Rosie! It can't be that bad! Whatever is the matter?"

"I had a letter... from Belinda, Jules, and oh, it made me long so for home, you cannot imagine. It is all so *strange* here and big and... and *cold*. There is nothing of *us* here at all."

"There will be, Rosie, dear," Julia said, flopping to the floor beside her and wrapping her arms around her. "It will take time, but we will make *this* our home, just as much as Fullers Road was. It will be different but it will still be our home because we will all be here."

"But we will not," Rosie wailed. "I shall be married to some lord or other, and you and Angie and Bella will marry too, and Johnny will be at Cambridge, and Will is bound to marry, too, and bring some horrid aristocratic lady into the family and everything will be different. Do you not see? Not like when Ted and Allie married, because they lived just down the road and we saw them almost every day. But suppose I marry someone from... from Cornwall, say, or Wales, then I shall be torn away from you all, and how should I bear it? I wish we could go home, Jules, truly I do. I am not sure I want to marry a lord... or anyone grand."

"Then you shall not. You shall stay here with Mama and Pa and me, for I shan't ever marry, you know."

"You will, Julia. Of course you will. It is a woman's duty to marry."

"But first she has to find a man willing to marry her, and who would ever have me? Depend upon it, I shall be just like Aunt Madge in a few years, grumpy and bitter, trailing round with the family trying to be helpful. And my first lesson in helpfulness would have to be remembering to carry a handkerchief around with me, for yours is sodden and I have none to offer you. What a useless spinster aunt I shall be!"

Rosie smiled wanly.

~~~~~

'To Miss Fletcher, Chadwell Park, nr Ware, Hertfordshire. My dearest friend, Is this not the most delightful surprise? It was Ricky's idea to write to you the very day of your departure. He says that the mail coach travels much faster than any private conveyance, and so such a letter will be waiting for you the instant you walk through the door of your new home. I hope it is so, indeed, for if you are a little overwhelmed by the grandeur of Chadwell Park, which sounds by Mrs Fletcher's account to be very grand indeed, then perhaps this will cheer you a little. And if your new house is wonderful and your mind is fully occupied with pondering its wonders, then do remember your friends back home, and send us an account of it all. Oh Rosie, I so long to hear of it from you! Is it everything you expected? Are the rooms beautiful? And tell me of the journey, too, for I have never been anywhere except to Grandpa at Newcastle now and then when he was thought to

be dying, although it was all a take in and he is still with us. And now he claims to be ill again, can you believe it? But there is no other news to report. The talk is all of your departure, my dear friend, and how sad we all feel, as you may imagine. Also there is more talk of Camilla Weston, but you know all about that, and there is nothing new to say of her, so I shall not waste paper on her. Do write as soon as you have time, to describe your new home in the most minute detail. Ricky sends his best regards to you, as do I, your most affectionate friend, Belinda.'

3: Early Days

The afternoon stretched interminably. They would eat late, Julia already knew, for the servants were accustomed to a seven o'clock dinner, and Mama did not like to disrupt their usual practices on the first day.

"We shall have everything just as we like it in a day or so, I am sure," she had said, "but just for today let them do as they usually do. We will dress at six and eat at seven."

Pa had sighed, and sent his man Enoch to find the remains of the hampers of food that had travelled with them.

By the time the hour arrived to dress for dinner, Julia had unpacked most of her things, filled drawers and presses, and arranged her few ornamental possessions on her dressing table and mantelpiece. She chose a gown, and sat and waited for Sarah to bring hot water for washing. She waited for half an hour.

Eventually, Sarah came in at a rush. "So sorry, Miss Julia, but there's no more hot water to be had, just enough for the mistress and Miss Rosie, and Master Will's that upset about it. I don't know how it is, with a great big kitchen like that and fires everywhere, yet there's hardly enough hot water for two basins, and now we're all behind."

"No matter, Sarah, you go and see to Miss Rosie, and Angie and I will dress each other. Off you go."

With a bit of a scramble, they were all down in the saloon shortly before seven. And there they waited, as seven o'clock came and went. As the clock on the mantel chimed the quarter hour with a sonorous sense of its own importance, Mama rose and rang the bell. It was a full ten minutes before the butler sidled into the room.

"Yes, madam?"

"What has happened to delay dinner, Keeble?"

"Some difficulty in the kitchen, madam. Mrs Sharwell should be ready soon."

The men groaned, and Julia jumped to her feet impatiently. "This is ridiculous! It is bad enough to make us wait in the first place, but the kitchen has had all day to prepare."

Mama smiled a little rigidly. "We must make allowances, dear. It is the first time they have cooked for us."

"But they cooked every day for the Plummers," Will said, crossly. "What is the difference? I am famished. Why can we not eat whatever is ready? They can send the rest up whenever the crisis has been dealt with."

"I do not think—" Mama began, spots of colour appearing on her cheeks.

"I agree with Will," Pa said. "We will eat now. Come, Lizzie."

He rose and offered her his arm, and although her lips set in a thin line, she had no choice but to comply. The butler bowed low, his face impassive, and held the door open for them to pass through.

In the dining room, the table was bare. They found Enoch engaged in a furious discussion with one of the footmen, while another footman appeared to be laughing at them. They all sprang to attention when the family entered, holding chairs for the ladies.

"There's no place for Dorothea!" Bella cried. "You told the man to set an extra place, I heard you, but he hasn't done it."

"I expect he forgot, with all the other calls on his time," Mama said. "Please lay an extra place beside Miss Bella, Keeble."

"Are you expecting a guest, madam?" the butler said in bland tones.

"It's not for you to question your mistress's orders," Pa said curtly. "You are always to lay an extra place when Miss Bella dines with us. Do it now, and if you value your position here, get some food on this table at once."

Enoch sprang to reset the table, while the butler and footmen departed without haste.

"Mr Fletcher, I would prefer it if you would leave the management of the servants on such occasions to me," Mama said in her placid way, when they had gone. "It is my responsibility to see that meals arrive on time."

"And it is their responsibility to obey your orders, at once and unquestioningly," Pa said immediately. "I don't like to see insolence, Lizzie, and so I tell you."

She laughed quite easily. "Insolence? You refine too much upon it, dear. There are bound to be trivial little difficulties, but we will all soon adjust to the new circumstances, you may be sure."

With Dorothea's place laid, Enoch rushed away to help transport the food from the kitchen wing, and before long a little train of servants arrived, each bearing a dish to set on the table, filling the room with welcome aromas. They all fell upon the soups with relief — something to eat at last! The soups were removed with joints of beef and mutton, and although they were black on one side and underdone on the other, everyone was too glad to see food to complain. Apart from Aunt Madge, of course.

After that, there was a second course, with an odd array of food, many dishes being unfamiliar to them.

"What is that strange stuff?" Julia said, as a footman placed a dish on the table near her.

"I couldn't rightly say, miss," he said.

"That one is glazed grenadines with endives," the butler said. "One of Mrs Sharwell's specialities, I fancy."

"It looks disgusting," Julia said. "Who wants to try it? Mama? Pa? Angie? Anyone?"

"I will try a little," Rosie said, her voice soft.

"Allow me to help you to the best portion, miss," the butler said, spooning great dollops of the grey sludge onto her plate.

"Thank you, Mr Keeble," she said, looking at it without enthusiasm.

Johnny smiled at her. "You are a brave soul, Rosie, but you need not eat it if you dislike it. I agree with Jules, it looks unappetising, speciality or no. These sweetbreads are more to my taste, and the wine is not bad. We must have a look round the cellar tomorrow, Will, and see where the gaps are."

"You are treating us to a splendid dinner, Mrs Fletcher," Pa said, with a warm smile, as he set to work on a dish of macaroni with chicken. "Are we to eat this well every day of the week from now on? Or is this a Market Day treat, as at home?"

"Oh... it is Friday, is it not? Market Day. Or it would be, if we were still at Sagborough."

"Aye, and we'd have Allie and Ted and all the bairns here, too," he said, sadly. "We miss them, don't we?"

"We do, Pa," Rosie said quietly, lowering her head.

"They will come to visit us in the summer," Mama said brightly. "It is all agreed. But as to having two courses every day... this is what the kitchen usually provided for the Plummer family, Mrs Graham told me, so perhaps we should do the same?"

"There's no need, not just for us," Pa said. "When we have guests, then of course you'll want to put on a good spread, but for the family, let's keep it simple, eh?"

"It shall be as you wish, Mr Fletcher, naturally." But Julia thought she was a little offended, all the same.

By the time dinner was finished, Julia was ready for her bed, but Mama insisted that they withdraw to a different saloon, and sit with their needlework while the gentlemen drank port and talked about... well, whatever men talked about when there were no ladies present. Rosie and Aunt Madge dutifully stitched, while Julia pretended to read a book and tried not to yawn. Angie discovered a pianoforte in the adjoining room, so she was happy. Bella was the luckiest of them, for Miss Crabtree came and took her away to bed.

Mama rang for tea at ten, but the men came through before it had arrived.

"Shall we have some cards?" Will said, rubbing his hands together gleefully. "Mama, will you make up a four?"

Julia brightened at once. Cards would be better than this dreary sitting about.

"Must you play tonight?" Mama said. "I thought for once we might just have a little music and conversation."

"Johnny will be off to Cambridge on Monday, so we must make the most of him," Pa said. "Julia, you'll play, won't you?"

"Willingly, but have we time? It will take an hour, at least, to track down a footman, and then the fellow will disappear into some subterranean maze for another hour, and if he manages to locate a card table, there will be no cards. It will be past midnight before we sit down to play."

"Really, Julia!" Mama said, laughing. "How you love to

exaggerate."

"Do I? You told Keeble this afternoon that we would want the tea tray at ten, you rang for it at ten and where is it? How hard can it be to prepare a tray of tea on time?"

"Never mind the tea," Will said. "We have port and brandy enough, and who needs tea, anyway? Tasteless stuff. As for a card table, we need no footman, for we explored thoroughly for all the essentials of existence while we were waiting interminably to be fed. Look!" He brought forward a small side table from a corner of the room, opened and turned the lid and there was a perfect card table. "And there are cards in the drawer, you see?"

"Are there fish, or must I fetch some money?" Julia said.

"Again, we are prepared, for we have our own fish, conveniently placed to be ready when wanted. In the cupboard over there, you will find Great-uncle Rowley's set, which he very kindly left to Johnny when he departed this mortal realm, if you remember."

"With the words, *'He has won them all from me many times over, so he might as well keep them,'* if I recall," Julia said.

"He was a terrible card player," Johnny said, grinning, as he drew chairs to the table. "There, you see? Who needs footmen? Perhaps we should run over to the kitchen and make our own tea. What do you say, Mama?"

"We might have to do that," Aunt Madge said, as the clock struck the half hour. "Look at the time! Half an hour late already. You will have to talk severely to them, Lizzie."

"I do wish you would call me Elizabeth," Mama said fretfully. "It is my proper name, after all. I do not mind Harry shortening it, for that is a husband's privilege, but I do not want the world to do so."

"Jack Glover always called you Lizzie," Madge said.

"He is my brother, and has known me since I was a baby. There is no doing anything about that. But my first husband's family never called me anything but Elizabeth, or Mrs Haygarth in public. They were always most correct."

Aunt Madge huffed, and said grudgingly that she'd do her best, but she didn't hold with it, and if there was no tea to be had, she would go to bed. And off she went, lips pursed as usual. Rosie asked if she might retire, too, and after a long discussion, she and Angie, and Mama too, all went to bed.

The card players sat on until after midnight in great contentment, steadily depleting the decanters, and not in the least worried that the tea tray never did make an appearance.

~~~~~

In the port-infused atmosphere of the night before, a firm plan had been made between Julia and the three men to make a complete circuit of the grounds the next morning. Their two hundred acres, the attorney had informed them, had a boundary of almost three miles in length, perfect for a leisurely stroll. Their enthusiasm was somewhat dampened the next morning by steady rain. Fortunately, the business of obtaining washing water and dressing took so long that the rain had stopped altogether by the time they set out.

"Now we have only an hour until breakfast," Will said

crossly, his breath clouding around him. "Hardly time for a thorough look at our new domain."

"We can walk briskly," Pa said cheerfully. "No penance in this chill air."

"There's no need to hurry," Julia said, "for breakfast will doubtless be late. Nothing else has run to time, after all."

"Aye, true enough," Pa said, chuckling. "Lord, if I'd run my warehouses on such dilatory lines, I'd still be scratching around for bales of wool in Yorkshire and wondering if I could pay the coal merchant on Lady Day."

"It is outrageous," Will said. "No hot water again today, and what did arrive was late. Lester says they are all in disarray below stairs, hardly knowing where anything is. You would think they were new in service. He is quite disgusted with them, but then he has very high standards."

"They will settle, in time," Pa said easily.

"I could settle them in two shakes of a lamb's tail if I were allowed," Will said darkly.

Pa shook his head, smiling. "Ah, you always were impatient, even as a boy. You could barely wait to be born, and your poor Mama only just made it back home before you were announcing yourself loudly. Arrived before the midwife, you did."

Will smiled ruefully. "I expect I just wanted to get on with life. There's so much pleasure to be had in this world, why would I not wish to join it as soon as I could? But seriously, Pa, someone needs to do something about the servants. They are more than dilatory, they are downright insolent, if you ask me. They enjoy keeping us waiting. Let me talk to them."

"No, no, no, you must leave it all to Lizzie. Her house, her servants, you know. She'll have a quiet word here and there, just point them in the right direction, you know the delicate way she has, and all will be as right as rain before long. Well, shall we walk down the drive first?"

The air was cold and damp, but there was not the bitter chill to which Julia was accustomed in Yorkshire. Under the bare-limbed trees lining the drive, a few brave snowdrops shyly bent their heads.

"Snowdrops already," Julia said. "So early!"

"Aye, the climate's milder this far south," Pa said. "Ah, there's the gate now. What a strange lodge that is, built like a Roman arch, yet people live in it. Which way shall we turn? Clockwise or widdershins?"

"Clockwise," they said, in unison.

A narrow track led off the drive, weaving in and out of stands of trees. A high wall separated them from the hamlet of Danes Green, although the spire of the parish church was visible, and smoke rose from several chimneys. In the still air, a cockerel crowed nearby, and a door banged. The distant clang of metal on metal suggested that the smith, at least, was already hard at work. After a short distance, the woods thickened and the village was lost to view.

Before long, they emerged into a clearing, frightening away a pair of deer. They had reached a corner of the estate, where a moss-covered wall rose to a height of some ten feet, with a door of wood and metal set in it.

"Where does that lead, do you suppose?" Johnny said. "Shall we look and see?" He turned the huge twisted metal ring to lift the latch and the door creaked open. Stepping through, he said, "We are just beyond the village. I can see the first houses. Pa, what is the house opposite? There are two very fine gateposts and a cosy little lodge. Nothing like as ostentatious as our fancy affair."

They all followed him onto the road. The gateposts were very fine indeed, made of bricks fitted in such a way that the pattern spiralled around and upwards. Ivy obscured the lower parts, but Julia marched across the road, and pulled at leaves and stems until she could read the name picked out in differently coloured bricks.

"It is Chadwell Manor," she called out. The ancestral home of the Plummer family, and their home again, now that they had sold Chadwell Park to the Fletchers.

The others followed her across the road and peered through the gates. And there it was, not a hundred yards away, its rows of fine Tudor chimneys all smoking vigorously.

"I wager *they* have plenty of hot water," Will muttered.

"You can ask them this afternoon when you see them for the shooting," Pa said genially.

"Will the whole family be there?" Julia said. "Maybe you'll meet my gamekeeper."

"Maybe we will," Pa said. "And maybe he'll dress like a gentleman this time, eh? Then we'll be able to recognise him." He chuckled good-humouredly.

"I think Sir Owen said it would just be himself and his elder son," Will said.

"Ah, well, we shall meet your gamekeeper some other time, puss," Pa said.

"Tomorrow, I expect," she said. "These southern folks aren't such heathens as not to go to church, are they? So you'll see him in church tomorrow morning, and he may even look like a gentleman."

~~~~~

'To Miss Jupp, St Peter's Road, Sagborough, West Riding. My dear Belinda, How clever of Ricky to suggest sending a letter at once, for there it was waiting for me the moment I arrived! Oh, but it made me weep just a little to remember you and Ricky, my two dearest friends in the whole world, after my own family of course. First of all, be assured that we are all well. Dreadfully fatigued after the long journey, of course, for five days in a carriage, be it ever so comfortable, is bound to leave one a little pulled. Mama is in heaven, for the house is just as she hoped. Oh, I must describe it to you, so that you will know just how we have risen in the world, to live in such a palace. The entrance to the grounds is marked by a great stone arch not unlike Micklegate Bar, but very Greek, with pillars and a big triangle over the top, which is a pediment, Miss Crabtree told us later. It is big enough to live in, for the gatekeeper and all his family came out to make their courtesies. Then a curving drive lined with trees and a bridge across a lake, and then the house. Oh, Belinda, you cannot imagine how enormous it is! It has only two stories, not counting the attics and basement, but it seemed to stretch to the skies, and there are statues even on the roof, if you can

imagine such a thing! It presents a very long face, with a multitude of windows, and then to either side and a little offset are two wings, one the kitchens and the other the stables. In front, there are two sets of steps to each side, very square, not curving at all. I do not think you can imagine all this from such a description, so I shall try to make drawings to send to you, just as soon as I can find my sketchbook. And then inside, everything is so fine and decorated - nothing is left plain at all. If there is a patch of ceiling or wall not used for any function, then it must be covered in latticework or swags of carved foliage or fruit or some other design. It is all very overpowering, and the ceilings so high and far away that one feels like a little mouse creeping about in the undergrowth in a great forest. And the worst of it is that everyone else seems to like it, or else, like Julia, doesn't care. Even Aunt Madge grudgingly admits that her room is commodious and well-appointed, and you know how little she approves of anything as a rule. So I am alone in hating it all. Perhaps that is too strong a sentiment, brought on only by missing you, my dearest friend. I feel very alone here without you. I have covered two sheets already and dare not impose any further costs on your long-suffering Pa, so I will stop now, and write more very soon. My dearest regards to you and to all your family. Pray give Ricky my sincerest thanks for urging you to write so soon. Your letter cheered me vastly. Your most affectionate and rather lonely friend, Rosie.'

4: *Sunday*

For the first time in his life, James looked forward to the Sabbath with genuine enthusiasm, and he knew precisely the reason why — he would see Miss Julia Fletcher again. He had met hundreds of society misses over the years, and every single one of them had bored him to tears. Until now. Far from boring him, she had made him smile... no, *laugh*, and he could hardly wait to see her again at church and observe her reaction to discovering that he was the rector, exactly the person she had said it would be her fate to marry.

How funny that was! And yet, perhaps it was prophetic, too. James had never had the least desire to marry, for surely marriage would be even more boring than bachelorhood, but to marry someone like Julia... that would be different. She would make him smile every day, he was convinced of it. He would never be bored with someone like that.

James would never be accounted a dandy, preferring comfort to fashion, but today he dressed with a little more care than usual. He took pains with his cravat, and rummaged through a drawer of muddled oddments for a pin suitable for the occasion. Then he donned his surplice and made his way to the church.

"Great heavens, James, whatever has happened?" Thomas Leadbetter, his curate, cried out when he saw him. "Is your clock running fast? Are you ill? We are not at all prepared, for there is a quarter hour yet before Frye even begins to ring the bell, and you are not usually looked for until some time after he has stopped, you know."

James chuckled. "Let me be piously punctual, for once, Thomas. I am sure such an event will not recur. Where is everyone? I had expected the church to be filling somewhat by now."

"Our parishioners prefer to have an extra hour in bed than to sit on hard pews for that time awaiting your presence, and who can blame them?"

"Am I so very slipshod, Thomas? Am I thoroughly despised for my lackadaisical ways?"

"Not in the least. You are very well liked, James, for your sermons are commendably short, although if the service commences more than an hour late, folk do get restless for their breakfast, you know."

"Promptness and short sermons. Very well. I shall try to do better on the former point. Do you think my congregation will arrive soon? I shall stand at the door to welcome them as they arrive, I believe."

"Have you smelling salts at the ready? They will be so astonished to see you that—"

"Yes, yes, you have made your point, you dreadful fellow. I am not at all sure why I suffer your impertinence, Thomas Leadbetter."

"Because I do all the parish chores that you find so abominably dreary?" Thomas said, grinning.

"You are my curate, so it is your duty," James said smugly, and swept off to take up his station on the church steps.

The truth was, he had no idea how he would contrive without Thomas to do everything that was needful for the good order of the parish. James was happy to turn up on a Sunday and read through a brief sermon he had extracted from a book, when he remembered, but to Thomas fell all the parochial care of the sick or poor or needy. For that he was paid the princely sum of one hundred pounds a year, room, meals and laundry included, while James spent his days in idleness and took in the full tithes of the parish, to the sum of fourteen hundred pounds a year. It was grossly inequitable, and yet Thomas, good man that he was, thought himself fortunate to be so well placed, for many curates made no more than fifty pounds a year and had to find their own lodgings and darn their own socks, too.

Before too long, the parishioners began to arrive, and James had the amusement of their expressions of surprise at seeing their rector not merely in attendance, but actually early for the first time ever. But he was rewarded, for a few minutes before the appointed hour for the service, and before Mr Frye, the sexton, had even begun to toll the bell to hurry along the latecomers, the Fletcher party arrived. They had walked from the Park, James was impressed to see, in a long and well-dressed train, with a few servants following behind them. Not the familiar servants, but perhaps these were the valets and lady's maids they had brought from the north.

James's attention was distracted by Mrs Reynell, who teased him coquettishly about his early appearance.

"Whatever can it be that calls you to your duties with such eagerness, Rector?" she said, fluttering her eyelashes.

Mrs Reynell would be considered a most desirable wife for many men, being a young widow of some considerable fortune, still in looks and unencumbered by infants, but James was not enticed. He would never be enticed by anyone who pursued him so determinedly, and had not a thought in her head beyond the limited scope of her house, her servants and her clothes. She was rattling away about some bonnet or other, a new one, seemingly, which she deemed important enough to keep mentioning. But he could not be interested in bonnets, except one, perhaps. His eye scanned the arriving troop of Fletchers... where was she? Was she even there? Yes! There she was, in a deep blue velvet pelisse and a plain straw bonnet with mismatched ribbons. He grinned when he saw her.

"We meet again, Miss Fletcher," he cried out, as the group advanced on him.

She looked, saw him, her eyes widened. "Mr Plummer! But you are... the parson!" Merriment lit her face. "I had no idea! I thought you were the gamekeeper, you know, and I know my mistake on *that* score, but I had not the least idea that you were in Holy orders. What a tease you are, to tell me nothing about yourself."

"I beg your pardon, but I could not resist, you see. Especially when you said it would probably be your fate to marry the local clergyman."

"Oh!" Her eyes widened in amusement. "I did say that, didn't I? What a good joke, not to tell me that is *you*. But you need not worry, sir, for I shall not hold you to it." And she laughed outright, then.

There was a gentle cough from an older lady in the party, who was smiling determinedly. "Julia, dear, where are your manners? Do, pray, introduce us."

"Oh — of course, you haven't met, have you? This is Mr James Plummer, younger son of Sir Owen and Lady Plummer, and vicar of this parish."

"Rector," he murmured.

"Rector? What's the difference? They are both clergymen, and so—"

"Julia," the older lady said in a firm tone.

"Oh, I beg your pardon, Mama. This is my father, Mr Harry Fletcher. My new Mama. My sisters, Rosie, Angie, Bella. That is my oldest brother, Will, over there, talking to that young lady. And this is my other brother, Johnny. My aunt, Miss Paton. And this is Miss Crabtree, Bella's governess."

"No need to introduce the governess, Julia," Mrs Fletcher murmured, the fixed smile never leaving her face.

"Why ever not?" Julia said, turning surprised eyes on her stepmother.

"Never mind that now, dear," Mrs Fletcher said hastily. "Is there someone to show us to our pew, Mr Plummer?"

"It would be my pleasure to do so," James said, rather pleased with this opportune suggestion, for he had been wondering how he might prolong the conversation without being too obvious.

He led them into the church slowly so that they might admire the fine arched nave, the carved font and the stained glass window commemorating the marriage of Squire Bellingham to the Lady Hermione Winfell in the year 1638, the high water of that family's fortunes. The squire had been so thrilled to have secured the hand of a duke's daughter that he had spent half her dowry on a memorial to record this triumph for posterity.

Mr Frye, who had just arrived, rushed to open the pew door. The ladies filed in and disposed themselves on the generously padded seats, and the two young men after them, but Mr Fletcher looked searchingly at James.

"Have we deposed your own family from this pew, Mr Plummer?"

"It is the Chadwell Park pew, and therefore it is yours, sir. My father would have it no other way. That is the Manor's pew, directly opposite yours."

" Much obliged to you, Rector. I look forward to your sermon. What is your text for today?"

"Um… it is not based on any specific text, rather it covers a broad spectrum of philosophical points," James said, floundering, for he had quite forgotten what he was to say.

From the back of his memory, a fragment emerged. "The theme is resolution."

"Resolution. Interesting. Thank you, sir."

James had no further excuse to linger, so he bowed and made his way back to the church door to receive another swathe of astonished parishioners, and to deflect the determined Mrs Reynell, who was more persistent than a wasp at a picnic.

His sermon went well, once he had quickly conned it to remind himself of the subject. He found himself unusually eloquent when he could look down from the pulpit and see the expressive face of Miss Julia Fletcher gazing up at him. Her countenance was never still, he found. Many of his congregation stared back at him blank-faced, or looked down at their prayer books, or simply gazed into space, looking bored. Well, he understood that. A few even fell asleep, and he understood that, too. Sunday was the only day of rest for the hard-working men and women of the parish, and if they took the opportunity for a little extra unofficial rest, who was he to blame them? They might sleep through his sermons if they chose.

But *she* did not sleep. She gazed at him from beneath a slightly squashed bonnet, its feather drooping as if it had been taken out in the rain and resented the insult. And the face below the bonnet was constantly in motion, smiling at his little jokes, falling into solemnity when he made a point of marginal profundity, and sometimes frowning, her head tipped distractingly to one side, if he said something she could not understand. On such occasions, he would repeat the point in simpler terms and then the frown vanished and the smile returned, like sunshine after a shower. It was enchanting.

He walked back to the Rectory afterwards in the highest of spirits.

"That went unusually well, did you not think, Thomas? I was on fire today, and only old Mr Beardmore fell asleep, that I could see."

"I am surprised you noticed him in his distant pew," the curate said. "Your eyes were fixed on a subject somewhat closer to the pulpit, I believe. But then she is very much worth looking at."

"Who can you mean, you old rascal? Who are you matching me to now?"

"Why, the Fletcher girl, of course. The heiress."

"Heiress? Is she?"

"Really, James! Surely you must know that she has fifty thousand pounds."

"Ah, I see. You mean Miss *Rose* Fletcher."

"Naturally. Beauty and money in one demure little package. What could be sweeter? But if not the beauty, who was it who caught your eye? The younger one is a dainty miss, too. Miss Angela Fletcher."

"Not her. The middle one. The one who mistook me for a gamekeeper."

Thomas stopped dead, and spun round with a crunch of gravel. "The *middle* one? The great tall one with the bonnet that looked as if she had sat on it?"

James chuckled. "Do you know, that is just the sort of thing she would do. Are you going to stand gawking at me all day, my friend? For I should like my breakfast before the sun goes down, and it is rather chilly just standing here in this wind."

Thomas chuckled and they moved on towards the Rectory, where the sight of smoke rising from several chimneys suggested that a good blaze was to be had within.

"Is that why you were so early to church today?" Thomas said, grinning widely. "I thought you were just keen to see the family who have displaced your father, but perhaps it was something more than that. You must be in love with the girl."

"In love? Heavens, no! Must a man be in love just because he enjoys a young lady's company? I should not wish it, I give you my word. Love is for fools, and brings nothing but disaster and grief in its train. Have I not seen enough of the effects of love in my own family? No, no, wish not such a punishment as *that* upon me, I beg you. But she amuses me so I might marry her anyway."

"Excellent," Thomas said cheerfully. "Then I shall have a try for the heiress, if it will not overset any plans of yours."

"It is nothing to me, but it might overset Father's plans. He has the heiress and her fifty thousand pounds marked for Michael."

"Then in that case, I shall settle for Mrs Reynell, for nobody else wants her, of that I am certain, and her eight hundred a year would be a great addition to my income," he said gravely.

"And the house," James said, with a commendably straight face. "Do not forget her house. You would be very comfortable there, Thomas, I am certain, and it is so conveniently placed directly opposite the church. Ideal for a curate, I should have said."

Chuckling together, they entered the house and made straight for the kitchen, and breakfast.

~~~~~

On Sunday evening, the Fletchers were all invited to dine at Chadwell Manor. This was a signal honour, they were given to understand, for the Plummers never entertained on the Sabbath as a rule, but there was no other day available before Johnny departed for Cambridge, and they wished to offer the hand of friendship to the whole family. Sir Owen was most insistent on the point.

Julia had briefly met the remaining members of the Plummer family at church, but now she was to spend a whole evening in their company and she was not sure just how enjoyable it would be. Angie was in alt to be dining out so soon, but Rosie was a bag of nerves.

"You need only be yourself," Angie said, as they gathered in Rosie's room with Sarah, their maid, to put the finishing touches to their ensembles. "Ooh, I cannot wait!" She twirled round happily, her skirt swirling elegantly around her.

Julia stood patiently, jewelled combs in hand, waiting her turn to be titivated. She wished she could twirl about like that, but she would be sure to catch her gown on some protrusion, or knock something over. No matter how hard she tried to stay as still as she could, watch where she walked and keep away from the furniture, it was no use. She never intended to fall or to drop things, but somehow such accidents happened to her all the time.

Sometimes, after yet another disaster, when Pa looked at her sorrowfully and murmured, "Oh dear, Julia," she wished she were small and dainty like Rosie and Angie. Not when she was striding about the countryside, for then it was delightful to have legs long enough to cover the ground at speed, and she could even keep up with the men. But at balls and dinners away from home, it would be pleasant to be elegant and ladylike, and not mortify her family with her little scrapes. She was never mortified herself, for if one was awkward and clumsy there was not much to be done about it, but it distressed Rosie so. She was a person of the greatest sensibility, and felt all the crushing humiliation of Julia's disgrace as if she herself had transgressed in some way. Poor Rosie!

They travelled the short distance to Chadwell Manor in two carriages, to be greeted by numerous footmen, a butler who held his head so high that he appeared to look down his nose at them, and all the gentlemen of the family.

"Welcome, welcome!" Sir Owen said. "Mrs Fletcher, may I offer you my arm? Be careful on the steps, one or two flags are a trifle uneven. Do come inside out of the chill wind. The ladies are all in the parlour, where there is a good fire to warm you."

Mr Michael Plummer stepped forward to offer his arm to Rosie, and then the gamekeeper offered his arm to Julia.

"Good evening, Miss Fletcher," he said. "I trust you are well?"

"Very well, Mr Plummer. Very resolute, after your sermon. Also very hungry. We're not used to eating at this hour. Does everyone here eat this late?"

"Six or seven o'clock is quite usual, although there are those who still prefer five or even earlier. In London, eight o'clock is not unheard of."

"Good heavens! I should expire from hunger if I— Oops!"

One foot caught a protruding part of the steps and she would have plunged to her knees, but somehow he caught her and held her fast, one arm around her waist.

"There, I have you now. Up you come."

And by some miracle, she was upright, her gown undamaged, the disaster averted. How astonishing. "Thank you, sir."

"Really, Julia," came the sour tones of Aunt Madge from behind her. "Do try for some decorum."

"Decorum," she said musingly. "Tricky."

Her gamekeeper laughed genially. "Come inside, Miss Fletcher. This is the great hall. You will see it properly later, for we are to dine here. This way."

A screen shielded most of the room from view, but the soaring roof was visible. Craning her neck to see the great wooden beams and carved ceiling far above her head, Julia slowly turned round in a circle. "It is like a cathedral," she said, awed. "Just like the Minster, only in wood, not stone."

"York Minster? Is it so? On a smaller scale, I should think."

"Oh yes, but such confidence, don't you think? Those great soaring arches — what sort of man could imagine such things, and then build them, and have them stand for hundreds of years? It is astounding."

"Indeed it is," he said, his ever-present smile widening. "I had never thought of it so, but it is indeed astounding. Have you been often to York Minster?"

"Several times a year. Ma used to love to listen to the music there, and it has become a family tradition. There is something magical about a choir singing in such a setting. The music seems to rise into the air and weave itself around the columns and fill every corner of the building, even into the highest point of the roof. It's wonderful."

"I can imagine it must be. I have attended service at Lincoln Cathedral, of course, but I must be a philistine, for I never once observed the music weaving itself around the columns in that way. What a wonderful image!"

"Come *along*, Julia! You are keeping everyone waiting." That was Aunt Madge, fussing as usual.

"Do forgive us, Miss Paton," Mr Plummer said smoothly. "The blame is mine, I fear, for delaying Miss Fletcher, but I was much interested in her remarks."

He smiled so charmingly that even grouchy Aunt Paton softened and smiled a little and murmured that it was quite all right and it was no wonder that dear Julia was riveted by such a fascinating old building. A footman took the ladies' cloaks and they moved out of the great hall into an inner hall filled with a fine staircase lined with carved balusters. Passing it by, they turned aside into a cosy inner room full of people and the light of many candles.

"Miss Julia Fletcher, Miss Paton," intoned the butler.

Lady Plummer came forward to greet them, and Julia was gently shepherded to a sofa where the daughter of the house sat — what was her name? Patricia, that was it. They were almost the same age, but Miss Patricia Plummer was as unlike Julia as could be imagined, for she was short and plump, with a white, rounded, almost featureless face that reminded Julia forcefully of a piece of dough, with two currants for eyes. Miss Plummer turned her expressionless gaze on Julia.

"Good evening, Miss Fletcher. You are well, I trust." Her tone was flat, the words less a question than a formality. Without waiting for an answer, she went on placidly, "You are pleased with your new home, I hope. I took the greatest care in arranging everything for you."

"Oh, that was your doing, was it?" Julia said. "I thought Lady Plummer—"

"Mama has been too distraught for such activity, naturally. The duty fell to me to manage all the arrangements. I hope everything is to your liking and the servants are giving satisfaction."

How to answer that without giving offence? But perhaps she ought to express her concern for Lady Plummer? She scratched around in her mind for a suitable form of words.

Fortunately Miss Plummer was not much interested in her answer, for she continued immediately in the same calm tone.

"Your eldest sister is married, I understand. Does she have children?"

This time, she was genuinely interested for she paused for Julia to answer.

"She has three children, two little girls of three and two, and a boy who is not yet one."

"How could you bear to leave them?" Miss Plummer said, and for the first time there was animation in her face. "Such a charming collection of infants! But you will have them to stay with you, I hope."

"They plan to visit us during the summer, and my eldest brother's family, also. He has four children."

"Four?" She threw a puzzled glance across the room to where Will was talking to another young lady, who was laughing at some jesting remark of his. "He is married?"

"Not that brother. I have another brother… a half-brother, really. A natural son of my father's," she added hastily, because the next question was bound to be about Ted's mother, and it was as well to get the matter out of the way at once.

"Oh." Miss Plummer's face lapsed into blankness for a moment, but almost immediately she perked up. "But he has children? Young children?"

"Four. Two boys and two girls. The eldest boy is just five."

"How delightful! Infants are so endlessly fascinating, are they not? Such dear, sweet creatures! How you must dote on them. And they will come to visit you in the summer — you must be counting the days until their arrival."

Now, Julia was not a hard-hearted girl, and was fond of her nephews and nieces in a casual sort of way, being very glad to see them for short spells and even more glad when they went away again. She had always assumed that they would become more interesting when they were older and able to conduct a rational conversation, and less apt to squeal and run about breaking things. The idea that she might dote on them and be pining for a reunion was a foreign one to her, so she was rather at a loss for words. Fortunately, Miss Plummer was supremely indifferent to her feelings, for she sailed on majestically.

"My own sister has only two children, but they are such darlings! Young Charles is six, but so well-grown for his age that I am certain he will be taller than his father in the fullness of time, and Letitia quite agrees with me on the point. As for Seraphina, she is..."

Julia felt her mind beginning to wander. She wished now she had paid more attention when the new Mama had explained the family in detail to her. Miss Plummer's sister was... Lady... Lady something or other, so who was Letitia? It was all too confusing. She heaved a frustrated sigh, and her eyes fell on Mr James Plummer across the room. He was standing beside Johnny and Pa and another man, but instead of attending to their conversation he was watching her, an amused smile on his face, almost as if he could read her thoughts. She could not help smiling back at him.

At once he set down the glass in his hand and crossed the room to her. "Miss Fletcher, we have a few minutes before the hour for dinner. Perhaps you would care to see the family's greatest treasure? It is in the library."

Mr Plummer's company was far more agreeable to her than that of his dull sister, but Julia was not so ill-mannered as to show it. "Miss Plummer is telling me all about her nephew and niece."

"Which she may do at greater leisure after dinner when the ladies have withdrawn. Patricia, you will not mind if I steal Miss Fletcher from you?"

Miss Plummer's face resumed its blank expression as she inclined her head in acceptance.

Julia rose and took Mr Plummer's arm. He led her back past the stairs and into the room beyond it. The library was dark, that was her first impression, all heavy panelling and a floor stained a deep brown to match, the few rugs not adding much colour. The glass-fronted bookcases were filled with serious-looking tomes, their titles picked out in thin gold letters on cracked leather covers.

In one corner, a few spluttering candles created a pool of light, and here stood Mr Michael Plummer with Rosie. Sir Owen was there too with Mama on his arm, but almost at once they turned and left, presumably having taken their turn at viewing the treasure.

"Shall we?" Mr James said, gesturing towards the lit corner.

"You have got up a rota between you, I see. Who is to

introduce Angie to the treasure?"

"Ah, yes. My father was a military man in his youth, Miss Fletcher, and the regimented life has never lost its charm for him. He plans every detail of the campaign. We all have our orders, even for a simple dinner engagement, each of us being assigned a lady to escort, and a correct time to show her the flag. Lord Charles is the one designated to take care of Miss Angela, but he may not deign to so demean himself. His brother is a marquess, you see, and that makes him too grand to be told what to do. Whereas I—"

He stopped abruptly, but Julia could supply the rest of the sentiment. "Whereas you are the younger son of a baronet and must do as you are bid."

He smiled down at her, his eyes twinkling in a manner that felt curiously intimate. They were almost alone in this darkened room, and it should have seemed improper but oddly, it didn't. Another man might have taken the opportunity to flirt with her, but he did not.

"Naturally I do as my father bids me, whenever it coincides with my own wishes," he said. "Now, what do you think of our treasure, Miss Fletcher?"

He ushered her forward, and she peered at what appeared to be a rag on the wall. "This old thing?"

Rosie turned horrified eyes on her. "Julia! It is the d'Auberne battle flag, last flown at Agincourt."

"On which side?" Julia said interestedly.

"Ours, naturally," Rosie hissed.

Beside her, the gamekeeper shook with silent laughter,

but his elder brother said stiffly, "The d'Aubernes are our ancestors who came to England with William of Normandy, Miss Julia. They have been loyal to the rightful king of England ever since. Their flag was retired after the last d'Auberne fell on the field at Agincourt, brought home by the Plummer cousins. They built this house as a shrine for their lost relative, and to display his flag with the proper respect."

"It would be more respectful to give the thing a good scrub once in a while," Julia said. "It's filthy. Is there a pattern beneath the dirt?"

Mr Michael Plummer immediately began talking about escutcheons and frets and dexter and sinister, mixed with an array of oddly assorted animals. Abruptly, he stopped. "Never mind. Let me take you back to the parlour, Miss Fletcher."

Obediently Rosie rested her hand on his arm and allowed herself to be led from the room.

Mr James laughed out loud, then. "You are a minx, Miss Fletcher," he whispered in Julia's ear. "On which side, indeed!"

"I could not resist," she said. "Is it time for dinner yet?"

5: A Wet Day

'To Miss Fletcher, Chadwell Park, nr Ware, Hertfordshire. My dearest friend, Ricky and I await your first letter with the greatest impatience, but I could not wait to tell you of the latest scandal currently enlivening our dull little town. The rumours about Camilla Weston are all too true, for she is in a difficult situation, as the euphemism goes. I am sure you know what that means, and I do not quite like to write it openly in a letter. If you do not know, ask Julia for Ricky says she knows a great deal that is rather improper. Anyway, it means that Camilla must marry at once, and there is some talk of one of the Fessell boys, but I cannot see that happening at all. The worst of it is that some people are saying it ought to be Will, that he has not behaved as he ought towards Camilla and must now set things right, but I cannot believe that. Mr Weston himself says there is no blame attached to Will, but you know how these rumours fly, once started, and I thought I would just warn you, so that Will might be prepared. Do write soon, my dear friend. Ricky goes every day to fetch the post himself in hopes of a letter from you. He sends you his best* *regards, as do I, your most affectionate friend, Belinda.'*

~~~~~

All Julia's optimistic plans for another long walk before breakfast were dashed by the sight of steady, drenching rain as soon as she ran to the window on awakening. Well, she would just have to find something else to do.

There was no point in waiting for hot water, or even tepid water, to appear from below stairs, so she washed in what was left in the ewer from last night, and dressed herself as best she could. Even after last night's huge meal, she was hungry. She was always hungry, but at home in Sagborough she had gone to the kitchen for something to put her on until the next meal. Why should she not do so here?

She made her way downstairs, seeing nobody, although somewhere a maid was clattering the fire irons. Entering the passage to the kitchen, she stepped from the deep pile of expensive rugs to plain druggets, and the oily smell of tallow candles. In the kitchen building, she could hear angry voices in the distance, and the sound of someone sweeping, but where was the kitchen? She knew only the short passage from the outer door where the gamekeeper had deposited her.

Taking a guess, she walked past several closed doors and then came to one that stood open. Inside, the butler lounged at his ease with one of the footmen, the pair laughing together over glasses of wine.

"It's a bit early for drinking, I'd have thought," Julia said to them genially.

They both drifted to their feet. "What are you doing

here, miss?" the butler said.

"Looking for the kitchen and some food, but I think I should have gone the other way."

"If you would care to return to your part of the house, miss, you may ring the bell and I shall bring you whatever you require," the butler said coldly.

"And wait an hour for you to turn up? A body could expire from hunger in a place like this. The cook will have baked the morning rolls, so I'll just help myself to a couple and clear off."

The butler drew himself up to his full height. "It is not for you to *help yourself* to anything you happen to fancy."

Julia's eyebrows rose. "It's not for you to give me orders, Keeble. I shall go where I like and help myself to whatever I like, and no *servant* will gainsay me. Where is the kitchen?"

For several seconds, Keeble glared at her and she wondered if even now he dared to defy her, but then he gave the tiniest nod to the footman, who said, "Follow me, miss."

"My name is Miss Julia or Miss Fletcher," she said. "I thought the housekeeper was merely badly trained, an exception, perhaps, but I see that insolence and laziness is endemic in this house. It was not so when Sir Owen and Lady Plummer were here, I'll warrant, because everything at the Manor runs to time with the greatest efficiency. You should remember who pays your wages, Keeble. If you don't like working for us, then find employment elsewhere, but if you choose to stay, then you will have to do better than this. We may be northern, and we may have been in trade, but we are not savages and we know the difference between good service and bad, and we don't tolerate the latter. Remember that."

And then she swept out of the room, head high.

~~~~~

'To Miss Jupp, St Peter's Road, Sagborough, West Riding. My dear Belinda, I hope you like my first drawings. One is of my bedroom — a whole room all to myself! I cannot quite like sleeping alone, but I suppose I must accustom myself to it, for Mama says it is how the gentry lives. However, when Allie comes to stay in the summer, we shall have to double up again. The other drawing is of what is called the gallery, full of old paintings and strange statues, to which I cannot do justice, but you will get a general idea. It is very peaceful for no one else goes there. I take your letters there to read and reread when I feel a little overwhelmed by everything. We dined last night with Sir Owen Plummer and his family at Chadwell Manor, and although they were very polite to us, I was uncomfortable all evening. Do you remember when Mrs Malpas told us of the time she dined with Lord and Lady Craston, and they were kindness itself, she said, and she knew Lady Craston when she was just a humble seamstress, so there should have been no uneasiness at all, and yet she felt as if she had no business to be there, mingling with such people as if she were their equal? Well, now I know exactly how she felt. I wish I were more like Julia and Angie, for they felt no discomfort at all. They seemed quite at home, and Mama, naturally, for she is gentry herself, but I could not be easy, despite all Mr Michael Plummer's efforts. Angie played her usual games, for she hid the salt cellar. I went hot and cold *when it was looked for and could not be found, only the spoon, despite the servants' efforts, for I was sure it was one of Angie's tricks, and she confessed it later. She hid it in a dish of pears, can you believe it! I do not know how she has the effrontery! Fortunately, Mama did not guess, but I think Pa did. As for Julia, she was laughing and joking with the other Plummer son, who is also the rector, but he is not at all a pious person, I think, for he encouraged Julia shamefully. She was not at all ladylike, eating from all the meat dishes just like the men, and then she was asking him about the servants and how long it takes them to answer bells and such like. I was quite mortified by it, I confess. But there, I suppose she will never change, and she will be as cross as anything today because it is raining and she cannot go out. I do not know how we are to occupy her inside the house. Must go — time for breakfast. Must not be late. Yours in haste, your affectionate friend, Rosie.'*

~~~~~

Julia wondered if she might have done more harm than good by her outburst towards the butler, but miraculously breakfast was on time, the coffee hot and strong, the mutton chops juicy and the toast cooked to perfection, since they prepared it themselves, just as they had always done at home. Mama had asked more than once for toasting forks to be put out for them, but Keeble had said that they had not yet found any. Today, they appeared, and there was great harmony in the breakfast parlour, despite the weather.

After breakfast, it was time to despatch Johnny north to Cambridge.

"This is a new experience, setting off after breakfast," he

said, grinning. "I shall be there in good time for dinner, too. You are far more conveniently placed now — three hours of travel instead of three days or more. We should have moved south long since."

Mama preened under such praise, but Pa merely reiterated the instructions not to overtax the horses, to find beds for the night for Murgatroyd and Young Jim, the coachmen, and to send them home in good time the next day in case the carriage was wanted.

"I shall look after them, never fear," Johnny said.

"Aye, I do fear it. Don't be taking them off to a tavern to drink the night away. I want them back safe and sound tomorrow."

Johnny just laughed, and with hugs from Mama, handshakes from Will and Pa, and tears from Rosie, he was persuaded into the carriage, and it rolled off into the driving rain.

Everyone else dashed back into the house to escape the chill damp air, but Julia lingered on beside Pa.

"He's happy about it, anyway," Pa said softly. "Are you happy, puss? You seemed to enjoy yourself last night."

"That was just Mr James Plummer's nonsense," Julia said. "He's a peculiar sort of rector, don't you think? He made me laugh. But the house... the estate...I love the space." She took in a huge lungful of rainy air, then threw out an arm towards the lake and the woods beyond. "Look at it, Pa. All this is ours — well, yours, I suppose, and Will's eventually. All this emptiness is ours. No warehouses hemming us in. No crowds of people. No mill chimneys belching out smoke to cloak us in darkness. I can *breathe* here, in a way I never could in Sagborough. Up there, I was always trying to escape from the town, from the narrow streets, the clamouring crowds. Here, I can walk in any direction and be free. It's wonderful."

"That's good," was all he said, and Julia forbore to ask the obvious question of him. Perhaps she did not want to hear the answer.

By the time they went back inside, everyone had vanished, but girlish voices were still audible from the parlour. Inside, Rosie was sitting stiffly in a chair so ornate it might as well be a throne, while Angie was twirling light-footed around the room.

"There you are, Jules! We are going on a tour of the house, since it is too wet to go outside. Rosie is going to test every chair for comfort and I am going to dance in every room. What will you do?"

"Look at the view from each window, to see if there is any sign it will stop raining soon," Julia said with a laugh. "Pa? Are you coming with us? What will you do?"

"Keep an eye on you three mischiefs, that's what I'll do. But I shall look out for a snug little room to make my own. I miss my office, and there must be a quiet corner somewhere in this barn of a place where I can set up my desk."

"Excellent," Angie said, with a final spin. "Come on. Breakfast parlour next."

Keeble and a footman were busy clearing the table, but they stood to attention, and made respectful bows. Julia thought the butler was eyeing her warily.

The room was already familiar to them, and was in addition too cluttered with furniture for satisfactory twirling, so they moved quickly on to the dining room. This, too, was not interesting to Angie, but the music room was far more appealing. Rosie played a little, while Angie danced and Pa applauded. Julia was not minded to dance, not unless it was absolutely unavoidable, so she sat on a wide window seat and watched the merciless rain washing down the panes in slithering rivulets.

After the music room was one of the principal saloons, and here Angie was thrown into paroxysms of excitement.

"The doors to the next saloon fold away," she cried. "Shall we try it? These three big rooms can be thrown into one to make a ballroom. Oh, Pa, we must try it! Can you make it open up?"

"I don't see a way, but the servants will know. Rosie, ring the bell for Keeble will you?"

"Heavens, Pa, we could find hammers and knock the walls down ourselves before anyone will come," Angie said, but Rosie obediently rang the bell and sat down expectantly to wait.

Julia pulled out her pocket watch. "It will be twenty minutes, that is my guess."

But she was wrong. Keeble arrived after a mere three minutes. "You rang, sir?"

"We did. We should like these rooms opened up to make a ballroom — my daughters want to see what it will look like."

"Very good, sir. I shall just summon a pair of footmen."

He left the room, but Julia held the watch ostentatiously in front of her, and the butler returned in moments. "Anthony has just gone to fetch Paul. They will be here very shortly. The release mechanism is hidden inside this false pillar, if you will observe, sir."

"Very ingenious," Pa said, bending to see.

Sighing, Julia stationed herself by the window again. She wished she had Angie's enthusiasm for dancing, but without her sister's delicate frame and gracefulness, there was no enjoyment in the exercise. Julia was just too large and clumsy for elegance.

The footmen arrived, the doors and a part of the wall were folded away into the pillars, and then the two men willingly knelt down and rolled up rugs, while Keeble moved chairs and small tables aside.

"That is rather a good ballroom, I believe," Pa said. "What do you lasses think?"

"Oh yes!" Rosie said, eyes shining. "It is almost as big as the assembly room at the King's Head."

"So it is. What about you, Julia? How many couples could stand up here?"

Julia tipped her head to one side, assessing. "Perhaps thirty, at a pinch. But where is Angie? She was the one who wanted the room opened up, after all. Why is she not here, trying it out?"

"Aye, she's vanished," Pa said. "I suppose she got bored waiting."

"It didn't take very long," Julia said.

"No, indeed, Mr Keeble has been very efficient," Rosie said.

Just then, the furthest door opened, and Angie slipped in.

"There you are, flower," Pa said. "What do you think of your ballroom, now that you see it?"

Angie spun round in pure excitement. "Oh, Pa! It is wonderful! This whole house is wonderful! I love it. I am *so* glad we moved here. How soon can we hold a ball?"

"Ask your Mama," Pa said, with a smile.

Rosie was dispatched to the instrument again, while Angie settled down to dance the full extent of the ballroom.

Julia followed her father out of the room. "Shall we have a look at the library?" she said. "That might do for your office."

The library was depressing. It was overpoweringly large, with massive armchairs, a vast secretary and a highly polished desk that could at a pinch serve a turn as a dining table. Open bookcases filled two walls, while glass-fronted cases occupied a third. Every single shelf was empty.

"Where are all the books?" Julia said.

"Sir Owen told me that they would be taking them back to the Manor. They came from there originally, and belong to the Plummer family, so they were not included in the sale. I'm no reader, so it doesn't bother me. Johnny is going to buy some when we go to London, but it will take a deal of books to fill these shelves, it seems to me." He sighed. "I don't see me ever feeling comfortable in this room, to be honest. Your mama tells me that I should receive gentlemen callers here, but it's not a place I'd care to spend much time, and we seem to have exhausted the possibilities of this floor."

They emerged into the passage again. Beyond the library was only the staircase, with a door to either side of it. One door was Aunt Madge's bedroom, Julia knew, but the other…

"What is in this room?"

"Another bedroom, I think," Pa said. "So many bedrooms!"

Julia pushed open the door and went in. The bed was the same heavy style as in all the bedrooms, but apart from a wardrobe and a small press, there was no other furniture and only one low cupboard under the curve of the stairs. She went immediately to the windows. One overlooked the front steps and the other the stables, where she could see Will talking to one of the grooms.

"This would suit you," she said.

"Your mama wants to keep it for a guest."

"We have more than enough bedrooms to cope with guests. Johnny's room is empty, and he could share with Will, as he's used to doing. Rosie and I can share, and Angie too — Rosie's room is more than big enough for all of us. That would free up three bedrooms for guests."

Pa laughed. "Don't you like being gentry, puss?"

"I'm still myself, gentry or not, and I'd still rather sleep with my sisters than alone. I've shared with Angie since we left the nursery, and Rosie moved in with us after Allie married. It's what we're used to."

"I don't like to go against your mama's wishes, puss."

"Except for yourself. You refused to let *her* sleep in a separate room, and she argued for it, I heard her."

Pa rubbed his nose. "That's a different matter, but... it's a good point. Do you girls truly want to share?"

"Oh, *yes!* Rosie came into my bed last night, you know, so I know she wants to, and it would be much easier for Sarah to dress us. You see, there are so many changes... so much to get used to... it would be the greatest comfort to us all to keep at least that one thing the same."

"Very well. We'll talk it over at dinner, and then we'll see. And perhaps if there are some spare rooms upstairs, Lizzie won't mind if I have this room for my own. My desk would fit perfectly under that window, and I can put a safe in that cupboard. The backgammon table would go over here, I think. Yes, this would do very well, if Lizzie doesn't object."

"Pa, it's your house."

"And your mama is mistress of it."

"But you are the master," Julia said, smiling. "Mama will tell us all how to behave and when it's proper to return calls and such like, but we have to be comfortable living here, or it just won't feel like home. And it is our home, isn't it?"

He nodded. "It is. It certainly is."

"Then we have to make it the home we want."

6: *Assessment*

James walked down to the Manor for breakfast. He did so more often than not, but today he knew he would be expected. There would be a full report to be made of the evening. Not that anything unexpected would emerge from it. Mother was determined to dislike the Fletchers and Father was determined to do his duty by them, no matter how vulgar.

Not that they were vulgar, not in the slightest. Fletcher himself was a trifle rough around the edges, but he was quick, that much was certain. He had picked up the kernel of one of Father's points instantly, and long before Charles or even Michael had grasped it. He was sensible on political matters, too. Not comfortable in his rôle as a country gentleman, but that would come. As for the rest of the family, it was hard to fault them, and he could not deny that their manners were the equal of his own family's. Well, except for Miss Julia, of course. The thought made him smile.

He had timed his arrival to be a little early, but even so,

they were all there, apart from Father, who would enter the breakfast parlour just as the clock struck the hour. As all the clocks struck, in fact, for they were required to run precisely to time. Father adjusted them every morning, to be sure of it.

"Well, last night went rather better than we had anticipated," James said brightly, sitting down in his usual seat. "They are not quite the savages we feared, are they?"

Mother moaned softly, a handkerchief to her eyes, and Letitia muttered, "Really, James! Have some compassion for Mama's nerves. She is quite overset this morning."

"James has not the least sensibility, you should know that by now, Letty," Michael said. "He never enters into anyone's feelings, no matter how deeply distraught they may be."

"One distraught person at a time is quite enough, one might have supposed," James said.

"You have not even the heart to be upset on your own account, when you had to suffer the awkwardness of attending Miss Julia Fletcher. Such a graceless girl, yet you showed not the least awareness of it. You feel nothing, nothing at all."

"You wound me deeply, brother," James said. "I was very cut up when my favourite hunter fell and broke his leg."

Michael huffed in exasperation, but Uncle Morgan chuckled. "Serves you right for stuffing him at that wall instead of taking the hedge, like everyone else. You were showing off, and got what you deserved by it."

"Not entirely true," James said. "It should have been *my*

fate to hit the wall, but somehow I sailed right over it and Legend took the brunt of it, instead. Rather fortunate for me."

"Or ill fortune for the rest of us," Letitia said waspishly. "It is a pity you did not break your head and spare us all your inanity."

"Ah, such sisterly affection. You would miss me if I were dead and buried," James said.

"Not in the least, I do assure you."

They would probably have continued in a similar vein for some time, for James was of a mind to be amused and Letitia was all too easy to tease, but just at that moment the clock struck the hour and Sir Owen strode into the room. The gentlemen all rose to their feet, sitting down again only when Sir Owen had taken his own seat at the foot of the table. The servants sprang into action, and for a while nothing was said except for polite requests for this or that dish.

When the servants had withdrawn, Sir Owen set down his coffee cup and looked around the table at his assembled family. "Now that we have seen the Fletcher family properly for the first time, I trust you will all agree with me that they are a respectable, sensible family, not such as any person of good breeding need be ashamed to acknowledge as an acquaintance. I have already discussed this with Lady Plummer, but now I say it to all of you. We *shall* acknowledge the Fletchers, all of us. Here in Hertfordshire we will offer them every courtesy, we will invite them to this house, and accept such invitations to Chadwell Park as they offer to us. London is another matter. I have explained to Fletcher that Lady Plummer cannot be expected to sponsor his daughters in society, nor shall I propose his sons for White's. They must make their own way in the world. Fletcher will not go into society in London, that will be left to Mrs Fletcher and the young people, but they have some connections, seemingly. If we encounter them, we will acknowledge them, just as we do here, but there is no need to go beyond that if we do not wish it, and they do not expect it. Michael, what did you think of Miss Fletcher?"

"She is... pleasant," he said tentatively.

"I thought her a very well-mannered young lady," his father said. "Even Lady Plummer could not fault her behaviour."

"But the rest of them, Sir Owen!" his wife said, lifting her damp handkerchief from her eyes. "The middle girl is a veritable hoyden, and the youngest looks as if butter would not melt in her mouth, but I am certain it was she who hid the salt."

"She moved my wine glass, too," Charles said. "I took a mouthful of water by mistake. Dreadful child."

"They are every bit as coarse as I had feared," she said. "No breeding at all, and to think that we are expected to deal with them almost as if they were our equals! It is too bad, too bad altogether. We have quite enough to contend with, crammed in here as we are and all the economies we have to make."

"Is it not pleasant to have the family under one roof?" Sir Owen said, in gentle tones. "And, as I have explained, my dear, the need for economy is removed now that we no longer have the burden of the Park. I concede that the

Fletchers have not your good taste, but then few people do."

"I thought they were amusing," James said, and perhaps he spoke rather more loudly than usual, for they all turned to stare at him.

"Amusing?" Letitia said in tones of astonishment. "You are impossible, James! How any person of refinement could consider such vulgar people amusing is beyond comprehension."

"Now that is too much, Letitia," Sir Owen said repressively. "I saw nothing vulgar about the Fletchers. Fletcher himself may not speak quite as we do, but his opinions are sound, and there is little to fault in the rest of the family. They may not possess the innate good breeding that Lady Plummer displays, but their manners were by no means displeasing. Charles, what do you think your brother the marquess would make of them?"

"Nothing at all, Sir Owen," Charles sniffed, "for I sincerely hope he will never be obliged to meet such people. They would certainly never be invited to Barrowsworth."

Sir Owen sighed. "Patricia?"

"They were polite," she said in her soft voice.

"Morgan?"

"That Miss Paton is a termagant, but the rest of them are tolerable, I dare say, if one has no better company. The men played a good hand of whist, I will say that for them. The father and younger son took twenty pounds from me."

"They took twenty pounds from Papa, you mean," Letitia said acidly, but Morgan only laughed. He had been sponging off his brother for so long that he no longer even pretended to feel guilty about it.

Sir Owen ignored the interruption. "Michael, having seen the young lady for myself, I can tell you that I would have no objection to Miss Rose Fletcher as a daughter-in-law, and her fifty thousand pounds would give you a very comfortable independence. You have my authority to pursue the matter, if you wish. As for the others, you may find that they improve upon closer acquaintance, but I will not disdain their company. Patricia, ring the bell for more coffee, will you?"

And thus was the Fletcher family disposed of.

~~~~~

The Fletchers conducted their own assessment of their new neighbours, in their own way. First, in whispered conversations in bedrooms, later in snatched bursts as they met about the house and then at greater length over dinner.

"I must say, they keep a very good table," Mama said, as the soup was removed with a haunch of venison. "So many dishes! And fish — I counted six kinds at least, not including the oysters. I do not count *them*, for anyone might serve oysters, after all. You admired the poultry livers, I believe, Mr Fletcher. I must ask Lady Plummer for the receipt. And the prawns! So delicious."

"And all laid out in a timely fashion," Julia said, throwing dark looks at Keeble, who was pretending to ignore the discussion. "Dinner served precisely to the hour. It is most agreeable not to be kept waiting for a meal."

"Oh, but one must make allowances, dear," Mama said quickly.

"Must one?" Julia said. "Why?"

Pa chuckled. "Now, now, puss, don't be plaguing your mama with your jokes. She's not used to your teasing ways, yet. Well, I thought them a fine, polite family. A little starchy, perhaps, but then their ancestors came over with William of Normandy so maybe they've a right to be starchy."

"No one has a right to be starchy!" Julia said.

Will chuckled. "You are always so refreshing, Julia. No obsequiousness with you, is there?"

"I should hope not, indeed. We have no need to bow down to the Plummer family, after all. They were desperate for money and we gave them some of ours. They should bow down to us, if anything."

"Really, Julia!" Mama said. "Your liveliness is misplaced, sometimes." When Keeble and the footmen had withdrawn again, she went on, "I did not think them starchy at all. Lady Plummer is exceedingly refined, and you girls would do well to model your behaviour on hers."

"Not on yours, Mama?" Julia said. "Surely we must be guided by you."

"If you only would!" Mama said, a hint of exasperation in her tone. "My manners are, I hope, above reproach for any society, but Lady Plummer has something more — an air of good breeding such as you will see a great deal when we are in London. It is a great condescension for her and Sir Owen to invite us to dine, and we should be grateful for it."

Julia said nothing to that, for there was no response that would not open her to reproof.

"I can't speak for Sir Owen," Pa said, "for he's a baronet, after all, and perhaps he's entitled to be condescending to mushrooms like us. Not that he was, not in the slightest. Very gentlemanly, I thought him, and honest, too. I can deal admirably with a straightforward man like that. But Lady Plummer wasn't always so grand. She was nothing but his quartermaster's daughter when he was in the army. Her mother was respectable enough, by the sound of it, but still, if Sir Owen's older brother hadn't died and made him the heir, she'd have been a lowly soldier's wife, with nothing to be condescending about."

"A lowly soldier? He would have been a general by now, I daresay," Mama said, slightly pink about the cheeks. "Perhaps he would have won some famous battles and been elevated to the peerage for his trouble."

"Perhaps he would and perhaps he wouldn't, but she'd still be a quartermaster's daughter," Pa said. "Don't be making these people out to be finer than they are, Lizzie. I'll respect Sir Owen as a baronet and Lady Plummer as his wife, but I've seen real lords and their ladies at Sagborough, and some of them are as friendly as you please, and nothing condescending about it. Take Lord and Lady Craston, for instance. They only know me through buying from my warehouses, but they always acknowledge me in the street and ask how I am. Not in the least starchy, even though he'll be a marquess one day."

"That is true, but the Marfords are not so friendly, nor the Harbottles."

"Well, they don't know us from Adam. They don't buy their silks and muslins from us, so how could they? But Malpas has occasion to deal with them, as mayor, and his wife's on calling terms with them. They find them easy enough to get along with. Not like us lower mortals, of course, but mostly they don't put themselves on too high a form."

"Why should they, just because they have money and houses and a fancy title?" Julia said impatiently.

Mama looked shocked, but Pa chuckled. "Aye, and we've got the money and the house, now, so the title's all that stands between us."

"And *breeding*," Mama said sharply. "There is no hiding their distinguished breeding, Harry. I will concede that Lady Plummer is no better than we are, but the Marfords... such exquisite manners!"

"They can be mannerly enough in society, when they choose to be," Pa said, "and some of them are good-hearted, I'll grant you, but there's no denying that some of them are arrogant, selfish creatures beneath it all. Old Lady Harbottle looks down on anyone below the level of a duke, and Lady Harriet Marford's pretty high and mighty, too — far too stiff-rumped for my taste. As for Lord Gilbert Marford — I can't tell you all the high jinks that he got up to, in his younger days, and no one to stop him. I tell you now, Lizzie, I'll not be happy if you push our Rosie towards a man of that ilk. I don't mind her marrying a lord, if one of them takes her fancy, but it's got to be a man we can all get along with, who'll treat her right and not make her ashamed of her background."

"Well, of course, my dear," Mama said stiffly. "That goes

without saying."

"And it doesn't have to be a lord," he went on relentlessly. "If one of these Plummer boys catches her eye, I'd not object to it."

"Not the younger!" Mama said hastily. "Not a mere rector. She can do better than that. But Mr Michael Plummer... who will inherit the baronetcy..." She turned speculative eyes on Rosie. "What did you think of him, dear?"

Rosie had a way of looking as if she would like to curl up into a ball, like a hedgehog, but she answered readily in her quiet way. "He was very agreeable, Mama."

"And he seemed most attentive, as I recall, both before dinner and during the meal. Very attentive indeed, and Lady Plummer *did* say... I thought nothing of it at the time, but she whispered to me quite confidentially after the meal that you seemed very quiet and unassuming. Which is true, of course, but if *she* looks kindly on you, then there is no knowing what may come of it. His attentions towards you were rather marked, now that I consider the matter. In fact, at table he quite neglected Julia on his other side, although possibly that was as much Julia's fault, for devoting all *her* attention on the rector."

"He is amusing, unlike the rest of his dull family," Julia said. "Although Sir Owen's brother was entertaining — what was his name? I forget."

"Mr Morgan Plummer, and he was quite rude," Aunt Madge said. "He kept presenting dishes to me and asking how I liked them, as if I had never tasted venison or teal before. He must think we are peasants who have never eaten anything but turnips, risen straight from grubbing in the earth. So insulting! I had to set him straight on a few points."

"I wish you would not, Madge," Mama said. "We are trying to find our new place in society, not alienate all our potential allies."

"I speak as I feel," Aunt Madge said, pursing her lips.

Just then, Keeble came in with another decanter of wine, so Mama said quickly, "Do try the Savoy cake, Mr Fletcher. So moist and delicate. Mrs Sharwell has such a light hand with bread and pastries. Or would you prefer the apple pie? Will, are you taking a gun out tomorrow? We could do with some game birds — whatever you can obtain."

"I have no arrangement with the Plummers," Will said. "I do not like to go about shooting indiscriminately, and I am not certain which coveys may be used."

"You could ask Mr James Plummer," Julia said.

"The rector? Is he the arbiter of what I may shoot on our own land?" Will said stiffly.

"He is the expert, since our gamekeeper is bedridden at present. He seems to take a gun out most days."

"Ah." Will's face lightened. "Perhaps I will call upon him before breakfast tomorrow, then."

"And what are your plans for tomorrow, my dear?" Pa said to Mama. "The carriage will be back by noon, if you wish to go a-calling."

"After breakfast, I am to go through the linen cupboard with Mrs Graham," she said, with a little sigh of pleasure.

"Later, I must certainly call upon Lady Plummer, to thank her for her hospitality. The girls will go with me, and you, if you wish to come, my dear."

"Am I needed?"

"It would be an appropriate attention, if you have nothing else to do."

"I shall have nothing else to do," he said gloomily. "There is nothing in this house for me to do."

"You could find out why there is never enough hot water," Julia said.

"Julia, dear, that is a matter for the servants," Mama said sharply. "I am sure Keeble will resolve the issue soon."

"No, I think it's a matter for a man with a practical nature," Julia said. "Sarah tells me there are three coppers in the kitchen wing which should provide sufficient hot water even for Will's excessive ablutions, but no one seems to know anything about them. I'll wager any money that Pa can sort it out."

Her father chuckled. "Aye, I'll wager I can, and if I can't, I'll know where to find someone who can. That's my day settled then. Aye, I'll take a little port, thank you, Keeble."

~~~~~

'To Miss Jupp, St Peter's Road, Sagborough, West Riding. My very dear friend, I wish so much that I could see you and Ricky, and talk to you both, for you would reassure me, I know you would. Everything has become so strange here, and I cannot be comfortable about it. Pa and Mama have always talked of me marrying a lord, and I can quite understand why they

should wish it, since Great-aunt Petronella has increased my dowry so handsomely. It would be churlish to wish that she had not, but oh, Belinda, my good friend, I <u>do</u> wish it. Fifty thousand pounds! It is so lowering to feel that I must be worthy of her generosity and of Pa's confidence in me. You know how I feel the weight of their expectations, but Pa has always said he will not force me into anything. And then it always seemed so far off, and not to be thought of until after Easter when we go to London, and perhaps even then it will not turn out as Mama wishes. Perhaps we shall not be able to move in more elevated society after all. That was always such a comfort to me, as you know, that I might never meet any lords at all and so there could be no question of it. But now — oh, Bel, I hardly know how to say this, but Mama thinks that Mr Michael Plummer is interested in me, and Pa said he would not object, and I begin to feel the bars of the cage closing around me. I try to remember Ricky's advice to me — such wise words! — that I cannot be made to marry against my will, and certainly not anyone I dislike, but I should so hate to disappoint Pa when he is expecting such great things of me and I do not dislike Mr Plummer, not really. He is very gentlemanlike, and not in the least disagreeable, but still I cannot imagine myself married to him. Heavens, what a long moaning sort of letter this is! Be assured that we are all well and beginning to settle into our new home. I am sure there is no foundation for the worst of my fears, but there is no one here who truly enters into my feelings on the subject, not even Julia and Angie, and no one to whom I can talk. I so wish you were here. My fondest regards to you and Ricky, from your anxious and dispirited friend, Rosie.'

7: An Unexpected Encounter

James was restless. A whole day of rain always made him feel *'cabined, cribbed, confined'*, as Shakespeare had it, and he knew exactly what the fellow meant. He had once had the misfortune to take ship across the Channel to France, and he had never been so miserable in his life, with nowhere to go and nothing to do, and no view but the endless roiling sea and the awful prospect of hours more of the same torture on the return journey. If he could have taken wings like a bird, or found himself a balloon to carry him back across the turbulent water, he would have done so.

Being unable to shoot that day, or even to walk or ride far, he had made his sodden way to the hut and settled himself there to clean his guns and drink a little brandy and be miserable. And if he opened one shutter and sat gazing out to the High Field gate, it was not from any expectation of seeing Miss Julia Fletcher there, it was only that he might see when the rain cleared. Or so he told himself. But she did not come and the rain did not clear, and he returned to the rectory in the same dismal frame of mind as when he had left it.

The next day was blessedly dry, so he took some bread and cheese for his breakfast and set off early for the hut. With a dozen rabbits, some pheasants, pigeon and a brace of snipe in his bag, he returned to the hut and ate his victuals sitting beside the same window. This time he admitted to himself that he would be glad to see the swinging legs and dishevelled hair of Miss Julia. But again she did not come.

Eventually, he made his way down to the Park to deposit his haul at the kitchen door, where Keeble, in his shirt sleeves and polishing apron, came to meet him.

"How are you getting on, Keeble?" James said. "Settling in here?"

Keeble pulled a face. "I dare say we'll get used to their ways in time, Master James, but it's hard, very hard."

James looked at him thoughtfully. "Keeble, I hope you are treating the Fletchers with appropriate respect."

The butler's lips twisted into an expression that might have been a sneer. "I treat the mercer with all the respect appropriate to his station," he said loftily.

"That is precisely what concerns me," James said. "I would have you remember that Mr Fletcher may not hold the elevated rank of your former master, nor does he speak in quite the same manner, but, like all men, he should be judged by his actions. Does he mistreat any of you? Are his requirements onerous?"

"No, sir," Keeble said stiffly.

"Has he quibbled over salaries?"

"He has increased our pay, sir. Quite substantially."

"What of his man? He came with him from Yorkshire, I believe, so he knows him well. Does he speak ill of his master?"

"Not at all. He can't speak highly enough of him, and he's been with the family for thirty years now, and valet to the master for fifteen," Keeble said, adding reluctantly, "That says something for the mercer, I suppose."

"It says a great deal," James said. "Generous, reasonable... and rich, Keeble. Very, very rich."

"How rich is very rich?" Keeble said thoughtfully.

"From all I have heard, his income must be about ten times my father's."

Keeble's eyes widened.

"Precisely so. And you should bear in mind, also, that wealth like that means that the family is well accustomed to the finer aspects of good society — the best food and wine, for instance, and exemplary service from their servants. One would not wish them to gain the impression that southern servants are in any way inferior, would one?"

The butler drew himself up a little. "Certainly not, sir!"

"Precisely so," James said with a smile. "I knew I could depend on you to uphold the finest traditions of Hertfordshire, Keeble. I was sure that the little deficiencies of service of which I have heard are mere temporary hitches, soon to be overcome. Such as the tardiness of meals, and the lack of hot water, for instance."

Keeble pulled a face. "The hot water... that was Millwright's job, getting the coppers heated up, but he's gone and no one knows how to do it now. The master and the young master are down there just now trying to work it out."

James laughed. "Oh, is *that* the problem? No one but Millwright knew the knack? Well, well, well. I had better go and have a word with Mr Fletcher."

He found him in his shirtsleeves atop a ladder, peering at a bewildering array of pipes and valves and levers. Down below, Will Fletcher stood forlornly watching, while Enoch, Mr Fletcher's man, held his master's coat.

"Are you making any progress, sir?" James called up to Fletcher.

"A little, a little." He nimbly descended the ladder. "Good day to you, Plummer. Do you have any knowledge of these devices?"

"I am not familiar with such things," James said.

"Aye, I daresay," Fletcher said with a laugh. "I know how a copper works, but this is like no device I've ever seen. This is the copper itself, inside here, and the coals for the fire go down here, but usually there's just a wooden lid on top, not all these pipes and whatnot. I'm trying to work out how the water gets into the copper, but I shall need to look at where these pipes come from."

"And why the servants cannot explain it is more than I can work out," Will Fletcher said morosely.

"Now there I can help," James said. "There was a man who understood it, called Millwright, but he left a few weeks ago. There was a certain amount of coming and going amongst the servants before your arrival."

"Was there, now?" Fletcher said. "Didn't want to work for me after your father, I dare say." He chuckled. "Can't say I blame them. It must be a come down for them, after serving a baronet. So they've had to recruit a few new people, have they?"

"I regret to say that it is a little more complicated than that," James said. "There were two sets of servants, one here and one at the Manor. Mother wanted to keep many of her own people so some of the Manor servants moved here, and others who did not wish to stay left altogether. Keeble was butler at the Manor, but Mrs Graham was merely the upper housemaid here. The cook here is new, from London."

"Well, that accounts for a great deal!" Will said. "So we have a full set of servants, but some of them have never worked at the Park before."

"Most of them, I should say," James said.

"I imagine this Millwright would not object to coming here to explain the workings of these devices, for a fee," Will said.

"That would be feeble indeed," his father said. "Good heavens, Will, these are only water pipes. I know how a beam engine or a spinning jenny works, I can surely get water into a copper. Come on, let's find out where these pipes come from."

Looking for water pipes sounded too fatiguing for words, so James sent his compliments to the ladies and left the men to their work.

~~~~~

FEBRUARY

Now that the Fletcher family had settled into Chadwell Park, it had begun to seem rather more like home. It would never be quite the same as their much-loved house in Sagborough, but at least it was comfortable now that there was plenty of hot water and meals arrived more or less on time, apart from the one day when the dressing bell had vanished from the table in the hall and everyone had had to scurry about so that the fish wouldn't spoil. Poor Keeble had been in quite a stew about it, but the bell had turned up the next day in the library, of all places. They had all grown accustomed to the vast scale of the place, apart from Rosie, that is, who still occasionally hid away in the gallery, and was so overawed by the butler that she called him Mr Keeble.

For Julia it was the grounds which she had grown to love. She knew her way around rather well by now, and although it was delightful to have so much space in which to roam, she found herself drawn very often to the gate at High Field and the prospect of open country beyond. So much empty land to enjoy! After a few tentative experiments, on one frost-nipped morning she decided to explore a little further afield.

From the gate, she walked down the field and into a belt of trees. A clear track led through it, across a plank bridge over a stream and then out into open fields again, bare and ready for the plough. One such field sloped down to a five-barred gate, another powerful lure to a girl with a yearning to explore. She would walk down to the gate, she decided, observe what lay beyond and then make her way home again, for there was a chill breeze now and a distant rumble that might be thunder.

At the bottom of the hill lay a wide pool of dense mud, but by carefully placing her feet on a few dry tussocks under the hedge, she succeeded in making her way to the gate. The vista beyond was disappointing, just another field, although this one was pasture. There were no sheep or cattle, nothing but taller stalks of grass waving disconsolately in the breeze. It rose to another hedge in the distance, this one low and well-trimmed in one or two places.

A shift in the wind brought a louder rumble of thunder, yet there was not a cloud in the sky. While she was pondering this oddity, a streak of russet brown shot past her legs, through the gate and away up the hill. A fox! Enchanted at this unexpected sighting, she jumped on to the lowest bar of the gate to watch the creature's progress as it tore up the hill. Another oddity, for whenever she had seen a fox before, it had been slinking quietly along, not in much of a hurry. Whereas this fox—

The thunder was right behind her, and now she could hear dogs, lots of dogs, all yapping excitedly. A horn blasted practically above her head. With an exclamation, she spun round, tipped off the gate into the mud and—

What on earth? There were horses rearing, voices yelling, the horn again, a scream, a woman falling with a shriek. And dogs everywhere, streaming past her, barking their silly heads off, scrabbling under the gate and up the field... oh, the fox! They were chasing the fox. And all around her were angry men, yelling at her.

"What the *devil* do you think you are doing?" one red faced old man shouted, his horse dancing impatiently, as several men fussed around the lady who had fallen from her horse. "Get out of the way! Move aside, this instant. What are you doing here anyway?"

Julia did not embarrass easily, but she could see that she had quite spoilt the chase for the riders and had been about to make a grovelling apology. This attitude, however, irked her excessively.

"I am only taking a walk, as anybody might do," she said, her chin rising. "How could I know you would be coming this way?"

"Well, you should have known! You are a very stupid gel and should learn to keep out of the way."

"And you, sir, are a very rude man and should learn better manners."

He growled like an animal and raised his whip, but Julia only glared at him defiantly. She would not be cowed by a man like that. Perhaps he would even have struck her, but out of the surging mêlée of horses, dogs and shouting riders and grooms appeared the very welcome face of James Plummer, leading his horse. He was neither red-faced nor yelling at her. If anything, he seemed to be trying not to laugh.

"Miss Fletcher, are you unharmed? I saw you slip over."

"I'm only muddy, Mr Plummer, but I thank you for your concern." This was said with a glare at the red-faced man, before she turned back to James. "The lady who fell — is she hurt?"

"Mrs Reynell appears to be uninjured, apart from her pride, perhaps," he said, smiling. "She has a reputation as a bruising rider, who seldom falls." Then, to the red-faced man he said, "Sir Hector, I shall escort Miss Fletcher back to Chadwell Park."

"Do so, and teach her some common sense while you are about it. Hmm, Miss Fletcher, eh?"

Without another word he wheeled his dancing horse and rode away, shouting orders as he did so. The swirling mass of riders and dogs turned about and set off in a different direction.

A young man with the look of a groom rode up. Mr Plummer said, "Ah, there you are, Smith. You had better take Sorcerer home. I shall walk with Miss Fletcher." The groom took the horse's reins and rode off, leaving Julia and Mr Plummer standing facing each other in the churned pool of mud.

His face was creased into a wide smile. "Did you truly not hear us approach? I was at the back of the pack and could not see much, but you seemed oblivious."

"I heard a noise but didn't realise what it was. I *am* a stupid girl, I suppose. I shall have to make an apology to that man, whoever he was."

"Sir Hector Bellingham, squire, magistrate, leader of society in his own mind, and master of the hunt in truth. Heaven forfend that any innocent young lady should come between him and his rightful prey. Miss Fletcher, you are surrounded by mud. Allow me to rescue you."

And without waiting for her response, he waded through the swamp and scooped her up in his arms, carrying her to a dry spot. She laughed, for it was too ridiculous for words.

"Thank you kindly, sir," she said, when he set her down. "I'm not ungrateful, but I could have managed by myself, you know."

"Naturally you could, but only at the price of becoming even more muddy. Come, you are wet and this wind is bitter. Let us walk briskly."

Julia needed no second invitation, for walking briskly was her favourite occupation in the world. He took her by a different way, and in a very short time they emerged from a spinney to see the little cottage directly in front of them. Apart from the straggling hedge that provided some shelter from the wind, there was only an open woodstore to one side, and a privy a little apart. Where there ought to have been a garden, or at least a lawn, was nothing but overgrown tussocks of grass and brambles, and a narrow track leading to the door.

"Come inside and warm yourself," he said. "I can have the fire blazing in no time."

He opened the door and ushered her inside. There was only one room, divided into two clear areas. To the left of the fireplace were stone flags, a high-backed wooden settle and a plain deal table. To the right were colourful rugs, softly upholstered chairs and a sofa, and a polished sideboard, with a curtained compartment that was probably a box bed.

"Wet and dry," Julia said, getting the point at once.

"Exactly so!" he said with a wide smile. "I knew you would understand it. This is my gun store, so I am often wet through when I come here. Hang your cloak on the peg there and sit down while I open up the fire."

She perched on the edge of the settle, reluctant to inflict too much mud even upon such a forgiving surface, while he wielded the poker. The fire was well banked, but he brought it to flaring life in seconds, then added more coals. She had to admit the warmth was very welcome.

Turning to face her, he opened his arms wide. "Welcome to the hut, my refuge from the world. I have Madeira, sherry, brandy and port, or I can make tea, if you prefer."

"Brandy, if you please," she said.

"An excellent choice," he said, smiling. "That will warm you inside, just as the fire warms you outside. And would you like some toasted bread and cheese?"

"Ohhh! I should *love* some! We used to toast cheese for our supper all the time at home... I mean at Sagborough, but here we are far too grand for such simple pleasures."

"Well, I am not at all grand, and I love toasted cheese."

"You are not like the rest of your family," she said cautiously, wondering if he would be offended by such plain speaking.

He merely laughed. "You mean they *are* grand? I suppose they are a bit. Charles is, anyway. Lord Charles Heaman, brother to the Marquess of Barrowford, as he never ceases to remind us. The rest of them might seem a bit stuffy, perhaps, and utterly predictable and boring, but not grand. You must not let it worry you if they are a bit stiff at first. They have never met anyone quite like your family, that is all."

"Vulgar mushrooms, you mean?"

That made him smile again. "You are not at all vulgar! I find the Fletchers a refreshing addition to Hertfordshire society, to be truthful. I am very glad you came to liven us up, and relieve the tedium of life here."

Julia found him an odd sort of man, unlike anyone she had ever met before. The rest of his family were very much as she had expected the aristocracy to be, rather full of their own importance and somewhat distant, not people she could be at ease with. But James Plummer was different, or perhaps because she had first taken him for a gamekeeper she saw him differently. The barrier of rank that sat, invisible but immovable, between the Fletchers and the Plummers melted away when she was with him, and he felt more like an extra brother than a stranger. How curious that was.

He had found toasting forks, bread and cheese by now, so for a while they both sat in front of the fire and toasted and ate and laughed as they tried not to drip melting cheese everywhere. He was more successful than Julia was, and twice he reached out and deftly caught cheese that was about to fall on her gown. She could not remember the last time she'd had so much fun.

After a while, her immediate hunger sated and mellow from warmth inside and out, she said, "Is it so tedious, your life here? You have all this wonderful countryside to enjoy, and employment to keep you busy."

"Oh yes, my employment. Rector of the parish of St Hilary's. My flock to be tended, if I were so inclined. But I am very remiss in attending to my duties."

Another of those gentle smiles. He was not a man she would describe as handsome, but when he looked at her like that, and the firelight caught his brown eyes and made them glow, framed by a mass of soft curls, he was very attractive indeed. Nothing at all like any clergyman she had known before. Clergymen were stooped and elderly and disagreeable, not charming young men with a liking for toasted cheese.

"Why did you become a clergyman, then, if you find the work so disagreeable?" she said.

He gave a bark of laughter. "A very good question, Miss Fletcher. The answer is the obvious one — that I am a younger son, with no inheritance to anticipate, so I must needs earn my bread."

"You could have chosen a profession more to your liking," she said. "Johnny is a second son, too, but he is a Fellow at his Cambridge college, and will be a professor in time, or so he says. What made you enter the church?"

"Sheer laziness," he said, with that strange little smile that always seemed as if he were sharing a private joke. "My father was an army man before he became the heir to the baronetcy, and he assumed I would follow in his footsteps, despite my repeatedly expressed disinclination. The army always seemed too energetic a business by half, to me, not to mention the prospect of dying in some horribly painful way. The alternatives are even worse. The law requires too much book learning, and a government post would involve being polite to every nincompoop in Europe. Too fatiguing for words. But when I was fourteen, Mr Ames, the rector at the time, unexpectedly died. *'How about the church, James?'* my father said, and I felt I could manage that. Keep the necessary terms at Oxford, a little bit of effort to memorise the Thirty-Nine Articles and an interview with the bishop — surely that would not be beyond my capabilities. And so it has proved. But the best of it is that Father engaged a curate to take care of the parish until I was ordained, to whit, Mr Thomas Leadbetter, who is not merely a devout and pious clergyman, but an energetic and diligent parish leader, who likes nothing better than to minister to his flock, especially at inconvenient hours and during inclement weather. The parishioners love him, and who am I to come between them? So apart from an occasional sermon, which I copy from a book and then reduce to a tolerable length — my best effort was ten minutes, I believe — I have nothing to do but hunt and shoot and rescue young ladies who fall into muddy puddles."

Julia wondered if he was being honest with this description. Few men would admit to laziness, but it was true that he passed his days in gentlemanly pursuits rather than parochial duties.

"Don't you feel guilty, leaving everything to your curate?" she said.

He sighed. "I should, I suppose, but we are both content with the arrangement, so why worry? Have you dried sufficiently, do you think? I should perhaps return you to Chadwell Park before your absence creates alarm."

"There's no need for you to accompany me," Julia said.

"I know my way perfectly well from here."

"But I must follow the same route home, so we may as well walk together as not, do you not agree?"

There was no denying the logic, so they tidied up the hut, banked the fire again, and walked together to the High Field gate and thence down the park to the house, chatting companionably all the way.

8: A Visitor

'To Miss Fletcher, Chadwell Park, nr Ware, Hertfordshire. My very dear friend, you will never guess what has happened! Camilla Weston has run away! Can you believe it? Her father arranged a hasty marriage for her to a farmer near York, which is perhaps as much as she could expect, but she would have none of it and now she has gone, taking all the money her mother had saved for young Luke's schooling and the coal merchant's bill, and has quite vanished. Mr Weston seems to think she is gone to her aunt at Newcastle, and has taken off in pursuit, although whether to bring her back or to throw her in the sea and be rid of her once and for all is impossible to say. No time to write more, for Ricky is waiting to whisk this to the post office in time to catch today's mail coach, but thank you for all the sketches. Such a lovely house! I will write more tomorrow. Your good friend, Belinda.'

~~~~~

James returned to the rectory in the very best of spirits. What a girl she was, Julia Fletcher! The way she had stood up to

Bellingham was glorious, a moment to savour, beyond question. And then that intimate time in the hut, sharing toasted cheese and brandy, and talking as equals. He could not remember a time when he had spoken so freely to a woman.

There had only been one odd moment which occurred on the walk home. As they walked across the park, they had seen in the distance two female figures, one rather larger one walking ahead with a book in her hands, and a smaller one running about on the grass and weaving in and out of the trees, shouting as she ran. And the oddity lay in what she was shouting — *'Can't catch me!'*, she yelled, dodging about as if she were being chased. Yet no one *was* chasing her, and the larger woman was oblivious to the game.

"Who is that?" he said to Julia, only to realise the answer immediately. "Your youngest sister, Isabella, of course."

"Bella and Dorothea. The one with the book is Miss Crabtree, the governess. They try to take some exercise every day."

That was confusing. Was Dorothea the governess, then? Or was there another child hidden by the trees? It was strange, but he did not quite like to pry, so they continued on their way to the kitchen door, where he left Julia and went on to the rectory.

He found Thomas busy in the parish room, writing and humming. The parish room, filled with the dusty records too unimportant to be kept in the church and a collection of battered chairs suitable for the accommodation of all shapes and sizes of parishioners' rears, was too dreary a room for

James to venture into, so it had been left to Thomas to use as he pleased. In James's memory, however, it had not ever been a place of happiness. No one, he dared suppose, had ever actually *hummed* in there before.

"Are you quite well, Thomas?" he said, putting his head round the door.

The curate looked up with a wide grin on his face. "Indeed I am. Very well indeed, for I have been invited to a card party at the Miss Williamsons', and who do you think will be there?"

"Miss Williamson?"

Thomas tutted.

"Miss Ariadne Williamson? No, let me see... Mr Frye, Mrs Frye and the Miss Fryes?"

"*Mrs Reynell!*" Thomas said in a dramatic whisper. "This is my opportunity to charm the lady and her eight hundred pounds a year."

"And the house, Thomas. Never forget the house, directly opposite the church — so convenient for you! But why does she deign to join in a mere card party at the Miss Williamsons? It is not her usual style at all."

"No, but she is being enticed by the hope of your presence, I suspect. Your invitation is on the hall table. Since you contrive to avoid every other engagement where she might encounter you, I suspect she may be growing desperate. It is my hope that she will therefore be susceptible to someone more appreciative of her good qualities."

"Thomas, the house and the eight hundred pounds a

year are the *only* good qualities she possesses. She would make you miserable, you know it perfectly well."

"Only slightly miserable, with so much money in my pockets. Will you come, James?"

"To a card party involving Mrs Reynell? Not likely! But I wish you good fortune, my friend. Here, take some coins with you, for she likes to play high. It will not aid your cause if you have to decline the chance to join her table."

He opened drawers until he found the object he was looking for, a purse heavy with coins, withdrawing a number of them and placing them on the desk in front of Thomas.

"Fifty guineas?" the curate said, counting the coins. "You expect me to lose half my salary in one evening?"

"No, I expect you to win a few guineas to your own benefit, and return my fifty. And if you should lose some of this, it is of no consequence to me."

"You are the best of good fellows, James. But how went your day? Was the hunt enjoyable?"

"Very, for a multitude of reasons. An excellent, fast ride, for one thing. I also had the pleasure of watching Mrs Reynell thrown into deep mud, and Sir Hector bested by a slip of a girl. And the fox escaped his fate, which I cannot but feel a fitting end when he has given us such good sport."

"He will be caught next time, or the time after that, I dare say."

"Perhaps, but I respect his stout-hearted defence of his life. You do not enquire as to the identity of the slip of a girl."

"Judging by the brightness of your eye, my friend, I may make a guess. Miss Julia Fletcher?"

"Indeed. Enchanted by the passing of a fast-moving fox, she had climbed upon a gate, the better to observe him. It was unfortunate that most of the hunt had already decided to jump that particular gate. There was a degree of confusion and alarm, Mrs Reynell's mount reared at a most unpropitious moment, Miss Fletcher was startled and both ladies ended up in the mud. Sir Hector was most unchivalrous. He called Miss Fletcher a *'stupid gel'*, whereupon she told him he was very rude man and should learn better manners."

Thomas's jaw dropped. "She did not!"

"She did. It was glorious, utterly glorious, Thomas. A moment to savour. And so I was able to be the chivalrous one, and escort her to the hut to warm herself after her dousing."

"Alone? Or had she a maid or footman with her?"

"Neither. Ah, you disapprove, but remember that I am a man of the cloth, my friend. Surely I may offer aid to a parishioner in distress without raising any question of impropriety?"

"You can spin that story if you like, James, but her father may not see it that way. She may be a lady of great independence of mind, but if her father hears of this, he may insist on a wedding."

"Which is precisely what I want, Thomas."

The curate looked at him thoughtfully. "Truly? You are serious about this, then?"

"I am perfectly serious. The more I consider the matter,

the more convinced I am that marriage to Julia will materially improve my comfort."

"Good heavens, and I thought you were joking! But you are not in love with her."

"It is not necessary to be swept away by emotion. I like her very well, and I think she likes me, too, for she is quite at her ease in my company. Yes, we shall deal together most agreeably."

"Then you had better be careful not to stretch the bounds of propriety too far, James, for if her father forbids you from seeing her, you will be in the suds."

"Ah. An excellent point." James sighed. "You are, as always, quite right. I shall be more circumspect in future."

~~~~~

Julia was not in the least circumspect, and so she had no hesitation in telling the whole family of her encounter with the hunt, not diminishing her own responsibility for the débâcle. The new Mama was shocked, naturally, but Pa took it in his stride.

"Well, puss," he said, chucking her under the chin as they gathered in the saloon before dinner, "if you will go wandering off on your own, inevitably you will get into trouble occasionally."

"At least she only ended up in a puddle this time," Will said. "Last time it was the canal. Really, Jules, you are such a madcap girl. But it is a pity you set up Bellingham's back. I hope it will not turn him against me when I am ready to join the hunt."

"I shall write him a very handsome apology," Julia said, "and Mrs Reynell, too. I always acknowledge when I am in the wrong."

"So you do, puss, so you do," Pa said mildly, "but it would perhaps be better not to be in the wrong quite so often, eh? But you could hardly have known about the hunt, so little blame to you there. I'm more concerned with this Plummer fellow who escorted you home by way of this hut of his. He isn't making a flirt of you, I hope?"

"Not in the least. He was perfectly gentlemanly."

"Even so, you must be careful, Julia," Mama said. "These high-ranking gentlemen are more subtle than the young men you knew in Yorkshire, and he may be leading you astray without you being aware of it. You must consider your reputation at all times... unless... Julia, you get on well with him, which your father and I must approve when he is a neighbour and our rector, but you are not developing a *tendre* for him, are you?"

Julia burst out laughing. "Heavens, no! He is less stuffy than the rest of his family, that is all."

"Even so, it was not well done of him to seclude you away in this cottage or hut of his, with no one else present. I hope you will not permit such a liberty in future. Should you care for my advice on your letters of apology?"

"I shall write them myself, but you and Pa may read them before they are sent."

"And I shall convey them to the recipients for you, Jules," Will said. "My greys have been eating their heads off ever since they arrived. It will be a good opportunity to stretch their legs a little."

"Aye, you want to show off that curricle and pair to the neighbours," Pa said indulgently. "Good, good. So no harm done, we hope. Ah, Keeble, is dinner ready?" he added, as the butler sidled in.

"It is too soon," Mama said, with a glance at the clock. "What is it, Keeble?"

The butler looked harassed. "Begging your pardon, madam, but there is a lady arrived. On foot, madam. With luggage."

"A card, perhaps? Or a name?"

"She said—"

But such questions became moot as a bedraggled figure appeared behind the butler, her gown and cloak grimy, her bonnet drooping and stray pieces of straw in her hair. Camilla Weston, it seemed, had run away to Hertfordshire.

"Camilla? Great heavens, what a fright you look!" Will said, with more honesty than tact.

Her chin lifted a little, but with what dignity she could muster, she curtsied formally. "Mrs Fletcher. Mr Fletcher. I apologise for my unexpected arrival, but might I beg the favour of a bed for the night?"

Mama rose magnificently to the occasion. "Of course, my dear. Ah, Keeble, tell Mrs Graham to prepare the blue room for Miss Weston, and send up hot water at once. Send word to Mrs Sharwell to delay dinner for one hour. Come this way, Miss Weston. Do you have your maid with you?"

She swept Camilla out of the room, the butler in her wake, leaving the room in stunned silence.

It was Will who exploded first. "Well, of all the damnable nerve!"

"Language!" Pa said sharply. "Remember your sisters, if you please."

Will bowed gracefully. "I beg your pardon, sir, but the provocation was extreme. Camilla is incorrigible!"

"Whatever she is, she is here and our guest, so we will treat her with courtesy. However, her father will be frantic with worry, since he thinks she is safely with her aunt at Newcastle. Will, go and tell one of the grooms to be ready to ride with an express at once. It will not take me a moment to scribble a note to Tom."

The men left in haste, and Angie giggled. "What a to-do! Whatever is she thinking, coming here like this? Does she think to force Will to make an honest woman of her?"

"Hush, Angie. *Pas devant les enfants,*" Aunt Madge said sharply, with a lift of her eyebrows towards Bella, sitting quietly in a corner, watching them. She had been poring over a fashion journal with Dorothea, but now her face was solemn.

"I understand French perfectly well, and I am not a child," Bella said.

"Nevertheless there are subjects unfit for your ears," Aunt Madge said sharply. "Unfit for any lady's ears, in fact. You will none of you say another word. Bella, I shall take you back to the nursery. You will eat with Miss Crabtree tonight."

Bella's face fell. "Must I? Dorothea wants to meet Camilla."

"Another time, perhaps. You don't eat with us when we have visitors. Come along, and you can help me look for my green thread, for it is not in my work bag. I cannot imagine what has happened to it, for I am certain I placed it there this morning, knowing I would need it. Come, Bella."

Pulling a face, Bella rose, but as she crossed the room she whispered to Julia, "Tell me everything later."

Julia nodded, laughing.

"And *especially* why she has straw in her hair."

That evening was the strangest Julia could remember in many a month. Camilla, washed, dressed in an only slightly rumpled gown and coiffed by Hathaway, Mama's very grand lady's maid, smiled prodigiously, simpered at Will and brought them up to date with all the Sagborough gossip. All, that is, except the one subject at the forefront of all their minds. Mama was too ladylike to raise the subject, naturally, but Julia burned to know all the details, such as how on earth Camilla had made her way south, with only her maid and a couple of small bags. As to *why*, no one was in any doubt — she hoped to cajole or browbeat or trick Will into marrying her. For his part, no one could fault his courtesy towards her, but there was no warmth in it, and nothing at all to give her hope.

A little while later, when the Fletcher sisters were sitting in bed, cosily swathed in woollen wraps, sharing the gossip with Bella, there was a quiet knock on the door. Mama's head peeked in, a pretty little lace confection covering her hair.

"Julia, dear, will you come along to our bedroom for a moment. Your Papa and I would like a word." A frown crossed her face. "Bella, dear, do go to bed at once. Come, Julia."

Bella grinned, and scuttled out, as the sisters exchanged surprised glances. Whatever could it mean? Julia's first thought, as she lit a candle and followed her mama across the landing, was that this was related to her unfortunate encounter with the hunt, for why else would she be singled out, and at such a late hour? Perhaps Sir Hector had written to Pa, or even come himself to rail at her behaviour.

She had never before entered the bedroom that Mama and Pa shared at Chadwell Park. She had been familiar with every room at Sagborough, and knew intimately every quirk of the house, down to the cracked pane where Will had once thrown a book, and the burn mark in the rug in the nursery, where only Ted's quick thinking had stamped out the flames and saved the house from burning down. But here, so much was new to her.

The room was huge. Sitting directly above the dining room, it had the same oval shape and length, dominated by the vast canopied bed which loomed out of the darkness. Pale hangings at the head surrounded a mound of crisp white pillows, and a silk bedspread was turned back, ready for the occupants to take their places for the night.

Julia had a sudden image of Pa and Mama lying side by side in that huge bed. What would it be like to climb into a bed like that... with a man? Julia had rarely slept alone in her life, but curling up beside a sister was a cosy and comforting experience. Surely sharing a bed with a man would not be like that, for men were strange, alien creatures. A little frightening, in some ways, with their starched cravats and broad shoulders and their liking for fast horses... but perhaps that was only Will and Johnny. Pa wasn't like that, and nor was James Plummer. Now, why had she thought of him?

"Ah, come in, puss," Pa said. He and Will were standing beside the fire, Pa in an exotic banyan and a fearsomely large cap, and Will still fully dressed. "Come and sit down. We need your help."

"My help?" Julia said, startled.

"With the Camilla problem," Will said tersely.

"Precisely," Pa said. "Julia, sit here. Lizzie, do you sit here, close to the fire. You must not take a chill, my dear. You see, Julia, the last thing we wish to do at this precise moment is to create any sort of scandal, not even the least hint of one, with our first season in London on the horizon and such high hopes as we have for Rosie. Camilla's arrival is not best timed, to put it mildly. In Sagborough, everyone knows us and knows Camilla, too, but here..."

He trailed off helplessly, and it was Mama who intervened, pulling her wrap closely about her. "Camilla must be *contained*," she said meaningfully.

"Why not send her home?" Julia said.

"Because that would create exactly the sort of speculation we are trying to avoid," Mama said. "A girl arrives unexpectedly, and not respectably in a carriage—"

"How *did* she get here?" Julia said.

"By the common stage and a farm cart," Mama said, visibly shuddering. "If we send her away again at once, people will wonder why."

"Then Will must go away," Julia said, in reasonable tones. "If he isn't here, Camilla will soon lose interest and take herself away again."

"That was my thought, too," Will said, with a rueful lift of one eyebrow. "I could easily pay Johnny a visit."

"The last thing you must do is to run away!" Mama said sharply. "What could be better designed to raise the most intense speculation? Apart from which, the girl is quite likely to follow you, and that could be disastrous. No, she must be contained here."

"How are you going to do that — lock her in the cellar?" Julia said.

"Really, Julia, your whimsy is sadly misplaced, sometimes," Mama said, although Will and Pa both chuckled. "Not physical containment, obviously. What we have decided is that Camilla's visit must be seen as planned. We can say that she impulsively travelled here before she was expected, but that we hoped she would visit us at some time."

"No one at Sagborough would believe that," Julia said.

"But we are not at Sagborough any more," Mama said patiently. "We will tell everyone that Camilla is here by invitation, that she will stay for two weeks or so, after which her father will come to collect her... or one of her brothers. Your father will write to Mr Weston tomorrow to explain this, and he will arrange that part of it. But for two weeks, Camilla will be our honoured guest, and that is where your help is needed."

Julia had a dreadful sense of foreboding. "What *precisely* do you want me to do?"

"Take charge of her," Mama said promptly. "We will put it about that the two of you are bosom friends — for you are much of an age, after all — and you must look after her, and keep her away from Rosie."

"Rosie? Not Will?"

"Will can take care of himself," Pa said, "but Rosie is an innocent, and I don't want her having more to do with Camilla than civility requires. Angie, too, isn't properly up to the mark yet. But you're a sensible girl, Julia, and not likely to be distressed by Camilla's ways. I hope she won't expose you to anything shocking, but if she does, then she'll be on her way home within the hour. She knows it, too, for your mama has told her in no uncertain terms that she's to behave herself."

"Will you do it, Julia?" Mama said, in anxious tones. "I don't know what we shall be able to contrive if you will not."

"Of course I will," Julia said. "Anything to protect Rosie."

"Exactly so!" Mama said. "The last thing we want at this moment is anything that might *contaminate* Rosie's reputation."

"I don't want to contaminate Julia's reputation, either," Pa said sharply. "Julia, this won't be easy for you, and Camilla's no walker, so it will mean curtailing your own exercise for a while, too."

"It is only for two weeks," Mama said, "and it is all for Rosie, after all." She beamed happily at them all.

9: *Morning Calls*

Julia had never had a great deal to do with Camilla Weston before, although she had known her all her life, and they had danced past each other at innumerable assemblies and balls. Now it was her task to contain her, as Mama put it. It was Julia, therefore, who woke Camilla the next morning, saw that she had a cup of chocolate and washing water, and helped her choose a gown. When Camilla emerged, fetchingly if inappropriately dressed in flimsy muslin, Julia was waiting to show her the way to the parlour, where the ladies gathered before breakfast.

"How very pretty you look," Julia said, with complete honesty. Camilla had none of Rosie's ethereal beauty, or even Angie's delicate looks, but she had a wholesome appeal all her own. With rosy cheeks, wide blue eyes, hair that fell in a mass of dark curls, and a well-formed figure, she had attracted a host of admirers before she had even left the schoolroom. It was a pity she was the fourth daughter, and none of the others able to give her a helping hand in society, but nevertheless she would probably have married well enough if she had been able to resist what Aunt Madge called *'fooling around with everything in breeches'*. Usually, she added, *'Let that be a lesson to you girls'*, but since she never spelt out exactly what the lesson was, they were none the wiser.

Allie had been a shade more explicit. "Just make sure that no gentleman steps out of line when he pays you attentions."

Julia had never had a gentleman pay her attentions, or at least not beyond the easy flirtatiousness of the drawing room, so there had been no opportunity for one of them to step out of line, and she wondered sometimes what precisely that entailed. Not that she ever lost sleep over it. Having several sisters who were prettier and daintier and capable of wearing a gown for an evening without tearing a sleeve or dripping soup onto the bodice, she supposed it would never happen to her. She was the ungainly, clumsy one of the family, unlikely ever to inspire affection in a man's heart. Her only attraction was her dowry of twenty thousand pounds, but whenever a suitor's eyes gleamed avariciously in her direction, Pa would ask her if she liked the fellow, she would shake her head and Pa would see him off. It was precisely as she wished it.

Spending time with Camilla, however, gave her an opportunity to observe a different response from gentlemen. On Camilla's first morning, Mama ordered the carriage and she, Julia and Camilla set out to visit as many of their acquaintances as could be managed. The first call was to the Manor, where Lady Plummer received them with cool civility, and Miss Plummer without interest. Lady Charles was indisposed, they were told. It was odd how often she was indisposed when they called. Sir Owen and his sons were not present, but his son-in-law was, and he was drawn irresistibly to Camilla.

Lord Charles Heaman was tall, thin and haughtily aristocratic, mentioning his brother the Marquess of Barrowford at every opportunity. Mama had great hopes that this illustrious personage could be a useful connection when they were in London, although Lord Charles had said or done nothing to encourage such ambitions. Whenever Julia had met him before, he had looked down his supercilious nose at all of them, even Rosie, that most demure of maidens. But something about Camilla gave him animation.

He bowed over Camilla's hand, holding it for far longer than was necessary, and smirked at her in a manner that turned Julia's stomach. Yet Camilla seemed to enjoy such attentions, blushing and lowering her eyes and giggling at every feeble witticism. It was astonishing. Julia was relieved when Mama stayed only for the prescribed fifteen minutes.

Their next call was to Mrs Reynell, the widow last seen floundering in the mud during the hunt. But she had received Julia's letter, and was graciously pleased to be offered another abject apology.

"You will know better now than to wander about on hunt days, Miss Fletcher," she said.

"Indeed I will," Julia said genially. "Mr James Plummer is to advise me on which days I should avoid wandering."

"Oh. Mr James Plummer? Not your brother? He is to

take up hunting, is he not?"

Mama intervened smoothly. "He certainly hopes to, as soon as he has acquired some suitable horses. Our part of Yorkshire was less conducive to hunting, so he is excited to try what Hertfordshire may offer. Such an active young man, and he does love his horses."

"And handsome, too," Mrs Reynell said, her expression thoughtful. "He will have all the young ladies sighing after him when he goes to London, I make no doubt. He will be able to take his pick."

Camilla sat up a little straighter, her lips pursed, but Mama said quickly, "Will has no plans to marry for some years. He is but six and twenty, and no need to set up his nursery yet."

"Six and twenty? I had thought him older," Mrs Reynell said, losing interest. Since she was herself at least thirty, despite the careful use of rouge and powder designed to conceal her age, Will was no doubt too young to attract her as a potential second husband.

Again, Mama rose after only fifteen minutes, and it was back to the carriage. Since she insisted on calling upon the ladies of Danes Green in strict rank order, they now passed through the village for the third time, this time sailing past the Manor gates to leave the straggling lines of cottages behind.

Not a hundred yards further on, they came across a man in muddy clothing carrying a gun, a bulging game bag slung over one casual shoulder. Mama's gaze slid past him, but Julia knew him at once.

"Oh, look! There is Mr Plummer!" Rapping smartly on the glass, she waved enthusiastically and he looked up, beamed at her and— Well, he would have waved back, she was sure of it, but the carriage rolled majestically on its way and he was lost to view.

"A little decorum, Julia, if you please," Mama said, in her serene way. "It is for the gentleman to make his bow first to a lady, and you may then acknowledge him by a slight inclination of the head, nothing more. You should never wave or otherwise try to attract his attention."

"I beg your pardon, Mama," Julia said meekly. "I shall try to remember."

In a very few minutes they came to Fairstead House, the home of Miss Williamson and Miss Ariadne Williamson. The house was a large one, although with only modest grounds, but the two elderly spinsters who resided there were what Mama described as *'shabby genteel'*, having the house only for their lifetimes and without the income to support it or themselves with any pretensions to elegance, or even comfort. It was rumoured that they lived in two or three rooms for most of the year, only emerging from this seclusion to entertain when their nephew, Mr Richard Osgood, visited.

Since this gentleman was presently enjoying such a visit, the Fletcher ladies were shown into a previously unseen and rather imposing drawing room in order to meet the honoured guest. He was a young man of about thirty years, already tending towards stoutness, and although his greeting to the callers was all that was polite, his countenance was serious and unsmiling. Julia wondered whether he disapproved of them, or whether he was habitually so unwelcoming.

The Miss Williamsons were otherwise, chattering excitedly over each other to tell all the achievements already attained in Mr Osgood's life, and the rewards heaped upon him. He was a dean at some cathedral or other, having been singled out personally by the bishop for this honour, and commended by no less a personage than the Archbishop of Canterbury, or perhaps it might have been one of his subordinates, it was impossible to tell, but clearly there was no knowing how high Mr Osgood might aspire to rise. A bishopric, the ladies were certain of it, and who knows, perhaps higher still. They twittered happily together, and in their brown bombazine they looked like nothing so much as two little sparrows, chirping away.

The gentleman in question appeared not to notice all their praise, for he was talking in a ponderous way to Camilla, who looked a great deal less bored than Julia would have been. In fact, she was treating him to her usual performance honed over the years by being practised on a great many Yorkshire gentlemen. Whatever he said, she would respond in a suitable manner, whether smiling, or nodding, or opening her eyes wide and once gasping, as if in amazement. And the stiff and solemn Mr Richard Osgood, the pious churchman who might even be a bishop one day, visibly melted under the attentions of a pretty young girl.

His aunts took so long to elaborate on all the gentleman's perfections that Julia was beginning to watch the clock and wonder how soon Mama would rise with her society smile to take her leave. But abruptly Miss Williamson said, "But did you receive our invitation, Mrs Fletcher? We delivered it by hand so—"

"Yes, indeed I did," Mama said, and for the first time Julia could remember, she looked uncomfortable.

"Oh, then may we expect you at our little gathering? Just an informal card party for dear Richard to meet all his old friends... and his new ones, of course. We should be so gratified if you should honour us with your company."

Mama played with her reticule. "I... have not quite determined... this cold weather, you know."

"Oh, indeed, but we always have a good blaze, do we not, sister? Poor dear Richard is so troubled with his chest in the winter months, you see, and we could not be at all easy unless we took every precaution. You would be quite comfortable, I am certain of it."

Julia held her breath. A card party! How she would enjoy that, and so would Pa and Will and Aunt Madge, she knew. But if Mama had decided against it, for some unfathomable reason, then there was nothing to be done about it.

"If you are thinking it might be unsuitable for the young ladies," Miss Williamson went on, "pray be assured that we are most careful about such matters. There will be no excessive drinking, or gambling. Dear Richard is a man of the cloth and we would not dream of exposing him to anything the least bit irregular. There will be a number of ladies present, and Mrs Reynell is to grace our rooms for the occasion, and she would never lend her name to the least whisper of impropriety. And there will be some young gentlemen present. I can see that Miss Weston would love to come."

Camilla turned great pleading eyes on Mama.

"For myself," Mama said firmly, "I am not fond of evening engagements at this season, but the gentlemen may wish to brave the elements, and they may escort Miss Weston, if she wishes to attend."

Julia was not about to let Camilla go if she could not. "I should enjoy it, too, Mama, if you could spare me for the evening."

Mama glanced at Camilla, who was trying not to look triumphant, and then back to Julia. "Rosie will bear me company, so you may go if you wish, Julia."

The Miss Williamsons clapped their hands in glee.

When they were safely back in the carriage and leaving Fairstead House behind, Julia said, "I thought you wanted us to mix with the gentry, Mama. Miss Williamson and her sister are gentry, are they not?"

"Oh yes, but so poor! It would be cruel to invite them to dine since they cannot return the hospitality, so in that sense they are quite beneath our notice. A card party with a scrappy supper is not at all the same. I do not object to morning calls, for we accepted the acquaintance before we knew much about them and cannot repudiate them now, but there is no consequence to be gained from their acquaintance, and I do not want Rosie to mingle in such low circles. We cannot be too careful of her just now, when we all have such hopes of her. But you girls may attend the card party, if you feel you might derive some pleasure from it."

Camilla heaved a satisfied sigh, and murmured, "This visit is going to be more enjoyable than I had suspected."

Julia eyed her suspiciously, but Mama merely smiled and patted Camilla's hand indulgently.

As they drove back into the village, they again passed a very elaborate gatehouse, whose drive wound away into trees so dense that no house was visible.

"Who lives there?" Camilla said. "Is it a very grand house?"

"So I believe," Mama said. "Kelshaw Hall is the home of Lady Frederica and Mr Benjamin Kelshaw. Lady Frederica's father is the Earl of Pinner."

"Aren't we calling there? I thought we were calling on all the local gentry."

"We are not acquainted with the Kelshaws," Mama said stiffly.

Camilla's eyes widened, but she understood. Mr Kelshaw had not called upon Pa when first the family had arrived at Chadwell Park, and Lady Frederica had not called upon Mama. The Fletchers were too closely connected to trade, and therefore unsuitable persons to be acquainted with the daughter of an earl. It had stung Mama very badly when she understood the slight.

Julia said nothing, pondering the oddities of this new world in which they now found themselves, when perfectly respectable people could not be friends because of some perceived disparity in rank.

The ladies had barely removed their coats and bonnets, and settled to their usual tasks in the parlour, before a carriage arrived. Keeble sidled in with a collection of cards on a silver salver.

"Lady Bellingham, Miss Bellingham and Sir Hector Bellingham are in the hall, madam. Are you at home?"

Julia squeaked in surprise, and perhaps a little alarm. But Mama had been hoping that Lady Bellingham, at least, would seek her acquaintance, and so she answered swiftly.

"Yes, of course we are at home. Do show them in, and pray ask my husband to join us, if he is to be found. Well, this is a surprise. Julia, I fear you will have to make your apology all over again. I do hope he is not going to rant and rage at you."

"Unlikely if he has his wife and daughter with him," Julia said.

Mama's face lightened. "Quite right. This must be just a social visit, and not before time, either. This will expand our list of acquaintances considerably."

Angie, Will and Aunt Madge were elsewhere, but Mama, Rosie, Julia and Camilla all rose as the Bellingham family came into the room. Sir Hector was not a man who wasted time on unnecessary courtesies, for his eyes raked the room and lit on Julia. At once he strode across to loom in front of her. He was a large man in every sense of the word, and a brightly coloured coat did nothing to diminish his size. Julia quaked a little, but she lifted her chin to look him straight in the eye.

But he beamed happily at her. "There you are, young lady," he boomed. "That was a fine letter you wrote me, a very proper letter. All your own work, was it, or did you have a bit of help, eh?"

"Every word was my own, and I meant it, sir. May I say again how sorry I am—"

"No, no, no more of that, if you please. We were neither of us quite at our best that day, so I offer you my own apology in return. Shall we shake hands on it?"

And just as if she were a man, he held out his beefy paw to her. She had no hesitation in taking it and allowing her hand to be vigorously pumped and simultaneously squeezed.

"There now, we can be friends," Sir Hector said, sitting down on a sofa and patting the seat beside him. "I must say, I like a gel with spirit, and you have a devilish spirited nature, Miss Fletcher. Now, no colouring up, for I am sure you will not be missish over a compliment or two, and you will not mind my blunt speaking, I am sure. We have exchanged stronger words already, after all."

He laughed heartily, and Julia felt obliged to smile slightly in return, for the sake of politeness. Mama was too ladylike to show any sign of displeasure at such unmannerly behaviour, but Julia knew her well enough to be sure that she felt it, nonetheless.

Fortunately, Lady Bellingham and her daughter fluttered delicately into Mama's orbit, Aunt Madge and Pa came in not many minutes later, followed by Will, and then Keeble and a little procession of footmen with refreshments. In the general movement about the room, Sir Hector was captured by Pa, Will made a beeline for the Bellingham daughter and Julia was able to make her escape to sit a little out of the way with Aunt Madge.

The Bellinghams stayed for more than half an hour and

Mama was so pleased with this excessive degree of attention that she almost forgave Sir Hector for neglecting her so comprehensively that she had not exchanged a single word with him.

"He is only a knight, not a baronet, but still he is the squire and local magistrate, and thus a person of consequence in the county," she said happily. "I had thought Bellingham Green too far away for any acquaintance, but Lady Bellingham tells me there is a farm track they use to shorten the distance. Rather rough, of course, and impassable after too much rain for there is a ford to be crossed, but not too muddy at present. Hmm, three days, I think..."

"Three days, Lizzie?" Pa said. "What are you planning now?"

"I shall return Lady Bellingham's call in three days," she said complacently. "Any sooner would look too eager, but one must acknowledge the condescension of their visit with an early attention. And perhaps after that they will invite us to dine."

"Ah, you have such a subtle way of going about these things," Pa said, smiling fondly at her. "My father's rule has served me well enough for all these years. If a man takes three weeks to call on you, then you can take three weeks to return it."

Mama laughed. "That does well enough for gentlemen, I make no doubt, but ladies take more account of disparity of rank and the distinctions that must be made."

"I'm sure you're right," he said. "You usually are. Have you seen my newspaper — the London one that came yesterday? I was sure I left it on my desk, but it's nowhere to be found."

"Everything disappears in this house," Aunt Madge said darkly. "I have been all over looking for my scissors and where should I find them but in the library, and what they were doing there I'm sure I can't say."

Mama only smiled in her gentle way and shook her head. "It is this house, Madge. It has so many rooms that it is hard to remember where anything is. We shall grow accustomed in time, I am sure."

But Aunt Madge grumbled steadily for the best part of an hour, and nothing would appease her.

10: A Card Party

"I thought you were determined not to go," Thomas said to James, as they donned their cloaks at the rectory and awaited the Plummer carriage which was to convey them to Fairstead House. "Oh, never tell me that Mrs Reynell has cried off! And after I have been planning my assault on her affections these two weeks past."

"I know nothing of Mrs Reynell, but I do know that a certain young lady of my acquaintance is to be there."

"Miss Julia Fletcher? James, this is becoming a serious pursuit."

"I am going to marry her, Thomas."

"And does the lady know this?"

"Not yet. I do not intend to rush my fences, so I shall proceed in slow, steady steps. Then, when the time is right, I shall move in for the kill. Well... not an apt analogy, perhaps, but you understand me, I think."

Thomas frowned. "Have you spoken to her father yet? He may have ambitions for her beyond a country rectory."

"I shall talk to Fletcher when matters have progressed a little further, but he will not stand in her way, I am sure of that. Come now, Thomas, you do not imagine that Fletcher will turn me away just because I am a second son, do you? I am exceedingly eligible, you know. Not, perhaps, in London, but in Hertfordshire there are not so many bachelors of respectable family with a house and a good income. No, Fletcher will not gainsay me. Ah, here is the carriage now."

The carriage already contained Sir Owen, Lord Charles, Uncle Morgan and Michael, so James squeezed inside, and Thomas climbed onto the box beside Lawson to drive the short distance to Fairstead House. They were, of course, punctual to the minute, for Sir Owen would permit nothing less, which meant that they were almost the first to arrive. Only the Frye family, who were not quite gentry but admitted by virtue of distant kinship with the Williamson sisters, were there before them, wearing their very best clothes and excited faces.

Sir Owen's arrival was the cue for the wine to be broached, and soon after another gaggle of guests arrived, leaving James free to loiter near the door awaiting Julia. He was in rather a quandary, for if Mrs Reynell should come through it first, he might not be able to avoid her and there was a serious risk that she would dig her claws into him for the whole evening, and then his time would be entirely wasted. But it was not Mrs Reynell whose face appeared next, it was Miss Paton and an unknown young lady with rosy cheeks, followed by Mr Fletcher and Mr Will Fletcher, and finally… there was Julia. His future wife.

He was loath to rush forward in such a public place and draw attention to his courtship, but he did not need to. Julia looked around the room, saw him, smiled and waggled her fingers at him. After such a greeting, it was only courtesy for him to move towards her, make his salutations to the family and then offer her his arm.

"Would you like some wine?" he said. "Shall we steer towards the footman over there with the tray?"

"I'd better not," she said. "I shall be tipsy if I start drinking before I've even sat down. I like to have a glass of something beside me while I play, but you know how it is with standing about like this — sip, sip, sip and look at that, the glass is empty."

"There is some lemonade on the sideboard over there. That could be relied upon not to make you tipsy."

She agreed that it would not. As they made their way across the room, he noticed that the lace frill around her bodice was awry.

Leaning forward to whisper in her ear, he murmured, "There is something amiss with your lace."

"Is there? Oh! Stupid thing!" She turned to face the wall, then with one tug, the lace came free and she stuffed it in her reticule. "Let's hope Aunt Madge doesn't notice. She'd say I was showing far too much bosom now. She says it's very unattractive to flaunt so much flesh."

"Does she? She is mistaken, however," he said silkily, gazing with heroic self-control into her face. He too hoped that Aunt Madge would not notice, for she was liable to whisk her charge away to the retiring room to repair the damage and that would be a crying shame. Julia's eyebrows rose in astonishment, and he deemed it advisable to change the subject hastily before she asked why. "Your friend, the one with the dark curls... does she make a long stay with you?"

"Friend? Oh, you mean Camilla. Oh dear, I forgot to introduce you. I am so bird-witted sometimes. Should you like to meet her?"

"No, not in the slightest," he said promptly, making her laugh. "You are far more amusing company, I assure you. Besides, she is being very well entertained by Mr Osgood."

And so she was, simpering and fluttering her eyelashes, while the future bishop smiled and patted her hand in an avuncular way. This raised all sorts of interesting ideas in Julia's mind.

"Tell me about Mr Osgood," she said. "Is he rich? Oh — he's not married, is he?"

"Not married, and rather eligible, if that is where your thoughts are leading. He has two very good livings, worth fifteen hundred or so, and will inherit another two thousand a year from his father in time. I should have thought him rather a dry stick for your friend, who is..." He hesitated, groping for the most tactful description. "Well, she seems like an affectionate little thing."

"Oh yes, very affectionate! No, I should not have thought it a good match under other circumstances, but—" She stopped abruptly, blushing fierily, which intrigued him so much that he almost asked what she meant by it. But just at that moment, the door was thrown open once more, and a hush fell upon the room. With a slight sway of the hips, Mrs Reynell slithered into the room. Slithered? Where had that word come from? And yet it was apt, for was she not something of a snake?

She was rather an elegantly dressed snake this evening, her silk gown foaming around her feet, and her bodice devoid of the slightest hint of lace to hide her ample charms.

James could not resist. Leaning towards Julia, he whispered into her ear, "Your aunt would not approve of *that.*"

So it was that when Mrs Reynell's gaze fell upon him, she saw the two of them, heads together, laughing at the shared joke. It was perfect, he thought. Now the widow knows exactly where she stands.

But it was not quite perfect enough to avoid trouble. The widow's eyes flashed dangerously. Seeing her preparing to bear down on him, he hastily said, "The tables are beginning to form. Shall we join your father?"

Steering Julia as fast as was decent across the room and away from the widow, he scooped up Mr Fletcher and looked wildly about for a fourth. "Ah, Mr Kelshaw! How do you do, sir? Do you know Mr Fletcher? Fletcher, this is Mr Kelshaw, whose estate is just to the west of Danes Green. Shall we take that table over there, gentlemen? Miss Fletcher?"

And it was done, the crisis averted. He did not turn his head to see how well Mrs Reynell bore his escape, or whether Thomas intervened to soothe her, for he picked up the pack of cards on the table, and kept up a patter of no moment as he shuffled and dealt. But it was some time before he could relax and enjoy the pleasure of the game and Julia's company.

There was one unexpected outcome of his manoeuvrings. He remembered rather too late that Lady Frederica Kelshaw was a high stickler who would have nothing at all to do with upstarts like the Fletchers, and her dutiful husband had likewise avoided them. Now that they had been introduced, however inadvertently, they discovered certain interests in common. A casual enquiry by Kelshaw as to how the Fletchers were settling in at Chadwell Park brought forth a mention of the lack of hot water and the three coppers in the basement. Kelshaw's face lit up at once, and in no time at all the two were discussing pipes and valves and heaven knows what else, and from there to Kelshaw's favourite topic, water closets. Supper was taken up with sketches on scraps of paper and the evening ended with a promise from Kelshaw to call at the Park first thing the next day to determine the most advantageous locations for these wonders of the modern age.

And by dint of surrounding himself at every opportunity with Fletchers, and keeping Julia's arm firmly linked to his as much as possible, James managed to avoid exchanging even bows with Mrs Reynell for the entire evening. It was a triumph, and he returned to the rectory well satisfied with his endeavours.

~~~~~

Chadwell Park was now thrown into a bustle of preparations for the forthcoming season in London. Although there were many weeks yet before their departure, there was much to do, and Julia could not escape her share of the business.

Numerous boxes had been filled with the very best silk and muslin and jaconet and kerseymere that the warehouses of Fletcher's Import and Export Company could offer, brought south to be made up into gowns of every type imaginable. A famous *modiste* from London had been exclusively engaged to address the wardrobes of the Fletcher ladies, and this rather haughty personage and her two seamstresses had been assigned quarters in the main house, rather than the servants' wing. An unused bedroom had been fitted out with large worktables, and given over entirely to the enterprise. Several hours each day were therefore devoted to measuring and fitting, and the scouring of journals to divine the most flattering and fashionable styles.

Julia had little interest in these affairs, and for her part would have avoided going to London altogether, if she could. However, since she was kept busy containing Camilla and could not go on her long walks, the dressmaking was as good a way as any of occupying the otherwise long, empty hours.

One morning, it was Julia's turn to be fitted for several partly made gowns, so she was standing on a box while the seamstresses knelt on the floor, pinning hems, and the *modiste* tutted over her. Madame Farage made no open comment on the deficiencies of form before her. When it was Rosie's turn on the box she clapped her hands in delight, and smiled benignly on Angie and Mama, but Julia's ungainly shape brought only frowns and sighs.

"You look lovely, Jules," Rosie said, walking around to admire a ball gown from all angles. "You can wear such wonderful colours, and think how splendidly you will look going down the dance."

Julia raised her eyebrows at this, but there was no point contradicting Rosie. She had such a romantic view of the world that she saw everything in glowing terms.

"I cannot wait!" Angie cried. "So many ballrooms, so many dances! We shall have such a glorious time, dancing our way around London." She curtsied to an imaginary partner, and then danced her way elegantly around the room, deftly avoiding the numerous chairs draped with fabrics.

"And so many partners," Camilla said, lifting her head from the journal she was reading. "So many eligible gentlemen, so many lords, so many heirs to dukedoms."

Madame Farage tittered at this optimism, but Mama said calmly, "Many partners, we must hope indeed, but there are not so many heirs to dukedoms, and if there were, even Rosie could hardly aim so high. Julia, hold your arms up a little. Hmm, I am not quite convinced about that sleeve, Madame. A little more fullness, do you not think?"

"Perhaps, but we do not wish to widen the shoulders."

"That is true. You do have very broad shoulders, Julia. They are not your best feature. There was a style in the journal that arrived yesterday that might suit. Rosie, dear, would you run down to the parlour and fetch *La Belle Assemblée* for me? It is on the small table near the fire."

Rosie ran off at once, but she returned in a few moments, empty handed. "It is not there, Mama."

"Nonsense! I put it there myself, not an hour ago. Did you look on the big table?"

"Yes, Mama, and on both sideboards, and in the

cupboard."

"It must be there. I shall go myself."

But she had no more success than Rosie, returning puzzled and rather cross, and spent quite some time trying to explain the style she had in mind to Madame Farage by waving her hands vaguely in the air.

One of the consequences of Camilla's arrival was an increase in the number of gentleman callers. Julia could not quite see what the attraction was, or why men flocked around Camilla when Rosie was so much more beautiful, and had a dowry of fifty thousand pounds besides, but then, men were a mystery to her, she decided. Why, for instance, was Lord Charles Heaman such an assiduous caller nowadays? Or the two Plummer brothers? Mr Michael Plummer seemed attentive to Rosie, but that was understandable, for she was a very desirable bride for the heir to an impoverished baronetcy, but Lord Charles seemed most drawn to Camilla, which was odd in a married man. Odder still was that Mama seemed to encourage him, not interfering when he spent the whole visit at Camilla's side, although she had grumbled about him in the past, complaining at his discourtesy. His great crime, seemingly, was that he was deaf to her hints that an introduction to his brother, the Marquess of Barrowford would be a great kindness.

As for James Plummer, he seemed to seek out Julia herself. Not that she minded his company, and he never engaged in tedious flirtation with her, but she wondered at his coming very much.

"I am surprised to see you here again, Mr Plummer," she

said to him one day. "This spell of fine weather cannot last for ever and I had thought you would be out with your gun today."

"I went rabbiting before breakfast," he said with his pleasant smile, his eyes creased at the sides. Even when he was being serious, those creases were still visible, as if he liked to laugh a great deal and his face remembered. "I potted a few pigeons, too, and if conditions are propitious, I might go down to the river later to try for some fowl. There is plenty of time for sport without neglecting the pleasures of society."

The pleasures of *her* society? She chose to take it as such, since he always sought her out on these visits, but she had no wish to press him on the point, and perhaps oblige him to be more directly complimentary. Heaven forbid she should be thought to be flirting with him. Her eyes strayed to Mr Michael Plummer, making laborious conversation to a silent Rosie. "Your brother's visits are more understandable, I believe," she said. "He has not your enthusiasm for the pursuit of small birds and beasts."

"A man may have other pursuits in mind," Mr Plummer said, his frankness causing Julia's eyes to widen.

"Of course. Rosie is so beautiful, it is no wonder that every man should be drawn to her."

"Not every man is drawn to your sister," he said easily, "and beauty is not the only or even the best guide to a woman's desirability."

"Her dowry is the principal reason for her desirability, I imagine," she said mischievously.

He laughed merrily. "That is a consideration, too, and rather a substantial one, but again, not the only one." He leaned forward to speak more softly, as if he did not wish to be overheard. "When a man is considering marriage, Miss Fletcher, he must look first for a woman of like mind to his own, able to enter into all his deepest concerns and support him in his endeavours, a woman who will be a companion and helpmeet for all the years to come. And once he has assured himself of her suitability, then he must open her eyes to the future before her."

"Open her eyes? As if she is asleep, and needs only to be wakened and the banns may be called? I can assure you, sir, it will take a great deal more than *that* to persuade Rosie to marry your brother. Or anyone at all, perhaps."

He looked startled, but recovered himself with a laugh. "Oh, indeed. Michael is not quite at that point yet... nor may ever be. He must marry before too long, of course, to secure the line... or I must." He smiled at her. "We are *both* of an age when marriage rises to the forefront of one's mind, but Michael is still considering his options, I believe."

Julia was not quite sure what to make of this conversation, but she reported it to Mama as faithfully as she could remember it, as she knew she was expected to do.

"Well, it is no matter," Mama said with a lift of one shoulder. "In some ways it would be a shame to have Rosie snatched up before she has even spread her wings in London. The heir to a baronetcy is not to be despised, certainly, but I feel sure she can do much better."

They were in the withdrawing room after dinner, and

Angie, Rosie and Camilla were in the music room next door, while Pa and Will were playing backgammon. Aunt Madge had gone to see that Bella was safely in bed.

Lowering her voice, although no one was near enough to overhear, Mama went on, "How is Camilla? Not giving you any trouble?"

"No, not at all. She is behaving herself very well." Suspiciously well, Julia almost added, but perhaps that was unkind. The Westons were a wealthy family, but they had never moved in the level of society to which their wealth entitled them. It may be that Camilla was finding her stay at Chadwell Park rather congenial.

"She is attracting some attention from the gentlemen, would you not agree?"

Julia could not deny it, although it puzzled her. "Mama… she is not exactly *eligible*, is she? I mean, if a gentleman wished to marry her—"

"Julia, it is not for us to interfere in such matters," Mama said firmly. "If anyone wished to marry her, then it would be a matter between him and Camilla's father. But her *friendships* are certainly of interest to us, for we are responsible for her while she stays with us. I noticed Lord Charles paying her some attention, and that surprised me. Has Camilla mentioned him?"

"No, not at all."

"Hmm. Still, it is something to watch carefully. Be sure to let me know if anything arises."

"What sort of thing?" Julia said.

"Oh… well, if Camilla should happen to meet him anywhere… any private talk they may have… anything of that nature," she said with a vague wave of the hand.

"If the talk is private, I may know nothing of it."

Mama gave her a strange look. "I suppose so. But anything odd, you know? Keep me informed, for I stand in place of her mama."

Julia agreed to it, although the request mystified her.

11: Courtship

James's Sundays had settled into a pattern. He rose and dressed early enough to walk across to the church with Thomas, where they shared the duties of lighting candles in the church and ensuring all was in readiness for the office. Then they sat by the fire in the vestry until the congregation began to arrive.

"How goes your courtship of Mrs Reynell?" James said.

The curate pulled a rueful face. "Courtship might be too strong a word for it. After the great triumph of an hour playing whist beside her, during which time she devoted most of her attention to glowering at your back, a very little to her cards and none at all to me, she abandoned me at the first opportunity. I called yesterday to enquire if she had taken any chill from venturing out on such a cold night, and I swear to you, James, she looked at me as if I had crawled out of a swamp. The chill in that room was deeper than the frost on the ground outside."

James chuckled. "But you were not serious about her, so you cannot be too disappointed."

"I had no expectation of success, that is true, for she has always placed herself on a very high form. She would never deign to marry a mere curate on a hundred pounds a year, and with no prospects of a living. But I should very much like to marry *someone*, James. I am forty years old and staring into the not so distant prospect of old age, and a wife would be the greatest comfort to me."

"I had thought you content with your life," James said.

"And so I am, very content. I have work that suits my nature, in a position where I can be of some use to my parishioners, and an income that is more than adequate for my modest needs, since you very generously provide me with a roof over my head, and as much good food and excellent wine as I can consume. Your cast off clothes even find their way to me. I want for nothing, at least nothing material. But a wife! How I should love to come home each night to a wife."

"I imagine there are any number of parish women who would be more than happy to oblige you, if you would but look their way."

"Oh, certainly. Becky from Mr Grant's farm, for instance, or Margaret, Mrs Reynell's parlourmaid. The Manor dairymaid, too. And I would happily take any one of them, or even Molly, the Kelshaw's scullery maid, for I do not mind the squint in the slightest, but they are all of them penniless."

"A wife would not be such a great additional expense, would it? Given that the house and food are provided."

"That is perfectly true, and at a hundred a year, I could provide for a *wife*, just about. But there would be children, any number of children, and I could not bear to raise a family in abject poverty."

"I had no idea you were so serious about this," James said thoughtfully. "But the solution is a simple one. I shall increase your salary to—"

"No, no, no! That you must not do," Thomas cried. "I am more than adequately compensated, I assure you. The tithes are yours, and fitting for your station in life. It is not for you to deprive yourself in order to enable me to marry a scullery maid with a squint. That would be foolishness indeed. If God intends me to marry, he will provide a wealthy woman who will fall violently in love with me, and if he does not... then I shall be content. But let us talk of happier matters, and your own courtship. You have been seeing a great deal of the lady, I hear."

"How do you hear such things, Thomas?"

"Would it surprise you to know that the good people of St Hilary's parish take a proprietorial interest in you? In all the great families, to be truthful. Every time you call upon Miss Fletcher at the Park, one of the footmen will happen to mention it to his sister at the Manor, who will tell her mother, who then relates to everyone who passes her gate. Which is, as you may imagine, everyone in the village. So it is widely known that you are paying court to Miss Julia Fletcher, and your brother is unusually attentive to Miss Fletcher. There is great excitement at these promising signs, as you may imagine."

"The villagers approve, do they?"

"Well…" Thomas scratched his nose thoughtfully. "The ladies are not thought to be quite worthy of the Plummers' distinguished heritage, but their dowries are mentioned with respect, and there will be great satisfaction in seeing you both settled, especially after that business with Mr Michael."

James shook his head. "There are no secrets in a village."

"None whatsoever," Thomas said cheerfully.

"You must hear all the gossip as you go about here and there. You would know if aught were said that I should know about. Or my brother, for that matter."

Thomas looked uncomfortable suddenly. "Ah, gossip. Reports of your comings and goings are one thing, for anyone might see you enter or leave a house by the front door, but rumour and supposition… that I cannot like, nor will I repeat such things. But I will tell you that I have heard nothing to the detriment of your young lady, except that she spills her soup occasionally, which I dare say you already know. And Miss Rose is a paragon of maidenly decorum, by every account I ever heard."

James could pry no further, but he was left with the uncomfortable feeling that Thomas could tell him a great deal about the Fletcher family, if he chose.

~~~~~

'To Miss Jupp, St Peter's Road, Sagborough, West Riding. My dearest friend, I am in the direst straits, for Mr Michael Plummer continues to be attentive, calling almost every day when the weather is fit, and Mama has warned me that his *visits can only mean one thing and that I should prepare myself to receive his offer! I shall sink through the floor, I swear it, if it comes to that for I know that it is a very good match and he will be a baronet one day and inherit Chadwell Manor and be a person of importance in the county, but I do not want to marry him in the slightest, and my reasons are the most dishonourable in the world. I do not mind him, at least not much, for although he is very thin and looks as if he has been stretched, that is not his fault and not every man can have broad shoulders like Ricky. It is the house, Bel. I truly think Chadwell Manor is the horridest house in the world, for it is dark and poky, at least the rooms are poky, except for the great hall which is massive and gloomy and echoing, and there are all sorts of dark passageways and peculiar staircases, and there are ghosts! A man without a head has been seen, and a woman dressed all in grey and crying, only sometimes she is not seen, but only the crying can be heard. Miss Bellingham told me so, and although she has never seen anything herself, she knows many people who have, and I could not live in a house with ghosts, I could not! I should be too terrified to sleep. I cannot think what I am to do! I am in despair. My very best regards to you and Ricky, and oh, how I wish I were safely back in Sagborough with you both. Your frightened friend, Rosie. Post script — good news! We are to hold a ball after Easter! Is that not the most wonderful thing?"*

~~~~~

After the service, when James had shaken fifty or sixty hands and was thinking longingly of his breakfast, Michael sidled up to him.

"May I walk back over to the rectory with you? I should

like to talk to you, if I may."

"Of course."

Thomas's delicate sense of propriety took him off to the kitchen to prepare breakfast, leaving the brothers alone in the drawing room. It was a comfortable place, or had been once, but years of neglect had rendered it shabby. It was clean enough, for Mrs Pound and her daughter, who between them combined the duties of cook, housekeeper and housemaid, were conscientious, but the rugs were worn to nothing, and several chairs sported little tufts of stuffing where a tear had not been attended to. James no longer noticed, especially as he generally only sat there in the evenings, and candlelight hid a multitude of sins. Now he saw his brother's disdainful gaze, and looked at his house with new eyes. But it was of no consequence, for Julia would remake the place as soon as they were married. She would enjoy that, he supposed. Most women did.

James poured Madeira for his brother and waited for him to unburden himself.

"It is this business with Miss Fletcher," he began tentatively, then stopped.

"Is there any business to discuss at present?" James said, rather amused. Michael always made such heavy weather of things! "You do not seem to have made much progress so far."

"Tell me what I should do!" Michael cried. "Should I marry her, James? Do you think it would be a good match?"

"What do Mother and Father say?"

"Mother says nothing. Father assures me it is up to me, but he wants her fifty thousand, I can tell. I thought we were supposed to be secure financially now, but he still wants me to marry for money."

"One can always do with additional income, brother. The sale of the Park may have righted the ship and prevented us from sinking beneath the waves, but we are not yet away from the rocks. Another fifty thousand would set us up very comfortably, and even Father would have a smile on his face, under such circumstances. But he will never force you into it, Michael, you know that. He never has."

"I know, I know, it was my choice, and never a word of reproach afterwards. But he *expects* me to marry, and now that I am thirty... I am the heir, and it is my duty. And Miss Fletcher is... acceptable."

James sighed inwardly. *Acceptable.* Such an unenthusiastic word for a man to use about the woman he was considering marrying. Would he say that of Julia, that she was *acceptable* to him? How would he describe her?

Adorable. The word arrived unbidden in his mind, startling him. Good heavens! Was he... surely he could not be... falling in love?

"Do you like Rosie?" James said hastily, to distract himself.

"Of course. There is nothing about her to dislike."

"But you do not love her." A statement, not a question.

"Lord, no! That would be impossible. I shall never love again, that much is certain. Once in a lifetime is enough."

"What is it like, being in love?" James said.

"Agony. Sweet, blissful agony, a terrible maelstrom of hope and despair. There are moments of unimagined ecstasy, and moments so black that life is not worth living, and one swings between the two like a pendulum, quite unable to stop oneself." His thin face was afire with the memories, and James could only wish he had never raised the subject.

"One day you will recover, and be able to look back on it with equanimity," James said.

"No, I never shall, because I shall never forget," Michael said evenly, the animation draining from his face. "That is why I hesitate to marry. Marriage can never obliterate the past, you see, and my dread is that it will make the torment even greater. I cannot do it, James. I should have seen it at once, but I cannot do it. And yet I must! The succession is my responsibility."

"And mine also," James said at once, "and so I can set your mind at rest. You need not marry Rose Fletcher, or anyone, if you choose not to, for I shall soon marry and give Father the grandsons he needs."

"You? Marry?"

"Why do you sound so surprised?"

"You never showed any inclination before. But who? Oh, do you want the fifty thousand for yourself?"

James gave a huff of annoyance. Michael could be remarkably obtuse sometimes. "Of course not. Rosie is very lovely, but I want no empty-headed beauty at my side. I am going to marry Julia Fletcher."

Michael only goggled at him.

~~~~~

'Chadwell Park, Friday, Disregard my last letter, dear friend. It seems Mr Michael Plummer is not to offer for me after all, for he has not visited once this week, and Mama thinks it will all come to nothing now. Thank goodness! There is still London to be navigated, but I am reprieved for now. Your very relieved friend, Rosie.'

~~~~~

MARCH

Mama had deemed Camilla's two week visit such a success that it had been extended for a further week, and then to a full month, so that she could attend the Park's first ball. Julia was less happy with these arrangements, for if her rôle was to contain Camilla, the effect of it was equally to contain Julia herself. Apart from a few occasions when she had dragged Camilla out to take a turn around the gardens, and once when Pa had taken pity on her and taken her out for a walk, she had not even been outside for weeks.

The extended stay had a happy side effect, however. The clothes Camilla's father had sent from Yorkshire had grown rather tight — "We are feeding you too many sweet puddings," Mama had said cheerfully, if inaccurately — and so Camilla was to spend a day with Madame Farage and her helpers, being fitted out with somewhat roomier gowns.

This was too good an opportunity for Julia to miss.

"Mama, since Camilla will be busy with fittings all day, may I go for a walk?" she said at breakfast.

"Must you, Julia?" Mama said. "With all this frost, you risk slipping over and twisting an ankle."

"The early frost will have cleared by now," Julia said.

"But it might rain — or snow! We have not seen a single flake of snow since we arrived, and that cannot last."

"I shall not go far if it looks as if the weather will turn, but it is clear just now and I have had no proper exercise for weeks."

"You can walk about the house," Mama began, but Pa lowered his newspaper.

"That's not at all the same, Lizzie. Jules, there is no hunt today, I take it?"

Julia smiled. "No. Mr Plummer told me there won't be another now that the farmers are starting to sow."

"Then I can't see any objection. Your mama can spare you for an hour or two, I'm sure. I'd go with you myself, puss, if I hadn't arranged to meet Kelshaw this morning about those cottages."

"Mama?"

"Very well, but do not be wandering all over the countryside, Julia."

"I won't, Mama. Thank you! Thank you, Pa."

Oh, the joy of freedom at last! She bundled herself up in her old woollen cloak and a multitude of scarves, for despite her brave words the air was bitter, stinging her cheeks as she strode up the hill towards the gate. *Her* gate, as she had come to think of it. She could not rest her arms on its gnarled and pitted wood without remembering her first sight of James walking up towards her, with his gun in his hands and his dilapidated clothes. The memory made her smile. It was no wonder she had thought him to be the gamekeeper!

From the gate she walked down past the little cottage and across a narrow belt of woodland, then another field. On previous walks, she had turned aside at this point to follow a series of open fields, but the wind was so bitter today that she was minded to seek a more sheltered way. She made her way through a small copse, and on the far side of it, only a narrow strip of pasture, dotted with trees, separated her from the river, close enough now that she could hear it burbling melodically in the distance.

Climbing a gate, she began to cross the pasture, humming quietly to herself. Ahead of her was only solid hedge, too thick to scramble through, even if one had no regard for scratches and tears. But surely there was another gate...

It was as her eye followed the line of the hedge that she realised she was not alone. Not far away a creature, who had been grazing placidly, had now raised its head and was looking directly at her. A very large creature, with a massive head and an unfriendly light in its eyes.

Julia was town born and bred, but she knew a bull when she saw one. Slowly, very, very slowly, she backed away.

The bull raised its head a little more.

Careful step by careful step, she inched towards the gate and safety. Was there a gap in the hedge through which she might squeeze? There was not.

A few more paces, a little closer to escape. Back, back, back, her heart thudding painfully. The wind caught at her cloak, so that it flapped around her. The bull made a low growl, deep in its throat, like thunder, only infinitely more menacing. It took a step towards her.

A tree! There was a tree not far away, a fine spreading tree with a low branch just right for a tall girl to reach, if she jumped high. She was not far away now... if only the bull would stay where it was...

It took another step, then pawed the ground, tossing its massive head. And then it began to move...

Julia turned and fled, skirts held high, as fast as her legs could run. Behind her there were horrifying sounds but she did not look back, her eyes fixed on the prize ahead of her. Nearer... nearer... Her breath caught in her throat, her heart pounded, her legs ached... almost there...

The thunder behind her grew louder, with snorts and bellows, but she was there at last! She made a huge jump, grasped the branch, swung herself up and over it...

She was safe!

The bull crashed into the tree below her, shaking it so hard that she was knocked sideways, clinging desperately with arms and legs as she dangled below the branch, only inches above the creature below her. Another scramble put her on top of the branch again, inching her way nearer to the trunk. There she stopped, unable to go further, straddling the branch in the most unladylike manner.

Below her, the bull snorted, and pawed the ground,

rumbling deep in his throat, pacing round the tree. He was not about to abandon his quarry.

Julia gazed longingly at the gate, not thirty yards away. So close, and yet she could not reach it. Here she must stay until the bull gave up his vigil below and allowed her to escape.

But as she settled down to wait, the bull lowered his head and slammed it into the tree trunk, shaking her so violently that she almost lost her balance and fell.

Clinging desperately to her branch, there was only one hope left. She began to pray.

12: To Aid A Lady

James's fishing had not been as successful as he would have liked, but standing about beside the river had made him bitterly cold, and the prospect of a warm fire and a glass of brandy loomed large in his mind. This left him in something of a quandary, for he had hoped to catch enough for both the Park and the Manor. In the end, he decided that courtesy decreed he provide for the Park first, and perhaps he could spare a little for the rectory, too. Thomas was very fond of fish.

He packed up with fumbling fingers, for they were frozen to the bone, and began the short climb back to the cottage. It was as he made his way alongside the hedge bordering a newly-ploughed field that he became aware of a commotion on the other side of the hedge. The low growl of a heavy beast, the thump of hooves and something that sounded distressingly like a squeak of alarm. A lady's squeak. And that was the field where Mr Simpson kept his bull.

Abandoning his fish, he ran full pelt along the hedge

until he reached the gate into the bull's field. He was in time to see the bull and a lady running... dear God, no! It was Julia! But before he could move, she had reached a tree, jumped — such a brave jump! — and was safe. Or was she? The bull crashed into the tree. His heart stopped as she was dislodged and hung suspended above the bull's head. But she recovered, and made herself secure again. Lord, what a girl! Was there ever anyone to equal her for courage!

Again the bull attacked the tree, and now James had to act. Without a moment's hesitation, he climbed the fence and ran towards the bull, yelling. The bull stopped, turned its head, saw him.

"Come on, you stupid fellow! Try me instead! Leave Julia alone."

The bull merely stared at him. James stopped, waved his arms, moved backwards. Surely the bull would follow? Confused, the creature lowered its head, but stayed exactly where it was.

"Come on, now! This way, pea brain. You are supposed to eat grass, not pretty young ladies. Ah, yes, come on now, follow me."

Slowly, step by step, the bull moved towards him. James backed away slowly, leading the creature away from the tree and the gate, allowing Julia the chance to escape. He was taking a terrible risk, he knew that, and he was shaking inside, but it had to be done. There was no time to go for help, for Julia had to be saved, no matter the cost.

He moved slowly, but the bull seemed disinclined to follow, so he kept yelling and waving, and eventually the bull had moved far enough that Julia could drop to the ground and begin to edge towards the gate. He sighed with relief — the bull had not noticed her. She was going to escape.

It was at that point that the bull decided that enough was enough. With a roar of displeasure, he lowered his head and began to move towards James, faster and faster. There was not much he could do, but he was very close to the hedge now, so he backed himself as close to it as he could. Surely even a brainless bull would not be stupid enough to stampede straight into a thick, thorny hedge?

But he was. James leapt aside at the last moment, and the bull crashed into the hedge with a bellow of rage. James did not wait for the creature to disentangle himself, backing as fast as he dared towards the gate. The bull turned, stared at him, lowered its head again. With a terrible fear in the pit of his stomach, James realised he was not going to make it in time.

"Hoy! Over here, sap skull!"

Julia! Out of the corner of his eye, James saw her still inside the field, waving frantically. The bull stopped, raised its head, watching her. It was enough. Picking up speed, James made a last bid for the gate and safety. Julia did the same. The bull finally got moving again, snorting with rage, but he had left it too late.

With a final burst of speed, James and Julia reached the gate almost at the same time, hurled themselves over it and fell into a tangled heap on the far side. The bull reached the gate, snorted and stamped his feet, but he was thwarted.

James laughed. They were both alive and unscathed, and

had a story that would only grow in the telling. Beside him, he could feel Julia shaking with laughter, too.

"Quick! We must get away from here before he realises that the gate can be broken," he said, scrambling to his feet, and hauling her unceremoniously upright too. Hand in hand, they ran until they were safely in the trees and out of sight, then hurled themselves, still laughing, to the ground.

"Lord, that was close!" she said, sitting up. "Are you uninjured, Mr Plummer?"

"Perfectly... at least..." He stretched arms and legs experimentally. "Yes, I seem not be missing anything vital."

"Except your brain, perhaps," she said. "That was a singularly foolhardy thing to do, running into the field like that. Not that I am ungrateful, of course, but you could have been killed, sir!"

He grinned at her. "But I was not!" Jumping to his feet, he held out a hand to her. "Up you come, Miss Fletcher. It is too cold to be lolling about on the ground. Let us find a blazing fire, get warm again and recover our composure."

She took his hand, and he pulled her up, but she winced.

"You are injured!" he said, instantly contrite.

"My leg... the ankle. I must have scraped it. Oh dear!" Bending down and lifting her skirt, she displayed mud and blood mingled, and a badly torn stocking.

"Does it hurt?"

"Oh no, nothing to speak of! Nothing is broken, I think, merely banged against something... the tree or the gate, who knows. I can easily walk home."

"The rectory is closer, and I have ointments and bandages. I should not like you to return home in such a state."

She made no protest, so he led her to a narrow track, and thence the short distance to the road through the village. She limped along gamely beside him, refusing his arm to lean upon, but even so, he wondered whether Mrs Reynell was watching from her house across the road as they turned onto the rectory drive.

Opening the front door, he ushered her into the hall. She looked around her with undisguised curiosity. It was the first time she had entered his house, and he felt a rush of excitement at the thought. One day this would be her home, too, and as familiar to her as the Park. What would she make of it? Would she like it, or despise its shabbiness?

Even so early in the afternoon the hall was gloomy, so he lit a candelabrum, its flickering light leading the way to the kitchen. When she saw it, she laughed out loud.

"Oh, this reminds me so much of home!" she cried turning slowly round. "Not like the Park — that's so big and... and *cold.* If I go into the kitchens there, they look down their noses at me and tell me I shouldn't be there. Isn't that silly? As if I can't go anywhere I like. But the Fullers Road house always felt warm and comfortable and welcoming. I could go to the kitchens there and Mrs Black would always have something just out of the oven for me to try, and the kettle was permanently on the fire. But where is your cook? Don't you have any servants?"

"We have Mrs Pound and her daughter Janet, who come in every day except Sunday to keep us straight. They are usually gone by early afternoon, except on laundry days, but they prepare a dinner before they go. You see those pots over there? We just need to put them to heat up, and *voilà!* Dinner is served. Lightwood, my valet, usually does that. He is the only servant who lives in, although he has gone to Ware today. Will you sit? I shall heat some water and find bandages and so on."

She perched on one of the battered chairs at the kitchen table while he poked life into the fire and set the kettle to heat up. Then he searched around for cloths, a bowl, some strips of linen for bandages and a jar of ointment. It was a long time since he had needed most of these things, so it took some searching to track everything down. By the time all these supplies were laid out on the kitchen table, the kettle was steaming.

Filling the bowl, he dipped a cloth into the warm water and sat down beside her. "You have a scratch on one cheek. May I clean it for you?"

"Thank you."

She closed her eyes as he dabbed gently, and he wondered if she were feeling awkward at such intimacy. He felt rather breathless himself, and oddly shy to be so close to her.

"Miss Fletcher," he said tentatively, when he had washed and dried her cheek, "it is one thing to clean your face, but I am tolerably certain your parents would look askance at me if I were to tend to your injured leg."

"But you're a clergyman!"

"I am also a single man, and it would be most inappropriate for me to remove your stocking, as I should need to do."

"Oh. I suppose it would. I can do it myself."

"Excellent. When you have tended the wound, would you like some toasted cheese?"

Her face lit up. "Ooh, yes, please! Running away from bulls is hungry work, isn't it?"

He laughed, and rose, saying, "I shall go and investigate the cheese store. I shall be gone for... shall we say ten minutes? Will that be enough time, do you think?"

She agreed, and was already bending down to lift her skirts as he lit a candle and hastened from the room. She was such an innocent, of course. Removing her stocking, even to tend to an injury, was quite outside the bounds of decorum, but they should not be alone together at all, if he were being honest. Still, it hardly mattered, for he planned to marry her.

The very thought of it made him smile inside as he loitered in the cheese room. His wife! Julia was a strange creature, so brave and bold and straightforward, without an ounce of malice or deception in her, but he would never, ever be bored with her. She would light up his life and provide some purpose to it, driving away the dreariness for good. He had been drifting along for far too long, but now he fizzed with energy, excitement crackling in him like sparks of lightning. He laughed out loud as he imagined her arriving at church for her wedding, bonnet askew and sleeve torn.

But he was moving along rather fast in his mind, maybe too fast, for he was sure she had not the least idea that she was an object of romantic interest to him. She saw him as a friend, no doubt, a comfortable and, he hoped, an agreeable friend, somewhat akin to a brother, perhaps. It was time to give her a broader hint of his plans.

He must have been too impatient, for when he returned to the kitchen she was still busy with her ministrations, her bare leg resting on the chair where he had sat just minutes earlier. She had her back towards him, so he stood, trying to catch his breath, watching her as she rubbed in the ointment, then wound the bandage haphazardly around, tore the end and tied a knot. Picking up the stocking, with a shrug she stuffed it into her muddy reticule, then jammed her boot back on.

Some sound of his alerted her, for she turned round with a smile, lowering the injured limb to the ground so that her skirts covered it. "There you are! It's safe to come in, for I'm modestly covered once more."

Modestly covered, to be sure, but oh, that smile! A man could throw himself at her feet for a smile like that. And then he laughed at himself for harbouring such grandiose sentiments.

"Was it a bad scrape?"

"No, nothing at all to it, when all's said and done. Did you find the cheese?"

"Good heavens, I quite forgot. Wait a moment."

Armed with bread, cheese and toasting forks, they

pulled a couple of chairs nearer to the fire, and toasted and ate and talked... how they talked! He told her about the few fish he had caught that day, still lying beside the hedge where he had thrown them to rescue her. She told him a great deal about Sagborough, and their house there.

"Do you miss it?" he said, when the toasting had dwindled to nothing.

"Sagborough? I miss the convenience of running out to a shop before breakfast, but I don't miss the noise, the bustle, the smoke. What I miss most, I think, is the familiarity of everything. The church, and our pew. Meeting friends on the street. My favourite walks. Knowing where everything was, and what would happen, the predictability of life. Here, every day there's some new surprise. Oh, I know we'll get used to it eventually, but the Park is so big and grand and overwhelming. I like your house better, I think."

"Do you?" That was an unexpectedly good sign. "I like it too, although sometimes it feels like temporary lodgings. I spend so much of my time at the Manor — I am there most evenings, and sometimes for breakfast, too. I should like to be more... established here. Get some permanent servants, set up my carriage, make some improvements to the house, dine at my own table once in a while with white linen and silver spoons and cut glass, instead of in the kitchen. Would you like to see my dining room?"

She said she would. He picked up the candelabrum, and led the way. It was perhaps the best room in the house, but it seemed drab to him, and unwelcoming. He tried to imagine the table with all the leaves added, its surface groaning with a multitude of dishes, but he could not.

"It is so antiquated," he said, looking around the room with disfavour. "I really need to toss everything out and start from scratch. New furniture, new rugs and curtains, new silverware and plate — everything brand new."

"Expensive!" she said, laughing. "And you an impoverished clergyman, too."

"Not so impoverished as all that," he said. "As rector, I take all the tithes, worth around fourteen hundred pounds a year. Father has the presentation of St Agnes, too, so whenever Mr Hasswell goes to his eternal rest, I shall have another four hundred a year. A very tidy income for a country parson."

"More work for your curate, I suppose."

That was a hit, indeed, rendering him silent. Yes, poor Thomas would have all the extra work of the second parish, but he planned to increase his salary. Perhaps it would be enough to enable him to marry. That would go some way to assuaging James's guilt for the shameless way he neglected his duties and allowed Thomas to shoulder the entire burden.

"Are you going to refurbish the rest of the house, too, since you are so rich?" she said, with a mischievous grin. Lord, those lips! He had a sudden urge to sweep her into his arms and—

That would never do. What was the matter with him? That encounter with the bull had rattled his brain, he was sure, for he was not normally so addle-pated.

"Perhaps. Tell me what you think. This is the parlour. Across here is the parish room, but I leave that to Thomas.

And this is the drawing room."

"This is a pleasant room, with a view of the church, too. A clergyman should always be able to look out of his window at his own church, don't you think? To remind him of his duties. Or his curate's duties, in your case."

"Do you disapprove?"

"Oh, it's not for me to approve or disapprove, Mr Plummer. You must manage your life as seems good to you. If Mr Leadbetter is content with the arrangement and your parishioners too, who am I to cavil at it? But I think it's sad that you have this fine house, and you seem to live in the kitchen... when you are even here. It's not new furnishings you need, it's *people* who make a house a home."

"You are quite right," he said. Then, throwing caution to the wind, he went on, "What I need is a wife and family."

And because he could not resist her for a second longer, he cupped her face in his hands and kissed her firmly on the lips.

For a moment, she froze. Then she pushed him sharply away.

"What did you do that for?" Not angry or shocked or distressed, just puzzled. A little indignant, perhaps.

"For the same reason I showed you the house and told you my income, so that you will be prepared."

"Prepared? For what?"

"For when I offer for you. So that you will know how to answer."

Her jaw dropped. She really had not had the least suspicion, despite all his attentions lately. "You're mad," she said. "Completely mad. I thought you were my *friend*, James Plummer, and now you've gone and spoilt it. I'm going home."

"I shall see you back to the Park."

"No, you won't! I've had quite enough of you for one day, thank you very much."

And with that, she swept out of the room. He heard her struggling to open the heavy front door, and then it slammed shut and she was gone.

"Well, James, you made a mull of *that*," he murmured to the empty room. "But at least she knows now."

13: Intentions

Shock put wings on Julia's feet, for she fairly flew home, her injured leg barely noticed. What was he thinking, kissing her like that, and then telling her, as cool as you please, that he was going to offer for her! And all the time she had *trusted* him!

She took the front steps two at a time, wrestled with the doorknob for several moments before she could get the front door open, and then stormed into the hall. No one was in sight, but then she hadn't expected it. In other houses, a footman or the butler would be lurking nearby, ready to sweep into action, and at Sagborough, Enoch would materialise. Here their servants were never where they were supposed to be.

She half ran up the stairs to the sanctuary of her room, slamming the door shut behind her. The nerve of the man! To talk about the house that way, and his income — as if she cared about that! And then to tell her calmly that he wanted her to be ready with her answer when he offered for her.

Well, she'd be ready with her answer all right, and it wouldn't be the one he wanted.

What did he want? That was an interesting question. He'd never made love to her or even flirted in the way that most men did, as if it was expected of them. He'd never given the least sign… although he had called several times, quite formally. She'd supposed he was there to support his brother's tepid courtship of Rosie, but perhaps he'd come on his own account after all. Perhaps he really did want to marry her, but what on earth for? He'd taken pains to tell her that he had money of his own, but still, twenty thousand pounds was a substantial dowry. Even she, with her ungainliness and torn gowns, might be a prize worth having for the second son of a baronet.

Well, this was one prize he would not get into his insolent hands, for all his pretty little house and his fourteen hundred a year and his schemes for more servants and a carriage. Even his kiss, warm and gentle and enjoyable as it was, would not win her. That it *had* been enjoyable she could not deny, and for a while she was lost in a pleasant reverie of a man with warm hands against her face and laughter lines round his eyes and hair waving softly round his face… and his lips on hers. She sighed. It made no difference, of course. One couldn't marry a man just because he kissed one in a toe-curlingly delicious way. That would be too foolish for words, even if the memory of it was rather overwhelming and made one feel just a little sad that it would not be repeated.

Gradually her indignation melted away, and by the time Rosie and Angie appeared, and Sarah came to dress them for dinner, Julia was her usual composed self. Her leg was throbbing distractingly, and she was perhaps a little more thoughtful and less chatty than usual, but no one noticed. It was not until dinner was well under way and the soup was removed with some fish that she was roused from her torpor.

"Ah, excellent," Pa said. "Mr Plummer delivered the fish not two hours ago, straight from the river, so it could not be fresher. No waiting for the weekly barge to make its way up the canal here, eh? Lizzie, will you try some? It looks beautiful."

"He recovered his bag, then," Julia said. "He had to abandon it when we were attacked by the bull."

This casual remark caused cries of astonishment, and Julia was obliged to give a full account of the whole incident, which she did with dramatic enjoyment. But when she came to the events of the rectory, she could not hide her outrage. Concealment was not in her nature, so it never occurred to her that perhaps a kiss and a declaration of intent might be private matters, and not a subject for the dinner table in full view of the servants.

"And then he *kissed* me," she squeaked, her voice rising. "Can you believe it? And when I asked him what he thought he was doing, he said he wanted me to be prepared for when he makes me an offer. I never thought he could be so foolish. I gave him a piece of my mind, I can tell you."

Angie clapped her hands in glee. "Jules! You have an admirer! I do believe you will be married before any of us. Whoever would have thought it?"

But Pa frowned, and Mama said calmly, "We will talk about this later, Julia. Will, would you please pass me the lamb cutlets?"

Only then did it occur to Julia that it might have been better to say nothing about it.

Mama was not one to make a drama out of anything, so dinner was completed and the ladies removed to the withdrawing room as usual. Rosie was asked to perform on the pianoforte, and after a brief interlude when the music she had set aside for the evening could not be found, they all settled down to their usual pursuits. Any attempt by Angie to raise the interesting subject of Mr James Plummer was firmly squashed by Mama.

"It is not your concern, Angie," she said repressively. "Mr Fletcher and I will discuss the matter at the appropriate time."

Aunt Madge sniffed. "What did she do to encourage him, that's what I'd like to know."

"Thank you, Madge, that will do." Mama never raised her voice, but there was a sharp edge to her tone that even Aunt Madge recognised. Not another word was said on the subject.

Will appeared shortly before the tea tray was expected. "Mama, Julia, Pa would like to see you in his office."

Julia was certain she had done nothing worthy of censure, but even so she was nervous as she followed Mama down the hall. Will padded along behind them.

"Why are you here?" she said. "It's not really your concern, is it?"

"It might be," he said, then grinned at her. "If he has mistreated you, it will be my job to call him out."

Julia laughed, but Mama spun round. "This is no laughing matter, Will," she said frostily.

That only increased Julia's gloom. Pa's face was serious, too, when they entered the office.

"Well, puss, this is a pickle and no mistake. You'd better tell us exactly what happened at the rectory."

"I've told you what happened — he kissed me, and despite what Aunt Madge says, I did *not* encourage him."

"It is not just the kiss," Pa said. "It's the whole thing — you being in the rectory with him, and your mama not with you, nor your sisters, not even a maid. Were there any servants there?"

"No, but... Pa, he behaved very properly, considering the circumstances. He didn't remove my stocking, or anything like that."

"Remove your stocking!" Will said, laughing. "Really, Julia, what a crazy girl you are."

"That will do, Will," Mama said. "Julia, tell us precisely what happened, from the moment you entered the rectory."

So she told them, exactly as she remembered it, everything that had been said and done, and even now, she could see nothing wrong in any of it. Apart from that kiss, of course. That had changed everything.

When she had finished, she was dispatched back to the withdrawing room, with the instruction to say nothing to anyone, and although Pa and Mama and Will were closeted together for another half an hour, when they emerged nothing further was said on the subject.

"Let me look at that leg of yours, Julia," Mama said.

Meekly, Julia followed, and as Mama washed and applied salve and rebandaged, she said, "Your father and I are agreed that there is no harm done to your reputation from today's little encounter. Mr Plummer has behaved very properly towards you, apart from that kiss, of course. Was that your first kiss?"

"Heavens, no."

Mama chuckled. "He should not have done it, but... better it should happen to you than to Rosie or Angie."

"Oh yes! Rosie would have agonised over it and felt she had committed a grave sin, and Angie would have spun a fairy tale out of it, with herself as the tragic heroine, naturally. Whereas it just made me cross with him."

"And you told us all about it, although perhaps it is best not to say such things in front of the servants."

"No, Mama," Julia said contritely. "I didn't think."

"You so rarely do, Julia dear. Incurable honesty is not precisely a fault, but when tempered with a modicum of restraint, may be accounted something closer to a virtue."

~~~~~

James was watching the rain sheeting down through the drawing room window, and trying to discern the church through the murk when a footman, bundled up in a thick cloak, splashed up the drive. James answered the door himself, to be handed a brief note.

'James, Pray be so kind as to attend me at your earliest

convenience. Sir Owen Plummer.'

Such a request, however politely worded, was not one to be ignored. Delaying only long enough to put on his thickest greatcoat, he made his way to the Manor.

"Sir Owen is awaiting you in the library," Jefford told him.

The butler would not lower himself to display any open sign of curiosity, but he must be wondering, and he would understand the significance of the library, a room only ever used for the most formal of occasions.

James knocked, waited for his father's brisk, "Enter!" and went in. The room was chilly enough to make him shiver. A fire had been hastily lit, for it blazed up the chimney, but had not yet made any impression on the temperature in the room.

"You wished to see me, Father?"

"Thank you for coming so promptly, James. Shall we sit?" He gestured to the matching chairs set either side of the fire. "I have had Fletcher here this morning, regarding his daughter. Miss Julia. He wishes to know what your intentions are towards the young lady."

"My intention is to marry her, Father. I intimated as much to her yesterday."

"So you offered for her?"

"No, I told her that I plan to offer for her."

"It is the same thing, a declaration. Is there cause for you to feel obligated?"

"Certainly not. I *want* to marry her."

His father's eyebrows rose slightly. "I see. For what reason?"

James gave a bark of surprise. "Because I like her, of course. She will suit me very well."

"At what point did you arrive at that conclusion?"

"Almost the first moment I saw her. I believe I told you how I met her, the very day her family arrived. She had walked up to the High Field, and was sitting perched on the gate when I left the hut. I decided then that I would marry her."

"That seems a whimsical decision," Sir Owen said.

"Well, let me modify my words. I decided that I would get to know her better, with a view to discovering whether I should like to marry her. I decided I should, and yesterday I chose to make my intentions known to her."

"Ah, so this is not just a spur of the moment decision, or a matter of setting right an improper situation. That is to your credit, I suppose, but I must say, James, you seem to have managed the business very ineptly."

"I know it, but courting one's future wife is not something one does often enough to become practised in the art."

His father gave a rumble that might have been laughter. "One must hope so, indeed. You are serious about this, then?"

"Perfectly. Father, you do not object, I take it?"

Sir Owen sighed. "If you like the girl, then I shall not stand in your way. She is not so prettily behaved as her sisters, but I detect no harm in her, and her dowry will see you very comfortable. I warn you now, however, your mother will *not* like it. She would be relieved to see Michael turn his back on the eldest sister, for all her fifty thousand pounds, and she is as inoffensive a creature as ever breathed. Lady Plummer cordially dislikes the rest of the family, and will not be at all pleased to have a permanent alliance with them. However, you are of age and the young lady too, and if it is what you want, then so be it. And if the two of you can provide me with a grandson, then I shall be more than content, since Michael has not done so. Have you told him of your plans?"

"I have. He asked my advice regarding Rosie Fletcher, and I told him not to worry about it if he dislikes the idea. But what had Fletcher to say? Did he play the heavy-handed father, come to insist I do the honourable thing?"

"He was very reasonable about the whole business. All he wanted to know was whether you are sincere. He does not want you making a May game of the girl."

"I must go and see him, I suppose. Do the thing properly. I had not planned to make my formal offer quite so soon, but today is as good a day as any other." James laughed. "May I borrow the carriage? I shall have to change into decent clothes, and I should not like to arrive mud-bespattered for such an important occasion."

"By all means. Ring for Jefford, will you? And James — be sure to let us know the outcome."

"There can be only one outcome, surely?"

His father gave a wintry smile. "In my experience, where ladies are concerned one can never be sure of anything."

~~~~~

Rosie was hiding in the gallery again. She went there whenever there was a letter from Belinda, or after Mr Michael Plummer called, or just when she felt low, which happened with increasing frequency. Julia knew now where to find her, sitting on the floor half hidden by a statue, usually crying, the latest missive from Belinda clutched in her hand.

"I am learning to be a proper maiden aunt, you see," Julia said, passing Rosie a clean handkerchief. "I am prepared for all crises. Almost all crises, anyway. Smelling salts! I don't have smelling salts. I shall ask Aunt Madge to supply me with some."

Rosie smiled wanly. "But you are not going to be a maiden aunt, Jules. You are going to marry Mr James Plummer."

"I wish you will not listen to Angie's nonsense. Of course I'm not going to marry him. What's upset you this time, Rosie dear? Has Belinda written again?"

"Not yet. You will say I am being silly, Jules."

"I never say that. I'm the silly one of the family, remember? Tell Auntie Jules all about it."

"Oh, it is so trivial but... my music keeps disappearing. It has happened three times now, and Aunt Madge's scissors and Pa's newspaper, and the funny little porcelain bird on the table in the music room, which just vanished, and Camilla found it in her bedroom, of all places. It is so unsettling."

"It's just the servants playing games, I expect. They don't like us very much, but they have to do what we say, so this is their way of having a little fun at our expense. Who is that calling?"

It was Will's voice, from the landing. "Julia! Where are you hiding, sis? Come on out, for you are wanted."

Julia jumped to her feet and peered round the curtain at the end of the gallery. "What is it, Will?"

"Pa wants to see you in the library."

"In the library? What is he doing in the library?"

"I have no idea, but he wants you, and the servants have been all over the house looking for you, so I should get down there sharpish if I were you."

Pa was gazing solemnly at the empty bookcases, row upon row of bare shelves. An empty library was a dispiriting place, and even though Julia rarely opened a book, she felt there ought to be at least a few of them in a room dedicated to books.

"Ah, there you are, puss. Well now, I have Mr James Plummer in my office, all dressed up and came in the carriage, too, so he'd not present himself to you muddy, so you can guess what he's about. Doing things very correctly, asking my permission first and now he wants to speak to you."

Julia pulled a face. "But I don't want to marry him. Can't you deal with it, Pa? You've done that for me before."

"Aye, when they were ineligible or were out and out fortune hunters, but he's neither of those. A baronet's son and an independent income, and he's a pleasant young man. I can't dismiss him out of hand. It's a very good match, to be truthful. I'd be happy for any of your sisters to do so well."

"You don't feel I have to marry him... that I'm compromised in some way, just because I was alone in the rectory with him?"

"Lord, no. I don't hold with such nonsense, forcing two people to marry if they're not inclined for it. If he'd been leading you astray, I'd have something to say about it, but he hasn't and you have enough good sense not to get yourself into difficulties, puss. I've never worried about you in that way, and it seems he's not here from any guilty conscience. He appears to want you for your own sake, and I like him the better for that. Now, if you won't have him, that's an end to it, but I think you owe it to him to tell him so to his face. With Rosie... well, I might intervene because she's soft-hearted and might be swayed against her better judgement, but you're a sensible girl, Jules."

"Must I see him?"

"When a man has wound himself up so far as to humble himself before the lady of his choice, he likes to see her face when he makes his pitch for her hand. It's a nerve racking business, I can tell you. It's only civil to hear him out. All you have to do is let him say his piece, then you thank him for the honour, much obliged and so forth, but you're not minded to marry. Be polite, and don't quarrel with him, puss, because we don't want any breach with the Plummers. And I shall be right here if you need reinforcements. Understood?"

Glumly, she nodded. There was no escaping it now.

14: A Dinner Party

James looked very smart, that was Julia's immediate thought. He stood beside the fire, gazing thoughtfully into its flames with one foot resting on the fender, and she had never seen him look so elegant. That brought an unexpected burst of pride — he had done this for her! Even though his attentions were unwelcome, yet it was gratifying that he had gone to so much trouble on her account.

He looked up and smiled, deepening the creases round his eyes.

"Julia!" He crossed the room towards her, hands outstretched.

"Mr Plummer." She dipped into a formal curtsy, then swiftly thrust her hands behind her back, out of his reach.

He only smiled the more. "You want to be formal, do you? Then so be it. Miss Fletcher, you know why I am here. Your father will have told you. I had hoped to give you more time to grow accustomed to the idea, but your father and mine got together and there we are. To speak plainly, I am by no means loath to settle things at once, so here I am. My dear Julia, you said yesterday that you thought we were friends. I thought so too. Indeed, I believe we have been friends from the moment we met at the High Field gate, and it is not merely my fancy, I trust, that we have only become better friends since that day. We get on so well, perfectly matched in every respect, that it is surely but a small step to become a perfect match in truth, as husband and wife. You know that I can keep you comfortably, and you know what your home will be. I have explained all of this to your father, and he is satisfied on these points. It would bring him great pleasure to see you established here, taking on the Plummer name, which is an honourable one and not to be despised. He tells me that Mrs Fletcher, too, would approve the match, and my own father would be glad to see me settled. So you see, it is a match with everything in its favour and nothing against. What do you say? Will you honour me with your hand, Julia? Will you be my wife?"

The smile had never faltered. There was not the smallest sign of anxiety in him, so he was in no doubt of her answer. Even as he waited for her to respond, he was still smiling. Why was he so sure of her? Perhaps centuries of aristocratic certainty infused him, making him sure that a mercer's daughter would not dare to refuse a baronet's son.

Well, he was wrong about that.

"I thank you for the honour you do me, sir, but I have no wish to marry."

Even then, the smile remained. He was so sure of himself! "Take a little time to think about it."

"I don't need time! My answer won't change. I don't want to marry anyone, and certainly not a clergyman. I'd make a terrible clergyman's wife."

"And I am a terrible clergyman, so once more we are well matched."

Julia huffed in annoyance. "You shouldn't joke about such things! It's not something to be proud of. I don't want to marry you — I don't want to marry at all! I am content with my life just as it is, and nothing you say will make me change my mind. I should be glad if you would leave now."

He made her a formal bow, respectfully low. "It shall be as you wish, and you need not worry that there will be any awkwardness between us, for we shall continue as friends, just as we have always been. Nevertheless, I shall continue to hope that one day you will appreciate how perfectly we are suited. I do not yet despair of winning your hand. I bid you good day. Pray give my regards to Mrs Fletcher and your sisters. I shall call again to see them soon."

And with that he was gone, leaving Julia torn between irritation and admiration for his insouciance.

~~~~~

Julia's proposal was the wonder of the day, and the only topic of conversation amongst the ladies of the household.

"I do think you should have married him, despite him being an impoverished vicar," Angie said, dancing around the parlour with excitement, "for just think how cosy you would be with your fourteen children, squeezed into that little parsonage. We would bring you baskets of food, you know, to rescue you from starvation."

"Nonsense, Angie," Mama said briskly. "Mr Plummer may be a clergyman, but he is a rector, not a vicar, and has a very good income, with the prospect of more. He can keep a wife very well, I assure you."

"Are you disappointed, Mama?" Julia said.

"I am certainly disappointed for poor Mr Plummer, who must feel your refusal acutely, and it would have been a comfort to have you so well settled, and so near to us. It would have been a very good match, Julia."

"She will not get another offer as good as this, not if she waits a month of Sundays," Aunt Madge said darkly. "But that is how she is, always going her own way and not a thought for anyone else."

"I can't marry a man just to please other people," Julia said. "That would be foolish indeed. I don't want to marry at all."

Mama laid down her needlework. "I do not quite like to hear you speak so decidedly on the subject, Julia. Mr Plummer may not be the man to excite your admiration, but there will be plenty of other men who will appreciate your good qualities and you should not turn your back on the very idea of marriage, not at your age."

"Very well," Julia said demurely. "I shall wait a little longer before I don my spinster's cap."

"Oh, tush!" Mama smiled at her. "You are one and twenty, years away from such considerations, and who knows what might happen? You may meet someone in London, perhaps. Now that the idea of marriage has been put before you, the prospect may appeal a little more."

Julia pulled a face. "London! I wish I needn't go at all."

"If Mr Plummer is so very disappointed, he may try again," Angie said happily.

Aunt Madge sniffed in derision, but Mama smiled. "Indeed he may. Perhaps we should invite him to dinner."

Julia could not endure such nonsense, so she sought refuge in the schoolroom, but even there she found Miss Crabtree, Bella and Dorothea discussing the interesting situation, peppering her with questions about Mr Plummer. Julia took a book and went to hide in the gallery.

~~~~~

James drove back to the Manor not at all disheartened. To be sure, she had turned him down in the most uncompromising of terms. *'I don't want to marry at all!'* Well, he had time. Several weeks yet before she went to London, and he was quite prepared to follow her there. If she preferred a sophisticated London beau to a country rector, then he could show her a different side to his nature. He could be equally at home in town, if he chose.

Only one of her remarks gave him pause. *'I am content with my life just as it is.'* That was a poser. Mr Fletcher was a man of great wealth, who could afford to keep any number of unmarried daughters in great comfort. He was an indulgent father, too, and would never press any of his children to marry unwillingly. He had made that quite clear when they had talked that morning.

"Julia's a sensible girl," he had said, "and she knows her own mind. It would be a good match for her, I'll not deny that, and better than we might have expected for her, but I'll not push her one way or the other. If you can persuade her to marry you, then you'll have my blessing and the full dowry, but if she won't have you, she'll hear no reproach from me. It won't bother me in the slightest if she never marries, so long as she's happy."

So how was he to win her over? She had no need to marry, and no wish for it, either. If he was to succeed, he would have to offer her something she could not find at home. If her own establishment and the prospect of children were not enough, what else could entice her away from her comfortable life? And the only inducement would be himself. He had to make her fall in love with him, and his sanguine spirit was entirely confident he could do it.

The whole family had gathered in the parlour to await his return and hear the outcome. His father merely nodded, his face impassive, but Mother raised her handkerchief from red-rimmed eyes to cry out, "Thank goodness!"

"You disapprove, Mother?" James said politely.

"Every woman of any sensibility must disapprove," Letitia snapped. "Every feeling revolts at bringing such a creature into the family. She cannot even speak properly, and her manners border on the wilful. Whatever were you thinking, James?"

"I was thinking that she would suit me very well," he said mildly. "I like her, and I have every intention of bringing her round eventually."

His mother moaned softly.

~~~~~

One outcome of Julia's proposal was more positive. Mama had been attempting for some time to return the Plummers' hospitality by inviting them to dinner, but there had always been some excuse. Lady Plummer was indisposed, or there was something infectious in the nursery, or the weather was too uncertain for them to venture out at night. All their other new acquaintances had enjoyed the bounty of their table and afterwards applauded politely at the young ladies' performance on the instrument, but the Plummers were the principal family of the neighbourhood, and the greatest prize.

Now, however, a brief note was received by Pa from Sir Owen informing him that a renewal of the invitation would be received with pleasure, in the interests of continuing amity between the two families. An invitation was dispatched within the hour, and a reply received just as promptly, brought by Sir Owen himself and his two sons.

It was the first time Julia had seen James since the proposal, but he was just as usual, his own relaxed self, the only difference being that he didn't seek her out at once, as he had always done before, but made himself agreeable to Mama and Aunt Madge first. He *was* agreeable, Julia was honest enough to acknowledge. She could not fault his manners, and when he finally made his way to her side, she was comfortable enough to meet him without any awkwardness.

"I shall be so glad to dine here again," he said, when the preliminary greetings were done. "Mother is dreading it, of course, to see another lady take her place at the head of the table, but Father is adamant that it would be insulting to refuse again. He very much wants to be on good terms with your family, and would regret any issue which might preclude that."

Was that a veiled reference to Julia? "We would all regret that, Mr Plummer," she said promptly, and was pleased to see him smile at her words. There was nothing of resentment in his manner towards her.

Mama was in a fever of excitement over the dinner with the Plummers. All of them were to come, and the greatest triumph was to have Lord Charles Heaman in her house.

"A real lord!" she said about twenty times a day. "Everything must be perfect for a real lord."

"Isn't it his brother who's the lord?" Julia said, amused. "Isn't Lord Charles's title just a... oh, what is it called?"

"A courtesy title, yes, but he is still a *lord*, Julia. Not a peer of the realm, I grant you that, but a lord is still a lord."

"I thought you didn't like him much, since he won't introduce you to his brother."

"But perhaps he will, if I feed him well enough," she said, beaming.

The ladies were informed that they were each to wear one of their new dresses. Julia rolled her eyes at the fuss, but Rosie, Angie and Camilla twittered happily, and spent hours in their rooms, laying out gowns and shoes and brooches and ribands. Julia left it to Mama to choose for her, but when she saw her reflection in the cheval mirror, she could hardly believe what she saw. It was the colour, she decided. Gone were the washed out blues and yellows that made her look ill. Her gown was a vibrant turquoise that shimmered between blue and green in the flickering candlelight. A net over gown sparkled. The bodice was shaped to make her look slimmer and more elegant.

"Oh, Jules, you look so pretty!" Rosie breathed.

"No, no! Not pretty, but... stylish," she said musingly. "I look surprisingly ladylike. How long will it be, do you suppose, before I tear something, or spill wine onto it?"

But for the moment, she was inspired to move slowly and, she hoped, gracefully, although still avoiding the furniture in case she tripped. There was no point inviting trouble.

Pa and Mama were waiting for them on the landing.

"Ah, here are my lovely ladies," Pa cried, kissing Rosie, Julia and Angie soundly on each cheek, and then for good measure kissing Mama, too. "*All* my lovely ladies. What a fortunate man I am to have such a fine family."

"You are very smart too, Pa," Angie said. "A new waistcoat, I see. You look quite splendid, and Mama too. How grand we all are tonight!"

Even Aunt Madge had been persuaded, grumbling at the extravagance, into a new gown, and Camilla looked charming in carmine, the dark colour and looser fitting concealing her increasing girth. Will looked exactly as always, arriving in the saloon in his London fashions just as the Plummers' carriage was heard on the drive.

They arrived, Mama and Pa went out to the hall to greet them, they returned and were announced by Keeble in ringing tones, enjoying the moment. Julia had taken up her usual position near the window, as far as possible from the door. From there, she watched the Plummers enter the room. Sir Owen, as serious as always. Lady Plummer, moist-eyed, gazing round the room as if to see what changes had been made. Michael, pale and looking anxious, as usual. Patricia, expressionless. Lord Charles, exuding aristocratic hauteur. Lady Charles, prune-faced. Creeping in at the back, Thomas Leadbetter, invited at the last minute to balance the excess of ladies. But where was—?

There he was, looking remarkably stylish. She had grown so used to the gamekeeper, with his battered hat and mud-coloured coat that she'd never noticed how smart he looked when he dressed for the evening, every inch the baronet's son. He had a remarkably good figure, she decided, broad in the chest but not too broad, and with legs that looked extremely well in stockings and silk knee breeches.

His eyes scanned the room, he saw her, he smiled. He made his greeting to Mama, and then to Rosie, but his eyes kept flitting back to Julia. Then, almost as if he couldn't help himself, he set off across the room determinedly towards her.

"You look lovely," he said.

This was such a shockingly direct remark, and spoken in an unusually serious manner for him, that she was speechless, and for some moments they simply stared at each other. Then, in a rush, he went on, "How is your leg now? No infection, I trust. You must be very careful to keep it clean and change the bandages every day. One cannot be too vigilant against infection in such cases. Has the surgeon attended to it? There is a physician I can recommend in Ware if you should want... Oh dear. I am babbling, am I not?"

He smiled so charmingly that Julia laughed out loud. "My leg is entirely healed, Mr Plummer, and no hint of infection has dared take root therein."

He laughed too. "I am glad to hear it. I was fishing again earlier today, so I doffed my hat to our friend the bull as I passed by, and wished him a good day."

"From the other side of the hedge, I hope."

"From three fields away, Miss Fletcher. I dared not go closer, in case he remembered that I had the temerity to evade him once and thought to rectify the situation."

"And did he reply to your civil greeting?"

"Not a word. He had not even the courtesy to raise his head from the patch of grass with which he was engaged. Dreadfully rude. I cannot imagine what the world is coming to, when bulls are so ill-mannered. It was not so when I was a boy, I swear."

She giggled, and there was a warmth inside her to find that it was just as he had said, that there was no awkwardness between them. How pleasing that was!

In no time, it seemed, Keeble was announcing dinner, and what could be more natural but that Mr Plummer should lead her through to the dining room and then sit beside her? And why should he not, after all, for were they not the best of friends?

Lady Plummer was gazing avidly around again, and Julia

said in a low voice to Mr Plummer, "Is your mama pleased or displeased with the room? I cannot tell from her countenance. We have made few changes, so it is very much as she left it. I hope she does not find it too distressing."

"She is merely astonished by the number of candles," he said at once. "Grandfather was never particularly generous with light, but since Father inherited, candles were one of his biggest economies. We could scarce see what we were eating. But you have all the rooms lit up as bright as day, and very pleasant it is, too."

"It must be very disagreeable to be forced to economise," she said.

"I imagine you have never had to do so."

"No, never. Not that we could have anything we wanted, for Pa always wanted to justify the expense. If a chair broke, he'd see if it could be mended before he'd lay out money for a new one. Mind you, he spoilt us girls. There were always little treats, and new gowns when we wanted them, although the materials came from his own warehouses, so I dare say it cost him very little. He's careful with his money, but he says it's because he can remember being poor... or at least, a lot less wealthy."

"That is a sensible attitude," Mr Plummer said, "but he has become a little more profligate of late, buying this house and undertaking the season. London is shockingly expensive. Shall you and your sisters be presented at court?"

"Heavens, no! Nothing so grand. Mama has a connection who will introduce us to a few people here and there, so we'll paddle about on the fringes of society and hope that Rosie is noticed."

"She will be noticed. You will all be noticed," he said, with a smile that lit up her insides like a bonfire.

Somehow, and she couldn't say quite how it was, the meal passed in a flash. All her stepmother's carefully planned dishes, spread over two courses, with six removes and a final array of sweetmeats and nuts, made no impression on her. All she knew was that they talked, although what they talked about was impossible to recall. She was both surprised and disappointed when Mama rose to lead the ladies away. It was to be hoped that the gentlemen would not be long at their port.

There was a dull hour in the withdrawing room, then the gentlemen returned and the tea tray was brought, but Mr Plummer was intercepted by Mama, so there was nothing for Julia to do but sit and drink her tea, and watch everyone else.

Aunt Madge and Mr Morgan Plummer were squabbling gently in one corner, and Lady Charles, Lady Plummer and Miss Plummer were whispering in another. Camilla and Lord Charles were very cosy together, poring over a book, but sitting a little closer than politeness required. Julia had spent enough time with Camilla to recognise the signs of flirtation in her. She was leaning towards Lord Charles, gazing into his bedazzled face as if he were the most fascinating man in the whole world, and he was foolish enough to believe himself to be so. He whispered something into Camilla's ear, but then to Julia's relief he rose and left the room.

None of this would have alarmed Julia in the slightest, for Camilla was an outrageous flirt and nothing seemed to curb her behaviour. Mama didn't even try. But when Camilla looked about her in the most furtive manner a few moments later, and then rose and left the room, all Julia's senses tingled with apprehension. Setting down her teacup, she quickly crossed the room and followed Camilla into the passageway. She was just in time to see a wisp of Camilla's distinctive gown disappear into the library.

That was puzzling. There was nothing at all in the library to entice Camilla inside, for there was not even a fire lit. Julia walked down the passage to the library door, but it was closed, with no indication that anyone had passed that way. Confused, she hesitated, wondering if perhaps she had been mistaken. Perhaps Camilla had gone round the corner to Pa's office?

But then, while she dithered, she heard a sound from inside the library. She could not say what sort of sound it was, but it sounded almost like a moan, as if someone were in distress. Resolutely she opened the door and went inside.

Near the fireplace, a candelabrum burned on a table, casting a little pool of light, but the rest of the room lay in deep darkness and nothing else could be distinguished. The sound came again, very close at hand, followed almost at once by, "Shhh!" Silence fell, although Julia thought she could detect breathing.

"Camilla? Are you all right?"

Silence.

Julia carefully made her way to the candelabrum, only banging her shins once on a footstool. Lifting the light high, she scanned the room, then slowly moved towards the spot behind the door where she had heard... something. A noise, a voice hushing someone or something and then breathing.

There was nothing behind the door, only one of the ornate pillars found in several of the rooms. But wait! A crack in the wall... a gap... a door, carefully decorated to blend into the wall, but now slightly ajar.

Julia wrenched it open, to see the startled faces of Lord Charles and Camilla.

"What are you doing?" Julia cried, holding the candelabrum high.

Lord Charles gave a strangled cry, turned and fled into the darkness behind Camilla, up a winding stair that Julia had known nothing about.

Camilla calmly rearranged the bodice of her gown which had become disordered. "Well, what a spoilsport you are, Julia. Can't a girl have a little fun without you screeching all over the place?"

"But he's already married!" Julia said. "He can't help you."

"No, but— Oh, never mind. You're such a simpleton, you wouldn't understand. There, I shall have to do. Shall we go back to the withdrawing room? And don't tell a soul, all right? Especially not your mama."

"She'd be horrified by what you were doing."

To Julia's amazement, Camilla laughed. "She'd be horrified you interfered, more like. Come on, I'm dying for some tea."

15: The Morning After

The rest of the evening passed in a blur. There was music and then cards, and after some interminable time the carriages were ordered. There was no more conversation with Mr Plummer, but Julia could not think about him when Camilla and Lord Charles were so much on her mind.

After a sleepless night, she awoke with heavy eyes and aching head.

Pa took one look at her at breakfast, and said, "What you need, young lady, is some fresh air. Do you want to walk down to the village with me? I have men in at Mr Green's cottage attending to the roof, but you can have a chat with Mrs Green and see if there's anything else they might need. I've never had tenants before, so I'd like to take good care of them."

"I always thought the landed gentry had tenant farmers," she said.

Pa chuckled. "Aye, so they do, but Sir Owen kept all the

farm land for the Manor, and kindly gave me the cottages and houses, which bring in a trifling amount of rent and need all manner of repairs to make them habitable."

"So he bamboozled you?"

"No, no. Nobody bamboozles me, puss. His attorney was suspiciously vague about the properties, so I sent my own man to look into it before I agreed to the arrangement, and then reduced the price accordingly. It suits me, though. Floors and walls and roofs I understand, but farms are beyond me. If I had farmers, I'd need a bailiff to deal with them and it would be all too easy for bamboozling to be going on right under my nose, and me none the wiser. You'll come then, will you? It's raining a bit, but you won't mind that."

Julia didn't mind at all. They walked briskly down the drive to the village, spending an hour at the cottage as Pa climbed happily up and down ladders while Julia sat in Mrs Green's front parlour drinking cheap tea and eating biscuits, as assorted small children wandered into the room, giggled and ran away again. Mrs Green smiled fondly at them, and when Julia asked her how she managed with so many children, she just said, "Ah, but they're darlings, aren't they? And the older ones help with the youngsters, so they're no trouble at all."

As they walked back home, Pa said, "Did you find out what they might need?"

"Meat, mainly. They only have meat on Sundays and then it's usually cheeks or trotters or some such, that we only have as a side dish. They'd enjoy some cutlets or a leg of mutton, perhaps. And decent tea," she added, pulling a face.

"What do they live on, without meat?"

"Cheese. Eggs, I expect, to judge from the chickens in the garden. Bacon. They raise a pig every year to salt away for the winter, although some years they can't get a piglet. I expect they'd like coal, as well. It was poor stuff they were burning. Are all your cottage tenants so poor?"

"No, but Green had a fall, seemingly, and broke his arm, so now he can only do odd jobs. Maybe I can find work for him at the Park."

"He could wind all the clocks. There are dozens of them, and no one ever remembers to do it until they stop. The eldest child is nine or ten, so he could help in the kitchen. Mrs Sharwell is always grumbling that she's run off her feet."

"That's settled, then. And now, puss, you can tell me what's on your mind, and don't pretend there's nothing, for I hope I know my own daughter better than that. Is it Plummer? For you seemed to be getting on rather well last night, and then you went very quiet."

"No, it's not him. I'm not sure I should tell you."

"Anything you can't tell your Pa is not something you should be doing," he said.

"It wasn't me who was doing it, and I don't like telling tales," she said.

"One of your sisters? No, it must be Camilla, for she's a little minx. I can see I've hit the nail on the head. Come on, puss, tell me all about it and then you can be easy. No use letting it fester and upset you."

"It *was* Camilla," she said, and then the whole story

tumbled out.

"Well, that settles it," Pa said grimly. "I'll write to Tom Weston this very day, and tell him to take his daughter and her nasty little ways far from my girls. I'll not have that sort of thing going on under my own roof, and so I'll tell him. I never wanted her here in the first place but your mama thought she might find a man daft enough to want to marry the chit. Well, it's no matter what she thought, now, is it? I'm surprised she hasn't got rid of the little baggage already. What did she say when you told her all this?"

"I haven't told her."

Pa stopped dead, so that Julia had to stop, too. "Not told her? Why ever not? She's taking care of the girl, after all."

"Because... because of something Camilla said, and I don't believe it, but I don't know why she'd make it up, either," Julia said miserably.

"What did she say?" Pa said gently. "Come now, Julia, let's have no secrets in this family."

Julia nodded. "I told Camilla that Mama would be horrified at what she'd done, and she said... she said she'd be horrified that I'd interfered. As if it was all planned, and Mama *wanted* Camilla to let Lord Charles do those things to her. But that can't be so, can it? Mama would never condone such a thing."

"I'd like to think so," he said, but there was an odd tone in his voice that Julia had never heard before.

When they reached the house, Pa said, "Wait for me in my office, puss. I'll find Camilla and Mama, and then we can sort this out once and for all."

It took a little while to gather the ladies, for Camilla was not dressed, but eventually they arrived and Pa related everything that Julia had told him, with no roundaboutation.

"Well, Camilla? What do you have to say about it, eh?"

"It was only a bit of fun, Mr Fletcher. No harm in it, and if Julia hadn't been spying on me, no one would have known anything about it."

"Don't you dare blame Julia for this! She was asked to look after you, as a guest in our house, and she was rewarded for her kindness by sights that no innocent young lady should ever see. Well, I'll not have you in this house a moment longer. Go upstairs and pack. You leave today."

"I'll need money for the stage," she said.

"You'll go in my carriage. I'll write to your father to explain, and I'll not pull my punches, either, although what he's to do with you now, I can't imagine. You're a disgrace, Camilla Weston. Julia, ring the bell for Keeble, will you?"

"He's here," Camilla said, as she opened the door. "Listening at the keyhole, I expect." With a giggle and a whisk of her expensive new skirts she was gone, unrepentant and unashamed.

"Yes, come in Keeble," Pa said. "Tell Murgatroyd and Young Jim they're to have the big carriage at the door in one hour. They're to take Miss Weston and her maid back to Sagborough. Well, don't stand there gawping, man. Off you go and see to it."

"I had better go and supervise the packing," Mama said,

sidling towards the door.

"Not so fast, madam," Pa said. "Before you go, you can explain to me why Camilla thought you'd object to Julia putting a stop to her intrigue with Lord Charles. And don't pretend not to understand, because I've seen for myself how you've thrown the two of them together these past weeks, and not even tried to stop that girl from flirting with him. Flirting! Ha! If only that were all."

Mama flushed, twisting her hands and gazing anywhere but at Pa, but in the end she said in a low voice, "I thought that if Camilla could work on Lord Charles, then perhaps he would agree to introduce us to his brother, Lord Barrowford, and just think what doors *that* would open for Rosie!"

"And Camilla agreed to do it?"

"She was very amenable. She hasn't a shred of morality, you know."

"So you asked and she agreed? Nothing more than that?"

Mama squirmed, there was no other word for it. "If she were successful, I said I would give her two hundred pounds. And the new dresses, of course."

Julia gasped. For an instant, she thought that Pa would explode, but then he visibly controlled his anger. When he spoke, his voice was unnaturally even. "You had better see to Camilla's packing."

She disappeared without a word. Silently, Pa strode to the sideboard where the drinks tray waited, and poured two glasses of brandy, pushing one into Julia's hand.

"I shall talk to your stepmother about this later, and explain to her exactly why her actions were so wrong, although I think she knows perfectly well. I don't need to explain it to you, I know that."

"No, Pa."

"It is a shocking thing that my own wife should be so misguided." He sighed heavily, waving her to a chair beside the fire and sitting himself, leaning forward and cradling his glass. "I wonder if I did a very wrong thing in uprooting you all and moving down here, for Lizzie's mind is now filled with plans for Rosie to marry well, and everything must bow down to that imperative. I'll be happy if it happens, of course... if she finds a man she can love and respect amongst the nobility, but if Lord Charles is typical of the species, that doesn't augur well, does it?"

"They're not all like him, though. Lord and Lady Craston are lovely. I was with you once when you met them on the street and they stopped to talk just like regular acquaintances, and not a bit of stiffness about them, even though he'll be a marquess one day and they were wildly fashionable."

Pa's face softened. "That's true. There are good and bad in the aristocracy just as in the merchant class."

"And they have less reason for being bad, with the privileged life they lead," Julia said.

He chuckled. "Ah, puss, you're such a comfort to me. I love all my children dearly, and I hope I never have favourites, but you're the one I turn to when I want reassuring that we've not changed, despite all the fancy new clothes and the big house. You and I haven't changed. Our heads may enjoy the Hertfordshire rain, but our feet are still firmly planted in Yorkshire. I never objected when your grandfather insisted on you all having what he called a proper education, for I knew what he was about — making a clear distinction between the legitimate children and the illegitimate son. So Ted went off to the grammar school, just like I did, but Will and Johnny went to Harrow and Cambridge, and you girls had a whole succession of fancy governesses with prim mouths and ladylike ways. And somehow, it drove a wedge between me and them. Sometimes I wonder if there's very much of me left in any of them. But all that education didn't work with you. Oh, you learnt a few things, but you're still a good Yorkshire lass at heart. And for all your stepmother's a proper lady with her manners and her fancy way of talking, she doesn't have one quarter your good sense."

"Now, that isn't true at all, Pa," Julia said. "You're just cross with her for now, but you'll kiss and make it up, and then you'll be more reasonable about it. You're spending a lot of money and Mama's putting a lot of effort into launching Rosie into society, so it's natural that mistakes get made along the way."

"You see? So much good sense." He chuckled again, leaned back in his chair and took a long draught of brandy. "Such a comfort to me, puss. I'm glad Camilla's going. I never liked her being here, and I liked still less dumping her on you, but now she'll be gone and you can do as you please again. Plenty more long walks, eh? And this close to Easter, the weather will be improving every day."

It was a delightful thought. But first, there was another

matter niggling in Julia's mind. "So how about we have a look at this secret stair that Lord Charles used to escape?"

Pa smiled broadly. "What an excellent idea."

~~~~~

James returned from the evening at the Park filled with optimism. He was a naturally buoyant person, never downhearted for very long, so Julia's rejection of his suit had not dented his plans in the slightest. He had taken her by surprise, that was the problem. Seeing herself as the awkward middle sister, she had not expected to be courted seriously, but he had sown the seed of the idea in her mind, and surely it would grow day by day. All he had to do was to pursue her with energy, and sooner or later she would succumb. Such a good start last night! No one, least of all Julia herself, could doubt the rightness of the match after an evening like that. It was a pity he had been drawn away after dinner, but it had given her the opportunity to miss his company. She had been subdued and even a little pale later on, so perhaps she was already softening towards him.

So full of energy was he, and so keen to continue his wooing at once, that he determined to call at the Park that very day. He had the excuse of thanking Mrs Fletcher for her hospitality, and if his enthusiasm was interpreted in another light, then that was all to the good.

Thomas went with him, for he too wished to pay his respects. He was not often invited to dine at the principal houses of the parish, since his father was only a grocer in Ware, and he was eager to display his gratitude.

They had barely emerged from the rectory when they

spied Miss Crabtree and her charge emerging from the woods, their arms full of daffodils and primroses.

"What a delightful vision," Thomas said gallantly, doffing his hat and bowing to the ladies. "Miss Crabtree, you are overladen with blooms. May I assist you?"

"How kind you are, Mr Leadbetter. If we had known how splendid the flowers would be or how many we would be tempted to pick, we should have brought a basket. Perhaps if you can manage these?"

They shuffled the flowers between them, only dropping a few, and set off down the road. James felt he could not be less chivalrous than his curate.

"May I carry some for you, Miss Isabella?"

"No, thank you. I can manage."

"What are you going to do with all these?" he said as they followed Thomas and Miss Crabtree towards the entrance to the Park's grounds.

"Put them in vases, of course," she said, with a touch of scorn in her voice.

"Forgive me, that was a foolish question. They will brighten the house considerably. Spring flowers are so cheerful, I always think, with their vivid colours."

"Dorothea thinks so, too," Isabella said. "Yellow is her favourite colour, like the sun. I prefer the autumn. Orange, red, gold, brown — the colours of fire."

"You call Miss Crabtree by her Christian name?"

"No, I call her Miss Crabtree."

That was a puzzle. "Then who is Dorothea?"

"She is my friend. Do you have a favourite colour?"

"Hmm, let me see… I like green, I think. All the shades of green, from the bright green of the first shoots of spring, through the deeper greens of summer, the delicate shades of the willow tree… oh, and that silvery green on the underside of leaves, or the dark green of pine needles."

She smiled. "Yes. Those are all lovely. Miss Crabtree and I are to paint these yellow flowers, but I can add lots of leaves around the edge of the paper, in different shades of green. That will look very pretty, I think. Dorothea will like it."

They had crossed the bridge over the lake by this point, and Isabella and Miss Crabtree, accompanied by a surprisingly willing Thomas, turned off for the kitchen wing and the gardeners' room, where the vases were kept. James continued up the drive to the front door, where a footman opened the door to him within moments of his knock.

"Good morning, sir."

"Enoch, is it not? Is Mrs Fletcher at home?"

"Yes, sir. Mr and Mrs Fletcher are in the parlour."

From somewhere above came the shrieks of girlish glee. "The young ladies are at home, too, I surmise," James said, wondering if Julia were one of the shriekers.

Enoch pursed his lips in a manner so like Lady Plummer that James almost laughed.

After relieving him of his greatcoat, hat and gloves, Enoch led him to the parlour door. "Mr James Plummer, madam," he intoned, as James passed into the room.

Julia was there! James could not suppress the smile of delight on his face, even though he immediately berated himself for such unsubtle behaviour. But then, why should he not let her see his pleasure in her company? It would do his cause no harm at all, and might induce her to look on him more favourably. But good manners dictated that he not rush across the room to her at once. He made his bows to Mrs Fletcher, and to Mr Fletcher too, not forgetting Miss Paton, and made a pretty enough speech thanking them for their hospitality.

Mrs Fletcher smiled invitingly, and gestured to the seat next to her. "We so enjoyed your company, but I fear it was rather a long evening. I do hope Lady Plummer is not too exhausted today."

"I have not seen Mother this morning," James said.

"Oh, of course. But on the journey home... she was not too tired?"

Since she had spent the short journey berating the Fletchers comprehensively for their food, their dress, their manners and even their management of the servants they had inherited, without so much as a pause for breath, James was able to answer with perfect truthfulness, "No, she was not in the least tired."

"And your father? Lord and Lady Charles? Miss Plummer?"

"All in their usual spirits, Mrs Fletcher, so far as I could tell." She nodded, waiting expectantly, so he went on, "My father said it was a splendid evening, and he particularly enjoyed the Miss Fletchers' musical performances. He especially mentioned Miss Angela — he said that she sings like an angel."

"How very gratifying," Mrs Fletcher said. "I shall be sure to tell her so, for Sir Owen must have heard some most superior performers, and therefore his opinion is especially valuable."

Another burst of girlish laughter from above prompted James to say, "Where is Miss Angela today? And Miss Fletcher, and Miss Weston, also. They are quite well, I trust?"

For some reason, Mrs Fletcher blushed. "Oh, perfectly, perfectly, but Julia is here, you see."

A little burst of pleasure shot through him. There was his excuse, neatly wrapped in ribbons with a bow on the top. "So she is. I shall just go and pay my respects."

Mrs Fletcher nodded approvingly, and although Miss Paton glowered at him every step of the way, he crossed the room to the seat by the window where Julia was sewing.

And she smiled up at him. It was working! He was making progress with her.

16: Stairs And Attics

Julia watched James approach. She had no desire for his attentions as a lover, but she would have to be made of stone not to be flattered by his obvious pleasure at seeing her.

"Miss Fletcher."

"Mr Plummer."

"I am come to enquire if you are quite well, and took no chill after standing beside the open door as we were leaving."

She burst out laughing. "What fustian! You are come over here to find out why Angie and Rosie are rushing about squealing. You must have heard them."

He laughed too. "Curses! I am found out! But do tell, for I am afire with curiosity." Lowering his voice, he added, "And your mama seems disinclined to enlighten me."

"We have discovered a secret stair that connects the library to the basement, the schoolroom and the attic. Angie and Rosie have spent hours creeping up and down as quiet as mice, and then leaping out. Their first victims were Bella and Miss Crabtree, who screamed in the most satisfactory manner. However, Miss Crabtree decided that one such disruption was sufficient excitement for one day, and she took Bella off for a walk. Bella was somewhat disgruntled not to be permitted to participate."

"Are you forbidden also, or are you not minded for creeping about secret stairs?"

"Mr Plummer, I have been known to fall down entirely ordinary stairs, ten feet wide and perfectly straight. To attempt a narrow, winding stair would be tempting Providence, I feel."

"You are wise. The stairs are far too dangerous, to my mind. When the house was first built, a chambermaid tripped on one of the spiral stairs and fell all the way to the basement, breaking her neck. Ever since then, they have been closed up and the servants forbidden to use them. The family know of them, of course. How did you discover them, for they are well concealed?"

"Them? *One* of the spiral stairs?" Excitement pulsed through her. "There are more?"

He leaned forward to whisper in her ear. "Four in all. Would you like to see the others?"

Wordlessly she nodded.

"If you can find an excuse to go to the Blue Saloon, I will show you."

Instantly she rose and crossed the room to where her mother sat, placidly chatting to Mr Leadbetter, who had appeared from somewhere with a posy of daffodils in his hand.

"Mama, Mr Plummer wishes to tell me about the drawing of Lincoln Cathedral in the Blue Saloon. May we go and look at it?"

"Of course, my dear," she said, smiling indulgently. "Just leave the door open. Enoch will be in the entrance hall."

Julia curtsied demurely, and led the way down the corridor.

"Your mama is very trusting," he said, and she could hear the amusement in his voice.

Opening the door to the Blue Saloon and ushering him through, she said, "She still hopes to make a match of it. Besides, you're the rector, and thus an upstanding and honourable gentleman. Aren't you?"

"Naturally, and if there are any angry bulls to be found in the Blue Saloon, I am the very man to protect you." Another burst of laughter emanated from somewhere upstairs. "Who are they terrorising now?"

"Each other. Mama forbade them from leaping out at the servants, so now they take it in turns to sit in one or other of the rooms connected by the stair, while the other tries to guess which room to jump into. It may seem a pointless sort of game, perhaps, but Angie is always ready for a game, no matter how simple, and as for Rosie, this is the first time since we moved here that she has laughed. Poor sweet Rosie! She has found it all overwhelming, and I have to tell you that your brother's attentions were by no means the least of it. Even

Mama is relieved that he seems to have drawn back."

"Yes, poor Michael! Your sister is so lovely and well-mannered that he was tempted, but he could not bring himself up to scratch in the end. It seems they are both happier for that choice. Ah, here is the drawing of Lincoln Cathedral, which is rather a good one, except that the artist has placed the clock on the wrong tower. That disposes of the Cathedral. Now, the door to the stair is in that pillar. Can you see it?"

"No, but now that I know how the one in the library works…" She felt around the decorative leaves that covered the lower part of the pillar until she found the latch. "There! Oh, it is just the same. I suppose it connects to the bedroom just above."

"And the basement and attics. Shall we explore? Then I can show you the other two stairs."

She hesitated for a moment. There was no need for him to show her, after all, for he could tell her where the other two stairs were. Besides, although Mama did not mind her being alone in a room with James when the door was open and Enoch right outside, she was very sure that she would object to her scuttling about in the basement and attics with him. But he was already lighting a candle.

"We shall go down to the basement first, and I shall lead the way so that if you trip I can catch you, but you must be very careful. These stairs are dreadfully narrow. Pull the door shut behind you."

He entered the stair, and with a bubble of excitement rising inside her, she followed him in and closed the door. At once the darkness enclosed her, the wavering candlelight already several steps below. Fear caught at her, but he turned and smiled up at her.

"All right?" he said, holding out his free hand to her. "Keep to the outside, where the steps are widest."

She took his hand, warm and reassuring, and picked up her skirts with her other hand. Slowly, step by winding step, the candle flame dancing, they made their way down into the darkness. The air was dank and cool, years of accumulated dust clouding up around their feet. Twice they stopped while he cleared away a cobweb across the full width of the stairs. At the bottom, he pushed open a door and Julia's nose was assaulted by a familiar smell.

"The apple store!"

He chuckled, raising the candle high to show her the towering wooden racks, half empty now. "Pears, too, in the autumn, but I expect they are all gone now. Onions and roots in the next room, potatoes the one after that. There is a proper ice house, too, connected by a tunnel. Do you remember the small mound in the centre of the parterre, the one with a temple to Diana on it?"

"Diana? Oh, the goddess statue. That's the top of the ice house? How ingenious."

"It's not a very good ice house, more artistic than functional. The one at the Manor is better. The other stairs are at the other end of the basement, so we must creep like little mice in case there are any servants about. The senior servants have rooms down here, as well as the boot room and mending room, so they come and go."

He took her hand again, and since it was still dark, she made no protest. As they crept along, from time to time they passed an open door where a window flooded them with light, or occasionally a lamp lit up a dark passageway, but most of the basement was as black as night.

At the furthest end a pillar, decorated in a more austere style than the ones above, revealed another stair, and James led her upwards.

"We are now just outside the dining room," he whispered as they rose one floor. Up again and then, "The big oval bedroom — your parents, I presume." Up yet again, and he threw open the door to a room filled with light. They were in an unused bedroom with the afternoon sun pouring in through the windows.

"The attics are full of bedrooms. Grandfather loved to fill the house with visitors. Hmm, the shutters should not be opened like that. Someone has been up here recently, and not the housemaids to judge by the dust."

"That's odd," Julia said, pointing to a lacquered vase on the washstand. "There is one just like that in the library. I wonder why this is here, when there are no other ornaments."

She wandered across to the window, gazing out across the drive and the lake. "I can see the High Field gate... oh, and is that the chimney of your little cottage, just peeping above the trees there?"

He came up behind her, looking over her shoulder. "I believe it is, yes."

"Was it a gamekeeper's cottage originally?"

"No, the gamekeeper has a place on Manor land, and always has done. The hut was built as an office, if you like, while the Park was being built. All the wood and marble and bricks were stacked up around it, and the architect worked from there, and even slept there, very often. Afterwards, it was taken over by Uncle Cecil, Father's elder brother."

"Did he use it as a hunting base, like you?"

James laughed. "In a way, although his quarry was a little different."

"Ladies, then."

"Opinions differ as to whether they would qualify for that epithet. Females of a certain type, shall we say."

"But you don't do that." It was not posed as a question, for she was fairly confident of the answer, but she waited with some nervousness for the answer.

He answered without hesitation. "I don't do that. I may not be a very good clergyman, but I have always tried my level best to follow Christian principles."

She was surprised at the burst of relief she felt. Assuredly she would like him less well if he were a libertine.

He was still directly behind her, not touching her, but so close she could feel his breath on her neck when he spoke, little puffs of warmth that somehow made her shiver. His voice was low and soft, and she knew what he was going to do an instant before it happened.

His arms slid gently round her waist, and his lips

feathered against her neck. It was the lightest of kisses, but she felt the effects of it reverberating through her whole body. This would never do!

"This is most improper, Mr Plummer."

"I know." And he kissed her again, more firmly.

She moved out of his arms, and he released her instantly. When she turned to face him, he was smiling. Oh, he shouldn't smile like that! Not that amused little smile, his eyes crinkling up in that way that made her instantly want to smile back. It was unfair, that he should be so charming, so agreeable.

When she and Allie and Rosie, and later Angie too, had curled up in bed together on cold winter nights like kittens in the nest, they had talked sometimes about the perfect man. Not necessarily to marry, because that had seemed like a far off possibility in those innocent days, but the sort of man they would like to fall in love with them. Handsome, naturally, and tall, with fair hair and an aristocratic mien like a Greek god. Wildly rich, rich enough to shower them with jewels.

James was nothing like that, and yet...

She knew she should move away from him, but somehow the gentle smile and those eyes with the little creases round them held her in thrall. No, not move away, she should run away as fast as her legs would carry her, or else—

His arms slid round her waist again and he kissed her full on the mouth, and she melted into his embrace as if... as if...

At that precise point, her brain gave up the unequal struggle and forgot its purpose. Without a thought in her head, she was all warmth, all feeling, all tingling delight, right down to her toes. She could feel wisps of his hair curling against her cheek, his hands firm on her back, restlessly stroking her, she could hear her own heart racing inside her, a wild, insistent drumming. It was... it was...

It was altogether too much.

Breathlessly, she made the smallest movement and again he released her instantly.

"Julia..." He made it sound like a caress.

Her head was spinning, but she must make an effort to recover her composure. He mustn't think he'd won her over. "You're not going to get silly and start talking about marriage again, are you?"

He only laughed at her. Nothing dented *his* composure. "Not if you dislike it," he said. If anything, the smile widened a fraction. "But one day you will realise how perfectly we are suited."

"No, I *won't!*"

"You will, Julia, I promise you, and then you will be happy for me to be silly and talk about marriage."

"How can you possibly be so sure?"

"Because we *are* perfectly suited. I have never met anyone I liked so well as you, and I know that you like me. It would be hard for you to deny, frankly, after what has just passed between us."

"It doesn't mean I want to *marry* you! I've told you already, I don't want to marry anyone. I wish you would believe me. Why do you persist in this stupid idea?"

For the first time, the smile slipped. "Why? I... I am not sure, but if I do not—" He sighed, and some expression she'd never seen before passed across his face. But then he recovered himself, and went on smoothly, "My plan is to make myself agreeable to you in every possible way until you succumb to my blandishments, as you inevitably will."

So smug! She was not sure whether to slap him or storm away in a huff. Instead, for some reason she could not begin to understand, she laughed. "You are incorrigible, James. I—"

James? Since when did she call him by his Christian name? No, no, no, this would never do! He was spinning his seductive webs around her and she must resist... at all costs she must resist.

"We should return to the Blue Saloon."

"This way," he said, as imperturbable as ever.

~~~~~

James left the Park as soon as he decently could, striding down the steps, the skirts of his greatcoat flaring. Thomas followed him out, half running to keep up with him.

"What has set you all on end?" he puffed.

"Nothing. I am going for a walk."

He turned aside onto the path through the rose garden and down to the lake, then up and up to the High Field gate. Springing over it in one quick movement, he headed for the hut.

What a fool he was! All this time, he had told himself

complacently that Julia was no more than an amusement, a distraction in an otherwise depressingly boring life. Then she had cut the ground from under his feet. *'Why do you persist in this stupid idea?'* she had said. And he had no answer to give her.

He knew what a true gentleman would do when his suit was rejected in such uncompromising terms— he would bow politely and withdraw, being no more than coolly formal from that day forth whenever they should happen to meet in public. He did not pursue her relentlessly, seek every opportunity to be with her, and he certainly did not take her in his arms and kiss her repeatedly and at earth-shaking, heart-wrenching, utterly glorious length.

He groaned. Oh, that kiss! And she had not resisted in the slightest. What a woman she was! So sweet and delightful and unpredictable and funny and frighteningly lovable.

No, more than that. She was adorable. He adored her, loved her, wanted her... *needed* her. He could not see how he could get through his miserable, lonely life without her. How was he to survive if she would not marry him? He had to convince her, he simply had to. Why did he persist, she had asked him, and the answer was staring him in the face — because the alternative was unthinkable.

Crashing open the door to the hut, he slammed it shut again, hurled himself onto the sofa and gave himself up entirely to the memory of that kiss.

~~~~~

'To Miss Fletcher, Chadwell Park, nr Ware, Hertfordshire. Dearest Rosie, Camilla is home! No one foresaw it, for we all

thought she was to stay with you until after Easter at least, to attend your first ball at Chadwell Park, but here she is back in Yorkshire and no one knows why. She is going about just as if nothing unusual has occurred, saying not a word about why she left or how she arrived home. Her father was as surprised as anyone to see her, seemingly. And there is talk of him sending her to her aunt in Carlisle, but she will not go! Can you believe it! The girl has no discretion, for Emmy Malpas saw her yesterday and was quite shocked at the increase in Camilla's girth. Poor innocent Emmy had not realised until that moment, it appears. Do please write as soon as you can to tell us what scandal broth she has brewed this time, for there must have been some reason for her to return home in such a hurry. We have been very gay here, for the Malpases have their cousins visiting. You will remember Ruth Malpas, I am sure. She is grown into such a pretty girl, although very serious and religious. She is very taken with Ricky, as you might guess for he has all the girls sighing over him these days. Mrs Malpas is in great hopes of a match. We were glad to receive your last letter which seemed to lay to rest your fears regarding Mr Michael Plummer, but we would both be glad to know that the withdrawal of his attentions is permanent. Ricky asks me to remind you that you do not have to marry anyone you do not like, which of course you know, but with your sweet, compliant nature you may feel an obligation. We are sure you are too busy with preparations for your departure for London to write, but we would welcome a few lines to assure us of your continued good health. Oh, and the ball! Do tell us all about the preparations for the ball. How excited you must be! We want to know all about it, if you can spare the time to write. Your devoted friend, Belinda, and

Ricky sends you his best regards, as always.'

~~~~~

'To Miss Fletcher, Chadwell Park, nr Ware, Hertfordshire. Ricky makes me write again, and pray apologise to your Pa for the extra postage, but he wishes me to tell you - that is, Ricky not your Pa wishes me to tell you that no matter how taken with him Ruth Malpas may be, she is nothing at all to him. He is adamant about that, and insists that I write straight away to tell you so, although why it could not wait until my next letter is more than I can guess. He is very upset with me for passing on what he calls scurrilous rumours although it is only what everybody is saying. Anyway, it seems that Mrs Malpas will be disappointed again, if Ruth is not to have Ricky and poor Emmy still does not take, for all her father's money. It is very sad, for she is a sweet girl. Your affectionate friend, Belinda.'

17: The Ball

Easter brought Johnny back to the Park, and a new, more lively air infused the house. Will now set about increasing the stables with some diligence, and so the two brothers rode here and there inspecting riding horses and hunters, adding a gig and a barouche to the carriage collection and taking on two new grooms.

For the ladies, the approaching ball was now the only topic of conversation. Every one of their new acquaintances was invited, even the Miss Williamsons, not forgetting their nephew Mr Richard Osgood, for eligible young men were in somewhat short supply.

Julia was amused by Mama's mental contortions over Lady Frederica Kelshaw. She had never been formally introduced to her ladyship, but Pa was fast friends with Mr Kelshaw, and Will had several times encountered the Miss Kelshaws out riding with Miss Bellingham.

"They desperately want an invitation, Miss Bellingham

says," he told her. "There are not so many balls in these parts that they would willingly forgo the opportunity to dance, and they are not to go to London this year."

"I cannot invite ladies with whom I am not acquainted," Mama said fretfully. "I should love to have them all, naturally, but the proprieties must be maintained. I do not know what may be done about it."

"We see them every week at church," Julia said. "Surely Mr Kelshaw could contrive an introduction?"

It transpired that Lady Frederica was not so unnatural a mother as to deprive her daughters of the opportunity to dance. An introduction was effected on Easter Sunday, Mama made her a deeply respectful curtsy and her ladyship graciously intimated that an invitation to the ball would not be viewed unfavourably. The invitation was written and sent that very afternoon, and an acceptance received the following day.

Mama's joy was now complete, and the rest of the family scarcely less so. Angie was in alt at the prospect of an entire evening given over to dancing, and Rosie too glowed with happy anticipation. Even the men looked forward to the occasion, Pa for an evening of cards, Will for a room full of young ladies to flirt with, and Johnny to meet some of the local gentlemen and discuss the political topics of the day.

Julia herself could not view the forthcoming ball with any pleasure. She was not a natural dancer, so for her the main purpose of the evening was something akin to torture. She had not minded the Sagborough assemblies, for there she was among friends, but here she was surrounded by strangers who would see her for the country bumpkin she was and judge her for the least misstep. If she could have sat out every dance and watched those more competent execute the steps, she would have been quite at ease, but Mama would never allow it.

She was grateful that James secured her hand for the first two dances several days before the event. He at least would not despise her if she turned the wrong way, or trod on her own gown. He would probably only laugh about it.

Once again, the supply of new gowns was raided to clothe the ladies, and Julia had an even more frighteningly delicate dress to wear.

"I shall be sure to tear it," she said gloomily. "Look how flimsy the silk is. I said so when Madame Farage proposed it, as I recall. I shall be terrified to move in it, let alone dance."

"You will have no difficulty if you remember to hold your head high, put your shoulders back and move with graceful steps," Mama said, with all the complacency of someone who had never torn a gown in her life.

They had not invited anyone to dinner before the ball, on the grounds that anyone left out would be mortally offended, but it made the evening a shade less nerve-racking to Julia. In the short window between the end of dinner and the expected first arrivals, the Fletcher family walked in some awe through their new home, now transformed into a place of magical wonders. Candles blazed from every sconce and chandelier. Small lamps filled with sweet oils filled the air with perfume. The saloon doors were flung wide, furniture and rugs removed and the floor chalked with delicate patterns ready for the dancers. To one side, the musicians were setting up their instruments on a small dais. Flowers and potted plants filled odd corners and created semi-private alcoves for those not dancing. "Our very own ballroom," Angie sighed.

Every other room was pressed into service for cards or supper or retiring rooms. Footmen swarmed everywhere, their own supplemented with grooms, hired extras from Ware and a few offered by neighbours. The drive was lined from gate house to front door with torches. Even the terrace was lit for the occasion, with tables piled with shawls for the ladies brave enough to venture into the frosty night to view the stars.

But all too soon Julia found herself dragooned into the receiving line outside the saloon, as the first carriages were seen proceeding up the drive. The Miss Williamsons and Mr Osgood were among the earliest arrivals. The two ladies looked like blackbirds today, with their matching black gowns and not a bit of colour to liven them up, twittering about being rushed. "He is so keen not to miss a single dance," one of them said, and indeed their nephew seemed to be in an enthusiastic mood, striding ahead of them into the ballroom.

After that, there was a steady stream of guests in their finest attire, jewels sparkling at the ladies' throats and arms, and brightening the gentlemen's neckcloths. The musicians were warming up, and Mama was herding the three girls towards their duty to open the dancing, when Mr Richard Osgood descended upon them, his face transformed. Gone was the happy smile, replaced by great anxiety.

"Is it true? Surely it cannot be true?" he cried, grasping Mama by one arm so that she started back in surprise, her mouth round with astonishment. "Miss Weston... she is not here?"

Ah, so that was it. Mama carefully removed his hand from her arm and gave him a sympathetic smile. "Ah, yes, how we all miss her, so lively as she was... is! We had hoped she could stay a full month with us, but she had to return home. Such a pity."

He deflated like a balloon. "Return home? Somewhere in Yorkshire, is it not?"

Angie and Rosie were already in the ballroom, and Mama's hand was steering Julia firmly in that direction too, but she could not but feel sorry for Mr Osgood, who had journeyed here from whichever cathedral city he called home for the express purpose, it seemed, of offering himself as a partner to Camilla Weston. Poor besotted fool!

"Sagborough," Julia called over her shoulder as she was towed away. "Her father is Tom Weston, a mill owner."

As she left Mr Osgood behind, he was pulling a notebook and pencil from an inner pocket.

The Fletcher sisters took their places at the head of the first set. The Plummer brothers were their partners, and a nephew of Sir Hector Bellingham was escorting Angie. Will and Johnny led out the Miss Kelshaws. Other couples quickly joined them and the dancing began.

Julia had to concentrate hard during the dance, for being so near the top of the set meant that she was dancing a great deal and there was little opportunity to relax. James kept up a patter of inconsequential talk at first, but after a while, he said, "Would you prefer me to keep silent?"

"If you would not mind," she said, although feeling rather foolish. "I can only think about one thing at a time, and I feel it ought to be my steps rather than the fish you hope to catch tomorrow."

"It shall be just as you wish," he said, with his charming smile, and after that said not a word, apart from occasionally murmuring, "To the right," or, "Take my hand now."

When she had muddled through both dances and he was leading her back to Mama's station at the head of the room, he said, "May I claim you for a later dance? We can sit out if you wish."

"I should be honoured, sir," she said demurely, torn between exasperation at his persistence and relief that she would be able to avoid one set of dances, at least.

"The supper dance, if you are not already engaged?"

"I am not already engaged."

"Excellent!"

And there was that smile again. It was strange how it warmed her inside whenever it appeared. It was not that she was waiting breathlessly for him to smile upon her, but when he did so, she felt soothed, somehow, as if the fractious little spikes of irritation she always felt at a ball were less spiky.

She found herself much in demand as a partner, despite her lack of skill. It was a compliment to the hostess of the ball, she presumed, that the single gentlemen should seek to dance with the daughters of the house, even so unrewarding a partner as herself. As a consequence, she was delighted to see James weaving his way towards her to claim the supper dance.

"You said we might sit out," she said, as soon as he had tucked her arm in his.

"And so we may, if you would like." The smile flashed across his face. "Where shall we sit? Would you like some lemonade?"

"No more lemonade, I beg you! Mr Leadbetter has been most assiduous in fetching refreshments for the ladies, so I am completely free of thirst just now. Shall we sit by the window? A little air would cool me better than my fan, I believe."

"We could spend a few minutes on the terrace," he said. "No longer than that for it is very cold tonight, but if you wrap up warmly, you will not take a chill."

"Very well, but no silliness, James."

She cursed herself for her carelessness in addressing him by his Christian name, but he said gravely, "No silliness, I promise."

He took a shawl from the pile and wrapped it around her shoulders, opening the French door for her to step outside. Two braziers had drawn clusters of refugees from the dance, and the torches spilt pools of light around the perimeter, but there were still shadowy corners for those seeking to hide from observation. James was not such a one. He led her to the balustrade directly beneath a torch, where they could be clearly seen. Below them in the garden little could be discerned, but Julia stood and gazed out anyway, as if the shapes of trees and flowerbeds would materialise out of the gloom if she only stared hard enough.

Beside her, James was silent too, but whenever she glanced at him, he was looking at her, his face serious.

"What is it?" she said, smiling to lighten the strangely solemn atmosphere. "Have I offended you?"

"No! Not in the least." But there was no answering smile, which gave her a twitch of alarm. "It is too chilly out here. The wind has turned to the east, I believe."

"What does that mean?" she said.

"Bitter cold and perhaps snow, who knows. Let me take you back inside."

She allowed him to tuck her arm in his, his other hand resting on hers firmly enough that she could feel the warmth of it even through her glove. They turned and moved back towards the door, passing one of the braziers. A woman's clear voice rose from the huddle of people gathered around it.

"She is a brazen hussy! Why, did you hear that she—?"

Someone hushed her, and the whole group fell silent, eyes focused on the ground or the flames, anywhere but at Julia and James passing by.

Julia knew. "They were talking about me, weren't they?" she said, as soon as they were back in the warmth of the ballroom.

Without answering, he ushered her to a secluded pair of chairs, half hidden from the room by foliage.

"Tell me the truth, James."

"I believe they were talking about you, yes, but no one takes any notice of such gossip."

"What sort of gossip?"

He sighed, and she suspected would have refused to answer if he could. "About us," he said slowly. "It has been rumoured that you are... *setting your cap* at me, as the vulgar expression goes."

"A brazen hussy. Well. I have been called worse, I suppose. But how does such a story get about when there is not an iota of truth in it? You know better than most how inaccurate it is."

That brought a wry smile. "Indeed, the boot is very much on the other foot, so to speak. But no one says such things to me, or to any of my family, so there has been no opportunity to say so. Thomas does what he can to squelch these tales as he goes about the parish, but I am not sure if it helps. He may be seen as partisan, as my curate. But we will all be gone to town soon, and the rumours of Hertfordshire will be left behind."

"We?" she said, grasping the most surprising part of all this. "You are going to London too?"

"I go most years," he said easily, with a flicker of his usual smile. "This year I have more reason than most."

"Aren't you supposed to minister to your flock... or something of the sort?"

"You know how useless I am at ministering, or any part of my parish duties. Thomas ministers far better than I, and no one will miss me in the slightest, I assure you. "

She should have been irritated by his unwelcome persistence, but oddly she was not. At least she would have one friend in the foreign country that was London in the season, one person who would merely laugh if she tripped over or spilt her wine.

"Give no thought to these stupid rumours, Julia," he went on. "Hold your head high and ignore them."

And for fully half an hour she did exactly that. Instead, they watched the dancing, admiring Rosie's beauty and Angie's elegance. They teased each other about bulls and fox hunting. They talked of London and what delights she might enjoy there — not the balls and routs and other uncomfortable society events, but the parks and theatres and great buildings and the lions at the Tower of London.

"Vauxhall Gardens," he said, his face animated. "You cannot imagine how much fun it is. Music and dancing, for those who wish it, and strolling about under the coloured lanterns, and *fireworks*. Have you ever seen fireworks, Julia?"

"Oh yes. Mr Malpas, the Sagborough mayor, had some once, when he held his first ball. He has one of the fancy new mansions on the York Road, and he had a ballroom put on the back, so we were all treated to a display of fireworks. But that was the only time, and I should very much like to see such a thing again. What about a balloon ascension? I read about one in the newspaper and there was even a little drawing of it, but I'm sure the artist got it wrong, for the balloon looked huge and the people in the basket hung below it were so tiny. Have you ever seen one?"

"Several, and the balloon is indeed huge. It is a great sight to behold, as it gradually fills with hot air and rises up from the ground like a sleeping monster."

"Have you ever been lifted up in a basket like that?"

"Heavens, no. Far too dangerous for a coward like me."

"You are not a coward," she said, shaking her head at him. "I have seen you challenge a bull, remember."

"Ah, but that was for you," he said smugly. "There is nothing I would not dare for you."

She laughed. "No silliness, remember?"

"I beg your pardon, Miss Fletcher. Pray forgive my unwarranted outbreak of silliness. It will not happen again."

And she could only laugh again, and shake her head, as much at herself as at him. She should have given him a set down, but she found herself absurdly pleased by the flattery and quite in charity with him.

Then it was time for supper, and that was where everything unravelled, for Mama was white-faced and distressed, and when Julia, in all innocence, asked what was the matter, Mama hissed, "You! It is all your fault!" and her eyes filled with tears.

"What have I done this time?" Julia said, in a low tone, for the dining room was crowded.

"*That woman* is saying such things about you! And it is all true, so how can I hold my head up, even here in my own house? And what will become of poor Rosie, with such a slur against our good name?"

Julia homed in on the one point of interest. "What woman? Who is saying this?"

"It hardly matters," James began, but Mama would not be silenced.

"The widow," she whispered. "Mrs Reynell. She knows you were inside the rectory, quite alone with Mr Plummer, for fully an hour, Julia, and you may imagine what construction she places upon *that.*"

Julia looked around the room for the widow, and there she was, not ten feet away, whispering into Lady Frederica's ear. Her ladyship looked shocked, and just at that moment, Mrs Reynell raised her head and looked directly at Julia, an expression on her face so akin to triumph that Julia was seized with the urge to wipe it from her countenance immediately, preferably with a heavy object.

She could not commit violence, at least not in her stepmother's dining room, but she had to do something. Rage boiled through her as she looked at the insufferable woman gloating over her. It was insupportable to sit tamely by while lies and false rumours were spread about her. Thinking before she acted was not in her nature, nor was circumspection, not when she was angry, and she was angrier at that moment than she had ever been. Shaking off James's warning hand and ignoring Mama's plaintive, "No, Julia!", she moved with quick steps to tower over Mrs Reynell where she sat, glass of wine in hand, looking up at her insolently.

"You've been telling tales about me, haven't you?" Julia said. "If you have anything to say about me, why don't you say it to my face, like an honest person would? Well? No, I thought not. Too cowardly. You'd rather whisper behind my back. It's disgusting. You should know better at your age than to spread such malicious gossip, without even bothering to find out the truth. Don't you know how much damage and hurt such falsehoods can do? And to be telling your lies right here, under this very roof, where you're a guest and have received nothing but generosity and kindness — that's unconscionably ill-mannered to people who've never done you the least harm and only want to be friendly. You're a nasty, wicked woman, that's all I have to say about it."

Mrs Reynell gazed up at her, mouth hanging open. Not a sound could be heard in the whole room. Into the silence, Julia spun on her heel and stalked out of the room.

18: Consequences

Julia stormed off to her room and paced about there for some considerable time, fuelled by her outrage that anyone, and especially a neighbour she'd regarded as friendly, would do such an unspeakable thing. From time to time drifts of music told her that the ball was continuing unhindered, despite her outburst, but she could hardly go back downstairs again. She dared not show her face in front of everyone. As she paced, she imagined Mama, struggling to put a brave face on it and pretend she was enjoying herself, and Pa would be frowning. She could almost hear his words — "I'm disappointed in you, Julia, very disappointed." He so rarely called her by her full name, only when he was unusually pleased with her or very cross indeed. Even James, who laughed at all her foolish bumblings would hardly be laughing now. What must he think of her? Why oh why could she not have held her tongue, just this once?

Because silence would have been worse. If she had said nothing, it would have emboldened that nasty widow, and bullies like that deserved to be set down. And now at least people knew it was all lies.

It was small consolation. Gradually as she paced, her anger trickled away and she began to cry. What had she done? She had ruined the ball for everyone — for Mama, most of all, who so badly wanted to be part of this society, who wanted Rosie to marry well. Rosie... had she damaged Rosie's chances, just by being alone with James for an hour? Surely the world was not so vindictive! Rosie would go to London and be her sweet, beautiful self and everyone would love her, for how could they not? Yet the niggle of unease would not be suppressed.

Eventually, she undressed herself as best she could and crawled into bed, where at least she could cry in comfort.

Somewhere in the small hours, Rosie and Angie crept into bed beside her, one either side, and hugged her tightly, Rosie weeping too.

"Mama would not let us come up to see you," Rosie whispered in the darkness. "She said we must carry on as if nothing had happened."

"What a horrid woman Mrs Reynell is!" Angie said. "To spread such nasty rumours about you and Mr Plummer."

But Rosie clucked agitatedly. "She was misguided, perhaps, but I am sure she meant no harm. She could not have known the hurt she was causing."

"She knew," Angie said.

Rosie and Angie were worn out from hours of dancing, and had besides consciences clear of all recriminations, so they were soon asleep. Their slow breathing, usually such a comfort, now only served to remind Julia that she was wide awake and her own conscience was anything but clear. So she turned this way and that, now crying a little, now quiet and always remorseful.

Tomorrow she would have a great heap of apologies to make, but for one night, there was nothing she could do but cry, and regret her intemperate actions.

The first light of dawn saw her sitting on the window seat, her forehead pressed against the cold glass. Slowly, the gardens coalesced out of the greyness, and then the ha-ha and the woods beyond. Frost shimmered on the lawn and dusted every bush. Even through the window she could feel the chill in the air. Winter had not yet relinquished its grip, although it had not been much of a winter. She missed the snows of Yorkshire. Oh, how she wished at that moment that she had never left the north!

A timid scratching on the door was followed by Sarah creeping in. "Madam would like to see you in her dressing room, Miss Julia."

"Now? Should I get dressed first?"

"She said right away, but not to disturb Miss Rosie and Miss Angie. Just you, miss."

Julia pulled her wrap tighter about her, and made her way to Mama's dressing room. It was a substantial room, as large as the bedroom Julia had shared with her sisters at Sagborough, and Mama had fitted up one end of it with comfortable sofas and a low table. Cups and a silver pot were laid out.

"Chocolate?" Mama said. "Come and sit down, Julia."

"Mama, I'm so sorry—"

She waved the apology away. "It is too late for that."

"Oh. But I must go and see Mrs Reynell."

"No." With a little shrug, she went on, "That bridge is beyond repair. We must talk about *you*, Julia."

"Are you going to send me away?" she said in a small voice. But even as she considered the humiliation, a part of her was exhilarated — she could go back to Sagborough! And then sorrow, for all her wonderful walks would be lost. It would be back to the canal, and the rough young men who hung about there. And in Yorkshire, there would be no smiling gamekeeper to bump into.

"Not that, no. Running away is not the answer. Julia, I want to talk to you very seriously now. Mrs Reynell may be a deeply unpleasant woman, but there is a kernel of truth in what she says. You *were* quite alone with Mr Plummer inside the rectory for a good hour— Yes, yes, *we* understand the reasons for it, but one can quite see how it must look. Mr Plummer is the rector, of course, and one should not suspect a man of God of misbehaviour, but he is also young and personable, and you have indeed been spending a great deal of time with him. There is enough of truth in the innuendo that we — your father and I — wish to nip it in the bud at once, before we go to London. There must be no shadow cast on Rosie's debut there."

Julia was silent, filled with foreboding. If they were not to send her away, how else could such tales be *'nipped in the bud'?*

"We will talk to you later, after breakfast, about what is to be done," Mama went on. "You will await your father's summons, and not go scampering about the countryside, do you understand? Stay in the parlour... no, your room will be better. Take a book to your room after breakfast, and stay there until you are sent for. Is that understood?"

"Yes, Mama."

"Very well. You may go."

Breakfast was an uncomfortable meal. Mama was silent. Aunt Madge was absent, despite having retired to bed after supper the night before. The men had all eaten early and gone out. Rosie and Angie arrived late, yawning, but they readily understood the chilly atmosphere. Only Bella, too excited by the ball to notice, chattered unstoppably about all she had seen by peering down from the landing and lurking on the stairs.

"Mr Leadbetter came to see us," she said proudly. "He brought champagne for Miss Crabtree, and lemonade for me and Dorothea."

And this made Miss Crabtree blush scarlet and mumble something incoherent.

Mama's toast, half buttered, paused in mid-air. "I hope you do not encourage Mr Leadbetter in any way, Miss Crabtree," she said. "A curate on a hundred pounds a year is not a man who can afford to marry."

"Oh no, Mrs Fletcher, I would never—"

"Not that I would not be very happy for you if ever a

man of means should take you in affection," Mama said, her voice softening. "Everyone should have their chance of happiness, in my view."

There was nothing Miss Crabtree could say to that, so she wisely remained silent.

After breakfast, Julia dutifully retreated to her bedroom with a book, although the last thing she was inclined to do was to read. She sat, then paced, then sat for a while more, as the clock impassively ticked away the seconds and minutes and hours. It was past noon when the summons came, Enoch bringing the news with a sympathetic expression.

"You're wanted in the master's office, Miss Julia. Madam's there, too, and Sir Owen and Mr James Plummer."

The Plummers. So. This was what was meant by *'nipping it in the bud'*. She was to be married off, whether she wanted it or not, for the least hint of scandal could not be allowed to taint Rosie.

Julia steeled herself. This was not going to be pleasant.

They were all there, just as Enoch had said. Mama and Pa stood either side of the fireplace. Sir Owen rose from a seat beside the desk to bow to her. And James lurked near the window, as far from her as he could get. All of them bore serious expressions. No, this was definitely not going to be pleasant.

Mama spoke first, an expanded version of all she had said before. Rosie's reputation must not be impugned by association, there was enough truth in the rumours to make denial impossible, so they must be stamped out in the only way now possible, by marriage. There was much more, about duty and obedience and doing the right thing, and how she knew that Julia would understand.

Julia understood only too well. She was to be sacrificed, whether she wished it or not, because a small-minded widow had taken it upon herself to make assumptions about her, and never mind whether there was any truth in those assumptions. She hoped she had always done her duty, and been obedient to her parents as much as she was able, but there was a line that she would not cross, no matter what.

"You cannot force me to marry."

"No, dear, but I know you would not wish to damage Rosie's prospects in any way."

"Rosie will be admired and valued and *loved* wherever she goes, regardless of what I do," Julia said. "And if society would set her aside because of some imagined misdemeanour by her sister, then the loss is society's, surely."

Mama winced. "That is not how these things work, Julia! We cannot afford any misstep at this stage, not given our background."

"You mean Pa coming from trade?" Again Mama winced, but Julia continued relentlessly, "We are who we are. People either accept us as we are or they do not, and if anyone chooses to reject us because of our *background*, as you so delicately put it, then that is not a person I could respect or would wish to know. I am sorry for my intemperate words last night, and I will say as much and more to Mrs Reynell, but I will not marry James, or *anyone*, on account of them."

Pa shifted restlessly. "I think you should reconsider, Jules."

"You too, Pa? Haven't you always said you'd never force any of us to marry against our will? Yet now you want to force me into this marriage, and all because of some imagined ill that might accrue to Rosie? Shame on you!"

"I will *never* force you, as you well know," Pa said tersely. "Nor can I, in law. No one can make you marry where you're disinclined. But I don't understand why you don't want to. You get on so well with James, as anyone can see. He's very eligible, of course, but that doesn't weigh with me. It's character that's important, and he's a man I can trust. I wouldn't be happy to hand you over to just any man with a lineage and a few pennies in his pocket, puss, but James would take good care of you, and you *like* him. So why won't you do this thing that's so important to your stepmother... to all of us?"

"I can't, Pa," she said fiercely. "I just can't. This is my whole life we're talking about, set against a momentary rumour swirling around and the possibility... nothing but a possibility of harm to Rosie's future. What difference does it make? Even if I were to marry today, would all these foul rumours simply subside of their own accord? Isn't it better to face up to them, fair and square, look them in the eye and say — judge me if you dare? Isn't that how you've always taught us?"

"Yes, but... everything is different now," he said, with a helpless lift of one shoulder.

Sir Owen had not yet spoken, but now he said, "Miss

Fletcher, you make your case with great spirit, and I can only admire you for it. You are correct that no one can force you to marry, nor can the deleterious effects of these events be determined with any accuracy. Society is fickle, and may reject your family for your perceived transgressions or may choose to ignore them. No one can predict the outcome. All I can tell you is that Mrs Reynell is very friendly with Lady Frederica Kelshaw, and her connections in London will undoubtedly be fully informed of your supposed misdemeanours in lurid detail. Notwithstanding that, no one would wish you to be pressed to marry against your will. It is clear to me that you have reasons for your views, although I cannot guess what they may be, and I have not the right to expect an explanation. I believe that I, and perhaps your parents too, should withdraw at this point and leave the discussion of this matter to those most nearly concerned — that is, to you and my son. Fletcher? Mrs Fletcher? Do you agree?"

Mama was reluctant, Julia could see that, but Pa was more than willing to withdraw and so Julia found herself for the second time left alone in the office with James.

"I shan't change my mind," she said crossly, plumping herself down on the nearest chair.

For once, there was no smile on his face. "I hope you will," he said quietly. "I think you do not fully understand the danger in which your family stands."

She jumped to her feet again. "If you are going to tell me that Rosie's prospects might be damaged because I once spent a full hour in the rectory kitchen with you without a chaperon, then you are fair and far off. It's ridiculous. Rosie will be judged by her own virtues, which are numerous. No one in London cares tuppence about me, or what I may or may not have done."

He was silent for such a long time that she wondered if he had run out of arguments. But then he sighed, and left his station by the window to stand beside her, taking hold of one of her hands.

"Dear Julia, you are so open and honest that you cannot imagine how… how *spiteful* the world can be. But if you will not marry me for Rosie's sake, then do it for your own…"

"No!" she cried, snatching her hand out of his grip. "No, no, a thousand times no! I've told you I don't want to marry, not *ever*, and nothing has changed my opinion on that. Nothing you can say will change my mind. No matter how well we may get along, that is no foundation for marriage. There has to be something more."

"Then how about love?" he said, his face riddled with anxiety. "Would that not make a difference? I love you, Julia! Marry me, and make me the happiest man alive, I beg you."

"Love? *Love?*" With that one word, all the muddle of emotions that had overwhelmed her in the last few hours, all the rage and fear and remorse and burning sense of injustice rose boiling to the surface. "You *dare* to speak to me of love? After all this? How can you do this to me, James Plummer? All this time you led me to believe we were just friends, and now you start ranting about *love!* Do you imagine I'll melt into a puddle of compliance, is that it? Suddenly I'll feel sorry for you or something? You're despicable! Do you understand how unfair it is to try to… to *blackmail* me into marrying you?"

"No, I never intended—"

"I hate all this! I've a good mind to follow Camilla's example and just run away from here, and escape from all of it. I'll go to live with Great-aunt Petronella. At least *she* won't hound and harry and coerce me to marry against my will."

"Julia—"

"Stop it! You disgust me! I was perfectly happy until you came along and disrupted my life. Why in God's name can't you just *leave me alone?*"

She ran for the door, raced up the stairs and hurled herself into her room, slamming the door. But the house was too confining. She couldn't breathe… she needed clean air and space to walk off her anger. Pausing only to change into her comfortable old half-boots and find her thick woollen cloak, she escaped down the secret stair and out of the house, striding away through the gardens before she was even missed.

19: *Unrequited Love*

James stood transfixed, too astonished to move. *' I was perfectly happy until you came along and disrupted my life.'* Was that how she saw him, as an annoyance who ruffled the placid waters of her life? Or was it merely her anger speaking? Surely she had been too receptive to his overtures to dislike him as much as her words implied? Perhaps he had completely misread her.

There was no point standing about like a wax-work, however. As he slipped out of the room, there was no one in sight. From next door came the sound of servants restoring the library to its usual state after it had served as a card room, but somewhere in the distance he could hear a voice singing... no, humming. Opening the door of the blue saloon a fraction, he saw that the room was still untouched after the ball. The floor bore the scuffed traces of chalk, while around the edges, chairs sat at odd angles, just as their occupants had left them, and every table and shelf bore abandoned wine glasses, plates, even a fan. The dividing doors were still tucked away into their concealing pillars, so he could see clear to the far end of the room.

A woman danced there... no, a girl, he realised. It was Isabella, her shape already womanly though she was but fourteen. She hummed to herself, eyes closed, as she moved through the steps. A cotillion, he thought, with seven imaginary partners. She lacked the almost magical lissomness of Angie, nor had she Rosie's serene beauty, but she would not disgrace herself in any company. James watched for some minutes, smiling at the contrast with Julia's awkward attempts. Every now and then, Bella murmured something to herself.

"Left... no, right. Jump a little higher, like this. Daintily, daintily, like a lady."

It was enchanting to watch, until she murmured, "No, Dorothea, gracefully, like this."

But there was no one else in the room. James crept away, puzzled and slightly disturbed.

~~~~~

Thomas found him hunched over the brandy bottle in the rectory drawing room late in the afternoon.

"Ah. She turned you down again, then?" Thomas said, fetching another glass from the sideboard and pouring a large measure for himself.

"And who would blame her for that? Not I," James said, with unaccustomed seriousness. "I should dislike it extremely if I were told to marry purely because a vicious woman was spreading rumours about me. False rumours, at that. Mrs

Reynell is such an unpleasant woman, and it is all jealousy. How ironic — the woman I want despises me, and yet *she*— You were supposed to seduce Mrs Reynell away from me, Thomas."

"I beg your pardon, but it could not be done. Even if she had deigned to look my way, she would be impossible to live with, fortune or no fortune. Did Miss Fletcher give you no hope at all?"

"None, but she was magnificent, Thomas," he went on, his head lifting at the thought. "She said we should face up to the lies. *'Judge me if you dare'*, she said. Is that not wonderful?"

"But the world will indeed judge her," Thomas said softly. "You know it as well as anyone, James."

"As to that, I cannot say, for the world is fickle and unpredictable, but she has such courage! Who could not love a woman like that?"

"Is this the time to remind you of your own words, my friend?" Thomas said, with a wry smile. "You were the one, after all, who said that love is for fools. Yet here you are, so deep in love you cannot even see the irony."

James refilled his brandy glass and took a long draught while he reordered his thoughts. It was true that he had chosen Julia dispassionately, because she amused him and relieved the boredom that sapped his spirits, and he had never intended to fall in love with her. Yet he had been drawn to her from the first moment he had seen her sitting on the gate, jauntily swinging one leg. She made him smile, always, and was that not the very foundation of love?

"The principle holds, I think," he said, "although whether a man must be a fool to fall in love or it is the falling in love which makes him so is more than I can say. Perhaps a little of both. I was a fool to fall in love, and I am still a fool for persisting even when there is but little hope of success."

"Ah, unrequited love," Thomas said with a satisfied smile. "The purest kind there is."

"Thomas? Are you a sufferer also? But who has won your affection? Not Mrs Reynell?"

The curate almost choked on his brandy. "Heaven forfend! No, not that perfidious woman. I have met someone so far above her in every way that I cannot quite believe it."

"Who is it? Come, Thomas, you must tell me. You know all my secrets, after all, so you cannot keep your own, not in an affair of the heart."

"You will not mock me?"

"I promise I will not."

"It is Miss Violetta Crabtree."

"The governess? Isabella's governess, who walks around the estate with her nose in a book? But Violetta — what a frivolous name for such a serious lady."

"She is not serious at all, James," Thomas said indignantly. "She has the most glorious sense of humour, quite subversive at times. And she knows Latin *and* Greek, for her father was a clergyman and a man of some learning, who did not hesitate to educate his daughters to the same high standard as his sons."

"But there is no hope of a future together."

"Oh, no. Certainly not. I have a hundred pounds a year, and she has savings of some two hundred pounds, that is all. Unless I can somehow obtain a living, there is no possibility of marriage. But we meet occasionally, mostly accidentally but occasionally by my contrivance, and I treasure such times, James. It is the greatest comfort to me to know that there is one woman in this world who does not despise me for my humble station in life, who talks to me as an equal, who sees me as *myself* and not just the curate."

"Then I wish you the greatest joy of your unrequited love," James said. "For myself, I still hope that mine will not always be unrequited."

"You are an optimist, my friend."

"I must be, for to surrender all hope would plunge me into a very dark place. I have no expectation that she will ever love me as I love her, but we are so perfectly matched in every way that it would be madness to give up now. No one will ever suit me so well. One day she will understand it, on that I am determined, and I shall not retreat until I have won her."

"How many times have you offered for her?"

"Formally, twice, but she was aware of my intentions before that."

"And she has refused you twice, but has she given you the smallest sign that she may one day change her mind? Any hint whatsoever?"

James was about to assert it staunchly, but honesty

made the words die on his lips. Sighing, he said, "Thomas, it puzzles me why I maintain my friendship with you, for surely your rôle now is to encourage me, not chip away at the foundations of all my hopes. No, she has given me no sign, quite the reverse, and yet it is impossible for me to accept. Now, do not mistake me, for I have no illusions about myself. I am no great catch, either in my person or in my rank in society. A second son and a clergyman, and with her dowry she could do much better, if she wished. But she does *not* wish. She likes me, we get along excessively well, and I flatter myself she enjoys my company above that of any other — yet she rejects me. She rejects the very idea of marriage, and that must be overcome. What else should a woman do with her life but marry, and create a new family? How can she bear to contemplate a life of spinsterhood? It is a mystery to me. Women are strange creatures, Thomas. I understand them not."

Thomas having nothing to add to this assessment, they lapsed into silent contemplation of the brandy. James's contemplation was not pleasant. For all his outward confidence, he could not forget Julia's face as she had raged at him. *'You disgust me! I was perfectly happy until you came along and disrupted my life. Why in God's name can't you just leave me alone?'* She had never been angry with him before, and it was painful to recall. Even though he understood that her ire was a response to the situation in which she had found herself and he could not blame her in the slightest, he had borne the brunt of it.

For the first time, it crossed his mind that perhaps Thomas was right. Could it possibly be that he would never succeed with Julia? His casual decision to marry her had been thwarted at every step. Even with both her parents and his father, not to mention the spiteful tongue of Mrs Reynell, to encourage the match, she had rejected him in no uncertain terms. His foolish scheme to make her fall in love with him had failed utterly. James's character was naturally sanguine, but even he could find no cause for optimism in his present situation. She would not have him, and that was an end to it.

This reverie was disrupted by Mrs Pound. "You'll not mind if Janet and me get off early today, sir, but it's coming on to snow. Everything's ready for your dinner, and we'll finish sorting the linen tomorrow."

Thomas strode to the window. "Heavens, it is indeed snowing — and with Easter already gone by."

"Tis the price we pay for a mild winter, a late storm," Mrs Pound said, with resignation.

"Of course you must go at once," James said. "If it is still coming down tomorrow, stay snug at home. I should not like to think of you struggling through the storm just to rake out the ashes."

James was not minded to struggle through the storm himself, so he chose not to dine at the Manor that evening. It was a relief, for he knew that Letitia and his mother would be cock-a-hoop to have evaded once again the prospect of the mercer's daughter joining the family. Uncle Morgan would tease him unmercifully and Michael would all but weep over him in sympathy. No, he could live without his family for one evening. He ate in the rectory kitchen with Thomas and Lightwood, James's valet and general handyman, where they enjoyed an array of dishes left by Mrs Pound and a rather good bottle of claret.

After dinner, Lightwood stretched out in a chair beside the fire for a nap, but Thomas and James settled down with the cribbage board and the remains of the claret. They were almost on the point of waking Lightwood so that they could all go to bed when there was an almighty hammering on the front door, accompanied by the doorbell clanging and voices shouting.

"I expect old Mr Downes has had another turn," Thomas said, getting up at once. "That will be young Downes wanting me and my prayer book."

But he returned moments later with Mr Fletcher, bundled up in greatcoat and scarves, rimed with snow, his eyes wild.

"Is she here? Do you know where she is, Plummer? For we are at our wits' end, I can tell you."

Fear tore through James. "Julia?" he said hoarsely.

Fletcher nodded. "She went out earlier this afternoon, but she's not back and no one knows where she's gone. You were the last to see her. Did she say anything — anything at all?"

Frantically he ran over their conversation in his mind. "No... no, nothing. Well, only some joke about running away to an aunt."

Fletcher uttered a low moan. "No! She would not... would she? Which aunt? Where? She has several..."

James frowned, trying to remember. "Petronella?" he

hazarded.

Fletcher groaned again. "Yorkshire! If it were Annie in Brighton— But no, that can't be right. She's taken nothing with her, no bag or box. Nothing but her old cloak and her walking boots."

"If I were planning a trip to Yorkshire," James said thoughtfully, "I would catch the northbound stage coach at Ware, and—"

"Yes, yes, but—"

"—if I were in a hurry, I would walk across country to the Wheatsheaf, and pick up a lift from there. Far shorter than the road."

"Yes, but—"

"I would not burden myself with bags."

Fletcher sat abruptly on the nearest chair. "Then she is out walking… in this weather?"

"It would take her an hour and a half… perhaps two hours. Maybe less, for she is a fast walker."

"I don't think there was time. The snow's been falling for hours. She'll be out there somewhere… my poor Julia! She always says she never gets lost, but in snow…"

James had no words of comfort to offer. Terror clutched at his heart, and worse, guilt. This was his fault! He had pushed her beyond endurance, and now she was lost in the snow, freezing to death not five miles from her home. Dead! His lovely Julia, dead in the merciless storm.

"She would have sought shelter as soon as the snow

started." That was the calm voice of Thomas, and it brought James back from the edge of despair.

"Of course she would," he said, grabbing at this sliver of hope. "There are plenty of barns along the way... a few cottages, or even Fairstead House, if she thinks of it. She may have taken shelter there."

"So she may," Fletcher said, relief in his voice. "Will and Johnny have gone to the Manor, but if she is not there, we must go on to Fairstead House. I must *know*."

"I will go there," Thomas said, jumping up. "What about Kelshaw House?"

"It seems unlikely, but..."

"We must try everywhere. Might she have gone to the church to pray? Lightwood, will you go and see? Check the vestry, too."

"You are kind souls," Fletcher said wearily. "Thank you."

"Will you have a brandy, sir?" James said, after Thomas and Lightwood had gone.

"I think I will. Thank you."

James fetched the half empty brandy bottle and a couple of clean glasses, and poured generous measures.

"Leadbetter is right, of course," Fletcher said, sipping his brandy. "We must look everywhere we can. I even went to ask Mrs Reynell — I thought Jules might have gone there to apologise. But if she is not in the village... we cannot get to the Wheatsheaf in this weather. Not until the morning, and only if the snow stops."

"It will not last long, I think," James said, with more assurance than he felt.

He brought out some bread and cheese, with the thought of toasting them, but that only reminded him of happy times in Julia's company. At that moment, he would have given up toasted cheese, and a great many other indulgences too, to know that she was safe.

In time, Lightwood returned, and then Will and Johnny Fletcher, and finally, covered from head to foot in snow that melted and dripped all over Mrs Pound's clean kitchen floor, Thomas Leadbetter. None had any news to report. Wherever Julia had gone, it was not to any acquaintances in the village.

"Will you stay here for tonight, sir?" James said to Fletcher. "The snow is not easing at all, and the road is becoming treacherous."

"I thank you for your kindness," Fletcher said, "but I must report back to Mrs Fletcher, and reassure her as best I can. We have lanterns, and our route home is an easy one to follow, even in driving snow."

"Let me come with you, to help guide you. I have walked to the Park in snow more times than I care to remember over the years."

"You are very good, Plummer, but we will not lose our way in so short a distance. It is but a step to the gatehouse, and so long as we stay between the trees lining the drive we shall do well enough. We are from Yorkshire, after all, and no strangers to winter weather."

"Try not to fall in the lake," James said.

They laughed, taking it as a joke, and were soon gone,

leaving James with three more people to fret over.

"Stop worrying," Thomas said. "There are three of them, and the young Fletchers will look after their father."

"May I worry about Julia?"

Thomas hesitated. "I am not sure I can stop you, but you have always said she is sensible, James. She will have found shelter. It is not as if Hertfordshire is some desolate wilderness, after all. It is impossible to walk more than a quarter of a mile in any direction without seeing a habitation of some sort, and no one would refuse to take in a young lady caught in a storm. She will be sitting snug as you please in a farmhouse or labourer's cottage, you may be sure."

"Of course she will. Of course. Bound to be. She is too sensible to persevere once the snow started. Naturally she would have made for the nearest safe refuge. Where is that map, Thomas? Let me see if I can determine the most likely places to try tomorrow."

Willingly, Thomas fetched the parish map, and then the one for St Agnes, as well, which included the Wheatsheaf, and James pored over them eagerly, trying to work out the route Julia might have taken and which barns and cottages were situated near enough to provide shelter.

Eventually, when even James's feverish study had subsided to a dull resignation that they did not know and could not guess where she might be, Thomas tentatively suggested that they retreat to bed.

"You will want to be up at first light, I am sure. Best to get some sleep while you may."

It was, of course, an eminently good suggestion, except

for the small impediment that James could not conceive of sleeping while Julia was out there somewhere, trapped by the snow. He meekly withdrew to his room, therefore, but made no attempt to ready himself for bed, dismissing Lightwood with a curt wave of the hand. And then he built up the fire and slumped in the battered chair beside it, bathed in the ghostly light of the flames, while his mind ran and ran in circles.

No matter how much he tried to concentrate on the probability that Julia was safe and warm somewhere, his imagination threw up pictures of her lying in the snow, curled up under a hedge in the pitiful attempt to shelter, or huddled under a tree. He told himself repeatedly that she would not have abandoned all prudence just because she was angry with him. She was a good walker who knew the byways around the Park intimately, and she would have seen the bad weather coming in. Of course she would be safe! Yet despair and grief gnawed at him like a physical pain. He could not bear it if she were to die, and all because of him! She would not run away, surely! It was madness...

But if she had not gone to the Wheatsheaf, where would she have gone?

He sat up abruptly. If she had not gone towards Ware, then perhaps she had walked to her favourite spot, the place she returned to over and over — the gate at High Field. And if she had gone *there*, and set off in almost any direction, then there was one obvious sanctuary that would draw her if she were beset by snow — the hut.

He padded downstairs, found his boots and greatcoat, lit a lantern and crept out into the night.

20: Home

The snow had stopped, all but a few drifting flakes. Not that it mattered, for James could find his way to the hut blindfolded, if need be. Out to the road, walk alongside the rectory wall and then the church wall, past the Park gatehouse and then if he could not see the outline of the rough track that connected the hut to the road, he need only follow the boundary wall up the hill.

The snow was not deep, although it had drifted against the Park wall somewhat, so he struggled up the hill. He had forgotten how many brambles grew against the wall, so his coat was snagged every few paces. After a while, the clouds began to break up and moonshine showed him the outline of the track, and then the way was easier.

The hut lay in darkness, no chink of light emerging from between the shutters. As he drew near, he realised the futility of his journey, born of nothing but his own desire to be doing something — *anything* — rather than sitting around being eaten alive by terror. Julia could not be here, surely. It was too close to the village, so she could easily have made her way to safety. What a fool he was! She was probably snug in bed at the Wheatsheaf, and would laugh heartily to hear of his wasted journey.

He lifted the latch, went in and raised the lantern to look around.

She was there, stretched out on the sofa, fast asleep. The light roused her, and she stirred.

"Mmm? What is it?" She opened her eyes fully, saw him, pushed herself upright. "James?"

He was momentarily speechless, torn between overwhelming relief that left him weak, and indignation that she was here, fast asleep, as if nothing at all was amiss.

"What's the matter?" she said. "What time is it? Have I missed dinner?"

"Missed dinner?"

She chuckled, stretching and rising slowly to her feet. "It must be late, for you've brought a lantern. Mama will flay me alive if I've kept everyone waiting."

He could barely breathe. How could she make light of her situation, when her father and brother were scouring the countryside for her? When her life was all but despaired of? Had she truly no idea of what she had done?

"Kept everyone waiting?" he said, in a low rumble that was almost a growl, so that her eyes widened in surprise. "I should think you have, yes. Have you the slightest idea of the trouble you have caused? Your father has been looking everywhere for you."

"Whatever for? He knows I never get lost. Is it very late? I'd better get home."

The pitch of his anger frightened him. To give himself time to calm down a little, he busied himself lighting candles and throwing logs on the fire, until he felt he could answer her with a degree of composure.

"It is two in the morning, Julia."

"What? Two o'clock? No! Surely not!"

"It has been snowing steadily since shortly after you disappeared and—"

"Disappeared! I went out for a walk, that's all. For goodness sake, James, don't be so hysterical. I was cold, I came here to warm up, I fell asleep. When I woke, it was snowing so I stayed here. I suppose I must have fallen asleep again. Is it really two in the morning?"

"Yes, it is, and your father has been frantic with worry for you. He thinks you are lost in the snow somewhere."

"Well, that's just stupid!" she cried. "As if I would ever get lost in the snow! Pa knows that perfectly well. What a lot of fuss over nothing!"

"You are the most selfish, troublesome creature alive." He was so angry, he shook from head to toe. "You leave without a word to anyone, and here you are, completely unconcerned about the trouble you have caused. Your father is worried sick that you were caught in the snow, possibly freezing to death somewhere between here and Ware, and here you are, warm and snug and not the slightest bit apologetic about it."

"Ware? What on *earth* would I be doing going to Ware? Honestly, James, you must have windmills in your head tonight. And what are you doing wandering around in the middle of the night anyway?"

"Looking for you, idiot! Your father looked everywhere else."

"Well, I'm very sorry if Pa was worried about me, but he should know me better than to imagine I'd be caught out in a snowstorm. For heaven's sake, I'm from Yorkshire, I know all about snow! This is ridiculous. But if it's two o'clock, there's no point in worrying about dinner, is there?"

James boiled with impotent rage, grabbing her by the shoulders and giving her a little shake with every word. "Julia Fletcher, you are the most troublesome, annoying, frustrating, vexing, ungovernable, tiresome, *maddening* girl I ever knew!"

She gazed at him defiantly, her breathing heavy and her eyes — oh, her eyes! How they flashed at him. Fiery anger tore through him, beyond his ability to contain it. In that moment, he loved and hated her with equal force.

Without any conscious thought, his arms wrapped tightly around her, and he fastened his lips on hers with ferocious intensity, surrendering to the power of whatever emotion held him in its grip. It was a kiss like no other he had experienced, so passionate, so furious that every thought was swept from his mind and there was nothing but this primeval compulsion, although to what end, he could not tell.

Gradually, he became aware that he was meeting no resistance to this outpouring of rage, for she held herself quiescent in his arms, not quite returning his fervour, but accepting it without the slightest protest. And slowly, slowly, as her yielding warmth comforted him and his anger trickled into nothing, the kiss became something else, quieter and gentler, a thing of sweet tenderness between lovers.

Lovers? No, that was just his own ardent wish misleading him...

With a groan of despair, he released her and staggered back to collapse onto a chair, head in hands. There were no words, nothing at all he could say to her now.

For a long time he sat thus. When he dared to raise his head, she was sitting too, her hands composedly resting in her lap, her face calm. He could read nothing from her expression, not in this gloom of flickering candles and firelight.

Cautiously, he tried his voice. "It will be too difficult to walk across the Park, but if you feel you can manage the path to the village, I ought to get you home." Not bad. He sounded almost normal.

"Yes."

She sounded almost herself, too. A little subdued, perhaps, but not angry. For both of them, that kiss had wiped away their argument. He felt scoured clean, somehow. Whatever had they quarrelled about anyway? It seemed a trivial, distant thing, now.

"The snow is not deep, so it should be an easy walk."

"Yes."

She did not move. Restlessly, he went to the window and opened the shutter a crack. "The moon is out, so we will be able to see the path clearly."

"Yes."

"Shall we go?"

For answer, she stood, pulling her cloak tightly around her. She had not even removed it when she lay down.

He tamped down the fire and extinguished all the lights except his lantern, holding the door open for her. Then they set off on the walk down the hill, into the village and then through the gates of the Park, where the trees along the avenue had kept the snow to a mere sprinkling.

It was so strange to walk beside her without speaking. She had always chattered to him in the easiest manner imaginable, but now she had nothing to say. Whenever he dared to look at her, the expression on her face was placid. There was a stillness about her that he could not interpret.

They crossed the bridge over the lake and made their way up to the front door, where James banged vigorously with the knocker, and rang the bell for good measure.

"No one will hear," she said.

"The butler's and housekeeper's rooms are directly below the front door, so one of them will hear," he said, knocking and ringing again. "Eventually."

But it was not Keeble or Mrs Graham whose hands wrestled with the bolts and locks, not two minutes later. When the door opened, it was Mr Fletcher's face, animated with a mixture of hope and terror, which peered out at them, his night cap askew. He saw Julia, he gave a cry of joy, and threw the door wide.

"Jules! My darling girl!"

He opened his arms and she rushed into them, both of them crying, talking excitedly, hugging. Then more figures appeared in the hall behind them, ghostly pale in their night wraps, candles wavering in the draught from the open door. Julia was enfolded by excited female voices and more tears and drawn further into the house.

James slowly made his way down the steps, quite unnoticed, and trudged wearily home.

~~~~~

Julia lay awake for most of what remained of the night, as Rosie and Angie slept quietly beside her. She had slept away half the day and some of the night too, as her exhaustion caught up with her. Now she was wide awake.

She was calm. After the turbulence of recent days, she had reached an oasis of tranquillity, all the high emotion drained out of her.

James *loved* her. He had told her so and she had not believed him, but last night...! Good heavens, she had believed him then, for she had seen it for herself. First his anger, an anger not founded merely on the inconvenience of searching for her, but something more deep rooted. When she had first opened her eyes and seen him standing on the threshold, lantern held high, his face had been suffused with joy. He had sagged against the door post with relief. And then, when she had shown no contrition, he had exploded with rage. Even then, she hadn't understood.

But when he kissed her... oh Lord, what a kiss! She had

not had the least inkling until that moment that a kiss could be more than the gentle affection she had experienced with James in the attic. Then he had been all softness and caressing tenderness. But this latest kiss… it was like nothing on earth… so powerful, so all-encompassing, so *passionate*.

Passion… love… the love of a grown man for a woman. For her, Julia realised in wonder. How was it possible that any man could feel such an overwhelming emotion for someone like her? For Rosie, yes, so beautiful and good as she was. Or even Angie, as dainty and graceful as an angel. But for herself, with all her odd ways? It was hard to credit. Yet it was so.

It made no difference to her determination not to marry, but it changed her. It changed everything.

After such a disturbed night, everyone rose late to a subdued breakfast. No one berated Julia for the panic she had inadvertently caused. Her apologies were waved away airily.

"You are safe and sound, puss, that's all that matters," Pa said.

Even Mama smiled at her. "You will not want to go for your usual walk today, I imagine, Julia," she said, her voice gentle. "There is still snow lying, and I should be glad of your help with the packing."

With the ball over and their removal to London only two weeks away, there was now an orgy of sorting and planning and packing, for the first boxes of precious new gowns were to be dispatched in two days.

"There is still much to be bought once we arrive," Mama said, a smile of happy anticipation on her face. "Madame

Farage is progressing wonderfully with gowns, but we shall need stockings, shoes, gloves, hats... oh, so many hats you will need! Today we will make a start on Rosie's boxes."

Julia could not think she would be much help with packing, for she would be sure to do it wrongly and crush the delicate fabrics and carefully constructed sleeves. Nevertheless, she willing followed Mama, Rosie and Angie upstairs, and prepared to submit to a day of tedium.

Enoch knocked on the door shortly before noon. "Master wants to see Miss Julia in his office."

Julia's stomach clenched in fear — not again! Surely it could not be James importuning her yet again? "Is anyone with him, Enoch?"

"No, miss, he's quite alone."

"Has anyone called on him this morning?"

"No, miss."

It was safe, then. Pa was indeed alone, standing gazing out of the front window over the steps and down towards the lake.

"You wanted to see me, Pa?"

"Come here, puss, and tell me what you see."

She crossed the room to stand beside him and looked out at the view. "I see my favourite walk, across the lake and up the hill to the High Field gate. I see freedom."

He chuckled. "Aye, I can understand that. Now, for me it represents responsibility. A burden. All that land to be cared for, and tenants depending on me. And yet... so much space.

So much greenery and fresh, clean air. My office in Fullers Road overlooked the street, with all the noise and wagons rumbling past at all hours. In the summer, I couldn't open the window for the horse dung not cleaned up swiftly enough, and the rest of the year there was smoke lying, sometimes so bad I couldn't see old Mr Hagger's house opposite. And yet, when we first came here, I couldn't sleep at night or read the newspaper of a morning because it was so *quiet.*"

"But you like it now?" Julia said tentatively.

"Aye, I do. It's home, isn't it? Your mama's happy, so I'm happy too. Will and the girls are looking forward to London, and Johnny is going to fill the library with books. Everyone is happy except you, puss — and Madge, but nothing makes her happy, so we can disregard that."

"Pa, the only thing that makes me unhappy is being dragooned into marrying."

"Yes, that was wrong of us," he said ruefully. "I just thought— but it makes no difference. If you won't have him, you won't and that's an end to it. You won't be troubled in that way any longer, and we'll just have to live with whatever damage this Reynell woman can cause us. I went to see James this morning, to thank him for bringing you home to us safely, for he vanished before I got a chance last night. We had a long chat. He's distraught, poor fellow, for he feels it's all his fault that you were driven out into the snow."

"It was my own silly fault, not his."

"If he had not angered you, he thinks you would never have left the house. But we will not quarrel over who was the more at fault, for we are none of us quite blameless in the matter, it seems to me. We agreed, however, that your wishes must be respected and you must on no account be pressed further. On that we are determined. Henceforth, you may decide your own path, whatever makes you happy. I know you've never liked the idea of London, so if you don't want to go, you need not."

"You mean I could stay here?" she said, brightening. Oh, the joy of not having to face a ballroom full of imperious aristocrats and expose her ineptitude to the world!

"If you like. Madge would stay with you, for propriety. Now, don't pull that face. You have to have a chaperon, you know. Or you could go back to Sagborough, and squeeze in with Allie and Ted. Or even Aunt Petronella, if you really want. You don't have to decide at once, puss. Take your time to think it over."

"I'd like to stay here," she said instantly. "We'll soon have better weather and I can walk every day. I'd love that, if Aunt Madge would not be too put out."

"She's not much minded for London, either," he said. "She says she'd feel like a fish out of water, not knowing the ways of these grand London folks, yet she'd feel obliged to go everywhere with you girls. But if you stay here, your mama will only have Rosie and Angie to manage."

"Who are far better fitted for society than I am," Julia said with a wry grimace. But then she had an uncomfortable thought. "But what about James? Will he feel... would it...?"

"Upset him if you stay? You'd not see much of each other, unless you go out of your way to bump into him. Only at church, and occasionally when you're out walking."

Not see much of him? That didn't sound like much fun.

"Jules, when I called on him this morning, he was writing a letter to you... to explain a few things, he said. To write the words he can't say to you. I said I would deliver the letter to you... if you want it."

He reached into a pocket and pulled out a neatly folded letter, bearing only the words, *'Miss J Fletcher'.*

Numbly, she took it from his outstretched hand. "What does it say?"

"I haven't read it, puss. I should, of course, or your mama should, and James expected me to, but I'd rather not. Whatever he has to say to you, I think it should be for your eyes alone, don't you?"

Mutely, she nodded.

"Then off you go and find a quiet corner to read it. I'll be here if you want to talk about it."

Outside the office she hesitated. Where should she go? Her bedroom was awash with gowns and boxes. Johnny and Will had set up the billiard table in the library. Aunt Madge was supervising the replacement of candles in the saloon. The gallery—? Oh, but there was a far better place. With a smile, she crept into the blue saloon, opened the door to the secret stair and began to climb.

The attics were freezing. She remembered the bedroom at the far end, filled with afternoon sunshine, and hurried along the passage, the glass roof lighting her way. The bedroom was just as she had last seen it, except that the lacquered vase on the washstand was gone. In its place was a piece of sheet music — how strange!

But she could not think of that now. Dusting off a chair, she sat and tore open the letter.

'*My dearest, most beloved Julia, Forgive my presumption in addressing you thus, and in the form of a letter, but it is impossible for me to say all that is in my heart when you are with me, for my tongue ties itself in knots and my brain turns to porridge. Pray allow me, then, to speak freely to you in this way, as I now must or my heart will surely burst. Perhaps you will never see this letter, but if it should reach your eyes, I beseech you to accept it in the humble spirit in which it is written. For some weeks I have been in relentless pursuit of you, regardless of your wishes in the matter. You have been charity itself, but you have made your feelings very plain on the subject, and I can only apologise with the utmost sincerity for the discourteous manner in which I have disregarded your expressed wishes. You have your reasons for not wishing to marry, undoubtedly, and even though I do not understand what they may be, I must and will respect them. Be assured that I shall pursue my suit no longer. You will be free from any further importunings on my part. I cannot change my own nature, however. I can no more stop loving you than I can cease to breathe. Julia, my dearest love, I lay my heart at your feet. There it will remain, and if you should choose to disregard it, I shall understand, but if ever the time comes that you see me in a different light, you need only reach out to me and I will be at your side. Such an outcome would delight me beyond all things, but however much I may wish it to come to pass, I no longer have any hope in that direction, and so my greatest desire is that you be free to make your own life, however it best pleases you. Whether you marry in the future, or whether you never take that step, then I hope and pray that you will always be happy and well loved and cherished. I remain and shall always be your devoted and affectionate friend, James Plummer.'*

21: Surprising News

Julia sat quite still for a long time, reading and rereading her letter, emotions roiling through her. Gratitude, primarily, to be so well loved, but also guilt, that she had brought him to this pass. James had always been such a buoyant man, who raised her spirits with every word, every smile. Yet his letter was humility itself, as if all the lightness of spirit had been scoured out of him. Was it truly her doing that had brought him so low? She had never meant to! How could she have helped it? There was nothing she could have done to avoid this outcome.

With all her heart, she wished she could have him back, the cheerful gamekeeper who had teased her by not telling her that he was one of the Plummers, or that he was the rector. She had joked that it would probably be her fate to marry the local parson, and he had smiled and said nothing and left her to find it out for herself. She smiled now as she remembered, but such sweet memories only made her feel worse. Tears trickled down her cheeks, but she dashed them

A Winter Chase: The Mercer's House Book 1

angrily away. She never cried, and she would not cry over James, no matter how much his words churned her up inside.

' *Julia, my dearest love, I lay my heart at your feet.'*

How could she be unmoved by such a declaration? She would have to be made of stone. Uneasily she was aware that it was in her power to relieve his suffering instantly. It would be the simplest thing in the world to agree to marry him, and he would smile at her again, his eyes creasing up in that charming way they had, and he would be happy.

If only she could explain it to him, how terrified she was, how impossible for her to marry anyone, least of all a good, kind man like James. He deserved better than a reluctant wife, filled with guilt because she had inadvertently caused him pain. That was no reason to marry.

Eventually, the cold seeped into her bones and she was forced to return to warmer parts of the house. This time, she used the servants' stair, and as soon as she reached the bedroom floor, she heard Mama's voice high with distress. Tucking the letter into her sleeve, she opened the door to find Mama and her sisters on the landing.

"Julia! There you are!" Mama cried as soon as Julia emerged. "Wherever have you been? We were frantic with worry in case you had—"

Of course! Every time she could not be found instantly, they would panic. "Oh, Mama, I am so sorry!" Impulsively, she threw her arms around her stepmother and hugged her tight. "What a thoughtless, thoughtless girl I am! Of course you were worried."

289

"There, there, dear," her stepmother said. "It is of no consequence, so long as you are safe. Ah, Mrs Graham, there you are. Pray tell everyone that Miss Julia is found. But where were you, dear? So that we may know where to look in future."

"I was in one of the attic rooms."

"The attic!" Angie cried. "What on earth were you doing up there?"

"Looking for a quiet place to be alone," Julia said. Then, because she was reluctant to mention her letter hidden in her sleeve, she added, "I wanted time to myself to think."

"But why—?" Angie began, but Mama cut her off with a wave of her hand.

"Julia has much to ponder at the moment. We must not deny her the right to solitude, if that is what she needs. All I ask, Julia, is that if you should decide to leave the house, you tell me so."

"Of course, Mama. I hope I know better now than to disappear without a word. Especially if it should be like to snow," she added, head dutifully bowed.

Angie snorted with laughter but Mama had no sense of humour. "I should hope you would not go out at all if it is like to snow, Julia."

"No, Mama," she said meekly.

"Rosie, Angie, back into your room, and help Hathaway and Sarah with the packing. Julia, a word in my dressing room, if you please."

Dutifully, Julia followed. As soon as the door was closed, she burst out, "Mama, I am very sorry—"

Mama laughed and waved her to silence. "Julia dear, you spend half your life apologising. Enough. Sit down, dear. I wondered what your father wished to say to you, that is all. I know he went to see Mr James Plummer this morning. Was there anything new?"

"He will not be paying his addresses to me any longer," she said, and wondered quite why that made her feel so downcast. She would still see him, after all, but without any silliness, so she should be pleased.

"Oh. Perhaps it is as well."

"And Pa said..." She hesitated, knowing that Mama was so keen on London. "He said I might stay here if I wished and not go to London, and Aunt Madge would chaperon me."

"And do you wish that?" Julia nodded, and Mama sighed. "I thought you might do so. Your father and Madge and I discussed it, and Madge does not mind staying with you."

"You aren't cross with me?" Julia said quietly.

Mama gave her a sideways look. "Julia, I should love to take you to town with us, if only to show you something of the wider world beyond the confines of your life thus far. All you have ever known is one small northern town and a tiny corner of Hertfordshire. In town you would meet a very different society, one that might appeal to you."

"A superior society?" Julia said mischievously.

"In some ways, yes," Mama said seriously. "Not in all.

London manners are very elegant, but the aristocracy is not always sound on questions of morality, so one must be cautious. But you would have enjoyed the sights of London, dear. It is a wondrous place indeed. However, if you are minded to stay here, I shall make no objection, you may be sure. It will make our stay in town a little easier."

"You will not have to worry about me tripping over my own feet in the cotillion, you mean," Julia said cheerfully.

"That was not what was in my mind, Julia. It is Mrs Reynell's insinuations that concern me more. If you are not to marry Mr Plummer, there will be whispers following us to town. Your absence will enable them to die down more quickly."

"Ah, yes. Mrs Reynell. Is there anything you wish me to do, Mama, anything that would help?"

"Apart from marrying, there is nothing that can help," she said crisply. "Water under the bridge, Julia. We must live with the consequences of that woman's malice, I fear."

~~~~~

James had Mrs Reynell on his mind, too. If he could have announced his betrothal to Julia, the foul rumours would have died down, but now they would fester and he could not allow her good name to be besmirched. Yet what could he do about it? Mrs Reynell was a respectable widow, whose word would be accepted without question.

He was sitting glumly over a glass of Madeira in the kitchen when Thomas came in, stamping snow from his boots.

"The thaw is setting in already," he said. "Snow never

lasts long at this time of year. We are almost into April, after all."

"Look what you've done to my clean floor, Master Thomas," Mrs Pound said, wiping floury hands on her apron. "Janet's just mopped that."

"Not to worry, Mrs Pound. I shall mop it again."

He did, too, whistling cheerfully as he worked, even while Mrs Pound grumbled on, pointing out tiny spots he had missed. Eventually, even her high standards were met, and Thomas subsided into a chair with a mug of coffee.

"Wine already, my friend? Is it truly so bad?"

"Mercer's been here, that's what's set him on edge," Mrs Pound said.

"Mr Fletcher? He came here?" Thomas said.

"He just wanted to thank me for taking Miss Fletcher home."

"Ah."

James answered the implicit question. "I shall not pursue Miss Fletcher any more."

"Ah."

"Now, that's a right shame," Mrs Pound said, as she rolled out pastry at the other end of the kitchen table. "Lovely girl, she is, no matter what that Mrs Reynell says."

"What exactly does she say?" James said. "No one repeats such tales to my face, but I should like to know."

"That Miss Julia set her cap at you from the day she

moved here, but there's no one'd blame her for that, not with you such a fine young gen'leman, an' all," Mrs Pound said. "And that she was in here alone with you for a whole hour, and me and Janet not here, and not even that Lightwood around to lend a shred of propriety. That's what she says. Not that you was up to no mischief, not with bloody cloths left for me to wash and bandages gone and the ointment used, and Mr Grimston's boy seeing everything that happened with that there bull in Boggy Meadow. Everyone knows you was telling the truth about all that."

"Everyone being the servants, I suppose," James said. "Whereas Mrs Reynell whispers in the ears of her acquaintances, who have not had the benefit of hearing the Grimston's boy's testimony, and are somewhat above the level of servants' gossip."

"Well, as to that, she's no better than a servant herself, that one."

"Mrs Reynell?" Thomas said, sitting up straighter. "Do you know something scurrilous about her, Mrs Pound? Oh, do tell!"

The cook looked uncomfortable suddenly. "I'm not one for gossiping, as you know, Master Thomas."

"Of course not, but a matter is only gossip if it is untrue," Thomas said sweepingly. "We are men of the cloth, Mrs Pound. We should know everything about our parishioners."

"Well, if you put it like that," Mrs Pound said. "And it *is* true. She came from Stevenage originally, Mrs Reynell, and my cousin has a place there, housekeeper to a very well-set-up gen'leman. A bachelor he's been all his life, but he always had… well, *women*, if you take my meaning."

Thomas yelped. "You cannot mean… that *Mrs Reynell* was his mistress?"

Mrs Pound blushed fiercely, an improbable sight on a woman of her mature years and as round as a dumpling. "I don't like to put labels like that on people, Master Thomas. Tisn't kind. She was his lady love, anyway, for about five years, so my cousin said. Early on she went away and when she came back, she called herself Mrs Reynell. There were two babes came along, but never a sight nor sign of any Mr Reynell. She never wanted no dealings with the babes, so her gen'leman sent them away somewhere. When he tired of her, and they always do, don't they? Well, he bought this house for her and here she is, giving herself airs as if she was somebody."

"Oh, but that is wonderful, Mrs Pound," Thomas said. "What a tale! But you need not worry that we shall reveal it to a soul. Our lips are sealed."

"Yours might be, but mine are not necessarily so," James said, with a grin.

"James! As a clergyman, surely you would not take advantage of such information."

"That witch has tried her very best to damage Julia's reputation. Is it right that she should get away with it?"

"As Christians, we should turn the other cheek."

"I am sorry to fall short of your high standards, my friend, but I have never been a very good clergyman, and clearly I am not a very good Christian either, for I feel only the

Old Testament will do for this occasion. An eye for an eye, Thomas, and a tooth for a tooth. I intend to have a friendly word with Mrs Reynell. Would you like to come and watch? You can defend me if she sets about me with a candelabrum."

Thomas chuckled. "That I should like to see. Let me get my coat."

~~~~~

APRIL

"Have you heard? Mrs Reynell has left the village," Angie said, bouncing into the breakfast parlour one morning. "Her carriage passed through the village not long after seven this morning."

"You were up early, flower," Pa said, eyes teasing over the rim of his coffee cup.

"I did not see it myself, naturally, but a great many people did, including Janet Pound on her way to the rectory, and she told the butcher's boy when he called, and he told Sarah, and Sarah told me. So it must be true," she ended triumphantly.

"You should not repeat servants' gossip, Angie," Mama said. "I suppose it is not known where she may be going?"

"Camberwell. Campbeltown. Camberley. Something of the sort."

"Camelford," Mama said. "She has a cousin there, I understand. Well, that is a relief. We shall not be plagued with any more nonsense from *that* direction."

"I expect she heard that Jules was to stay on here and

not go to town, and she was so horrified she upped and fled," Will said cheerfully.

"Am I so terrifying?" Julia said.

"Beyond compare, little sister. The way you stood up to her at supper that night was —"

"Thank you, Will, but none of us wish to be reminded of that night," Mama said briskly. "One may admire Julia's bravery without constantly speaking of it. Rosie, will you pass the apricot jam to your father, if you please. Mr Fletcher, what are your plans for the day?"

"Plans? We gentlemen of leisure don't have plans. Kelshaw might drop by later to show me his sketches for the new cow house."

Mama's eyebrows rose, but she said mildly, "And will you write to Brassington about the linens?"

"I will indeed, if you tell me precisely what I'm to say, or you could write to him yourself."

"A lady cannot write to a man of business so effectively as a man, my dear, and if you do not remind Brassington, I am certain that Mary and Anthony will forget, and the agency servants will not care about such details. I do not want to spend our first days in town chasing around draper's shops. Will, are you in for dinner tonight, not going into Ware for the evening?"

"I believe so, yes."

"And is your packing in hand?"

"Lester will do all that sort of thing you know. It is what I pay him for, after all."

Pa placed a hand on Mama's. "Lizzie, my dear, stop fretting. It will all work out, you may be sure. The London house is chosen, thanks to Will's efforts, the lease is drawn up, the servants are in place, Mrs Graham leaves tomorrow to arrange everything. Trust them to do their work properly."

"But I so want everything to be perfect. Our first proper season in town, and nothing must be allowed to go wrong, nothing!"

"And I want you to enjoy this famous season, and not worry yourself into a spin."

"She likes worrying herself into a spin," Julia said, smiling.

Her stepmother had the grace to laugh. "So I do, Julia, so I do. Ah, here is the mail. Thank you Enoch. One for you, Rosie, from Belinda Jupp."

"Lovely!" Angie cried. "Read it at once, and tell us all the news from Sagborough."

"Very well," Rosie said, neatly lifting the seal. "It says— oh! *Oh!*" And then, worryingly, "Oh dear."

"Whatever does it say?" Angie said. "Read it aloud, Rosie, do."

"Very well. *'Rosie, you will never guess what has happened! A man has arrived - no, a gentleman, a Mr Richard Osgood—'*"

Here she was interrupted by several squeaks of surprise from around the table. Even Mama raised her eyebrows a trifle.

"'—a Mr Richard Osgood, who arrived two days ago, travelling post, if you please, and before his feet even touched the ground in the yard of the Carrbridge Arms, he was asking for Miss Camilla Weston. After bespeaking his rooms and leaving his man to unpack, he got straight back in his carriage with one of the ostlers to direct the coachman, and drove at once to the Westons' house where he offered for Camilla on the spot. And even though he has been informed of her situation, he still wants to marry her and is to go to York for a licence so that he may carry her off with all due haste. And he is not the gentleman responsible for her present situation, for he never saw her until she went into Hertfordshire. Have you ever heard the like? Write at once and tell me more about him, for no one here knows a thing about him. Yours in astonishment, Belinda. Ricky has made me unseal this to add his best regards, which I forgot before. He thanks you for the description of your ball which sounds wonderful, except for—' Well, never mind that," Rosie added hastily.

"Great heavens! Richard Osgood!" Mama said.

"But he is a dean," Angie said. "Marrying *Camilla Weston!* He must be mad."

"He is in love," Rosie said.

"It's the same thing," Julia said.

"Well, I think it is romantic," Rosie said with a sigh. "To be so much in love that he goes racing up to Yorkshire in pursuit of her, and not be deterred by any obstacle. Camilla must be so thankful. How grateful I should be to find myself the object of so romantic an action, to have a man travel the length of the country to rescue me from a predicament."

"Is Camilla in a predicament?" Bella said. "What is this *situation* Belinda mentions?"

"Good heavens, is that the time?" Miss Crabtree said, jumping to her feet. "Come along Bella, Dorothea, we are late for our lessons. The globes, this morning, and then we must work at our Italian." And she hastened Bella out of the room.

"That child is so quiet, one forgets she is there," Mama said.

"She is not a child," Pa said. "Allie put her hair up at fourteen, after all, and dined with us even when we had company."

"Fourteen is far too young to know about Camilla's disgrace, however," Mama said serenely. "Besides, that was Sagborough. Things are different now. Sixteen or seventeen is time enough for a girl to make her debut in society."

"Poor Bella," Pa said.

Angie shook her head. "No, it is poor Miss Crabtree. Another two or three years of Bella and Dorothea."

"She doesn't mind Bella, or Dorothea," Pa said. "She understands about Dorothea, just as we do, if not better."

"But no one else does," Mama said. "Camilla may have teetered on the edge of society, but if she marries well and settles down she will be a respected matron. But Bella... who knows what will become of her?"

"She will be loved and have a home here, with her family," Will said. *"Always."*

22: *Reasons*

Julia was unsettled. Ever since she had read James's letter, she had felt oddly disconnected. It must be because all around her the preparations for London gathered pace, and she was left out of the whirlwind. It could not be because of James, for she now had exactly what she wanted, hadn't she? She would be *'free from any further importunings',* free to be his friend without any expectations from him or anyone else. And Mrs Reynell had gone away, so she was free of the threat of any further malice.

She was free. So why did she feel so restless? If she could just see James, see him smile at her again in that way he had that made her want to smile too, then she would be perfectly happy, she knew it. But he was nowhere to be found. She saw nothing of him on her walks, and although she often found herself passing the little cottage, the shutters were closed and no smoke emerged from the chimney. When the Fletchers occasionally went out for dinner, he was never amongst the other guests. But when he even failed to appear at church, Julia realised the dreadful truth — he was avoiding her.

With only two days before the departure to London, the rest of the family was busy making their farewells. Julia found herself standing a little aside, too disheartened to talk to anyone. She saw Sir Owen sitting on a bench near the lychgate. He was alone, too, waiting for the rest of the Plummers to finish talking to their friends. He smiled invitingly at her, and obediently she sat down beside him.

"You are not having second thoughts about remaining at the Park for the spring, Miss Fletcher?"

"No, not at all. There is nothing in London to excite me. The only pleasure it would afford me is to watch the enjoyment of my family."

"London's loss is Hertfordshire's gain, however. I shall hope to enjoy your company very often at the Manor."

"Do you not go to town yourself, sir?"

"I prefer the quietude of the country, Miss Fletcher. Lady Plummer likes to go, for she is enlivened by the spectacle of the *Beau Monde* in all its glory. Michael will also go in his eternal quest for a bride. And Lord and Lady Charles will go, of course, for all Charles's relations will be there. I shall visit them from time to time, but I never spend the whole season in town, not any more. But I shall not be lonely, for Patricia stays with me, to look after the children, and I have my brother, Morgan. And I hope that you and Miss Paton will bear me company, too, and dine with us sometimes."

"Thank you, that would be lovely. But... what about

James? He will be here to bear you company, won't he?"

"I cannot say what James will do. He can leave the parish in Mr Leadbetter's capable hands, so some years he goes to town but other years he does not."

"Is he well?" Julia said impulsively. "I have not seen him for a while, so..."

"He is well enough. You must not worry about him, for what happened is none of your fault. I am very sorry for James's sake that matters could not be otherwise between you, but no doubt you have your reasons for rejecting him."

"Marriage terrifies me!" she cried.

"Ah, yes, for a woman it is a daunting undertaking."

"Exactly so!"

"Every child brings a terrible risk. So many wonderful women are lost in childbed."

Julia chewed her lip. "No, that's not it, for such matters are in God's hands. Short or long, marriage is for my whole life and beyond, and I don't know how it would change me. I feel that... it would diminish me, somehow. That I would become a pale shadow of myself, subsumed in society's constraint of wifely duty and unrelenting motherhood. I am not like other women, Sir Owen. I don't sit and embroider, or paint watercolours of pretty vistas, or dream of the day when I have my own establishment. I'm not elegant or graceful or accomplished. My sisters are all those things, but I'm not and it doesn't worry me in the slightest. I'm *happy* as I am, and I don't want to change."

"And no man who truly loved you would ever want you

to change," Sir Owen said at once. "In my view, Miss Fletcher, a contented marriage requires only three things. Firstly, enough money to live upon comfortably, for nothing drags people down more than the dispiriting and endless quest for economy. Secondly, a degree of affection, and I do not mean romantic love, for that can lead one astray into the most improbable of matches."

Julia laughed, thinking of Camilla and the besotted Richard Osgood. "Very true!"

"Exactly so. But there must be a fondness, or liking. If one is to spend the rest of one's life with a person, it had better be someone agreeable. And thirdly, there must be consideration for the other, and that must apply equally to both. If one is always giving way to the other, then resentment may build." He lapsed into silence for a moment, but then he sighed, and continued, "Consideration for the other. With that, the marriage will endure and love will only grow."

"But how can anyone be sure of that?"

Sir Owen smiled. "No one can be *sure*, Miss Fletcher. Marriage can be unpredictable, just as with any other element of life. How philosophical we are become! I cannot help but feel that this is a conversation you should have with James."

"Would he want to talk to me? He's avoiding me, isn't he?"

"He is feeling a little sorry for himself just now, and shirks all company, not just yours. He spends most of his days up at the hut, but I believe he would be happy to talk to you

— to better understand your reasons for refusing him."

The various chattering groups outside the church now began to break apart, and Sir Owen was claimed by his lady. Julia joined the rest of her family and walked in pensive silence across the road to the gatehouse. There she stopped.

"Pa, Mama, would you mind if I go for a walk?" she said.

"Alone?" Mama said, frowning.

"If you have no objection. I shall not go far, just up the hill to the gate, and then back across the park. Please?"

"Aye, why not?" Pa said. Then, seeing Mama's concerned face, he added, "The exercise will do her good, love. She's been brooding too much lately."

With a quick word of thanks, Julia set off at once before Mama had time to say anything that might change Pa's mind, for he was very swayed by her views nowadays.

Overnight rain had freshened the air, and Julia breathed deeply as she strode uphill. The track leading towards the gate was edged with cheerful spring greens and yellows, cowslips and bobbing daffodils pushing through the detritus of last year's fallen leaves. Up and up she climbed, until the gate came into sight. But that was not her destination. Nearer at hand was the familiar ragged hedge that sheltered James's hiding place.

The cottage was silent and firmly shuttered when Julia arrived, and there was no smoke visible from the chimney, but chinks of light between the slats of the shutters suggested that James was within. She knocked, but when there was no reply, she lifted the latch and went inside.

Only a single candle lit the gloom, flickering in the draught from the door. The fire was out, nothing but a pile of ashes. At first, she could not see James at all, but as her eyes adjusted to the lack of light, she made out his outline, lying huddled in blankets on the sofa.

"James? May I come in?"

"Of course." He sounded tired. As he sat up and swung his legs to the floor, unfolding himself from the blankets, she could see that he wore no coat, and his neckcloth was untied, hanging limply from his throat. With his untidy hair and unshaven cheeks, he looked utterly lost. All his usual insouciance had drained out of him, leaving him oddly passive.

She had never seen him like this — vulnerable and hurting. With all her heart, she wished she could take him in her arms and rock him like a child until he felt better. But that would only prolong his pain. She could only say what she had come to say, and then leave him in peace. "I wanted to talk to you — is that all right?"

"Of course," he said again, and her heart somersaulted at the expression on his face. He looked so sad, as if he had lost all interest in life, all hope.

"Aren't you cold? The fire's gone out."

"Has it?" He shrugged. "I'm warm enough. Blankets outside, brandy inside."

Now she saw the bottle and empty glass on the table beside the sofa.

"There are no logs here. Will you fetch some?"

Wordlessly he rose and went outside, while she knelt at the fire, raking ashes and relaying the fire. When he returned with an armful of logs, she quickly lit the tinder. It blazed into life, bringing a ghostly red light to the room, making her shadow dance against the walls. He had slumped onto the sofa again, so she dragged a stool nearer and sat down in front of him.

"I went to see your father... to explain... why I don't want to marry. He... he said I should talk to you. If you will let me. I don't want to... to upset you... or—"

"It is all right, Julia," he said tiredly.

"So... I may stay? And explain?"

"I will listen to whatever you wish to say to me."

But his tone was so flat that she wanted to cry, and for a moment she could not speak. Licking her lips, she took a deep breath and gave a shaky laugh. "Now I don't know how to begin."

He smiled a little then, and her spirits lifted. "At the beginning, I dare say."

"Yes." She laughed again. "Very well. The beginning. That was Ted, I suppose. My half-brother, Ted, you know? My eldest brother." He nodded, so she went on, "I never thought much about marriage until Ted started courting Cathy. That was six... no, seven years ago now, and he did it very properly, very seriously. Ted was always serious. He went to see her father, and then he started calling on her, and taking her out and about. All very correct. She was only a mill manager's daughter, with no money to bring to the marriage and she was no beauty, either, but Ted knew exactly what he wanted. And the curious thing is that she changed. The more attention he paid her, the more she blossomed, somehow, until she was almost beautiful. She *glowed*, and on her wedding day she could not have looked more lovely. But then... the babies started coming, and all that disappeared. Now, you would never know how lovely she was. She looks tired and worn out and she is only twenty-six." She heaved a sigh. "And then there is Allie."

"Your eldest sister?"

She nodded. "Allie looks just as she ever did. She never glowed in that way, not even on her wedding day, but she used to be a happy, lively person. Optimistic. Things would always work out for the best — she truly believed that. But then she fell in love with Jack Ewbank. No one else would do, and so she set out to get him and she did, because Allie always got what she wanted. I suppose Pa spoiled us girls, because he was always indulging us — new gowns, bracelets, outings, whatever we wanted. Allie expected Jack to treat her the same way, but he's very careful with his money and he won't do it. Well, he doesn't have Pa's money, I suppose, although he'll have his father's brewery, in time.

"So Allie grumbles all the time. Nothing is ever right for her. She hoped Pa would help out, but he says she's Jack's responsibility now. And so she's miserable and Cathy's exhausted and I don't want to be like either of them, James, truly I don't. They both thought marriage would be wonderful, and it isn't, not for either of them. They fell in love, and... love deceived them, and what is left after love is gone?" She smiled a little. "Your father said as long as there is respect and consideration for each other, the marriage will endure and love will grow, but I don't see how it can!"

"My father is wise," James said, and now he sounded more like himself. "He has been married for a long time, through some difficult times, but he is unswervingly devoted to Mother, even though she has turned into quite a watering pot these last four years."

"Because of selling the Park?"

"Exactly. She loved that house, you see. We moved there when Grandmother died, some twenty years ago, and Mother became mistress of it. When Grandfather died and she finally became Lady Plummer, she felt she had achieved her life's ambition."

"And then your father sold it to us."

"Not immediately. We tried to find alternatives, but nothing came of them. Poor Michael set out to rescue us by marrying an heiress, and that ended disastrously. He was ill for a long time, so in the end Father chose to sell. He could not bear to be in debt. Building that house had almost ruined us, but Grandfather carried on as though nothing was wrong. It was a shock when we finally understood the enormity of the problem. Father was adamant that the debts must be cleared, and now they have been. He is solvent again for the first time in decades. Mother will come to understand that the sacrifice had to be made. Houses do not matter very much, in truth. It is people who are important, and I believe Mother still adores Father, despite everything. Outward appearances can be deceptive."

"I suppose that's true," Julia said. "One can't tell what

goes on beneath the surface. Perhaps Allie and Cathy are truly happy at heart. But how can anyone know? I am so afraid of losing *myself*, James. Pa lets me be just as I want to be, but a husband, even one as kind and gentle as you, would be different. *I* would be different. I would be responsible for your happiness and not just my own. Could I do it? The question is unanswerable."

"Marriage is bound to change one, but I think it must be a change for the better, ultimately. It would certainly change *me* for the better. Here I am, selfish and indolent and good for nothing, but you have made me understand myself as nothing and no one else before you had ever managed. If I had you to care for…"

His voice cracked, and she whispered, "I am so sorry, James."

In response, he smiled at her, and there was so much open affection in his face that her stomach flip-flopped again. Such a lovely man! Yet she was making him miserable.

He patted the sofa. "Come and sit beside me, Julia."

Willingly she did so, and he slid an arm round her waist. "How does this feel? Are you comfortable?"

"Yes."

"You have no aversion to my person, then?"

"Oh, *no!* I *like* you, James. I have always liked you. If I were to marry anyone, it would be you." He winced a little at these words, so she rushed on, "But I don't love you. I don't think I'm capable of loving anyone, not in that way. My family, of course, and friends… but nothing more than that. I can't love you as a wife should love a husband. I don't feel that… oh, I can't describe it. Allie used to say that her heart jumped about whenever Jack came into the room, and my heart doesn't do anything like that. I don't glow like Cathy did. I'm always very pleased to see you but… it's not the same. I'm fond of you, but—" She stopped, remembering Sir Owen's words. *A degree of affection*. That was all a marriage needed. Not romantic love, just a fondness. For a moment she quailed, and his face was filled with such grief that her heart ached for him. But she could not marry for mere fondness. "I never meant to hurt you."

"I know that." His lips quirked into a wry smile. "Nor did I ever mean to fall in love with you, but it happened anyway and now…"

"Now I've made you miserable."

He nodded. "The worst of it is… seeing you all the time."

"Oh. Do you want me to go?"

"No, no." His arm tightened around her waist. "No, it is not this kind of seeing you that troubles me, but when we meet publicly… I know how a gentleman is supposed to behave in such circumstances. I have to be polite and treat you with exactly the same courtesy as always, neither distinguishing you in any way, nor drawing attention to you, and doing nothing to distress you. And I cannot do it. I find it impossible to dissemble and pretend you mean nothing to me, dearest Julia. That is the dilemma I was pondering when you arrived, trying to decide what to do. Needless to say, I know what I ought to do, for your comfort and my own sanity. I must go away from here."

Some odd emotion skittered through her. "Go away? Where?"

"I have friends in Bath."

"*Bath!* You mean to go to Bath?" Her voice had risen in alarm. He was going away! "For how long?"

"Until I can face you again with some degree of composure. A few weeks... months... sometimes I feel it might take years."

"*Years!*" She jumped to her feet and paced across the room to the door, leaning her forehead against it. Why did she feel as if the earth had dropped away beneath her feet and she was falling into a dark pit? What was the matter with her?

"Julia...?" He had followed her across the room.

Spinning to face him, she whispered, "I'll miss you abominably. Who will rescue me when I get into trouble if you're not here? What is the point of going out for a walk without the possibility of bumping into you? How can I get through all the interminably boring dinners and card evenings without you to share a joke with? It will be horrid without you! You *can't* go away and leave me all alone!"

And somehow she was crying. Why was she crying? What was the matter with her? She had wanted to be free, hadn't she? Well, now she was, so why was she so upset?

"Julia..." He reached out for her but she held up her hands, as if to keep him at bay. At once his arms dropped.

"No, don't hold me. I have to *think.*"

"Do you want a brandy?" She couldn't see him clearly through the unstoppable tears, but his voice was gentle, almost caressing.

"No, no. Nothing. Don't *distract* me. James, it seems to me that if you stay here, you will be miserable, but if you go away we'll *both* be miserable, and that isn't right, is it? What is the point of us both being miserable?"

Wordlessly he watched her, his face unreadable.

"I can't bear to think that I'll never see you again," she cried.

Still he watched, his breathing rapid. One hand lifted, as if he would stroke her face, but then it fell to his side again. He said nothing, waiting...

"Whereas if we were married," she said slowly, with a shuddering breath, "you would be happy, and I would always have someone to rescue me and bump into on walks and share a joke with at boring evening parties. And afterwards, we would go back to the rectory and toast bread and cheese in the kitchen and... and that would be lovely, wouldn't it?"

He nodded slowly, and now she could see something else in his face. Hope, that was it. He was beginning to hope.

"And then we would go upstairs together."

He tilted his head to one side. "You are not afraid of that part of it?" His voice was low.

"No. Allie says it's wonderful."

He gave a bark of laughter. "Well, God bless Allie for that, at least. I am glad that she finds some happiness in her marriage. But in time, there would be children. How do you feel about that?"

"I don't feel old enough to be responsible for another human being, particularly not a tiny scrap of a creature like a baby. But if he grows up to be like you, with your smile and eyes that crease up at the corners—" Then she was crying too hard to speak.

"Julia."

This time he took her in his arms and she made no protest, allowing him to hold her tight while she wept onto his shoulder and soaked the linen of his shirt. He said nothing, but his arms were tight around her, warm and comforting. And her mind cleared as abruptly as mist fading on a summer morning. And finally, at long last, understanding dawned on her.

"You do realise what you've done, don't you?" she said into his loose cravat. "You've given it to me."

"What have I given you?"

"*Love.* I've caught it from you." She felt the rumble of his laughter.

"Like an infectious disease? Measles, perhaps."

"Some kind of horrid fever, that's what it feels like at the moment. I'm all shaky, just thinking about you going away. That's what this is, isn't it? Not heart-jumping, not like that, but... misery when you're not around." Wonderingly, she gazed up at him. "It must be love... mustn't it?"

He nodded. "Sounds like it."

"Is that how it is for you?"

"Well, I get the heart-jumping too, but the misery? Oh, yes."

She sighed. "James, I've been such a fool, thinking up all sorts of excuses and all the time... I think I must have been in love with you almost from the start, or well on the way to it. Even when I thought you were the gamekeeper."

"I certainly was in love with you. I remember seeing you sitting on the gate at High Field, swinging one leg, your hair busily escaping from your bonnet and I knew there and then that you were the one for me. Julia..." He shifted a little so that he could look into her eyes, his hands cupping her face. "Dearest Julia, my heart is at your feet, where it has been since that moment. Will you take it?"

"Only if you will take mine." She exhaled slowly. "Do you know, I came here to explain to you exactly why I can't marry you and now... Will you take care of me, James?"

"I will. I promise to rescue you from every rampaging bull and angry huntsman and jealous widow, and in return you must remind me when Sunday comes round, so that I remember to don my surplice."

"Do you forget?"

"I have been known to do so. You will help me to be a less terrible clergyman."

"I'll try. Oh, James, it will be all right, won't it? We'll be happy, won't we?"

"It will be all right. Our marriage will be whatever we want it to be. Oh, there will be trials, I have no doubt. Things will happen, perhaps we will quarrel sometimes and yell at each other."

"But then you will kiss me like you did on the snowy day, and we'll entirely forget what we were quarrelling about."

He chuckled. "Did you like that? The angry kiss?"

"Mmm. I like all your kisses, but the angry kiss was... wonderful." She sighed. "I didn't know until then just how much you cared about me. I'd seen you amused and light-hearted and gentle, but I'd never seen you passionate before. It was a revelation."

"Oh." He seemed surprised. "I thought I had gone too far, but it was wonderful, was it not?" Then he laughed. "Kissing you is always wonderful. Sweet and gentle kisses..." He touched his lips softly to hers. "Friendly kisses..." A firmer kiss. "Ardent kisses..."

The room fell into silence for a long, long time.

23: Family Matters

James was dizzy with joy. She was his at last! They walked hand in hand to the gate and then across the park to the house, saying nothing but every so often they would glance at each other and laugh in delight. At such moments, when he saw her face suffused with happiness, he was filled with such contentment that his throat tightened and he was not sure he would ever be coherent again.

The Fletchers were surprised of course, but after the initial cries of amazement, Mr Fletcher said, "Well, with Julia we've learnt to expect the unexpected." Everyone laughed, champagne was called for and there was general celebration.

"When will the wedding be?" Angie said, spinning like a top in excitement.

James and Julia exchanged glances. "We have not discussed that yet," he said.

"The sooner the better," Julia said. "Don't you think?"

"You will find no objections from me," he said, feeling

his already wide smile increasing still further.

"But not while we are in London, surely?" Angie said. "Rosie and I have to be your bridesmaids."

"We can return from London for a night or two, I expect," Pa said.

"What about wedding clothes?" Mama said. "I shall not see a Fletcher daughter married without proper wedding clothes. You can spend a week or so in town while we visit the warehouses, Julia, and then you can be married July. It is only three months, after all."

James's spirits sank again. Ah well, three months was not such a long time to wait, when they would have the rest of their lives together. After a while, he remembered that his own family was as yet unaware of his change in circumstances, so, after accepting an invitation to dine *en famille* at the Park that evening, he left for the Manor. He took the short cut across the deer park, hardly noticing his surroundings, his head was so filled with happy thoughts.

He found his mother and Letitia alone in the parlour.

"Good heavens, James, what are you about to be coming here in such a state?" his mother cried. "You look as if you have just rolled out of bed."

It was a fair comment, and pretty close to the truth. "I beg your pardon, Mother, Letitia. I only wished to—"

His father came in with a flurry of smiles. "James! How good to see you! Are you to dine with us tonight?"

"No, I—"

"He will have to put some effort into his appearance if he does," Letitia said coldly. "You insult us by appearing in such a dishevelled state, brother."

"I apologise again, Letitia. I have some news—"

"You have not even shaved today," his mother said.

"What does that matter?" Sir Owen said. "I for one am pleased to see him."

"I shall be pleased also when he is respectably attired," his mother said. "Go home and attend to yourself, James, and we shall see you at dinner."

"Will you please listen?" James said testily. "I am *not* dining here tonight, for I am engaged at the Park. I came here only to tell you that Julia has accepted me at last. Good day to you, Mother, Letitia, Father."

He bowed and would have made his escape, but Letitia squealed and his mother laughed. *Laughed!*

"You will not marry that hoyden, James Plummer."

"I hesitate to contradict a lady, but I will, Mother."

"They are both of age," Sir Owen said mildly. "Her family approve, and I have no objection. You will just have to become accustomed to the idea, I am afraid, Lady Plummer."

"Certainly not. We are not having Fletcher blood despoiling the Plummer line. Oh, I say nothing about the girl herself, although she is not at all what any rational person would care for, but the family is unacceptable."

"Because of the taint of trade, do you mean?" James said.

"That alone should render them ineligible in the eyes of any right-thinking person, and if you had any consideration for my feelings, you would never wish to form an alliance with the very people who drove us from our home and forced us into the most unpleasant economies." James and his father would both have objected to this gross misrepresentation, but she waved them to silence. "I say nothing about that, however. My wishes have never been considered. No, my object is otherwise — because of the taint of lunacy." Her tone was triumphant. "The youngest girl — Isabella, is it? — is quite insane. She talks to herself and believes that there is another person there. The servants have to set a place for this non-existent person at table, and the family fall in with the pretence, humouring her. No doubt she would become violent if challenged. The so-called governess is undoubtedly there to ensure the child is safely locked away at night, especially when the moon is full. I will not have insanity brought into the family, and that is an end to the matter."

There was a long silence. James looked at his father, whose usually impassive face was clouded.

"We had better talk about this," Sir Own said. "The library, James."

The library. He was taking it seriously then.

As always, the room was chilly from disuse. James busied himself with lighting a fire while Michael was sent for, for no matter of significance to the family could be discussed without Michael.

His face lit up when he saw James. "Brother! At last! Are you well? You look tired."

"I am well. I am engaged to Julia, Michael, but Mama will not have it. She thinks Bella Fletcher is crazy."

"Oh. Congratulations, but... *is* she crazy?"

"I hardly know her well enough to judge. I have seen her perhaps twice, at a distance, and once, very briefly, to speak to." He thought uneasily of Bella running about in the park, diving behind trees, as if hiding from someone, and then dancing all by herself but talking to an invisible dancer. When he had spoken to her, she had talked about the other girl as if she were real. There was some truth in what Mama said. "But she does not strike me as insane. Unusual, perhaps, but nothing worse than that."

"Nevertheless, it is a serious objection," Sir Owen said. "If Michael were married and with a string of sons to his name, the risk would be worth taking, but until that time... I will talk to Fletcher about this, but James, unless he is able to reassure me on this point, I must withdraw my approval for the match."

"I am of age, Father," James said, but without heat. He could see that his father would not be moved.

"That is so, and you are financially independent, but you are also a dutiful son. I hope you would not marry against the express wishes of both your parents."

"No, Father," he said sadly.

"Do not look so crestfallen. As soon as Michael is safely married and has an heir, there will be no harm in it. You can wait a little while longer, surely?"

"Yes, Father."

"I will do my very best to find a bride in town this year," Michael said. "There is bound to be someone who will suit me."

"Of course," James said, but his words were hollow. His brother had been looking for a bride for years without success, and why should this year be otherwise? All his hopes were destroyed, and he could not see any possibility of marrying Julia within five years. And would she wait? That was the question.

~~~~~

It was a very different James who presented himself in the saloon at Chadwell Park that evening. It was not merely the rumpled and disordered clothing which had vanished, but so had his buoyant spirits. When he had left Julia that afternoon, he had been happy, excited, sparkling with energy and enthusiasm. Now he was dejected again, the icy hand of fear clawing at his insides. He was going to lose Julia after all, and he could not see what to do about it.

"Whatever is it?" Julia whispered to him. "What has happened?"

"I must talk to your father," he said heavily. "I have a letter for him from my father. Perhaps this can all be cleared up very speedily, but if not, then I fear this must be a very long betrothal."

Pa took them both into his office, and read the letter from Sir Owen carefully, before showing it to Julia.

"Well, this is a setback, true enough, but it need not deter you, surely, James? You are of age, and not beholden to your father for income or position."

"No, sir, but you would not have me marry in the face of his explicit disapproval, would you? I am not the heir, but since Michael is as yet unmarried, my own marriage is a matter of some interest to the family, and if there *is* lunacy in the bloodline, you can well understand my father's hesitation."

"But it doesn't deter *you*, does it?"

James could not at that moment think of any circumstance which would deter him from marrying Julia. "Heavens, no! And if Michael fails in his quest for a bride yet again this spring, then I am quite prepared to defy my father and marry Julia anyway. It would be better, however, if he could be convinced that Isabella is not quite howling at the moon."

Pa chuckled. "You may see her behaviour and judge for yourself, for we dine as a family this evening, with no ceremony. Bella will be there, and so, possibly, will Dorothea."

"The legendary Dorothea," James said lightly. "I look forward to making her acquaintance."

They returned to the saloon, and everyone was there, excepting Will, whose manful struggles with his cravat always made him late. James bowed politely over Bella's hand and asked her how she did.

"I am very well, thank you, Mr Plummer," she answered composedly.

"And Dorothea? She is well, too?"

Her eyes narrowed. "Are you mocking me, sir?"

"Not in the slightest. Did she like the picture you painted of the primroses and daffodils?"

She smiled then, her face lighting up. He had thought her a solemn child until then, not plain, precisely, but with no animation to her countenance. When she smiled, however, he saw at once the resemblance to her elder sisters. "She liked it very much. She said she thought it was one of my best paintings ever, for I am not a great proficient in water colours, but it came out very well. I put leaves around the edge, just as you suggested."

"I believe the idea of that was entirely your own, Miss Fletcher," he said gravely. "I merely put the thought of leaves into your mind."

"It was a happy thought," she said.

Will arrived at that moment, some ten minutes after the hour, and Keeble, with an air of relief, announced dinner at once. James sat at Mrs Fletcher's right hand, as the guest of honour, but he had Julia on his other side, and across the table sat Bella and the empty chair for Dorothea. The footman gravely held the chair for the non-existent girl, and slid it towards the table, just as was done for every other lady present. When the dishes were passed around, Bella laid a little from several dishes on Dorothea's plate.

James watched it all without comment. He could quite see why his mother was so unnerved by such behaviour, for he found it a little disturbing himself. Yet the most chilling part was that no one else in the family seemed to think it at all odd. They would ask Bella if Dorothea would like to try the larded sweetbreads — "For I know that is one of her favourites," Angie said — and the footmen even poured wine to set before the empty chair.

And yet it seemed harmless enough. In every other respect, Bella's behaviour was irreproachable, that of a perfectly well brought up young lady who, if she were only to leave her imaginary friend behind, would blend seamlessly with the gentrified world her family now inhabited.

When the ladies had withdrawn, James and Will joined Mr Fletcher at the foot of the table, and Mr Fletcher showed his son the letter from Sir Owen.

"Lunacy!" Will said. "Bella is... a little odd, I grant you, but she is as inoffensive a creature as ever breathed. What harm does it do to go along with her little fantasies? Mama was always insistent that we should accept her as she is, and not try to make her conform to society's norms."

"And I've no quarrel with that," Mr Fletcher said. "Edith and I were of one mind on that subject. But if Bella's little fantasies, as you call them, are to prevent Julia marrying, well, I don't like that one little bit."

"Nothing will prevent the marriage, sir," James said at once. "Not unless Julia cries off, for I certainly shall not. It does mean a longer betrothal than either of us might wish, however. We must wait until Michael is safely married."

"But even then there is no guarantee that you and your heirs will be removed from the inheritance," Will said. "At what point will Sir Owen give his consent? When your brother marries? When his wife is with child? Or must you wait until he has two sons? It could be years — or never."

"Not never," James said. "I cannot tell you when my father will relent, but sooner or later he will."

"And you do not feel that this is the moment to rebel against your father's strictures?" Will said with a mischievous grin. "Fathers are not always right, after all, and a son must eventually learn to be his own man."

Mr Fletcher smiled at him, and acknowledged it.

"It may be so in your family," James said heavily, "but Sir Owen is a stickler for duty and obedience. He gave up his own much-loved career in the army to return home when his elder brother died, and he has never given less than his best for his family and the estate. He has made difficult decisions in recent years, as you are all too aware. Michael and I both live in dread of disappointing him in some way. Mother... well, Mother is different, less rational about certain things, but Father is so *reasonable.* He would never force either of us, or the girls either, into a distasteful marriage, nor did he push me into a career for which I am patently unsuited. He is the most accommodating of parents, in general. So when he *does* take a stand, I cannot ignore his wishes, and I am sure you would think the less of me if I were to do so."

"Certainly," Mr Fletcher said, "for I myself was forced to decide between obedience and my own desires, long ago. I chose obedience then and I still think it was the right thing to do."

"Then you understand my position," James said. "Julia and I must perforce wait a little while for our perfect happiness."

Mr Fletcher sighed heavily. "That's all very well, and I

like a son who honours his father as much as the next man, but my concern is Julia. She's always gone her own way, and she may not want to wait indefinitely."

The icy chill around James's heart tightened its grip. "Then so be it. I must do what I believe to be right."

"That is all any of us can do," Mr Fletcher said. "Shall we re-join the ladies? I think it's time we had a family discussion about this, and decide what we can do."

"There is nothing to be done," James said despairingly.

"Let's see about that, shall we?" Fletcher said.

~~~~~

As a young girl, Julia had once climbed a mountain, or perhaps it was no more than a large hill, but it had seemed very large and very high to her childish self. She had been obliged to walk and scramble a great distance before reaching the top, where Great-uncle Rowley had assured her there would be a fine view. And then, just as they trudged wearily up the last rocky slope, the mist came down and the view was gone.

Julia felt rather the same way now, as though she had come through a trying ordeal to reach some promised prize, only to have it snatched away at the last minute. She was too stunned to be angry with Lady Plummer, who might easily have spoken earlier when the marriage was first mooted, instead of waiting until it was all agreed and everyone seemed happy with it.

The long evening had been got through somehow. James was too well-bred to allow his feelings to interfere with civility, so he made conversation as if there was nothing in the world amiss. When he looked at Julia, she saw a softening in his eyes, and his voice changed, too. Had he always been that way with her and she had simply never noticed it before? Or perhaps it was a new development, but she decided that she liked it. Such obvious signs of his affection made her feel cherished and special. Pa had always loved her, of course, and told her so, but he loved all of them equally. James was the first person who loved her more than anyone else in the world. It was a strange feeling for someone who had always been a free spirit, going her own way and asking for nothing.

The four sisters, even Bella, gathered on the big bed that Rosie, Angie and Julia shared to discuss the dramas of the day. Julia had little to say. She would be married soon or late, and no amount of speculation would change the course of events. But the others waxed eloquent on the injustice of it all, and so Julia let them speak as they would.

"It is so unfair," Angie said. "First Mrs Reynell, and now this. You are so unlucky, Jules."

"Poor Julia," Rosie said tearfully. "To have found happiness only to have it snatched away again at once."

"It has not been snatched away yet," Bella said. "Only postponed. You will just have to be patient, Jules."

"Not my strongest suit," Julia said, pulling a face.

"Oh, but for Mr Plummer!" Rosie cried. "Such a charming man, and so in love with you... you can be patient for him, surely, sister? Poor, poor Mr Plummer."

"And poor me," Bella said robustly. "You will not leave me out of your lamentations, I hope Rosie, for I believe I am the worst maligned here."

"So you are, dearest," Rosie said, weeping afresh. "It is cruel of Lady Plummer to say such horrid things about you and blight poor Julia's prospects."

"It blights your prospects, too," Bella said. "And Angie's and Will's. One madwoman in the family casts a taint over everyone. You will all be viewed with suspicion in London, you know."

Angie gasped with horror as the full implications sank in. "*No!* We would not... would we?"

"Very likely," Bella said. "But it is quite all right, Angie. I know what I have to do."

24: A Quarrel

James breakfasted with his family at the Manor the next morning, not because he wanted their company especially, but half in hopes that a good night's sleep might have softened his father's stance. But there was no sign of it, and the meal proceeded in its usual leisurely way, with nothing much said beyond the customary discussion of everyone's plans for the day.

"Come into my book room, James," Sir Owen said, as he rose at the end of the meal.

"Very good, sir."

Sir Owen's book room was an ill-situated apartment at the side of the house, given an air of gloom by a large oak tree just outside. The room was too small to house more than a desk and a couple of chairs, but a narrow bookcase squeezed in behind the door was enough to entitle it to its name. The real book room, now designated a study, had been commandeered by Lord Charles for his own use the moment he had married Letitia, and Sir Owen had not liked to throw him out of it on his return to the Manor.

"Now then, James," Sir Owen said, sitting behind his desk and waving James to the opposite chair, for all the world as if he were an attorney or a bailiff, "tell me about your dinner last night."

"It was rather good, although there was only one course. The loin of veal was particularly good."

Sir Owen's eyebrows rose. "It does not become you to be facetious. Was the girl there?"

"Isabella? She was."

"And... the friend?"

"She was there too."

"James, if you make me drag every little detail out of you, I shall be convinced that everything Lady Plummer said is true. Give me a full account of her, if you please."

"I beg your pardon, Father. Let me tell you all that I can of her. The first impression is good. She is in appearance everything that a girl of fourteen ought to be, well grown and bidding fair to be as pretty and accomplished as her sisters, in time. I assure you, no one would see the least thing amiss with her. But at dinner... Mother was right about that. There was a place set for this friend of hers — Dorothea, she is called."

"Oh, she has a name, does she?"

"Naturally she has a name. The family makes no fuss about it, and the servants are clearly used to it by now. To be honest, it seems harmless to me, and rather charming."

"But not *normal*, James."

"Unusual, perhaps, but I would not describe her as a lunatic."

"You are hardly an impartial observer," Sir Owen said.

"I hope I would never let my own wishes colour my judgement," James said stiffly. "But in any event, it is your opinion which matters, not mine."

"And I must maintain my reservations until I have seen the girl for myself. She has attended church, I dare say, but nothing about her drew my notice. Next time, I shall look out for her. A little conversation with her will put me in a better position to judge."

"You could go to the Park and ask to see her," James said. "I am sure Mr and Mrs Fletcher would be pleased to oblige you."

"That would look too particular," his father said, frowning through bushy eyebrows. "One does not like to give credence to a rumour such as this by drawing attention to it."

"Father, the rumour is already circulating," James said impatiently. "A visit would only be seen as a conscientious attempt to verify or refute it."

"I shall see her at church," his father repeated. "I will not be rushed over this, James. Marriage is a matter of decades, so a delay of a few days or weeks is of little consequence. We are talking about the very future of this family, after all, a heavy responsibility which weighs on all of us. I must be certain of the case before reaching a decision. "

"Very well, sir," James said, dispiritedly.

But matters were taken out of Sir Owen's hands almost at once, when Jefford knocked at the door.

"Beg pardon, sir, but there are callers. Mr Fletcher, Miss Isabella Fletcher and a Miss Crabtree."

"Miss Crabtree?"

"The governess, sir. Mr Fletcher's regards but he begs the favour of a few minutes of your time, and Lady Plummer's also."

"Thank you, Jefford. Where are the visitors now?"

"I showed them into the parlour, sir, where the ladies are sitting."

"Tell Lady Plummer that we shall attend them there." When Jefford had left, he added, "It seems that I shall have my meeting with Miss Isabella sooner than anticipated. Shall we join the ladies?"

Despite the warmth from the fire, there was a distinctly frosty air about the parlour. The ladies were sitting bolt upright, stiff with disapproval, their faces blank, although to be fair to Patricia, that was her habitual expression, so she could hardly be blamed for it. Charles stood near the door, as if waiting for an opportunity to escape. Michael huddled miserably by the window, as far from everyone as he could contrive. Uncle Morgan cradled a brandy glass, looking amused.

Side by side on the sofa reserved for guests, Mr Fletcher and Miss Crabtree sat either side of Isabella. Fletcher was in the middle of recounting some detail of a meal — perhaps last night's dinner — but he broke off as they entered, and rose to his feet.

"Ah, Sir Owen, Mr James, there you are. I've brought Bella to meet you, so that you and Lady Plummer can see for yourselves how she is. At least, it was her idea to come, not mine. She wants to explain a few things to you all."

"I am very pleased to meet you, Miss Fletcher," Sir Owen said with a courteous bow. "Please be seated, Fletcher. Have you been offered refreshments?"

"They have," Lady Plummer said in frigid tones. "They declined."

"Aye, we'll not take up much of your time," Fletcher said. "Away you go, Bella. Say your piece."

She looked calmly around the room at them, utterly composed. "I am the youngest daughter in the family — the youngest child, in fact. Angie is only four years older than me, but it always seemed an insuperable gap to me. I was often ill as a child, too, so the others were always off doing exciting things while I was stuck at home, recovering from one thing or another."

"Aye, that's true enough," Fletcher said. "She was born early, so she was a sickly babe, and a sickly child."

"I grew out of that in time, but by then my four sisters were far advanced in education, and had become as close as any sisters could be. They shared two bedrooms, one big group. And I was alone. I slept alone, I was often alone in the schoolroom when they were taking lessons with the masters, or shopping with Mama. Even in a large family like ours, I was always alone. I badly wanted a sister of my own age... or a friend, perhaps. And so I invented Dorothea to keep me company — someone to talk to, to share my life with."

"Little one, I had no idea you were so lonely," Fletcher said, his voice wavering. "My poor child!"

"It is of no consequence, Pa. I solved the problem for myself, you see. Everyone was very understanding, and accepted Dorothea as a part of the family. Probably they suspected that I thought she was real, but that would be foolish. I know perfectly well that she is an artefact of my imagination. In Yorkshire, where people have known me all my life, no one thought anything about it. Oh, I expect they talked about me behind my back, but no one ever mentioned it so I imagined that people everywhere would be the same. Now, of course, I can see how odd it must look to you, and how it must worry you, now that Julia is joining your family. I should be mortified if my thoughtless actions were to harm her or any of my family. So I have come here to explain it to you, so that you will understand that I am not a madwoman. Dorothea does not exist, and you will hear nothing more of her, I promise you."

James listened with growing respect. Bella was but fourteen, but she was a sensible and articulate girl, a little solemn, perhaps, but clearly as normal as anyone in the room. Perhaps more normal than some, he conceded, as his glance passed over Letitia and then Patricia, before wandering to Uncle Morgan and Michael.

"Thank you, Miss Fletcher," Sir Owen said. "That is a very lucid explanation, and we are pleased to know more of your situation."

It was a dismissal, and Fletcher knew it. "Then we understand one another, sir, and need trouble you no longer. Come, Bella, Miss Crabtree."

They all rose, and James was struck with how at ease Mr Fletcher was, neither prideful nor unduly humble. There was no artifice about him at all, despite his roots in trade. He was a man who knew his own worth and was not cowed by the very different society in which he now found himself. And Julia was just the same, he thought with a flash of pride. His Julia! She was her father's daughter, and the equal of any woman in England.

James and his father both saw the visitors out, then returned to the parlour.

"Well, Lady Plummer?" Sir Owen said gently. "Are you reassured?"

"Certainly not," she said tartly. "The creature has been well rehearsed, and she speaks her lines with conviction, but that is as much as one can say. In fact, I would go so far as to suggest that this little performance makes her even more suspect in my eyes. She is clearly a conniving, slippery, deceptive chit of a girl, and the fact that her father is part of the deception makes it even worse. He clearly is incapable of recognising her insanity, and therefore the whole family is tainted. I wish we had never been forced into the acquaintance."

"Oh, this is ridiculous!" James cried. "She was perfectly sensible. Father, you agree, surely? You said her explanation was lucid."

"So it was. Too lucid, perhaps, for a child of that age to

have dreamt up," Sir Owen said. "I must agree with Lady Plummer on one point, at least, that she was told what to say. She spoke her lines very competently, I grant you that, but that is hardly relevant."

James paced across the room, too angry to be still. He found himself gazing at Michael's anxious face. "Brother, you will support me, will you not? Did she not appear to you as the very picture of rationality?"

Michael leaned back against the wall, as if he wished it would swallow him up and relieve him of the necessity of answering. "James, how can I judge? If Father and Mother think—"

With an exclamation of disgust, James spun round and strode away from him. "Father, tell me once and for all, will you now give me your blessing to marry Miss Fletcher?"

"I cannot, not yet. If Michael were married, it would be a different matter, but—"

James groaned in exasperation. "Do you not see what you are doing? Michael feels all the weight of his obligation to marry and continue the line, and now you are burdening him with the responsibility for *my* marriage, too! It is grossly unfair! He has suffered enough for this family, God knows. If I marry Julia, we can provide you with sons and Michael can take his time and find the wife of his heart, as I have done... as you did, Father. This nonsense about Bella is just an excuse, and you know it. Mother will *never* accept Julia, because her father was once in trade. She despises the whole family. Is it not so, Mother? Deny it if you dare."

"Why should I deny it? They are unworthy to mingle

with good society."

"You see, Father? Well, I have had enough. I will not be subject to your whims any longer, and I absolutely will *not* be party to any scheme which increases the heavy load that Michael has to bear. I shall marry Julia in my own time, and you will just have to accept that. Good day."

He stormed out of the room, collected his greatcoat and was away down the drive and half way home to the rectory before his rage had even begun to cool. It was insupportable! How dare his father hold him to ransom in this irrational way? Bella was no more insane than he was, and possibly less so. Which of them could honestly be called normal, anyway? Every man, woman and child on earth was different from every other, each with his own quirks and oddities. He would marry Julia at once, before she changed her mind.

His footsteps slowed as relief surged through him. He wanted to dance for joy, to shriek to the heavens that she was his... would very soon be entirely his, and what more could any man want? He stood, grinning from ear to ear, then laughing out loud. *She would be his!* There was no longer any obstacle, for he was as free as the air. High above him a pigeon clattered into flight with a shiver of leaves, and James laughed again. He was as free as that bird, and he knew precisely what he would do. He would go to the Park and find Julia, and settle a date for their wedding at once. Before she changed her mind.

He strode off again, but as soon as he passed the glebe he saw three people in the rectory garden — Thomas, Miss Crabtree and Isabella. They saw him, hailed him and Bella ran to open the gate for him.

"Good day again, Mr Plummer," she said. "Mr Leadbetter is showing us around your gardens, and then we are to go inside for tea and cake."

"That sounds a splendid idea, and Mrs Pound will have made a cherry cake today, I believe. But where is your father?"

"He has gone to talk to Mr Kelshaw about chimneys," she said, as if this were the most normal thing in the world, and perhaps in the Fletcher family it was.

James was wild to see Julia again, but this was too good an opportunity to find out more about Bella. He joined them, therefore, for the tour of the gardens, and then the rectory itself, for Bella was curious to see Julia's future home. When they had seen the principal rooms, Thomas and Bella went off to the kitchens to secure the promised cherry cake, and James took Miss Crabtree into the drawing room and lit the fire.

"It is a fine thing that your charge did today, Miss Crabtree," he said. "Was it her own idea, or yours?"

"Oh, entirely hers. She was horrified to think that her own actions might lead to such adverse consequences, and she determined at once to do whatever she might to alleviate matters. Was she successful in that regard?"

James laughed. "In one sense, she was. Her words did nothing to shift the opinions of either of my parents, but they served to convince me that no evidence would ever do so. My mother is adamantly opposed to any connection with a family so recently in trade, and my father is too concerned with the purity of the line. The end result was that I shouted a great deal and stormed out with the intention of marrying Julia as soon as the banns can be called."

"Oh dear," Miss Crabtree said. "Such a pity... to quarrel with your esteemed parents. I do hope the consequences of that will not be too dire."

"What is the worst that can happen?" James said cheerfully. "Only that they might never speak to me again, and I am not at all sure that I would not count that as a benefit."

"Oh, Mr Plummer!" Her voice was soft, for governesses tended not to have strident voices, but she was clearly shocked. "You will not be... disinherited? Cut out, somehow?"

"Heavens, no. Everything is for my brother anyway. I have no expectations. Well... a little money from Mother after her death, and the living of St Agnes, whenever Mr Hasswell should quit this earth, but even without those I have the living of St Hilary's, which provides an income more than sufficient to my needs."

"You will have Miss Julia's dowry, too," she said.

"So I will. I had forgotten that."

She smiled a little sadly. "Ah, how pleasant it must be to be so well provided for that the addition of twenty thousand pounds slips one's mind."

"A governess's lot is a hard one, is it not?" he said sympathetically. "Although I am sure Mr and Mrs Fletcher are generous employers."

"Oh, *yes!* I have no complaint whatsoever to make against either of them."

"And your charge? Is she troublesome?" he said lightly.

"Not in the least. She is a joy to teach, if you wish to know. I had the education of Julia and Angie too, for a little while, but Bella is the most rewarding of them. The older girls were already well-formed, their characters established, and needed no more than the lightest nudge from me, but Bella— She was like a little hedgehog, curled up around herself and hard to reach. But I had the very great privilege of helping her to uncurl herself and face the world. I understood her better than most."

"About Dorothea?"

She nodded. "Bella was a twin, you see. It was a difficult pregnancy, seemingly, and Mrs Fletcher was confined early. Bella was born quickly, but the second baby was not, and so he never drew a breath, poor little mite, and Bella was left alone. It is a strange thing, to be a twin, Mr Plummer. I had a twin sister who died when I was only three. I have no memory of her at all, but I *know* that she is gone. There is a yawning void in my heart where she used to live. In just that way, Bella *knows* that there is something missing from her life. So she invented Dorothea to fill the emptiness. Her mother understood, too, and together we managed to persuade the rest of the family to accept Bella just as she is. But now, perhaps, she is old enough to set aside that childish state and behave a little differently. Ah, this sounds like the tea arriving."

Janet Pound brought in the tea things, as Bella carefully carried the cake, and was allowed to cut it, while Miss Crabtree presided over the teapot. Thus passed a pleasant half hour, but James was becoming restless again to see Julia.

"May I escort you ladies back to the Park?" he said politely.

"Allow me to do so, James," Thomas said. "You will have other urgent matters to attend to, I am sure, now that you are betrothed."

"Nothing is more urgent than seeing my future wife," James said. "But there is no reason why we should not both accompany the ladies."

This happy plan was at once settled upon, and the four had not taken more than twenty paces from the rectory before they separated into two groups, Thomas keeping close attendance on Miss Crabtree while James had Bella on his arm. When they reached the house, he paused on the steps. A light rain was beginning to fall, but he could not let her go without expressing his gratitude. Her words had not achieved their intended objective, but indirectly they had set James free.

"I must thank you, Miss Fletcher, for speaking out so bravely today," he said.

"How could I do less, for Julia's sake?"

"Even so, it must have taken great courage to admit that your friend does not exist, and it was your own idea, I understand."

"Oh no," she said, turning guileless eyes on him. "It was Dorothea's idea. She does not want to cause any trouble for my sisters, so she told me what to say. From now on she will stay in my room, and I shall only talk to her at night, when we are alone. Good day, Mr Plummer. Thank you for walking home with me."

Dipping him a polite curtsy, she skipped up the steps and disappeared into the house, leaving James bewildered and confused.

25: No Compromise

Julia sat glumly in the parlour, laboriously sewing a torn ribbon back onto a bonnet. It was hard work, for her stitches were uneven and often had to be ripped out and done again. Rosie and Angie were practising in the music room, the pieces interspersed with much giggling, audible even from the parlour, interspersed with long silences ending in bursts of laughter. At least someone was happy. Julia had Aunt Madge and Mama for company, Mama engaged on some delicate embroidery work, and Aunt Madge methodically adding beads to the bodice of an evening gown.

Mama chattered away brightly, for she was quite excited, in her ladylike way, about the prospect of uniting the Fletcher and Plummer families.

"Such a good connection, dear. Such a long-established family, and they must know absolutely everybody. It will be very helpful to us in London, I am sure. And the connection to the Marquess of Barrowford... I have high hopes that Lord Charles will introduce us to his brother now. So you see how much good you have done, Julia dear, by accepting Mr Plummer. You have raised us all a little higher in society, and that will be so useful for Rosie."

"Not that she had a thought in her head beyond her own wishes," Aunt Madge said. "Never thinks of anyone but herself."

"There is nothing wrong with that," Mama said equably. "One must choose a husband principally according to affection, although paying due regard to suitability, naturally. Since Mr Plummer is eminently suitable, we must all congratulate Julia on making an excellent match. It is a pity about this business with Bella, but perhaps this visit of hers will do the trick. Julia, you have been constantly working and reworking that ribbon. You will have the bonnet shredded if you keep unpicking your stitches. Pass it to me, and let me see if I can tidy it up a little."

With relief, Julia gave her the bonnet, where a few deft stitches soon hid the tear, and became a jaunty little decoration which hid the damage far more effectively than any attempt of Julia's.

"I wish I could do that," she said.

Mama laughed. "Your talents lie in other directions. Now, dear, we have already settled that you are to come to town to see about wedding clothes."

"It hardly matters if we're not to marry for years," she said mournfully.

"Ah, you are a little out of spirits at the prospect of waiting, and who can blame you? But Mr Plummer will not want to wait too long, you may be sure, so deep in love as he is, and his father will not wish him to be miserable, so he will relent soon enough. Perhaps even now Bella's words are doing the trick, although one never quite knows with her. Did she tell you what she planned to say to Sir Owen?"

"Not a word."

Mama sighed. "Well, let us hope for the best, and an early resolution to the problem. And I have been thinking, Julia. Since you will be in town anyway, why not marry there? St George's in Hanover Square is such a fine church, and all the most distinguished families marry there."

"I should hate to be the centre of such a public spectacle," Julia said.

"Well, perhaps we could get a special licence and—"

"No. No fuss, Mama. I'd like to have the banns called in the regular way, and be married in St Hilary's by Mr Leadbetter, with Pa giving me away, and nobody there but family and a few village women."

She nodded in resignation. "I should have liked to show you off a little, but there, you never did enjoy being the centre of attention."

Miss Crabtree put her head around the door. "We are back, madam. It all went very well. Bella was a great credit to you."

"Thank you, Miss Crabtree. Well, there you are, Julia. Your sister has done her best for you, and we must hope that all will now be well."

Aunt Madge sniffed, but said nothing. Julia smiled at her.

"You disapprove of my marriage, don't you, Aunt Madge? You never thought anyone would ever want to marry me, and I confess I thought so myself. I'm as surprised by this as you could be. And the worst of it is that I shall be underfoot for ever more, because I shall only be down at the rectory. There is no getting rid of me now."

Aunt Madge smiled wryly. "I do think he is too good for you, true enough, but your pa will be glad to have you so close. You always were his favourite."

"Pa doesn't have favourites," Julia said. "He loves us all equally."

"Aye, and you a little bit more. He would rather you never married at all, but he will be glad to have you only a five minute walk away. He will be on your doorstep every day, you mark my words."

"And he'll be very welcome," Julia said, her chin rising.

"We shall all be glad to have Julia settled so close to us," Mama said hastily. Fortunately, the butler came in before Aunt Madge could escalate hostilities into a full battle. "Yes, Keeble, what is it?"

"Mr James Plummer, madam."

And there he was, a little damp from the rain, but his usual smiling self, his eyes seeking out Julia anxiously as he entered the room. He saw her, he beamed with joy, and Julia's was assailed by the most extraordinary feeling. Her heart leapt inside her, filling her with pure happiness. James was with her and all was right with the world.

Mama received him calmly. "Mr Plummer, how kind of

you to call. Do you bring us good news from the Manor?"

"I certainly bring news, but whether it is more of good or bad I leave you to decide for yourself. Miss Isabella made a strong case, but my parents remain unconvinced."

"Oh, that is a pity!" Mama cried.

"The consequence is that I am very much at odds with both of them, and am determined not to wait on their approval but to marry Julia whenever she wishes. So you may set our wedding date as soon as you like, my love," added with such a warm smile at Julia, that she blushed at the intensity of his gaze, and lowered her eyes.

"That is very disappointing," Mama said, fretfully. "Still, we must hope that they come round when they get to know Julia a little better."

She waved him to a chair, and he sat, quite at his ease, throwing Julia an occasional smile, his eyes drifting constantly towards her.

"I have no expectation of that," James said. "Mama is adamantly opposed to any connection between our families, and not because of Bella. That was just an excuse. I do not believe she will ever relent, and my father dislikes to oppose her. He may change his mind in time, but he wants to wait until Michael is married and I cannot allow that. Michael suffers enough from the pressure to marry as it is. He feels it extremely, yet he has not the temperament to go out and marry the first heiress who appears on the horizon. He tried that once and it almost destroyed him, and even now he is not yet fully recovered from the disaster. I would not for the world add the responsibility for my marriage to the heavy load he already carries."

"Your feelings do you credit, I am sure," Mama said, "yet it is the greatest pity that you should set yourself against your parents. Perhaps a short delay... until the autumn, say?"

James shook his head firmly. "I am determined not to wait any longer than is needful for Julia to order her wedding clothes and for the carriage to be built. My mother is beyond reach of reason and my father... well, he must do as he thinks is best for his family, but so too must I."

"Is there then no hope of a compromise?" Mama said. "Perhaps if you were to talk to your father—"

"Impossible. I have broken with him completely. If there is to be any talking, he must come to me."

Mama jumped up, so that James was obliged to rise, too. Julia had never seen her stepmother so agitated.

"But this is dreadful!" Mama cried. "Now they will cut us in town and we shall have no acquaintances worth having, and there will be no possibility of Lord Charles introducing us to his brother. Whatever are we to do?"

"Is that what concerns you?" James said. "But my family would never have been any help to you in town. Father rarely goes there, and you will not be on Mother's invitation list, you may be sure. As for Charles, he fell out with his brother years ago over some imagined slight, and they have not spoken since. You will have to make do with my acquaintances, few as they are, and your own connections."

Mama stared at him, consternation writ large on her face. For once she was completely speechless.

Into the silence, Julia said, "Mama, may James and I go out for a walk?"

"It is raining," he said, "but perhaps we could walk in the gallery for a while? Mrs Fletcher?"

"Oh... yes, if you will."

"I had better go with them," Aunt Madge said.

"A little time alone would be a kindness," James said smoothly.

"Ten minutes," Mama said distractedly. "You may have ten minutes alone, then Madge will chaperon you."

Julia was out of the room before she could change her mind, James hard on her heels. Behind them she heard Aunt Madge's grumbling voice.

"You are too soft with that girl, Lizzie."

"I do wish you would call me Elizabeth," Mama said, her voice fretful.

James firmly shut the door, and grinned at Julia. "Ten minutes," he whispered into her ear. "Better not waste them."

Hand in hand, they raced up the stairs and behind the curtain that partially screened the gallery from view, then down to the far end to be sure that no one lurked behind one of the many statues. Then she was in his arms, being held tight, so tight she could barely breathe, his lips pressed on hers.

She melted. Her insides felt like butter in the sun, her whole being infused with warmth as she stretched on tiptoes to return his kisses. After the first rush of passion expended itself, he kissed every part of her upturned face, murmured sweet endearments to her. Perhaps she murmured endearments of her own, but she was so enthralled she couldn't be sure.

Julia had enjoyed many moments of happiness in her existence. Seeing a rainbow, or the emergence of the sun after a storm. A long walk with Pa or quiet moments with Ma. The company of her sisters, and lazy summer afternoons with Johnny fishing for strange water creatures in the river. But she had never before experienced the glorious bliss of being held by the man she loved, being thoroughly kissed and adored and cherished. Joy filled her and overflowed until surely the whole gallery must be full of it, and the house too and the whole world. If she were any happier her heart would assuredly burst.

"James! It happened!"

He lifted his face from hers, smiled and softly kissed her nose. "What happened?"

"My heart jumped, just like Allie said. When you walked into the parlour, I felt... oh, a thousand things at once! And my heart just about jumped out of my body. It's really true — I'm in love with you."

He chuckled, and he was holding her so tight that she felt his body shake a little. "Oh, Julia, you are such a darling, I hardly have the words. Let us not wait too long to be married, my love, for I cannot wait to make you mine."

"Even when your family object?"

He frowned a little. "It is a strange thing, but I feel as light as air. I know I should be downhearted by the breach with my family but it is oddly freeing. I cannot quite account for it. It is as if I have been carrying a great weight on my shoulders all these years, so that everything I wanted to do — life itself, even — seemed like too great an effort. I could never be bothered to break away, and now that I have... now that you have all unwittingly inspired me to do it, I am fired with enthusiasm. I want to strip out the wretched interior of the rectory and make it into a home worthy of you, my dearest. *I* want to be worthy of you. It is time I started to take an interest in my parish, would you not say? Time I devoted myself to my responsibilities. I am ashamed to think of how indolent I have been. I am a disgrace to my profession, and it is my earnest intention to do better from now on. Will you help me, darling Julia? Help me to be a better man?"

"Only if you will help me to be better, too."

"As if you need any improvement," he whispered into her hair, and then he was kissing her again and that was the end of any rational conversation, until Aunt Madge's heavy footsteps drew them back into the mundane world.

James stayed for some time, for the usual rules for morning calls could not apply to a betrothed couple. Abandoning the gallery very soon after Aunt Madge's appearance, they retreated to the parlour, where he talked at length about all the improvements he intended to put in hand for the rectory, now that it was to have a mistress after so many years of bachelor existence. Aunt Madge scoffed at most of his ideas, but he answered her with lightness and commendable patience. Rosie and Angie, their music practice finished, joined in the discussion with enthusiasm, but Mama, unusually for her, had nothing to say to these plans.

"Are you quite well, Mama?" Julia said, eventually.

"Of course I am," she said.

"You seem a little out of sorts."

"Nonsense, Julia. How you do go on, sometimes. I am perfectly well, not in the least out of sorts."

James jumped to his feet. "It would not be at all surprising if you were, for here I am overstaying my welcome. You must have long wished me gone, I dare say, Mrs Fletcher."

"Oh, no, not at all. Not in the least, Mr Plummer. You must stay as long as you wish, but if you must go, at least come for dinner."

"You are very kind. But now I see how it is that I have stayed so long, for you have taken away the little clock that sat on the mantelpiece. It had a very pretty chime, and would have reminded me to leave a little sooner."

"Clock?" she said, frowning.

"A little porcelain affair with a shepherdess on either side. It was always above the fire in this room."

"I remember it," she said. "But why is it not there? I declare, it is too bad, the way things simply vanish in this house. No doubt it will turn up in the library or one of the saloons or even in a bedroom. But I will not have it! The servants make a May game of us, moving things from place to place like this. I will not stand for such underhanded dealings.

Rosie, ring the bell for Keeble."

"Mrs Fletcher," James said, sounding surprised, "I am sure the servants would not do such a thing."

"But they do! Who else can it be? They do it to annoy us, or perhaps they think we are too stupid to notice, but I will not have it! They will do as they are bid or else— There you are, Keeble. Where is the clock that used to sit on the mantelpiece?"

"I have no idea, madam. I assumed that you had moved it."

"Perhaps Mrs Graham took it away to be cleaned," James put in. "No one would move it without a good reason."

"Keeble, fetch Mrs Graham," Mama said. She was fairly quivering with indignation now.

"Mama, does it matter so much?" Angie said. "There are plenty of other clocks, after all."

"*Plenty of other clocks?* So you have plenty of jewels, I suppose, so it hardly matters if a few disappear? We have plenty of horses in the stables, so we will not miss one or two? Is that it? Foolish child! Mrs Graham, where is the clock that lives on the mantel?"

"Oh! It's gone!" the housekeeper said.

"We can all see that! But where is it?"

"I don't know, madam."

"Perhaps one of the housemaids—"

"None of them would move a valuable item like that

without my knowing it," Mrs Graham said sharply. "No more would one of the footmen move it without Mr Keeble knowing. If it's been moved, it could only have been one of the family."

"How dare you speak to me like that!" Mama hissed. "How *dare* you! No one in the family would move anything without asking me first. It could only have been one of the servants, and I suggest you set about finding out who it was, because if that clock is not back in its rightful place by dinner time, you will *all* be turned off without a reference. I will not tolerate thievery. Is that clearly understood?"

White-faced, Keeble nodded. Mrs Graham burst into tears.

26: *Reconciliations*

Mama sailed out of the room, head high, as Julia watched, aghast.

"Oh dear," James said mildly. "Well, Keeble, Mrs Graham, you had better set about finding this clock without delay."

"I don't know where to begin looking, sir, and that's a fact," Mrs Graham said tearfully.

"When things go missing, they often turn up in a different room," Julia said. "Have a good look around the rooms on this floor."

"Yes, Miss Julia." She bobbed a curtsy and scuttled away, Keeble in her wake.

"Is it true then what your mama was saying?" James said, with a frown. "That things regularly disappear?"

"Yes, but they always turn up again," Julia said. "Usually it's little things — scissors or a journal. I don't remember anything so valuable disappearing before."

"We should all of us join the search," Angie said. "This is a big house, and it might be anywhere. The wine cellar, or the kitchens, perhaps."

"That hardly seems likely," James said.

"But we have to do something," Angie said, dashing for the door. "I am going to make a start on the bedrooms."

"I am going to lie down until all this to-do has died down," Aunt Madge said. "Mr Plummer, you had best go home."

With these uncompromising words, she sailed out of the room.

"Yes, go," Julia said. "I will see you at dinner."

"Are you sure you do not need another pair of hands for the search?" he said. "I know every nook and cranny in the house, after all."

"I don't think we need to worry about nooks and crannies," Julia said airily. "The clock will turn up. These missing things always do."

He looked as if he were about to protest, but she gave a quick shake of her head and he smiled. "Well, you know best, I dare say. Good day, Julia. Good day, Miss Fletcher."

Rosie and Julia curtsied demurely, and he bowed himself out of the room.

"But we must do *something*, Jules," Rosie said, tears shining on her lashes. "How dreadful if the poor servants should be turned off."

"No chance of that," Julia said. "Mama will relent when she comes back down to earth, and Pa wouldn't let her do it, anyway."

"But what was the matter with her?" Rosie said. "I have never seen her angry like that, and... and unreasonable! She is usually so calm.

"Never mind that," Julia said. "There's no time to lose. Come on."

Grabbing Rosie's hand, she made for the door.

"Where are we going?" Rosie said.

"To find the clock, of course, but we have to be quick."

Out in the hall, Julia stopped. "Oh, botheration, no candle! Never mind, we'll just have to use the service stairs. Come on, quickly, Rosie."

"Are we allowed to?" Rosie said, although she let Julia pull her through the door and up the stairs.

"Of course," Julia said scornfully. "It's our house, so we can go where we like. I was going to use the secret stairs, but there's no time to get a candle. Up another level, Rosie."

"The attics?"

"The attics," Julia said firmly.

Cautiously, she opened the door and peered out. No one was in sight. "This way."

The bedroom at the far end was shuttered and gloomy, but there was still enough light to see that the washstand was empty.

"Bother. I was sure it would be here."

"The clock? This would be a good hiding place, for no one ever comes up here," Rosie said. "Certainly not the housemaids, for look at all this dust. Perhaps it is in one of these cupboards. Not that one. Nor that. Here it is! Julia, we have found it, but... you knew it would be here. It was you! You took it!"

"Don't be silly, of course I didn't, although I admit I suspected it would be here. No, leave it where it is, Rosie, and shut the cupboard door. Now we hide behind these curtains... yes, you that side, and I'll take this side. Now we keep quiet and wait."

And finally Rosie understood. Eyes wide, she slipped behind one curtain, her face pale even in the gloom, and Julia hid behind another. Then they waited. For a long time they waited, as occasional sounds drifted up from below. Someone shouting — Mrs Graham, possibly. Doors opening and closing with louder thumps than usual. Furniture being moved. The servants were searching with great thoroughness.

But eventually they were rewarded. Julia heard nothing, no footsteps, no swish of stiff clothing or creak of leather boots, not even heavy breathing. But there was a hint of perfume in the air. Someone dainty and light-footed, who washed in lavender scented soap.

It was Rosie who pushed her way out from her hiding place first.

"Angie!"

And so it was. She was kneeling in front of the cupboard,

with the clock in her hand.

"Rosie? Julia?" She laughed. "Well, you have caught me out, but not to worry, for I shall have this back downstairs in two shakes of a lamb's tail. You will not tell, will you?"

"Oh no, of course not," Rosie cried. "But why ever did you do such a thing, Angie dear? It seems... a little peculiar."

"It was just a little joke," Angie said. "Life here is so boring — no parties, one ball, hardly any dinners. I had to do *something* to liven things up."

"By stealing a clock?" Rosie squeaked.

"Not *stealing*, only moving from one place to another. I hide things up here for a day or two, then put them back but in a different room. Aunt Madge gets so cross, it is such fun to see."

"And cruel to tease her so... to tease all of us," Julia said sharply. "Rosie spent hours looking for that thimble, and presumably it was here all the time."

"My, how censorious you are getting now that you are to marry the vicar," Angie said. "But you will not tell, Julia? I should be mortified if Mama were to find out. You know what she is like."

"I shall not tell, no, but only because you are going to own up to it yourself."

"Never! Mama would be so cross! Why, she might even stop me going to London, and I shall absolutely *die* if I cannot go."

"And it would be no more than you deserve," Julia said

crisply. "But think about it, Angie. If you say nothing but simply put the clock back, Mama will still suspect the servants and that just isn't fair. They've done nothing wrong at all. You have to speak up if only to make sure that they are completely exonerated. Apologise handsomely, that always answers, in my rather extensive experience. Mama will be glad to have the affair settled without further disruption, you may be sure."

"Must I?"

"I believe Julia is right," Rosie said softly. "One should always own up to one's mistakes, and one should never, ever allow the servants to take the blame. Do you remember —? Oh, but you were probably still a baby, but Pa gave Will such a thrashing once when he broke a window and got Murgatroyd to take responsibility. He said that if Will had owned up to it like a man, he would not have minded, but it was the deceit and hiding behind a servant that irked him most. So Pa will be on your side, if you admit it honestly."

Angie drooped. "I suppose you are right."

They took the main stairs down to the parlour, where Angie sat glumly on the sofa, the clock on her knee, while Mama, Pa, Keeble and Mrs Graham were summoned.

"Ah, you've found it," Pa said at once. "Well done, Angie."

"Do not praise me, Pa, for it was I who took it in the first place. I have taken lots of little things these last few weeks, hiding them away and then putting them back in a different place. It was my misplaced idea of a joke, and I am very sorry for it. Mama, I never meant to cause such alarm. I realise now that it was a very foolish thing to do. Pray forgive me. Keeble, Mrs Graham, I hope that you will accept my sincere apology, and convey my regrets to all the other servants. It was never my intent to shed suspicion on any of you, and I deeply regret it."

"We're just glad to have the matter cleared up," Mrs Graham said.

"You young people will have your little jokes," Keeble said, with a smile. "Very amusing, and no harm done."

"Thank you, Keeble, Mrs Graham," Mama said. "You may go." There was no smile on her face, and even Pa looked serious.

"Well, flower, this is a to-do, isn't it?" Pa said to Angie. "Mrs Fletcher, what is to be done here? Is she to have bread and water for a month? Forty lashes of the cat o' nine tails? Hanged, drawn and quartered? It was a fine apology, I'll say that much."

"A fine apology! As if that makes it right. She must be punished, Harry, she must."

"Lizzie, no one thought anything of it when it was just my newspaper that disappeared, or Madge's scissors. The clock was a mistake, I'll grant you, but she owned up to it at once and apologised. I'd be glad to leave it at that, and forget all about it."

"I am sure you would, but how will she ever learn if she is to receive no punishment? She will think she can get away with anything."

"She learns by seeing that her actions have distressed

you, and upset the servants too. She will not do anything of the sort again, will you, flower?"

"No, Pa, never, I swear it."

"There, you see?" Pa said. "Nothing further is needed, surely."

"Harry Fletcher, you are too soft with them by far," Mama cried. "Over-indulged and spoilt, that's what they are. Anyone can see it, but will you listen? You never listen, not even to your own wife! Oh, I can't bear it!"

And in a most un-Mama-like way, she burst into tears and stormed from the room.

Pa's eyebrows rose. "Hmm, what's put her so out of frame? She's not normally so melodramatic."

"She was upset earlier when James told her he'd quarrelled with his family," Julia said. "She seemed to think we'd have no acquaintances in London."

"Ah. She was rather depending on that connection," Pa said. "I'll give her five minutes to calm down and then we'll have a little talk. And Angie — best keep out of trouble for a while, eh?"

~~~~~

Lightwood had obviously been watching out, for the rectory door opened as soon as James approached it.

"Sir Owen is in the drawing room, sir."

Was that good news? Probably not. "Ah. Has he been here long?"

"About an hour, sir. I took in a bottle of the best brandy. I thought you would wish it."

An hour. Definitely not good news. "Thank you, Lightwood, that was well done. An hour, eh? Better face the music, I suppose."

Sir Owen was standing at the window, glass in hand, gazing out at the wilderness that had once been a lawn. "What happened to the fellow who used to do your garden?"

"Broke his leg about two years ago and went to live with his daughter at Bishop's Stortford. I suppose I should get someone else."

Sir Owen turned to face James, his expression serious, but there was nothing to be read into that. He was always serious. "You need a housemaid, too. This rug has not been beaten for some time. You live in some chaos, James, but I expect Miss Fletcher will sort things out in the house."

"We will sort things out between us," James said neutrally. "And if not, we shall muddle along tolerably well, no doubt. Have you been offered some cherry cake?"

For the first time, a glimmer of a smile crossed his father's face. "I have never been fond of cake, as you well know. The brandy is excellent, though. You keep a good cellar, at least."

James laughed. "Most likely it came from your own cellar. You gave me a great many bottles when I was first ordained, remember? That was probably the last time you were in this house."

"It is, and that is remiss of me. One of many ways in

which I have been remiss as a father. No, no, do not deny it. You are a grown man, and I should not attempt to impose my will on you. I strongly dislike quarrelling with my own son, James, and should very much like to repair the breach. Will you shake my hand?"

"With all my heart, Father! I dislike being at odds with you, too, but I must tell you that I will not change my mind. I intend to marry Julia at any date of her choosing."

His father nodded. "I understand. You must do what you feel is right, as must we all. I have Lady Plummer's feelings to take into account, and... James, I cannot openly set myself against her. Marriage, as you will discover for yourself, involves making accommodations. As in war, one must decide when to march into battle and when a tactical retreat is in order, so for her sake I will not make any public acknowledgement of your betrothal. You do not need my approval, so nothing need be said about it. But I wish you great joy of your marriage, and I hope that your first-born will be a means of reconciliation with your mother. Will you take a drink with me? For there is a matter upon which I should welcome your advice."

James could not be more astonished. His father asking his advice? Wordlessly he replenished his father's glass and poured brandy for himself, gesturing his father to a chair.

"You said something very profound this morning," Sir Owen said.

"Did I? It must have been an accident."

"You speak lightly, but in my view it was profound, yes. You spoke of the heavy burden that Michael has to bear, and it is true that, as the eldest son, the duty falls to him to continue the family line. That much is indisputable."

"Is it so?" James said thoughtfully. "I would take issue with it, however. With hereditary titles, there are heirs apparent and heirs presumptive, and we see with the King's own children how little they regard their duty to continue the family line. If Michael falls short in the matter of heirs, then I step forward, and if I too fall short, there is Cousin Sydney and his five younger brothers, and two of them have sons now. Michael is not the only hope for a continuance of the family."

"That is perfectly true. You think, then, that I am too hard on Michael?"

"Not at all, sir. I think that *Michael* is too hard on Michael. He desperately wants to fulfil your expectations and make you proud of him."

"And yet I wish only to see him happily married, no more than that."

"To someone suitable, and preferably wealthy."

"Well… yes, naturally, but—" Sir Owen frowned, considering the point. "It is a matter of temperament, perhaps. Michael is not so easy-going as you are, James. For you, it is easy to disregard my expectations."

"What did you ever expect of me except that I would take up a profession? I only baulked at the army, a career for which I am manifestly unsuited. I am better fitted to the church, but I never tried to do it well. That is your great legacy to both of us, Father, that you set us an ideal we could never hope to achieve. Everything you do is done well. The house runs as smoothly as a well-oiled clock. Efficiency is your watchword. Michael despairs because he can never reach your standard, and I chose not even to try. We have both been in your thrall our whole lives. It is only now that I have found Julia that I can begin to see how to become the man I ought to be. I would like Michael to have the same chance — to meet a woman who inspires him."

"And yet you set out to court Miss Fletcher almost on a whim," Sir Owen said.

"I did. She made me smile, Father. Every time I see her, she makes me smile, and I pray that one day Michael will find someone who makes him smile, too, for God knows he has smiled little enough lately. Three years ago, he thought he had finally found the way to earn your approval, by marrying a woman rich enough to restore our fortunes without selling the Park. It would have pleased you and Mother, and it would have satisfied Michael's desire to do his duty. His failure nearly killed him, he still feels it deeply and I would see him relieved of that burden. I very much hope my marriage will do that. It would help if you would explain that to him... tell him that he need not continue his desperate search for a bride... that he need not even go to town, if he does not wish it."

"Surely he knows that? He must be aware that I should never wish him to marry against his inclination."

"And yet you pushed him to try with Rose Fletcher."

"A pretty and well-mannered girl with a fortune? An excellent opportunity, if he had liked her."

"He wanted to do it to please you, Father, that is all. I think it would help if you explained to him that you want his happiness above all else. That you want him to marry for love, as I am doing, and as you did too, after all."

For the first time, Sir Owen's face softened. "That is true. Lady Plummer was not well-born, and was certainly not what my own father wished for me, but even at twenty she was a perfect lady — *my* perfect lady. And look how well she fulfils that rôle now that she is entitled to the rank. An excellent wife and mother, and I will not say that she is entirely wrong to be concerned about Miss Isabella Fletcher. Only time will tell whether those fears are justified or not. Very well." He set down his glass and rose briskly to his feet. "I shall talk to Michael as you suggest, James, and I shall inform Lady Plummer that he may not be in town this spring and she should not plan to introduce him to any young ladies, as she is wont to do. That should resolve the matter. Good day to you, James. I am glad we have had this little chat."

So saying, he marched out of the room, leaving James bemused but not unhopeful.

~~~~~

'To Miss Fletcher, Chadwell Park, nr Ware, Hertfordshire. Rosie, we are in such an uproar here as you cannot imagine, and it is all Camilla Weston's fault again. The Romanies came back as they always do at this time of year, and one of them turned up at the Westons' house on a fine black horse and demanded to see Camilla. A great tall fellow, but most uncouth. Naturally he was refused admittance, but he yelled in the street and threw stones at the window until she came out, whereupon he scooped her up onto his horse and rode off with her!! And she was laughing, and kissing him, and since it is the same Romanies who were here last autumn, certain

conclusions must be drawn. Mr Weston went off to their encampment to talk to the fellow, but Camilla would not leave her paramour and so Mr Weston returned home and struck her name from the family Bible and she is nevermore to be mentioned in his hearing. What a wicked girl she is! Poor Mr Osgood is most distressed, although beginning to realise, perhaps, that he has had a most fortunate escape. Ruth Malpas is helping him to overcome his grief, and since he is a dean and she thinks reading sermons is the height of enjoyment, I would think they are well suited. Such excitement! Your most astonished friend, Belinda. Post script ~ The Malpases have taken a house in London, so you will have some acquaintances there, at least. I hope you have a lovely time. Do write as soon as you arrive to tell me what your house is like. Post post script ~ In all the to-do, I forgot to send my congratulations to Julia. I hope she will be very happy, although I do not think a vicar sounds very exciting, myself. However, a Romany would be a little too exciting. Something in between would be best. Post post post script ~ I almost forgot to send Ricky's regards to you but you know how fondly he thinks of you, and it does not need to be said, although he pesters me every time I write to be sure to mention it, so now I have done so.'

27: Connections

Dinner that evening was almost entirely consumed by discussion of Romanies and their seductive ways, and how Mr Osgood, a dean and upstanding pillar of respectability, could ever have wanted to marry a wild girl like Camilla Weston, and how thankful he must now be to have escaped that fate.

"What sort of girl is Miss Ruth Malpas?" Mama said.

"She was used to be a great deal of fun," Julia said, "but Allie says she is grown very sanctimonious. If she is making up to the dean, then I should say they will suit very well."

"'*Making up*'? What a vulgar expression, Julia," Mama said.

"But you will not let me say that she is throwing her cap at him, either, even though she is, by the sound of it."

"You may say that she displays a marked partiality for Mr Osgood, perhaps, or that she appears to enjoy his company. Was there any other news from Sagborough? Anything unconnected with Camilla Weston?"

"Belinda says that the Malpases have taken a house in town, so we will have some acquaintances there, at least," Rosie said.

Mama dropped her knife onto her plate with a clatter. "The Malpases! And Emmy, no doubt. So we shall have to have our parties cluttered up with a man who imports rugs and his vulgar family."

Pa carefully laid down his knife and fork. "Mrs Fletcher, let us understand one another rightly here. Jacob Malpas is one of my oldest friends, and is also Mayor of Sagborough, a position of great honour. Ruby Malpas and her daughter are good-hearted, inoffensive souls, and if they're in London this spring, we'll treat them with all the courtesy and respect due to them. I'm not so far removed from the business of importing and exporting myself as to disdain the company of others of similar background. You will displease me greatly if you offer them any slight."

Two spots of colour flared on her cheeks, but she answered at once, "Indeed, I would never do so, but you must admit that it is not the sort of connection with which Rosie should be surrounding herself."

"I hope my daughters will never be ashamed of their Sagborough friends," Pa said with dignity.

"Of course not, but this season is so important. Rosie must make a good first impression, and if she is to marry into the nobility, as we all hope, she must distance herself from any reminder of trade."

"Which is why I'll not go into society with you," Pa said. "That I understand. But we must not cast off all our old

371

friends in order to secure new ones."

"If I may suggest…" James said tentatively. "Everyone in town has a great variety of acquaintances, and they are not all invited to the same events. Mrs Fletcher might arrange a musical soirée, perhaps, for the more sophisticated of your acquaintances, and an informal card party for old friends like the Malpases. That way, there is no slight to anyone, but one is not obliged to introduce an importer of rugs to a marquess."

"There now, Mrs Fletcher," Pa said. "That is the way to do it."

"That is all very well, but how are we ever to know any marquesses?" she said fretfully. "We shall not know a soul from good society, and how we are to meet anyone is more than I can say."

"You once said to me, Lizzie, that Rosie would only have to drive through Hyde Park at the fashionable hour," Pa said. "She'd turn heads wherever she goes, you said, and we've ordered the carriage for it already. What is it we've ordered, Will?"

"A barouche, and very fine Rosie and her mama will look in it too, with their new bonnets and parasols."

"Is that true, Mr Plummer?" Pa said. "Will a drive through Hyde Park turn heads?"

James glanced at the blushing Rosie, and smiled. "Indeed it will. I have no doubt that Miss Fletcher and Miss Angela will attract a veritable deluge of admirers and each will be able to find one amongst them who makes her smile. For that is surely the real objective, is it not? For your daughters to be happy, whomsoever they choose to marry?"

Rosie smiled tremulously up at him, as Pa robustly said that of course it was, and no one was going to force Rosie to marry anyone she disliked. Even Mama looked a little happier, although she still had a tiny crease of worry on her forehead. Poor Mama! She'd been so keen to meet Lord Charles's brother, and now it looked as though there would be no marquesses on the guest list. But for the rest of the family, there was nothing but pleasure to be anticipated in London.

For Julia, London was of little interest. She would spend a week there being fitted for her wedding clothes, but otherwise she would be at home, the mornings spent in long, rambling walks with James, evenings at the Park or the Manor, and in a few weeks, she would be married and move into her new home.

She could hardly wait.

~~~~~

A few days later, Julia and Aunt Madge spent a whole day at the rectory, notebook in hand, determining what needed to be done. Aunt Madge was disposed to disapprove of every element of the rectory, from the smoking kitchen chimney to the cobwebby attics, and all points in between. Looking around the drawing room, she grudgingly admitted that some of the furniture was of good quality.

"No worm, anyway," she muttered. "I should have expected a great deal of worm, but there, it seems Mr James has been lucky. You will have to find a housemaid who knows her trade, not these local women. Someone who has been properly trained. The Pound women are all very well for two bachelors, but it will not do for you. Make a note of that — housemaid. What do we have so far?"

"Housekeeper, footman, a halfway competent cook, a housemaid."

"Gardener," Aunt Madge said, looking disdainfully out of the window. "One armed principally with a scythe and pruning shears."

"Gardener," Julia repeated dutifully, writing it down.

"Lady's maid, of course, but Lizzie will find someone for you in London."

"Lady's maid. I suppose we can leave James to decide on grooms."

"Who attends to the horses at present?"

"Lightwood, his valet. And Mr Leadbetter, I suspect. He does everything else around here, why not stable work as well?"

"Hmpf. But there will be carriage horses as well, so you will need a proper groom, to act as coachman as well. Add it to the list, Julia."

The knocker sounded on the front door. Julia made a move to answer it, but Aunt Madge said, "Wait for one of the servants, dear."

"But Lightwood is in the stable, Janet has gone to Ware to shop and Mrs Pound is making pastry."

Aunt Madge harrumphed, but made no further protest as Julia went to open the door. It was Sir Owen Plummer.

"Good morning, future Papa-in-law! I'm afraid James isn't here just now."

Sir Owen's face creased into a most unaccustomed smile. "Good morning, future daughter-in-law. Is he expected home soon?"

"I believe so. He has gone out with Mr Leadbetter to call on the old lady at the Kelshaw home farm who is like to die at any moment, and then Mr Hasswell at St Agnes, who has a fever."

"Ah. Unfortunately, he will arrive too late to do more than say a prayer over the poor man's body. He died in the night, as I have just had word."

"Oh dear. Will you come in, sir? My aunt is here."

"By all means. I had best wait for James, to make sure he knows. It is unexpected, for Hasswell was younger than I am, but there, we never can tell when our time is up."

The Madeira had barely been poured, and Aunt Madge had gone off to the kitchen to see about tea, when James and Mr Leadbetter returned.

"Father! Have you heard? Mr Hasswell is dead."

"I came to tell you of it myself, and to congratulate you. Four hundred a year — a timely addition to your income, James. Once the funeral is over, I shall write to the bishop and St Agnes will be yours."

"I have a better idea, Father. I should like to recommend Thomas for the living."

Mr Leadbetter froze, his gaze flicking from father to son

and back again.

"Leadbetter?" Sir Owen said. "St Agnes has always been intended for you, James."

"I know, but I hardly need the income. St Hilary's tithes combined with Julia's dowry gives me a very good income, more than enough to meet our modest needs. You would not wish me to live in luxury while Thomas goes on year after year as my curate on a hundred pounds a year. The living of St Agnes would enable him to be independent... to marry."

Sir Owen looked from one to the other, then nodded briskly. "Very well. It shall be as you wish. I congratulate you, Leadbetter. I had better return to the Manor. Lady Plummer will wish to hear the news without delay. Good day, James. Leadbetter." With a little smile, he added, "Good day, future daughter-in-law."

James calmly sipped his brandy, but Mr Leadbetter sat as one stunned.

"Are you quite well, Mr Leadbetter?" Julia said, trying not to laugh at his shocked expression.

"I... perfectly... quite well... merely..."

James rumbled with laughter. "Poor Thomas! How wicked of me to spring such a thing on you without the least warning."

"Oh... no... no... too generous, but..."

"I have had the idea in my mind for some time, but I did not want to get your hopes up, for Hasswell might have lived for another twenty years, after all. But now you will be able to marry at last."

"Marry..." He cleared his throat. "You will not mind if... if I go to the Park to tell Miss Crabtree of my good fortune?"

"Of course not. Off you go."

He went, reached the front door, came back for his forgotten cloak, then left again.

"Miss Crabtree?" Julia said in wonder. "Is that the way the wind is blowing?"

"It is. Thomas has wanted to marry for years in an abstract sort of way, but the idea became a more material prospect when he got to know Miss Crabtree better. They will live very comfortably on five hundred a year."

"Five hundred? I thought St Agnes yielded four hundred."

"You cannot imagine I can do without my curate, do you? No, he will still have a hundred a year from me."

"Pa will give Miss Crabtree something when she marries, as well. A sum of money, or an annuity. He is very generous towards former servants. This is all very well, my love, and I am delighted for them both, but Aunt Madge will be back at any moment with the tea things. Are you going to kiss me or not?"

"Oh, let me think about that..."

But he did not have to think for very long.

~~~~~

The procession of carriages leaving Chadwell Park for London was rather impressive. The small carriage, the larger travelling coach, a hired post chaise for the servants who could not be squeezed into the first two vehicles and finally a luggage wagon. Julia, James, Aunt Madge and Bella stood on the steps waving, while Miss Crabtree stood with Anthony, the one remaining footman, in the doorway.

"Well, there they go, off to the delights of town," James said cheerfully, as the cavalcade began its ponderous journey. "This evening they will dine in the fully-staffed splendour of Grosvenor Square while you are left to the tender mercies of a couple of kitchen maids. Are you quite sure you have no regrets about staying behind?"

"A couple of kitchen maids and Aunt Madge," Julia said, "who is a better cook than Mrs Sharwell, truth be told."

"And I shall go and see what those kitchen maids are up to just now," Aunt Madge said. "Nothing good, I wager. Bella, back to the schoolroom with you. Anthony, you are the butler now, so off you go and begin butlering."

They all scattered to their appointed tasks, leaving Julia and James alone on the step.

Julia laughed and shook her head. "Dear Aunt Madge! She is enjoying having the management of a house again, I suspect."

"How can one tell?" he murmured. "Is there a slightly diminished level of crossness about her?"

"That is just her way," Julia said. "You will grow accustomed to her, just as I shall grow accustomed to your Uncle Morgan, who is every bit as grumpy, I should say."

"True enough. What a pair they are! All families have their crosses to bear, and mine perhaps has more than yours.

I apologise in advance for inflicting them upon you. Shall we go back inside, and you can tell me about this house in Grosvenor Square?"

"I'd much rather talk about our house," she said, suddenly shy, as they entered the empty hall.

"I had much rather not talk at all," he whispered, scooping her into his arms, and raining kisses upon her upturned face. "Dearest Julia, I am going to make you so happy."

"I believe you," she said as soon as his kisses allowed, although a little breathlessly. "I shall do my very best to make you happy, too."

"Well, of course you will! How could it be otherwise?"

"I'm not very ladylike or accomplished or any of the things I'm supposed to be, and I know nothing at all about keeping house. How will I ever manage?"

"You will ask your Aunt Madge for help, of course. I am sure she would be delighted to oblige. Julia... my darling girl... you must not worry about trivialities. Thomas and I have muddled along in the rectory for years, so I am sure that you and I can muddle along too. And we shall be muddling along together, and what could be cosier than that? I grew up in a highly regimented household, and I find I have a great fondness for muddling along."

She laughed a little, but said quietly, "You will not mind, then, if I break things and spill things and tear things and trip over things? I am dreadfully clumsy, you know."

He kissed her forehead, then gently cupped her face

with his hands. "Julia, dearest, I fell in love with you *because* you do all those things. If I had wanted a refined and accomplished and ladylike wife, I could have married any time these last ten years, but I did not. Conventional women who conform to society's rules bore me to tears, whereas you... adorable, enchanting you... have held me in your hand from the very first moment I saw you sitting on the gate, swinging your legs. I love you exactly as you are, my darling girl. You must never, ever change."

"Then you mustn't change, either. I love *you* just as you are, too."

"Well, I should like to be a better clergyman, and once Thomas is gone to St Agnes, I shall have to be, but I hope I shall not change so very much otherwise. I shall still go shooting and fishing and hunting whenever I can, and I will still hide myself away in the hut on wet days, and I shall still toast bread and cheese, but now you will be beside me."

"Not the hunting, perhaps," she said, laughing. "Hunting and I don't agree, remember? But the rest... yes, please!"

"I can teach you to shoot, if you like."

"Me and guns? You must be mad!"

"Fishing, then. That is a pleasant, gentle occupation on a fine day. One sets up the rod and then lies back on the river bank to await developments, and if one has a charming companion to lie beside on the river bank..."

"That does sound pleasant," she said. "I shall be well compensated for missing London, I think."

"No regrets, then? No second thoughts?"

She slipped her arms around his neck and gave him his answer in unequivocal fashion, without a single word being spoken.

THE END

The next book in the series is *A Spring Dance,* wherein the Fletcher family arrives in London for the season, and Will meets a lady unimpressed by his claim to be a gentleman. You can read a sneak preview after the acknowledgements, and find out more at my website.

Thanks for reading!

If you have enjoyed reading this book, please consider writing a short review on Amazon. You can find out the latest news and sign up for the mailing list at my website marykingswood.co.uk.

Family trees: Hi-res versions available on my website under Extras.

A note on historical accuracy: I have endeavoured to stay true to the spirit of Regency times, and have avoided taking too many liberties or imposing modern sensibilities on my characters. The book is not one of historical record, but I've tried to make it reasonably accurate. However, I'm not perfect! If you spot a historical error, I'd very much appreciate knowing about it so that I can correct it and learn from it. Thank you!

The great houses: Most of the houses I describe in the books are creations of my imagination, or 'generic' styles of a particular era, but sometimes I base them on real houses.

These are the principal houses of this series:

Chadwell Park, Hertfordshire: based on two separate designs from Vitruvius Britannicus and Georgian Architectural Designs.

Chadwell Manor, Hertfordshire: invented.

Grosvenor Square, London: based on several designs of real houses.

Royal Crescent, Bath: based on plan of no 20.

Chaseley Court, Huntingdonshire: based on Fountains Hall, near Ripon, Yorkshire, but I added a couple of wings and a gallery.

Isn't that what's-his-name? Regular readers will know that characters from previous books occasionally pop up. There are mentions in this book of several Sagborough residents. The Harbottle family (including Nell, her son Louis and Nathan) of Percharden House were seen in *The Widow*. The Marfords, Lord Carrbridge's extensive family, were seen throughout the *Sons of the Marquess* series, and in *The Seamstress*. Mr Malpas, the mayor of Sagborough, his wife and daughter Emmy were in *The Seamstress*. Lord and Lady Craston (Ferdy and Fanny) were in *The Seamstress*.

About the series*:* A family grown rich in the wool trade. The landed gentry they've displaced. And the gentle daughter whose beauty will open the door to an even greater prize - the nobility.

The Fletcher family is moving from Yorkshire to a mansion in the south of England. After generations in trade, can they escape their roots and be admitted to the leisured world of the gentry?

Their new home is Chadwell Park, in Hertfordshire. **The**

Mercer's House.

Book 0: The Mercer: the rich merchant and the poor widow. *(A novella, free to mailing list subscribers).*

Book 1: A Winter Chase: the wild daughter and the reluctant clergyman.

Book 2: A Spring Dance: the flirtatious son and the prim paid companion.

Book 3: A Summer Game: the mischievous daughter and the strait-laced gentleman.

Book 4: A Michaelmas Truce: the cross spinster and the even crosser bachelor.

Book 5: An Autumn Courtship: the intellectual son and the flighty socialite.

Book 6: A Christmas Betrothal: the beautiful daughter, the unhappy son and the lost lover.

Any questions about the series? You can email me at mary@marykingswood.co.uk - I'd love to hear from you!

About the author

I write traditional Regency romances under the pen name Mary Kingswood, and epic fantasy as Pauline M Ross. I live in the beautiful Highlands of Scotland with my husband. I like chocolate, whisky, my Kindle, massed pipe bands, long leisurely lunches, chocolate, going places in my campervan, eating pizza in Italy, summer nights that never get dark, wood fires in winter, chocolate, the view from the study window looking out over the Moray Firth and the Black Isle to the mountains beyond. And chocolate. I dislike driving on motorways, cooking, shopping, hospitals.

Acknowledgements

Thanks go to:

Allison Lane, whose course on English Architecture inspired me.

Cara King, whose course on Regency dance also inspired me.

Dr Octavia Cox, whose podcast on the class of the Bingleys in Pride and Prejudice clarified my thoughts about the Fletchers.

Shayne Rutherford of Darkmoon Graphics for the cover design.

My beta readers: Barbara Daniels Dena, Quilting Danielle, Melissa Forsythe, Rosemary Paton

Last, but definitely not least, my first reader: Amy Ross.

Sneak preview: Book 2 of The Mercer's House: A Spring Dance

LONDON, THE FIRST DECADE OF THE 19TH CENTURY

APRIL

Will's heart swelled with pride as he descended from the carriage in Grosvenor Square. *Grosvenor Square!* The very heart of Mayfair, and therefore of London, of England and of the world. Here resided some of the greatest names in the country, and now his was to be counted amongst them. Mr William Fletcher... no, William Fletcher, *Esquire*, of Chadwell Park in Hertfordshire, and now of Grosvenor Square in London. To be strictly truthful, the town house was only leased from an elderly gentleman too frail to travel to it any more, and it would only be home from Easter to the end of July, but it was all Will and his family needed to establish themselves in society.

He gazed around the square with avid eyes, drinking in the sight of the pretty gardens in the centre and the many elegant buildings stretching to the skies. Three or four stories, not counting the attics and basements. The Fletchers' house had only three stories, and was not so wide as some others around the square, but it was sufficiently imposing. He had chosen well.

The black-painted front door with its shining brass doorknob opened, and out streamed footmen in neat livery and wigs. Oh, this was very good! Will hoped their neighbours were watching the spectacle of their arrival. Two carriages for the family, two more with luggage to be directed to the mews. Grooms emerged from the entry to hold the horses, while the footmen assisted the alighting ladies, whose eyes were round in wonder at their new home.

His stepmother descended first, eyes sparkling with excitement, although she said composedly, "This is a very pleasant location, Will. It will be delightful to look out at the trees. A square with gardens — that is very satisfactory."

"I am gratified that you approve my choice, Stepmother," Will said. "The house has its own garden, too."

"So you mentioned. After the open grounds of Chadwell Park, we should have felt sadly confined without a little greenery around us. And we are not so far from Hyde Park."

"It is a comfortable walking distance."

She laughed. "I hope we will drive there in the barouche."

Will's two sisters left the carriage next, their dainty figures elegant in fashionable travelling pelisses. Rosie's face was full of wonder.

"Oh, Will! It is enormous," she whispered. "So many windows. So many rooms. How will we ever fill it?"

"We will have visitors, I dare say," Will said grandly. "Besides, we need plenty of space for all the entertainments Stepmother has planned for you, Rosie. The drawing room will be full of your admirers."

Angie danced around him with glee. "And *my* admirers, Will. I am determined that Rosie shall not have them all. So this is Grosvenor Square! I like it very much. We shall have so much fun here!"

Will's father was the last to descend, looking the house over with the practised eye of the man of business. He had been a mercer for most of his life, and was not at all ashamed of his roots in trade even though he was now a member of the landed gentry. "This is a pretty part of London, Will. I'd no idea there were places like this, with their own gardens in the centre. I'd imagined it like St Ethelreda's, with the square built around the alms houses. Very pleasant. How far are we from the City?"

"I am not sure... two or three miles, perhaps. Why?"

"I'll want to visit my friends there," his father said. "That's a fair step to walk, though. Well, shall we go inside? Mrs Fletcher?"

He held his arm for his wife, the gentrified new wife who had persuaded him to buy an estate in Hertfordshire and become a gentleman. Together they ascended the few steps to the front door and passed into the hall.

"Oh, this is very spacious," Stepmother said, gazing around. "I expected it to be cramped, but it is not at all. And the stairs are well-placed... this is very good."

"There is a study or office in here," Will said eagerly, throwing open a door. "That would do very well for Pa, do you not think? And the library next door. Mr Bravington has left most of the books for us. And the dining room through here, and the morning room beyond."

They followed him from room to room, exclaiming over the well-appointed fitments, the imposing ceilings, the pillars and alcoves and niches. The furnishings were of good quality although a little old fashioned and faded, but that was not unexpected in a rented house. Will led the way upstairs to the main drawing room, which ran the full width of the house. The windows gave onto the square, the trees in the centre showing their vivid spring greenery.

"This is delightful!" Stepmother cried. "So large! And a fine view over the gardens. Well done, Will! You have made an excellent choice."

"This is perfect for dancing!" Angie cried, humming as she launched herself into a lively reel.

"Indeed it is," Stepmother said, laughing. "Such a splendid room, and another room next door for cards or music or whatever we want. This is splendid, Will."

"We would have room for thirty couples, at least," Angie said, sweeping Rosie into a country dance.

"Perhaps not quite so many," Stepmother said, "but twenty or twenty-five without crowding, the musicians just here, perhaps. Cards in the library and supper in the dining room and morning room. Perfect! We shall not need to hire a room for our balls after all. What is beyond this second drawing room...? Oh, another one! Goodness, we shall be quite spoilt for entertaining rooms."

Will was gratified by so much praise, but also thrilled to see his family here, in the heart of Mayfair. Undoubtedly they looked the part. Stepmother was elegantly attired, the present fashion for long, narrow skirts flattering her still slim figure. And the girls were exquisite, Rosie with her ethereal beauty and Angie daintily graceful, the two of them looking like a pair of pixies, wandered in from a woodland glade. They would be a triumph in London society.

It took them a full hour to exclaim over every room, to choose their bedrooms and to convene in the drawing room again. The ladies ordered tea, and Will poured brandy for his father and himself.

The tea had arrived and been poured, and Will was on his second glass of brandy when the door opened and a woman entered at a rush, a footman behind her laden with parcels.

"Oh, my goodness, you are here already! Such good time you have made, and I not here to greet you, but I had no notion that you would be here before five at the earliest. Yes, Thomas, take my purchases upstairs." She was as thin and shapeless as a broom handle, with a worn-out face and a grovelling manner that Will disliked on sight.

"It's not above forty miles," Pa said irritably. "Hardly a long day."

"Oh, but you must have left so early," the woman said.

"Never mind, cousin," Stepmother said. "You are here now, and that is all that matters. Cousin, this is my husband, Harry. This is Will, and here are Rosie and Angie. This is my cousin, Lady Failsworthy."

Will made her a perfunctory bow, for she was not at all what he had expected. When his stepmother had spoken of her cousin, a relation of her first husband's family and the widow of a baronet, she had made her sound very grand, but this poor dab of a female looked better suited to a rôle as housekeeper in some provincial squire's household. Yet she had been engaged — paid, in fact — to introduce them to her acquaintances in society.

"How were they all at Berinsfield?" Stepmother said. "You left them well, I trust?"

"Oh... they are all very well. All in the best of health, to be sure."

"Even Hugo's eldest? Have the spots gone away already?"

"Spots?"

"He had the measles. You cannot have forgotten already, Pandora."

"Oh... oh well, measles... is it so? I did not know. But I have not been at Berinsfield just lately. I have been staying with my... um, a friend, in Newcastle."

"I did not know you had any friends in Newcastle, apart from our old governess, Miss Clark," Stepmother said.

"Well, yes, Miss Clark is the very one. Such an old friend, and not in wonderful circumstances now, so she was glad of the company. It was a kindness to visit her. But I am not quite up-to-date with all the latest news from Berinsfield. The measles, and so forth."

"I wonder you did not tell me so, for I have been addressing my letters to you at Berinsfield. I should have been glad for you to convey my regards to Miss Clark, and I could perhaps have put a guinea under the seal, if she is in financial distress. But no matter. You have been here for some days now. Have you found everything in the house satisfactory?"

"I have had to give a little hint to some of the new servants, naturally. When one hires from an agency, one never knows what sort of training they may have had. And the kitchen — I have paid particular attention to the kitchen, advising the cook, you know. A man in the kitchen! Whatever were you thinking, Elizabeth dear?"

"He is a French man-cook," she said indignantly. "*Highly* recommended. I do hope you have not offended him, Pandora."

Lady Failsworthy went rather pink. "Indeed, Elizabeth, I hope I am more diplomatic than that. I have merely informed him of the sort of dishes that a refined family might choose."

"A refined family like the Haygarths of Berinsfield Manor, I suppose," Will said, amused. "Do you think the Fletchers of Chadwell Park are not refined? What do you imagine we eat, nettle soup and turnips, with pigs' trotters on

Sundays?"

The pinkness deepened. "No, indeed I do not, Mr Fletcher, but the cook is very... um, *French*, and he would put such strange food on the table. Nothing anyone might recognise. You will not want to eat such hodgepodges, I am sure."

"It is precisely because of his ability to put French *hodgepodges* on the table that I engaged him," Stepmother said crisply. "What have you ordered for dinner tonight?"

With the descent into domestic trivia, Will and his father beat a hasty retreat to the office, where a couple of footmen were summoned to rearrange the room to his father's satisfaction.

"This is a larger room than I have at Chadwell," Pa said, spreading his arms expensively. "And I like to be overlooking the street again, just as at Fullers Road, although the view is better than the sight of old Mr Hagger's house, and the mill wagons rumbling past. Look, that is a fine carriage going by, and a military man riding beside it. What sort of a soldier is he, would you say?"

"Hussar, I think, although I cannot tell you the regiment," Will said. "This is the best part of town, Pa. You will see such sights all day and all evening, too."

"Aye, you've done well to find this place. Mrs Fletcher likes it very well, I can tell, and that's what counts, not whether I can watch Hussars passing by. Goodness, look at that carriage, with the old lady all in purple, even the feathers. What is the coat of arms on the door?"

"I cannot tell you precisely, but it means she has a title... or the owner of the carriage has."

"Mrs Fletcher will like that, to have the nobs passing our very door. Ah, Enoch, there you are. Will you show these fellows how I like things? They've got the fire going very nicely, but I'd be glad to have this desk turned about, like so. And a table for backgammon, over there."

For a while, there was bustle and disturbance, but before too long everything was arranged just as Pa liked it, the brandy glasses were replenished and they settled down either side of the fire, just as they had done at Chadwell Park and at the Fullers Road house before that.

"Well, this is very cosy, Will. I'll like it well enough here, I dare say, so long as there's not too much of that French stuff. I like a good piece of meat fresh from the spit. There's nothing like it."

"I am sure Stepmother will order everything to your liking, Pa. She got into the way of it very quickly after you were married last year."

Pa frowned. "Will, I don't like to carp, because you know better than I do what's the proper way to go on, but I don't quite like you calling her *'Stepmother'* in that way. You could call her *'Ma'*, or perhaps *'Mother'*, if you prefer."

"But she is not my mother, and it goes against the grain to give that title to another lady."

"The girls do it. Look how prettily they call her *'Mama'*."

"But Ma was *'Ma'* to them, and Stepmother... the new Mrs Fletcher is *'Mama'*. It is a different term. I should be glad to address my stepmother in whatever way makes you happy, but not if it means giving her the same title as my real mother."

"You called your mother *'Ma'* often enough, just as you call me *'Pa'*." He sighed. "You still resent me remarrying, don't you, Will?"

"Not at all," Will said stiffly. "I confess I was suspicious of her motives at first, but once I understood how things were between you, I withdrew all my previous objections."

"You think I'm a fool, I suppose, to fall in love at my age, but there it is. My Lizzie makes me very happy, and I can only wish the same for you when your turn comes."

"I shall not marry for love, that much is certain," Will said, smiling at his father. "That sort of nonsense is all very well for the girls, and for you, if you wish it, but we are moving up in the world now, and I must marry for advantage. Rosie is destined to marry a lord, and I plan to marry a lord's daughter."

Pa chuckled. "I believe you'll do it, too. You have the charm of Old Nick himself. But what do you think of this Lady Failsworthy? A strange creature, I call her, and all those parcels she was laden with are set to my account, I don't doubt."

"True, but it was agreed that she might buy herself some fashionable clothes," Will said. "She has been living very quietly since her widowhood, and her wardrobe is out of date. If she is to introduce Stepmother and the girls to her noble acquaintances, then she must look the part."

"Aye, I dare say. I hope this will work, Will. Lizzie's set her heart on firing Rosie into the very best company, and she's pinning all her hopes on this cousin of hers. Or rather, she's a cousin of Lizzie's first husband. They sound very grand, the Haygarths. Not that they seem to come to London very much themselves, but they're proper gentry, unlike us, so they must know everybody. I just hope Lizzie won't be turned away at the door when she calls on Lady Failsworthy's friends. It would break her heart if she's snubbed by these grand people, after all this effort."

"It is a pity the Plummers will not help us," Will said. "After selling Chadwell Park to us, and receiving us in Hertfordshire with complaisance, I am sure we all expected to be part of their circle in town, too."

"Aye, that would have been for the best, but it was Sir Owen who was so keen to treat us civilly. Lady Plummer never liked us above half, and she's the one who's in London. We'll just have to do the best we can with Lady Failsworthy. She'll be able to open a few doors for us... or for you, anyway. I'll not be going into that sort of society."

"What will you do with yourself?" Will said. "You will be thoroughly moped sitting at home by yourself while we jaunt around to balls and routs and all manner of delights."

"Well, I'll not be sitting at home by myself, that's for certain," Pa said, chuckling. "Lord, Will, I've friends enough in the City who'll be glad to see me. All the people I did business with for years haven't just vanished. But I'll not tread on Lizzie's toes, that's for certain. I'll keep out of the way when she's entertaining. I'll only have my friends here when she's out for the evening with the girls. But you can invite your friends, too, if you want."

Will hardly knew how to answer him. "Oh... I dare say I shall not see them very much. We have drifted apart over the years."

"I hope you're not planning to drop your less elevated friends now that you're moving up in the world, Will. I'd be sorry to think you'd grown ashamed of men you were happy enough to spend time with in the past."

"I am not ashamed of them, Pa, but Stepmother is right about this. If we are truly to leave behind our roots in trade and become gentry, as we all hope, then we have to move in a different kind of society. When I was at school, I was a mercer's son and my friends were also the sons of men in trade — an attorney, a bookseller, a shipbuilder, a mill owner. The sons of aristocrats kept to themselves and ignored us. But now I am a gentleman, and if I am to establish myself in that society, I have to leave behind my past. It is not possible to have a foot in both worlds. I think you understand it very well. You are choosing to stay in the old world of trade, where you feel comfortable, but I have never been entirely at home in your world, Pa. I choose to leave trade behind and embrace the world of the gentry. That is what Grandfather wanted for me when he insisted that I be educated at Harrow and Cambridge, and that is what I want, also. It is my destiny, Pa. Just as Rosie's destiny is to marry a lord and connect us to the nobility, so mine is to use that connection to raise the whole family to a new level in society."

"You'll leave your old father behind you in the dust, then," Pa said sadly.

Will smiled. "I trust I should never be so ungrateful. You will always be my pa, however high I fly in years to come."

"Well, that's a relief. Pass the brandy, will you, and ring the bell for one of this army of footmen to light the candles. It's getting dark in here already."

~~~~~

'To Miss Jupp, St Peter's Road, Sagborough, West Riding. Dearest Belinda, How grand I am become! Grosvenor Square! I cannot tell you how much I like it here. Not that I disliked Chadwell Park precisely, but being in town again is so comfortable. Angie and I share a room at the front of the house, and there is a little desk — an escritoire, more properly — beside the window, so as I write I can look down into the street and the gardens in the centre of the square, which we are allowed to use. There is a railing all around the outside, but there is a key to open the gate, and Mama says we may walk there together sometimes, to take our exercise. I can see a path running around the outside, just inside the railings, and other paths leading inwards — so intriguing! There is a girl walking there now, with a splendid Negro footman behind her, wearing the most ravishing bonnet. The girl, I mean, not the footman, obviously, for just think how odd he would look with feathers curling around his face. I shall try to write more tomorrow, but I may be very busy, for we are to have dancing lessons. Oh, Belinda, such joy to be able to dance again, for there has been only one ball in all our three months in Hertfordshire. Is that not disgraceful? And now we shall have dancing lessons <u>every day</u> and soon there will be balls several times a week, and I believe I shall expire from pleasure. May you have as much happiness this spring, my very dear friend,

and Ricky too, of course, although pray tell him he is not to enjoy the assemblies so much this year, since I am not there to be his partner. Your affectionate friend, Rosie.'

END OF SAMPLE CHAPTER of *A Spring Dance; for more information or to buy go to my website marykingswood.co.uk.*

Made in United States
North Haven, CT
06 August 2022

22333206R00243